Praise for *All That's Left*

"*All That's Left* is a sprawling and fascinating story spanning generations, locations, and human experiences. It seamlessly blends the worlds of music touring, Canada's vast prairies, processing family trauma, and the healing power of our connection to animals. It's a captivating journey whose directions kept me guessing, and I loved being along for the ride. A highly recommended read by one of Canada's emerging literary talents."

—ELIZA REID, bestselling author of
Secrets of the Sprakkar

"Passionate, sometimes reckless, and always honest, Darby Swank is an enigma, even to herself. A talented musician, a horsewoman, and a survivor, she takes us on a ride from Edmonton's Whyte Avenue to the bar stages of Toronto and back to the family ranch in Saskatchewan. With a 'Jesus Horse Cult', a ruthless stalker, a lesbian preacher, and a family torn apart by silence, *All That's Left* explores obsession in its many forms, the sometimes-lethal results of the secrets we keep and the lies we tell ourselves, and the explosive legacy of domestic violence. A renaissance-like fusion of music, horses, sex and love, this page-turning story keeps us in the saddle and hanging on as we thunder toward Darby's full reckoning with both past and future."

—ANNE LAZURKO, award-winning author of
What is Written on the Tongue and *Dollybird*

"This wrenching novel grips you from page one. *All That's Left* takes a deep dive into what happens — sometimes supportive, sometimes terrifying— in the spaces between people. This is a story filled with tension and tempered with tenderness. Lisa Guenther understands relationships at their best, and at their worst. And she understands the ways that community and connection, music and art help us to pick each other up and carry on, as we must, when the unimaginable happens."

—Leona Theis, award-winning author of
If Sylvie Had Nine Lives and *Sightlines*

Praise for *Friendly Fire*

"Lisa Guenther's arresting blend of suspense, family drama, and the healing power of music makes *Friendly Fire* a captivating debut novel."

> —Theresa Shea, author of *The Unfinished Child*

"A well-paced character study with a strong sense of place."

> —Leo Brent Robillard, *Backwater Review*

"*Friendly Fire* is a remarkably honest and self-critical look at life in rural Saskatchewan."

> —Tom Ingram, *The Winnipeg Review*

"It's clear Guenther knows rural small-town life, and in this novel she paints a vivid picture of both its foibles and its merits."

> —Sharon Chisvin, *Winnipeg Free Press*

All That's Left

ALL THAT'S LEFT

A NOVEL

LISA GUENTHER

NEWEST
PRESS

This text is a work of fiction. Any similarities to real people, living or dead, is coincidental. Although real people and places are mentioned in this text, they are used fictitiously in the aid of the story.

Library and Archives Canada Cataloguing in Publication

Title: All that's left : a novel / Lisa Guenther.
Other titles: All that is left
Names: Guenther, Lisa, 1981- author.
Identifiers: Canadiana (print) 20230498132 | Canadiana (ebook) 20230498183 | ISBN 9781774390962
   (softcover) | ISBN 9781774390979 (EPUB)
Classification: LCC PS8613.U4473 A75 2024 | DDC C813/.6—dc23

NeWest Press wishes to acknowledge that the land on which we operate is Treaty 6 territory and Métis Nation of Alberta Region 4, a traditional meeting ground and home for many Indigenous Peoples, including Cree, Saulteaux, Niitsitapi (Blackfoot), Métis, Dene, and Nakota Sioux, since time immemorial.

Editor for the Press: Leslie Vermeer
Cover and interior design: Sarah Peters, Galley Creative Co.
Author photo: Billi J Miller

NeWest Press acknowledges the support of the Canada Council for the Arts, the Alberta Foundation for the Arts, and the Edmonton Arts Council for support of our publishing program. We acknowledge the financial support of the Government of Canada through the Canada Book Fund for our publishing activities.

NeWest Press
#201, 8540-109 Street
Edmonton, Alberta T6G 1E6
www.newestpress.com

No bison were harmed in the making of this book.
Printed and bound in Canada

To my mom, Patricia Guenther,
and to Edna Alford and Marleen Conacher

PART ONE
2002–2004

Where shall a man find sweetness to
surpass his own home and his parents?
In far lands he shall not, though he
find a house of gold.

—THE ODYSSEY
Robert Fitzgerald, *translator*

ONE

THE SOUND OF traffic on Edmonton's Stony Plain Road is almost soothing, like listening to surf on the shore. I dig my spoon into the top of my Blizzard, mine a huge chunk of ice cream laced with Reese's Pieces. Slowly suck the mess off my spoon.

For a moment, I'm just here, sitting at a hard plastic booth at Dairy Queen, letting the ice cream dissolve in my mouth, crunching the candy with my molars. Just a girl enjoying a frozen treat on an early September day. Not Darby Swank, crime victim, niece to a murderer, daughter to a coward. Survivor of the news cycle. My classmates at Grant MacEwan College have been tactful but distant, not asking about the black eye that lingered the first few days of class. Well, most of them have been distant. One girl, Ruby, immediately asked if I was okay, and it was all I could do not to start crying.

It could be worse. At first I worried my voice might have been damaged permanently, ending my singing career before it even began. However, the hoarseness faded quickly with vocal rest.

And so I am lucky. I am counting my blessings. But I am not okay.

I stare blankly across the street at the orange rectangular building where I'm supposed to be unleashing my musical creativity.

Once I had a well of music I could tap into, a source for my own songwriting. I could lower my bucket and haul up a new song.

That well sustained me through so much in my life: my mom's shitty behaviour and then her early death from cancer, bullies at school, my own shitty cheating on my nice boyfriend, Luke.

But since my uncle tried to throttle me a few weeks ago, the well has been dry, as they say. Or maybe it's been filled in, with rocks and chunks of concrete. Beyond repair.

It starts to rain hard outside, and the setting sun infuses the rain with gold. Stony Plain Road sounds even more like an ocean, with the traffic whooshing through the puddles. I'm not in Livelong anymore. Far from the lakes and the forest I know so well. Everything is okay right now, I tell myself. Uncle Will is in custody right now, no threat to me. I try to practise being present, as my new therapist suggested. Notice the solid floor beneath my feet, the hard seat of the booth I'm sitting in. The clean, cool plastic table I'm resting my arms on. I want to lay my head down, press my cheek against the smooth surface.

I linger in the Dairy Queen, licking the last bit of the Blizzard from the spoon and thinking about what I need to do next. I feel exhausted, so tired I don't even want to drive back to my shitty basement suite. At the same time I feel like a skinned cat somehow walking around in the world, sensitive to every breeze or temperature change. Vulnerable.

The bell above the door rings, and two girls walk in. They're both short with delicate facial features that would make them ideal for roles as fairies or waifs if they were actors. Both beautiful, in a slightly odd way, with green eyes that are set a little too wide apart and small noses that are a bit sharp. They are nearly identical, but the taller one has a golden tinge to her hair. It takes me a moment before I recognize the slightly shorter one as my classmate, Ruby, the one who asked me if I was okay on the first day of class.

I have to walk by them to get to the parking lot anyway, so I stop and say hi.

"Hey, Darby. This is my little sister, Amber."

Amber smiles widely, revealing sharp, pointed eye teeth. She gives me an outsized wave. "Hi!"

Amber turns back to the menu. "I don't know what I want." She sighs dramatically, then pouts, as though she is preparing for future disappointments.

Ruby turns back to me. "Whatcha doing? Wanna hang out? I was hoping to practise vocal phrasing with you. You're such a natural at it."

I know this is a pretense—Ruby is at least as good at phrasing as I am. I don't want to hang out. I want to sleep. But I don't want to be rude to the first person who's shown any interest in me in this city.

"Yeah, sure. Are we hanging out here, or ..."

"Want to come back to our place? I'll drive."

Amber's eyes widen. "I'll drive," she says.

"No, I called it."

"I still have the keys. Besides, I need the practice. You always drive."

"You two going to order?" I ask. "Should I get a burger to go?"

"No, don't do that, Mom will have supper. She'll be sad if we eat something else. She shows her love through food," says Ruby.

"It's her love language," says Amber.

"What the fuck is a love language?"

Amber and Ruby just stare at me, as though I'm from another planet. A planet called Rural Saskatchewan. Heat spreads from the base of my neck to my ears, my face, and I'm sure I'm blushing now.

"No one ever told you about love languages when you were growing up?" asks Amber, confusion and a little sadness in her voice. Who are these people? I wonder. Who talks about this stuff?

"Everyone has preferences for how they like to express and receive love," says Ruby. "Mom likes to do things for us—mainly cook. And she likes to tell us when she appreciates things we do. Dad's a doer, too, primarily, but he'll talk about it because the rest of us like words of affirmation. He also likes spending time with us—mostly playing music. I also like physical touch—hugging and that kind of thing. And Amber ..."

"I like gifts," says Amber.

"Oh." I don't know what else to say. Love languages seem like a foreign language to me. "Does everyone in Edmonton learn this in school or something?"

"Not really. Mom's a registered social worker. She has a master's degree and does family and couples counselling," says Ruby.

"What about your dad?"

"Red's an accountant," says Amber.

"You call your dad Red?"

"Everyone calls him Red," says Ruby.

"Are you ladies going to order something or what?" says a little girl standing behind us, maybe seven years old, sleek black hair in a ponytail. "My love language is ice cream, and I want it in my belly!"

"Ava!" Her mom turns to us. "I'm sorry."

"Don't apologize," I say. "She's right. Everyone needs to paint or get off the ladder."

Ruby and Amber order two medium Blizzards, both Smarties, and a box of Buster bars. After they pay, Ava walks to the till and asks for a large Oreo Blizzard.

"No, a small," her mom says to the teen working at the register. "You won't eat a large," she says to Ava.

"You can eat the rest," says Ava. Her mom relents.

We stand near the doors, watching the rain, as Amber and Ruby eat their Blizzards. Watching Ava reach for her Blizzard, Ruby says, "Now there's a girl who knows what she wants and isn't afraid to ask for it."

"Demand it, actually," I say.

"May we all chase our dreams with such determination," Ruby concludes.

"Ice cream is my love language, too," Amber sighs, then licks her spoon.

—

Amber drives aggressively but competently as she makes her way from the west side of downtown to her family's home south of Whyte Avenue.

"Have you driven over the High Level Bridge yet?" Amber asks as she switches into the right lane to pass a car trying to turn left at a busy intersection.

"No."

"Oh, we have to go that way then. It's downtown, but it won't be too busy this late in the day. I love the High Level Bridge. I love walking across it." And Amber tells us about standing in the middle of the bridge one summer afternoon, watching as a storm rolled in from the west. Even though I haven't walked across the bridge myself, for a moment I am there with her, feeling the wind pull at my hair and whip up the North Saskatchewan River below us. Smelling the rain, even tasting it on my tongue. And watching the bruise-coloured clouds swell, soon to fill the whole sky.

"Did you get caught in the rain?" I ask.

"Oh, yeah, but I was with my boyfriend at the time, so I thought it was kind of romantic."

Ruby, sitting in the back seat, snorts, rolls her eyes. Amber scowls at her in the mirror.

"What?" I ask. "Was he a jerk or something?"

"Oh, no, he was a very nice young man," says Ruby. "A very nice, gay young man."

"My sister thinks that because she's gay herself, she can tell when anyone else is gay or queer," says Amber. "It's super annoying."

"Well, he is gay, isn't he? And it's not because I'm a lesbian, by the way. It's because I pay attention to people." Amber shoots

Ruby a hurt look, and Ruby catches it. "Look, I'm sorry, I didn't mean to rub your face in it. You didn't do anything wrong, and you're not the first girl that's happened to. I just hated seeing him hurt you. And himself, frankly."

"Well, can you blame him, really? It's not easy being gay in high school here," says Amber.

"Yeah, I know. I get it. Remember when the Heathers broke into my locker and wrote slurs all over my textbooks and notebooks?" Ruby pauses, looks at me. "Their names weren't really Heather, we just called them that because of that movie from the eighties, about the school bullies."

"Yeah, got it," I say. "You know, no one in my school was openly gay. They would have been eaten alive. We were all raised to be so tough—girls and boys."

"Oh? In what way?" asks Ruby.

"Like, you dare not cry, unless you broke your arm clean off or something. Even then, you'd get more respect by being stoic."

"Oh? So is that what you're like now? Stoic in the face of incredible pain?"

I turn around so I can see Ruby. Her face and voice are neutral, a little like the therapist I started seeing last week. "Yeah. That's what I'm like now." I pause. "But I might not be like that forever."

Amber takes us down Whyte Avenue, a slow drive where we seem to stop every block for pedestrians or traffic lights. As we turn south and head toward the Mill Creek area, Ruby and Amber talk over each other as they tell me about the neighbourhood where they grew up.

"It's the best place to live, honestly. The Mill Creek Ravine— there's nothing like—" says Ruby.

"The pedestrian bridge is my favourite place in the whole world, it's made from the old rail—"

"They used parts of the trestles for the bike path through the rav—"

"It's called Mill Creek because there used to be a flour mill right where the creek—"

"Bill Bird built the flour mill," says Ruby. "Oh, here we are. Home sweet home."

Amber stops the car beside a blue minivan, turns on her blinker and reverses smoothly, backing into the spot between the minivan and a beat-up Camaro.

"Wow, nice parallel park," I say.

"Thanks," she says to me, then flashes her sister a smug smile in the rear-view mirror. Watching Ruby and Amber chatter and bicker triggers my only-child loneliness, my longing for siblings who never came. And then I start missing my dead: my mom, my Aunt Bea. Thinking about Aunt Bea makes me think of Uncle Will, and I'm back in the pasture, head spinning from a fall from my horse, the smell of dust, dead grass, and sweat almost overwhelming. Will looms over me, as though he's trying to help me up, and I reach for his hand. Then I spot the wedding band hanging on a string around his neck. He murdered Bea, I realize. And then he's throttling me and I can't catch my breath and the world is turning dark.

"Hey, Darby, are you okay?" Ruby has opened my door, is waiting for me to step on the curb. The honest answer is no, but I don't want to get into it.

"Yeah, I'm just a little warm. I don't handle heat well," I say. I swing my legs out of the car, feel the solid sidewalk beneath my feet, and look around me.

Elm trees line both sides of the Hodgkinses' street, branches forming a canopy. With the leaves turning, it's beautiful. The houses are old and small, but well-kept—what people call character homes. The Hodgkinses' home is a tidy white bungalow with a white picket fence around the yard. Well, mostly white—every few planks are painted a different colour. Dark blue, red, and yellow. Primary colours, I realize. The front door is painted blue, too. As we walk through the gate, I notice the steps to the front door are also painted in primary colours. A pot of white geraniums sits on each side of each step.

"I'm going to see if Mom needs help with supper," says Amber, scooping up the box of Buster bars and heading toward the house.

"Okay, I'm going to see what Red's doing. He's probably in the back," Ruby says to me. It takes me a moment to remember she's referring to her dad. "Coming, Darby?"

I follow Ruby around the little white house, past the rock garden overflowing with petunias, pansies, and dainty violets. The garage is sided with the same white vinyl as the house. "Stray Cat Strut" blasts from the windows.

Ruby doesn't bother knocking—he wouldn't hear us anyway, I guess. She jiggles the knob, then bumps her shoulder against the sticky door, tumbling inside.

I smell the pine before I even enter the garage Red has converted to a studio. Pine covers the walls and ceiling. Soft cork springs and retreats under each step. Everywhere I look, there are guitars. They sit in racks, hang on the walls. A couple of Gibsons and Fenders, but really odd stuff, too. One looks like a Martian's attempt to copy a Fender. And there are tons of Ibanez Artist Series models. He must collect them.

Red still has his back to us, large headphones wrapped over his orange hair. Ratty black T-shirt, khaki shorts, sandals, white socks pulled almost up to his knees. Ruby looks at the socks, looks at me, rolls her eyes. I smirk. Hoser Dad fashion.

But then I notice how he rocks that Gretsch. If I close my eyes, I would swear that Brian Setzer is in the room.

Ruby creeps up to Red, a cat stalking a bird. She grips his left shoulder, lifts the right earmuff, and screeches in his ear. He jumps, whirls around, and puts her in a headlock. "You rotten kid!"

Ruby laughs and laughs as he noogies her head. I feel my throat tightening, my stomach folding into itself. A mixture of anxiety and fear, although my head tells me that Red is no threat to anyone. And grief over my wounded relationship with my own family. I haven't talked to my dad since he helped me pack up my stuff weeks ago, and even then, I was monosyllabic. He'd stood in the yard, and I watched him waving at me in my rear-view mirror as I drove away. Instead of waving back, I shifted into third gear and looked at the road ahead.

Red notices me then, straightens up, looking a little embarrassed. Ruby's short hair stands on end from static.

"I'm Darby," I say. "I'm in Ruby's class at Grant Mac."

"Nice to meet you, Darby." He shakes my hand. His is warm, a little sweaty. "So you're going to MacEwan. Do you play guitar?"

"I do. Or I did. My guitar got stolen as I was moving into my apartment last month. I left my apartment door open while I was moving stuff in ..." My sorrow at losing my old acoustic Gibson returns.

"Well, we can't have that. A girl needs a guitar. Maybe I can part with something."

"Oh, no, it's okay. I don't need it for school, really."

"That's not the point. You miss playing guitar?"

"Yeah, I do." It's one of the few things that makes me feel connected to my dad, in a good way. More than anywhere else in the world, Dad looks at home on stage with a guitar. But even as I think about my dad rocking out at a dance at Turtle Lake, my brain flashes forward to his great betrayal—how he knew what Will had done, knew that Will had been beating Aunt Bea for years, but stayed silent. My throat starts to close as rage rises in me. The Bible says children won't suffer for the sins of the father, but that's not true.

My dad is not here, I remind myself. I'm at the Hodgkinses' home, and they had nothing to do with what happened to me or to my Aunt Bea.

"Mmmm hmmmm. Well, I could probably part with something," he says again.

"Like the Gretsch?" It's black and it looks like it's from the fifties. I know I can't afford it, but I'm drooling.

"No." He scowls at me briefly, then his face smooths and his eyes take on a contemplative look. "Let me think. What would be a good choice for you?"

He picks a cherry-coloured guitar from a nearby stand and lays it on an old card table. "This is a Harmony Rocket. It kind of has a Gretsch sound. Maybe something like a Gretsch crossed with a Gibson. Mellow. Woody. The neck pickup has a very nice jazz voice. That might work for you. We'll consider it."

Red shuffles around the room, evaluating his collection. Pauses in front of the Martian Fender, runs his hand along the sparkling white gold body. "No, the Eko's not right for her," he murmurs, and walks on.

Something red catches my eye. A bright sticker on the body of a blond, semi-hollow electric propped next to the south wall of the man cave. I walk toward it slowly, as though hypnotized.

The sticker is a rubicund devil woman, sitting in her pink underwear, grasping her ankles. She smiles at me with a confidence I can never imagine projecting. Her legs are strong, meaty, and her breasts nearly burst from the too-small bra. One strap slides down her shoulder. Long black hair tucked behind a pointy ear. Horns thrusting from the skin of her forehead. A sinuous tail snakes seductively in front of her thigh. Perhaps I should object to her objectification, but to me, she signals power.

I stroke the smooth wood body of the guitar. It looks like birch. A Yamaha SA800—I've never heard of this model.

"What about this Yamaha?" I turn back to Red and Ruby, who are both examining guitars on the north wall, next to the door.

"Aw, yes, the SA800. Very versatile. It's a jazz guitar with the guts of Jimmy Page's Les Paul. That might work for you." Red marches across the garage, picks up the guitar. Seems to weigh it in his hands, as though checking it for balance, before sliding the strap over his head.

"This is a copy of the Gibson ES-335. A sister to B.B. King's Lucille. Chuck Berry had another sister."

Red plays "Johnny B. Goode," then launches into "Blue Suede Shoes" with only a micro-second pause in between. Ruby dances with her feet glued to the floor, like the grooving toy flowers from the eighties. I tap my foot, hum, then start to sing a little.

"Okay, so when you have it on the back pickup, it sounds like the 355. Kind of thick, meaty. When you throw this switch, you use the front pickup. Usually people use the front for rhythm, back for lead, but it's up to you. These four knobs down here change the tone and the volumes on the front and back pickups, you see?"

I nod.

"Now, here's the neat thing. You like country? Yeah? Well, this guitar might work real well for you, young Darby, because when you push these knobs in, it switches from a dual to a single coil. You know what that means?"

He looks at me, his face full of anticipation like a kid on Christmas morning.

"No idea, Red."

His face falls briefly, like a cake gone wrong. But he quickly recovers.

"Push the knobs in, and you suddenly have that Fender twang." Red pushes in the two-tone knobs on the lower right of the guitar. He starts strumming "Folsom Prison Blues," throws his head back, and laughs like a maniac. A thin, crystal-clear twang cuts through the man cave.

"Whoa! Fun!" I laugh, too. Ruby starts singing.

"Wait, I'm not done yet, young ladies. If you pull the bridge pickup volume knob out—" Red pulls the lower-left knob "—you put the pickups out of phase. And then you have a Fender Strat!"

Red riffs "Texas Flood," channelling Stevie Ray Vaughn. The guitar sings with a slightly hollow chime.

"Darby, girl, this is your guitar. It even comes with your very own guardian angel," he says, pointing at the devil girl.

"How much?"

Red considers. "Well, it was eight hundred dollars new. I replaced the original pickups with real Gibson PAFs. Half the sound's the pickups. New tuning pegs, too—never would have stayed in tune with the originals. All that was probably a three-hundred-dollar touch ..."

I try to keep my face neutral, but I feel my mouth curving down with disappointment.

"But for you, future rock star that you are, five hundred dollars. We can work out a payment plan."

"Deal!"

"What are you going to name it?" Red smiles as he hands me the guitar.

I settle into the guitar strap and strum. Run my fingers over the devil.

"I think I'll call her Red," I say, smiling.

—

After showing me a few more features on the guitar, Red bows. "I better go help your mom finish supper," he says to Ruby. Then, turning to me, he says, "Darby, please stay for supper. We'd all love to have you."

I start to protest, but he's already out the door.

"You're staying right? I can give you a ride home after."

"Oh, I don't want to be any trouble."

"It'll be fine. Mom always makes enough for leftovers, so it's not like we'll be short on food."

"I don't know ..." I wrack my brain for an excuse, then stop. Why am I turning down what promises to be a good meal with people who've shown nothing but kindness to me, and who I share so many interests with? What am I bracing myself against? What am I afraid of?

"Hey, listen, Darby, you don't have to stay for supper. It's up to you. I can drive you home any time."

I inhale slowly, look at Ruby. If she was a horse, I'd say she has soft eyes—relaxed and wide, radiating kindness rather than worry or fear. I am safe here, I tell myself.

"No, sorry, I just get a little worried about stuff for no reason sometimes. I'll stay."

"Hey, don't be hard on yourself. There's always a reason, right?"

"Is there? I don't know, really. But I'll stay. I'd love to stay, actually. Thank you."

Ruby and I walk together across the yard toward the backdoor. The dandelions have gone to seed in the lawn, white puffballs waiting for a breeze to carry next year's crop to new soil. There are tufts of wilder grass grown high, feather-soft seed heads nodding in the early evening light. I look around and realize there's very little of the typical Kentucky bluegrass lawn—the space is filled with clover and what looks like vetch, and high bush cranberries line the fence, mossy rocks resting in their shade. The place looks wild, but not neglected, and a little less drought-stressed than other lawns in the city. It won't be long until a killing frost arrives and the snow buries it all.

"What do your neighbours think of your yard?"

"Oh, they're okay. Mom invites them to pick haskaps and saskatoons every year, and that keeps them happy. This is kind of a laid-back neighbourhood."

As we walk up the back steps, country music blasts from the kitchen. Dwight Yoakam singing about guitars and Cadillacs. Inside, Red is spinning a woman around the kitchen floor while Amber carefully manoeuvres past them toward the kitchen table with a stack of plates and cutlery.

Are these people for real? I didn't think families were like this outside the movies.

The woman sees me and releases Red's hands as she walks toward me.

"You must be Darby," she says, wiping her hands on her dark-blue jeans, before offering one. "I'm Beth."

She's a pretty woman, much like her daughters, with sharp features. But her hair is chocolate-coloured, cut into a blunt bob, and her bright blue eyes stand out against her darker skin tone. I wonder if she gets a lot of questions about her ethnicity. I remind myself it would probably be rude to ask.

We sit down for supper, and Ruby proceeds to educate me on the finer points of Ukrainian cuisine. The perogy-like dish is called *pedaheh*, she tells me, and best served with a cream sauce. "They should be soft," she tells me.

"Oh, wow, they are soft," I say, around a mouthful of food.

As I start to spoon my borscht, she clucks her tongue at me. "Add a little cream. It balances the beet flavour," she says, passing me some half-and-half.

I mix the cream into the purple soup, watch the colour soften, and try it again. The cream does cut the acidity. "Wow, if I'd known this years ago, I'd have eaten more beets," I said.

"I always knew I'd marry a Ukrainian gal," says Red, grinning at Beth. "I love the food."

"Dad makes the best cabbage rolls," says Amber. "Mom hates making them, but Dad loves them, so Baba taught him how."

"True story," says Red, reaching for more *pedaheh*. "They're not as good as Baba's, but they're not bad. I'll make them for you sometime, Darby."

Even though there are only four of them, the Hodgkins family is one of the loudest I have ever met. Constantly talking over each other, sometimes two or three people asking me different questions at the same time.

"Darby Swank ... is your family Irish?"

"Yeah, among other things ..."

"Any siblings?"

"No."

"How did you get into music?"

"My dad."

By the time Ruby and I start clearing dishes, I feel like I've been hit by a tornado. Like Dorothy, swept to an unfamiliar land where people seem to say what they're feeling and thinking with no hesitation.

"Your family is intense," I whisper to Ruby.

"Are we? What's your family like?"

"More reserved, I guess."

"Huh."

Ruby drives me back to my basement suite after we've finished cleaning up. After Amber's reaction to Ruby's demand to drive earlier, I'm on guard against sketchy habits, but Ruby is diligent. Traffic is light this time of night, so halfway through the drive, I let myself relax.

"I thought you were a bad driver for some reason," I say.

"I'm a great driver! But I have bad luck. Or maybe good luck, I don't know. I've had a lot of near misses. Once, a guy ran a red light and just about T-boned me at high speed."

"Oh, God. What happened?"

"He swerved at the last second, and I goosed it, so he just tapped my rear bumper," she says. "But it was scary."

I spend the rest of the drive watching for other vehicles.

Ruby watches to make sure I get into my building, and I wave at her as I open the door. As I walk into the hallway, I hold my breath. One neighbour has been smoking pot again, and someone else in the building has been cooking fish.

The door to my apartment is swollen with heat and humidity, the landlord tells me. I have to put my shoulder into it and shove hard, which leaves me stumbling. They painted and installed new carpet in my unit before I moved in, and the new paint smell lingers. I have to assume the last tenant trashed the place, as the rest of the building smells like musty carpet.

My answering machine is blinking. The first is from my ex-lover, Jack, just wanting to hear how I'm doing. "Call me," he says. The second is from my father.

"Darby, it's Dad. Just wanted to see how you're doing. Haven't heard from you in a while." He sounds tentative, hesitant. I wait, hoping for an apology, but there's just several seconds of silence, and then he hangs up.

I think back to that day in the pasture, when my own uncle almost killed me. I think about how my dad left me alone with a man he knew to be a murderer. Sure, he had a reason, an urgent one—he was hunting down a bear that had just killed one of our calves. He must have told himself I'd be fine.

But would another father have done the same? Would Red have knowingly left Ruby or Amber alone with a woman-killer? Even though I've just met them, I know in my bones that he would not.

I'm hot with rage. Strands of barbed wire wrap around my torso and tighten. The more I think about my dad, the deeper the barbs dig.

I deserve more than this short message on my answering machine, I think. Hands shaking, I delete the message.

—

I spend more and more time with Ruby and her family. One Sunday afternoon in early October I'm sitting on Ruby's bed as she twists my long, black hair into an elaborate updo while Amber applies makeup.

"I wish I had your lips," Amber sighs as she applies red lipstick with a little brush. "They're perfectly shaped."

I raise an eyebrow. "You and your sister look like fairy princesses and you're jealous of me?"

"Yes," she says. "We always want what we can't have. Okay, you're done! Your turn, Ruby."

"Just a sec, I'm almost done." Ruby pins one last piece of hair, and I relinquish my spot so Amber can work her magic. I study myself in the mirror. The summer sun has burned red undertones into my hair. I'm too thin. I look like I've lost muscle mass in the last several months. Amber's makeup makes me look good, though. The black eyeliner makes my eyes stand out, and the red lipstick is perfectly applied. Maybe I should start using a lipstick brush, I think.

Both Amber and Ruby opt for gold eyeshadow and metallic purple lipstick. Once we finish, we jam in Red's garage for a few hours, me on guitar, the three of us harmonizing. Amber is a decent singer, but she really can't hold a candle to Ruby's honeyed voice. And when my voice blends with Ruby's, it's like coffee and milk and cream.

"We should start a band," I say to Ruby.

"What should we call it?" Ruby asks.

"Something Edmontonish," says Amber.

"Magpies," I say. "The damned magpies, they're everywhere in this city."

"Magpie Apocalypse," Ruby says. "That's our band."

"Can I do your makeup and hair?" asks Amber.

"Yes," says Ruby.

That evening, as the three of us walk through the back door and into the kitchen, Beth is setting the table while Red checks the cabbage rolls in the oven. He's humming along to a song only he can hear.

"Stay for dinner?" Beth asks me.

"Yes, thank you," I say.

"It's going to be a few minutes," says Red, closing the oven door. The three of us go into the living room. I sit on the floor in front of Ruby, who unwinds my updo and starts braiding my hair. Amber and Ruby had been watching *Return to Snowy River* before I came over. Amber resumes the movie where they'd left off. It's the scene where Jim Craig and Denny, his loyal buckskin gelding, are racing after the bastards who've stolen Jim's herd of horses.

I sit cross-legged on the floor, spine against the couch, watching Jim lean back in the saddle as Denny plummets down the impossibly steep grade. I don't feel well. My chest is tight and I'm having trouble breathing. It's almost like I'm in the saddle. I can smell my own horse's sweat.

A gunshot blasts and Denny falters, slides down the mountain. Jim tumbles from the saddle and Denny rolls over him.

And suddenly I'm in the bush pasture again, falling over Bucky's neck. I can't breathe.

I close my eyes. Feel the floor under my sitting bones, touch the worn carpet. Inhale. Exhale. Smell the cabbage rolls. Feel Ruby's gentle fingers weaving my hair.

I fill my belly with Red's cabbage rolls and feel refuelled. After supper, Amber heads out to meet her new boyfriend at the movies. Ruby and I finish filling the dishwasher and are just about to head to the Black Dog for one drink (only one, we tell Beth) when the skies open and pour rain.

"Awwww, that sucks," says Ruby.

"We could have used that rain three or four months ago," I say, thinking about the dry, dusty summer, the forest fire. "Did I tell you I helped fight a forest fire this summer?"

"No," says Red. "But I think we'd all like to hear that story."

And so, instead of going to the Black Dog, we sit at the kitchen table, drinking beer from the can, and I tell them about the fire at Turtle Lake. I tell them how I worked with my friends and family and neighbours to protect homes, the heat and smoke scorching our throats, making our lungs hurt. I tell them about the sound of water bombers overhead.

"Were you ever afraid?" asks Ruby.

"Sometimes, at first, but mostly I was tired. And hungry."

Beth turns to me then. "Darby, I'd like to hug you. Is that okay with you?"

I nod, and stand up, and Beth wraps me in a long, warm hug. And then I don't want to go back to my empty apartment.

That night I dream that my horse, Bucky, is still alive. It's a dream I've had several times since he died this summer. We are at a ranch rodeo, waiting for our turn in the arena, when someone screams. I turn in my saddle and see a man dragging a girl, maybe thirteen, into an old pickup truck. Bucky whirls around and breaks into a run, and we chase them down the road. I wake up before I know if we will catch them, before I know who the girl is.

Who is the girl, I wonder. Is the girl me? My aunt? Neither?

I get up and make myself a cup of tea. It's two a.m. I'm still full of adrenalin, as though I've really been trying to chase down that truck.

The dream always stops in the same spot, mid-stride, but I know how the story really ends. My horse saves the day, running several miles to get me (the girl?) to safety. And how do I repay him? I stupidly turn him out in the same pasture where my uncle's stallion is running loose, having followed us after my uncle throttled me. And my uncle's horse runs poor Bucky into a barbed wire fence, where he suffers, tangled in wire, until my ex, Luke, and friend Sam arrive to find him and shoot him.

No one has a heart like a horse, I think. And we reward them so poorly for it. I cry silently, letting the tears roll down my cheeks, as I think of my beautiful sorrel gelding, his soft eyes and the wide white blaze dividing his face.

Two cups of herbal tea later I'm still wide awake. So is the upstairs neighbour, stomping around like a herd of cattle. I flip through the CDs Ruby lent me, select an album by The Doors, and pop it into my Discman. I climb back into bed and put on the headphones, listening to *Waiting for the Sun* until I eventually drift into sleep. This time my dreams are a mess of crowds and music and sand, everything blurry and not making sense, but I sleep until morning.

The next afternoon, Ruby and I are just coming out of our music theory class when a guy and a girl approach us.

"Hey, would you mind being in our video?" the girl asks. She has an open, friendly face and short, spiky hair.

"Umm, what's it for?" Ruby asks.

"My apologies," says the guy, who is short with long brown hair. "Let's start over. My name is Jason and this is my colleague, Charlotte. You can call her Char. We're students in MacEwan's Design program, and we need to shoot some film as part of our studies. All the students at the downtown campus are too uptight to appear on film, so we decided to head west, as they say, to the artsy campus. We'd love to get some footage of your singing, or even just talking."

"Well, sure, but it will have to be fast. We have to get to our voice class in ... fifteen minutes," says Ruby.

"That's fine. It's a nice day, so perhaps we can shoot on the steps outside, if you're amenable to that idea?" This guy talks like a forty-year-old, I think, but it's reassuring.

Ruby and I stand at the top of the concrete steps of the orange building while Jason quickly sets up their tripod below. Char shows us how to attach the small mics to our shirts.

"Okay, we're going to do a quick test. Tell us what you had for breakfast," says Jason.

"Coffee. Black," I say.

"Yogurt and granola," says Ruby. "The granola was homemade."

Char checks the video, then nods. "Good to go," she says.

Jason has us introduce ourselves and answer a couple of questions, then suggests we sing something. I look at Ruby.

"Brit?" I ask. She nods, then counts us in. We break into a slow, heartfelt cover of Britney Spears's "Lucky." When we finish, Char whoops.

"Wow, I hate Britney Spears, but I loved that," she says.

"Someday Brit will be seen as the Marilyn Monroe as our times," says Ruby. "Talented, beautiful, and ultimately tragic."

My first instinct is to roll my eyes, but I realize Ruby is dead serious. She has noticed my suppressed eye roll, and she looks at me dead on. "Fame can be a gilded cage, my friend. I just hope someone slides Brit a crowbar."

"You got all that?" Jason asks Char.

"Yeah, yeah."

I glance at my watch. "We're late for class," I say, removing my mic and handing it back to Char as a tangled mess, then follow Ruby through the doors.

—

Things get better and things get worse at the same time.

I love Edmonton. I love the industrial ring dividing the city from Sherwood Park, which lends a blue-collar vibe, or maybe an apocalyptic vibe, depending on your point of view. It was the first thing that really struck me when I drove in from Saskatchewan. I love the energy of the city, the white noise of the traffic.

But sometimes I feel like my energy is going to breach the brim. And at the same time, I feel like a raw nerve, just walking around in the world. Every lewd look from a stranger feels like a threat, leaves me shaking and angry. When I'm in my apartment, I check that my door is locked three or four times until I'm convinced that I remembered. I can't sleep past five a.m., even when I get to bed late, so I hop on the treadmill at the student gym, run off the nervousness. If the weather's good, I go for long walks, with jogging intervals, in the river valley. I love the smell of decomposing autumn leaves, the sight of the North Saskatchewan River. It's a little bit of wild winding through the city's heart.

Ruby and I meet up for tea one Sunday in mid October. We sit by the window, watching people walking up and down 124 Street wearing only light jackets. The sun warms our table.

"I feel like a cat in a sunbeam," Ruby says, stretching.

"I need to do something," I say. "Want to come for a walk?"

"No, sorry, I told Amber I'd hang out with her this afternoon. She's having a hard time at school right now. Her girlfriends are being bitches."

As we part, Ruby hands me an MP3 player. "I just about forgot. Dad put this mix together for you. Stride piano, swing piano. Lots of Fats Waller, I think, but I forgot who else."

"Thanks!" I hug Ruby goodbye. As I walk away, I put one earbud in and press play.

A magpie follows me as I walk toward the river valley, flying from storefront canopies to streetlamps, occasionally screeching at me as I walk by. Normally I'm annoyed by the hordes of magpies in Edmonton, but today I notice the bird's beauty, the iridescent black contrasted with pure white feathers, the way it tilts its head at me. I wonder what it wants from me. A scrap of food? A question answered? Or is it trying to tell me something important and urgent, something about a storm on the horizon or a child trapped in a well?

I feel good with the sun on my face. Relaxed, even a little sleepy as I descend the wooden stairs to the river valley trail.

Once I reach the trail, I pick up the pace. The air is cooler down here. It has an edge to it, a hint of winter. Brown and grey leaves blanket the ground, crunch under my sneakers, while nude tree branches frame the sky. Everything is still so dry. I wonder how much snow we'll get this winter. Hopefully enough to dampen the drought for next year.

Something rustles behind me. I whirl around, every muscle on alert. The bushes shake. A man with a long grey beard and a blue toque emerges from a hidden path, pushing branches from his face as he goes.

I can't breathe. I double over, hyperventilating.

"Are you okay?" He stands a couple feet in front of me. Starts to reach for me with one hand. I feel my legs shaking, and he drops the hand. He was going to touch my shoulder, I realize. I feel ashamed for being afraid of him.

I stand straight. "I'm okay," I say. I put both earbuds in, crank the music, walk back the way I came. Once I turn a corner, I run all the way back to the stairs. When I reach the top, the magpie is waiting. I'm sure it's the same one. It tilts its head, staring at me.

Suddenly angry, I pick up a stone to huck it at the bird. But the magpie is in the air by the time I straighten up, arm cocked. I underhand the stone into the brush.

I walk back to Jasper Avenue, hop on a bus heading west to my crappy basement apartment. I'm exhausted from days of little sleep and this nervousness that I can't shake. I lie down, hoping for a nap, but the neighbours are stomping around upstairs again. God, they sound like a herd of elephants. Are they being loud intentionally? Are they trying to drive me crazy or are they just super self-centred?

Defeated, I decide I might as well practise my guitar. But instead of using my headphones, I turn up my amp, just a touch. The stomping upstairs gets louder. I nudge the volume up another notch. Before long, they are thumping right above my head. Then pounding on my door. I don't answer, but I stop playing, don't make a sound.

"Hey! I know you're home!" It's a woman. She sounds frazzled. Upstairs, I hear the sound of a baby wailing. I say nothing. When she finally leaves, I plug my headphones in, practise silently. The baby wails for another hour, but they tread more quietly for the rest of the afternoon.

I feel both satisfied and bitchy. But most of all, I feel tired. I curl up in bed with the MP3 player and let sleep overtake me.

I sleep for a long time, until the drone of the apartment buzzer wakes me. I drag myself out of bed, feeling light-headed and groggy, and shuffle to the door.

"Hello?"

"Hey! You missed class today! Are you okay?"

"Hey, Ruby. What time is it?"

"It's five in the afternoon. Can you let me in please?"

"Yeah, yeah, sorry, come in."

Five in the afternoon? Did I sleep for more than twenty-four hours? How is that possible? I unlock my front door, walk into the kitchen, turn on the tap, and fill a big glass with water. I chug it and am refilling it when Ruby slowly opens the door, acoustic guitar slung over her back.

"Your neighbours left this on your door," she says, handing me a folded piece of yellow foolscap. A short message spelled out in block letters: *PLEASE KEEP IT DOWN. WE HAVE A LITTLE BABY. YOUR NEIGHBOURS, GEOFF AND RHONDA.*

Ruby looks at me questioningly and I tell her the story, feeling a little self-righteous. When I finish, there's a long, awkward pause.

"That seems out of character for you," she finally says. "And then you missed class today. How are you doing?"

"I've just been really tired. I finally slept."

"Did something else happen?"

I think of my fright at the homeless man in the river valley and shame bubbles up from my stomach, catches in the back of my throat. "No, I've just been tired."

"Okay. But you know you can talk to me, right? We're friends, and I care about you."

I feel something inside me starting to crack open. I'm afraid of what will come out.

"Really, I'm okay."

"Okay. Well, listen, I've been trying to learn that Neko Case song you like, 'Deep Red Bells,' but I can't quite get it. Will you sing it with me?" She swings her guitar around and starts to play. I can't resist the song—I start to sing. Ruby harmonizes effortlessly.

The song makes me feel like a vulnerable child. It makes me think of Bea, and Will, and my father. I feel alone and small, but also simultaneously not alone, because Neko wrote this song, and she must have felt, at some time, exactly how I feel now. Like a mouse trying to hide from the predators, but also watching carefully. Seeing all the horror and sorrow and grief and beauty and love that is out there in the big world. Seeing the others who didn't make it, who are missing, but also knowing that someone cared about them, that their lives mattered. That my aunt's life mattered, and my life matters, too. And there is strength in that, I think. There is strength in knowing.

When we near the end of the song, singing about the bells' thunderous ringing, all the pain and fear and grief that has been festering deep inside me breaks open and pours out. I lean against the kitchen counter, but my knees buckle and I slide to the lino floor sobbing. I feel Ruby's arms around me, and I bury my face into the soft place where her neck meets her shoulders, smell her vanilla lotion, and am reminded of my mom baking cookies, some of the few memories where she was gentle with me. I cry until the tears and mucus leaking from my body have left me dry, and then I pull back from Ruby and see the mess I've left on her shirt, and we both start laughing.

TWO

I'M TROMPING UP the steps of the orange MacEwan building one morning when I hear someone calling my name. I turn around and see two vaguely familiar faces. The filmmaking students, the ones who interviewed Ruby and me two or three weeks ago. I'd completely forgotten about them.

I stand awkwardly, halfway up the steps, hands shoved in my coat pockets, thin wool gloves not offering enough protection from the chilly, wet morning.

The young man reintroduces them both. Jason and Char. He tells me that the interview turned out and they'd like to make a short about me.

"Sorry, a short? Like, a short documentary?"

"Yeah, yeah. Just about your story, you know ..." He trails off. They want to talk about my aunt, I realize. About what Will did to her, to us.

"I don't know. The only one I'm talking to about all that is my therapist," I say, trying to make a joke out of it.

"It's still going to be about you," says Char. "About how you survived and how you're still making music. It's going to be your story. It's an important story, and we want to help you tell it."

"Can Ruby be in it, too? We're starting a duo."

"Yes, that's perfect," says Jason. "We'd love to film you practising together, playing some live shows."

I hesitate. Is this really what I want? But then I think, why am I hesitating? I have nothing to hide or be ashamed about. The shame belongs to my uncle. And maybe I will feel better if I talk about it more.

"Okay, I'll do it."

Both Char and Jason break into wide grins. I write my email, my phone number, and Ruby's number in Char's notebook, and she gives me a business card with her contact info. She is serious about all this, I think.

"This is going to be great, Darby," says Jason. "We'll be in touch."

—

Later that same day, right after our music theory class, Ruby suggests I move in with her family.

"Really?" I'm caught off guard by the suggestion.

"Well, you're over all the time anyway. You'd save money. My family likes you. And you're not getting along with your neighbours."

All these things are true, but something about it feels risky. At my therapist's suggestion, I'm trying to pay attention to how my body feels in these moments. My jaw is clenched, my core braced, as though I'm waiting for something to hit me, I realize. But why would I react this way to a kind offer from a friend, who just wants to help and spend more time with me?

"Let me think about it."

That night, alone in my apartment, I make a box of Kraft Dinner for supper and survey my basement suite. I have nothing hanging on the walls. The few photo albums I've brought are still packed away in boxes. Although the flooring is new and the paint fresh, there's no natural light. It's like living in a hole. It's not a home, and I feel lonely here.

The Hodgkins place isn't my home either, but at least it feels like somebody's home.

By the end of October, I'm settled into the Hodgkinses' tiny spare bedroom off the kitchen. Their old cat, Rescue, is initially displeased that I've taken over his bed, but he forgives me, snuggling into the bend of my knees each night.

The Hodgkinses' house is busy. Both Red and Beth work full time, Red as an accountant. He does a lot of work at a lower rate for non-profits, I soon learn.

Sometimes, if no one else is around, I talk to Beth about what happened with my aunt and uncle. She mostly just listens, but she also teaches me a few exercises to release tension and stress. Holding on affects the nervous system, she tells me.

"Picture your uncle's face on a basketball. Now kick that ball far, far away, right off this continent, right out of your life."

I imagine his stupid head flying over the Pacific, landing in northern Russia, getting stuck in a snowbank, his face turning blue with cold. Something inside me unclenches slightly, like a fist opening.

Amber seems to be constantly running in the back door, grabbing a snack from the kitchen, and then leaving in a rush for drama, or choir, or to hang out with friends. Ruby and I are in and out at all hours, too. When we're not at school, or not playing music, we're watching live music.

But even with the sometimes-frantic pace of the household, it's a comfortable space. The Hodgkinses laugh a lot, more than my own family ever did. There's always good food in the fridge, even if we don't have time to sit down for supper. On Saturday and

Sunday mornings, the whole family is up early for a big sit-down breakfast of Tex-Mex omelettes.

One day after school Ruby and I walk into the garage to jam and discover an old bench piano.

"Dad, he is such a collector," Ruby says, shaking her head.

I sit down, warm up, play some ragtime, and then try to pound out a few bars of "Finger Buster," a stride classic. My playing sounds clunky and out of time so I stop.

"No offence, but you're a way better pianist than guitar player."

Ruby doesn't mean anything by it, but her comment needles me. For weeks, it keeps me awake.

And so when the Hodgkinses' house is quiet and dark, I slip into my jeans, sweater, and thick wool socks and tiptoe into the garage. I turn the amp down and practise, quietly. Sometimes I play for an hour, sometimes two. But I always sleep after I'm done.

—

It's a Saturday night in November and I'm at the Sidetrack.

Ruby, her new girlfriend Cate, and I snag a spot in one of the sidecars, close to the stage. Alyssa, who Ruby knows from high school, swings by to drop off our drinks before we've even put in an order. She seems to have a sixth sense for what we'd each like.

I love the local band, all MacEwan alumni, that swings us around the dance floor. More people from MacEwan join us. We dance in shifts, always leaving a few people to watch our drinks.

Tonight I feel really good, even though I've been drinking more club soda than alcohol. I still haven't written a song, but I can feel something inside me building, a pressure that will need to be released somehow, soon. It will, I hope, come out in song.

We party until last call. After Alyssa and the other staff shoo the rest of the riff-raff out the door, our crew sits down with the bar staff, swapping stories and laughing and drinking. One of the bartenders tells a good joke, and Cate sprays beer out her nose. I laugh harder than I've ever laughed my entire life.

Then I see the mouse. It creeps out from the sidecar, scurries to a stray nacho chip on the floor. Cate laughs again, her laughter coming in sharp, short barks. The mouse pauses, looks at us to see if we're dangerous, then goes back to its nacho.

I wonder what it's like to be invisible. It's not something I can do, not with my profession. Yet there must be a safety in it, I think. Not worrying about attracting the "wrong attention" and being hit on by creeps, something that happens nearly every time I go out with Ruby. Together, we're like asshole magnets, and it makes us both edgy.

Being invisible isn't something I'd want to do all the time, but I wish I could wield it like a superpower or a cloak.

—

In early December, Christine, my therapist, tells me she'll be going on maternity leave in the new year. I eye her round belly, try to figure out if I'm feeling disappointed or relieved.

"I can transfer your file to one of my colleagues," she says.

I try to imagine starting over with a new therapist. No.

"That's okay. I think I can handle it from here on out."

"Is there anything else I can help you with? Do you have any questions?"

"What do I do when I feel really angry?"

Christine warns me not to suppress it, as it will just fester over time. "You need to acknowledge it, and then find a way to release it. You're a very physical person—try to find something active you can do with the energy that comes with that anger. Anything else?"

There are still so many things on my mind. How am I going to tell my father I'm not going home for Christmas? Will the Hodgkins family get tired of having me around? Will my uncle's lawyer negotiate a plea, or will I have to testify at his trial within the next year or so?

"No, thank you. Have a good Christmas. And congratulations."

"Okay. Listen, Darby, if you ever need anything, don't be afraid to phone us. Don't be afraid to ask for help. You don't need to be strong all the time."

I find the boxing gym three days later, walking south of Oliver Square. The sign says *Moe's Boxing*. Who is Moe? I wonder.

The gym is in a basement, below a dental office. Inside, the music is turned down low, almost drowned out by the rhythm of people hitting heavy bags. I expected it to be grimy, dimly lit, but the floor gleams under the fluorescent lights. A young fighter is in the ring with his coach, throwing punches at his coach's padded hands. The coach suddenly swings at him, and the fighter ducks, pops back up, and throws another combination.

"Can I help you?"

I turn to the young man at the desk.

"I'd like a membership."

—

My old lover, Jack, comes to visit me before Christmas. Funny, I never thought I'd have a "lover," but that's what Jack is, or was. He was never really a boyfriend—too juvenile a descriptor. He wasn't a one-night stand, either. Lover seems too fancy sometimes, but then I remember the electrical feeling of his fingertips brushing my skin, and there's no other word.

Still, because I've never been sure how to think about him, I haven't made any effort to call him since I moved to Edmonton. So I'm surprised when I get an email from him asking me to call him.

Jack in on his way to St. Albert to stay with family, he tells me over the phone. We agree to meet at a coffee shop near Oliver Square after I finish class.

More than anything, Jack is part of what happened at home, and that's really why I haven't been able to talk to him, or anyone else, for that matter. He was the good part, the part that helped save my life, the first person I called and the one who drove me to the hospital. But thinking about him makes me think about everything else that happened, my uncle killing my aunt, then trying to kill me. Not to mention that I still feel a little guilty for cheating on Luke with Jack. I haven't talked to Luke yet, or his sister Jen, either, even though Jen and I were once best friends.

Altogether too much drama that I wish I could just forget.

Because of the bus schedule, I get there about a half hour early. Order a large coffee, find a seat facing the door, and wait. Finish my coffee, think about leaving, but decide to order a herbal tea instead.

I'm standing in line when Jack walks in. He looks around the busy coffee shop, not seeing me until I wave at him. As our eyes connect, he smiles.

Jack wraps me in a gentle hug. "It's good to see you," he whispers in my ear. I shiver.

He orders a large coffee for himself. His coffee cup is overfull, and a little slops over the side as he mixes in a mountain of sugar. He sips at the excess coffee before walking back to our table.

Even though we haven't talked in months, it feels good and natural to talk to him. He fills me in on everything that's happening at home. Mostly gossip about customers at the Horseshoe, the little restaurant he runs at Turtle Lake.

I wish I could easily move between Edmonton and home like other students do. My home is such a minefield, I can't imagine any armour would make me feel safe.

We sit there for hours. Jack buys more coffee for himself, more herbal tea for me, and some dainty little desserts that neither of us touch.

"You miss waiting tables at the Horseshoe, Darbs?"

"Uh, no. Not at all."

"You miss me?" he asks, suddenly serious.

"Yes, I do." I *do* suddenly miss him, even though he's right here in front of me. Maybe I miss how I felt a few months ago. Sad but safe, and in love. Or at least in lust. I've lost all my lust, until this moment.

He reaches across the table, places a hand over mine. Heat builds in the centre of me, starts to spread to my toes, my fingers, my ears and lips.

He doesn't say anything more about it, but I know what he's thinking. We haven't seen each other since September. We don't talk on the phone. Our relationship has run its course. Like a river reaching the sea. It's not that anything's gone wrong between us. It's just turned into something else.

Jack doesn't ask me how I'm doing, not once. But I catch him looking at me, eyes all soft and worried, and I know he knows that I'm struggling. I kind of hate how he can do that, how he's been able to do that from the first moment he met me. It makes me want to cry, and that's the last thing I want to do, especially in public.

"Jack, stop it. Stop looking at me that way."

"Okay, tough guy." He smiles like a devil and his eyes lose that gooey look.

Just as I'm starting to pull on my coat, Jack puts a hand on my arm.

"Wait. I have something for you."

He digs around in his backpack, comes out with a flat rectangular box. It seems heavier than it should be for such a small gift. The wrapping paper is rocket ships and astronauts.

I raise one eyebrow.

"It's my nephew's birthday tomorrow, and I didn't want to buy two rolls of wrapping paper."

"Always the practical one, aren't you?"

He shrugs.

Inside the box is a black horseshoe, mounted on silvery barn board. I recognize it instantly. It's the one that hung over the doorway of the Horseshoe, the restaurant I worked at for years and years.

I'm suddenly holding back tears.

Jack pulls me into another hug.

"Take care, Darby, and make sure you hang it the right way so it doesn't lose its luck."

THREE

THREE WEEKS BEFORE Christmas, I mail Dad a short letter, telling him that I'm fine but I won't be coming home for Christmas. I don't explain why. I also email my old friend Jen, apologizing for not calling her since the summer. I type out my new cell phone number and the Hodgkinses' land line and sign off, not expecting much of a response.

But the next day, a new message from Jen sits in my inbox. I open it.

> It's okay, I should have emailed you, too. I've been very busy, lots going on with Mom and the whole trial. We should talk sometime.

I wait two days before replying.

> I'm also sorry for being such a bitch to your brother.

Jen responds before the day is out.

> Don't call yourself that.

I've decided to stay out of it, as much as I find the
whole thing hurtful and disrespectful. If you two get
back together again in the future, I don't want to hear
anything about it. But I don't think you will.

The last line intrigues me. Why is she so certain that we won't get together again? Then catching myself, I wonder why I would think I'd have another shot with Luke.

I spend Christmas with Ruby's family. They try to make me feel welcome and included, buying me tons of gifts (CDs, red lipstick, scarves, books). But acid burns the back of my throat constantly as I try to hold back the tears, the loneliness, and look cheerful and grateful. And I can't stop thinking about the pre-trial machinations surrounding Will.

After Christmas, I decide to reach out to Jen, again. Buoyed by the hopeful tone of the initial emails, I call her. I swallow my pride and apologize again for not calling her since the summer. And for cheating on her brother.

"You know, I think this is the first time I've heard you apologize genuinely for anything," she says.

I almost start to argue with her but think better of it. "I am really sorry about it," I say. "I suppose I should apologize to Luke."

"He's already forgiven you."

"Really? He was always too good for me."

"I can't believe I'm saying this, because I said the exact same thing to Luke, but maybe you should think more of yourself. You were never right together, but you can be right with someone else. Besides Jack." A long pause, as though she's holding something back. "Okay, so what's up? Is this about Will?"

"The justice system is ridiculous, Jen."

That's when she asks the question that sticks in my brain like a burr.

"It depends how you view it. Is it a legal system or a justice system? If it's a legal system, it's near perfect. If you set the bar at justice, well, there are issues. Justice is a messy concept. Not everyone in the system wants it."

"Well, you got that right. Will certainly doesn't want it, and neither does his lawyer."

"His lawyer is just doing a job that someone has to do. She needs to test the system, to make sure the Crown can prove their case."

"How noble of her to do that tough job that pays so well."

Will's lawyer, Vivian Simon, does a media scrum after every hearing on the courthouse steps. I don't have to see her on TV, thank goodness, but Jen emails me links to news stories and even attaches scans of clippings from various Saskatchewan papers. Vivian doesn't talk about the facts of the case in detail, but she tries to portray my uncle as some kind of victim. Reading the clippings one morning on Ruby's Mac computer, I spit my coffee all over the keyboard and cough out the rest for the next couple of minutes. Ruby comes in and sees the mess, and I try to apologize, but she waves it away, gets a bunch of paper towel, cleans it up, then reads.

"Wow," she says. "This lady has nerve. 'My client is suffering from a serious mental illness. His condition is worsening rapidly in the inhumane conditions he's being kept in.'"

"I didn't know being an asshole was a mental illness," I say, finally able to talk.

"Your uncle sounds like a sociopath."

"You think everyone's a sociopath. But yeah, you're probably right about him."

"Actually, maybe he has borderline personality. It's hard to know. Do you think he feels remorse?"

"I'll be sure to ask him at the next family dinner."

I call Jen again to ask if there's anything I can do about Vivian's media campaign.

"Well, there's nothing stopping you from talking to the media except common sense," says Jen. "You know his lawyer will scrutinize everything you say publicly and use it when you testify."

"Right. But anyone who's not testifying should be fine."

"What's your goal here?"

"I just want people to know my aunt was a person."

My next call is to Bea's agent, Pauline Brooks. "I've been thinking about it, too," she says. "It sends me into a rage every time I read about him in the paper. 'Poor Will, he's not thriving in prison.' Where's Bea in all this?"

"Exactly," I say. "She's invisible. Or worse, just the pretty dead woman."

"Did you know that Saskatchewan has one of the highest rates of domestic violence in Canada? I mean, everyone has a story."

"So what do we do about it, Pauline?"

"Well, I was thinking we'd start with a show of Bea's work. At the Chapel Gallery in Battleford. In fact, we could do that show during the trial. Did they set a date yet?"

"Yeah ... it starts the second week of January." All this will mean missing classes. But I must testify anyway, and I want to do this.

"That's perfect. That will give us time to plan. I'll call the Chapel. And I'll call some of my media contacts, too, and make sure Bea isn't lost in all of this."

Over the next several months I think about the trial, my uncle, and the opening constantly. When I'm at the boxing club, it's Will's face I picture as I slam my fist into the heavy punching bag, sending it swinging.

Pauline's campaign is so successful that the national media pick up the story. Jen keeps sending me newspaper clippings, often with some commentary. As the winter wears on, we talk on the phone weekly, then twice a week. They've been discussing the case in one of Jen's classes. It seems surreal.

"No one can understand why my mom didn't say something, and they expect me to explain it," she says to me one night. I think of Jen's mom, Lena, and the sickening moment I realized that she knew Will had been abusing Bea for years. I'd been so angry at her.

This is the moment I realize that Jen's parents let her down, too, although the consequences were particularly harsh for me. Jen seems to be using the whole experience, and the anger it's generated, as rocket fuel for her legal career. She's at the very top of her class, could go into any field and have her pick of firms to intern with and eventually work for. But she is angling for family law, she tells me.

"Why family law? I mean, it sounds God-awful to me."

Jen is silent for a long time. "I know this isn't entirely rational, and probably not healthy, but I want to fix things. Most of all, I want to fix what happened to Bea. I'll never be able to do that, but maybe I can help other people."

"I want to rip it all down," I say. "I'm so angry sometimes it scares me. I mean, I just want to fucking hit someone when I think of Will's assholery, and our parents covering for him. I think about it all the time, blow by blow. Fuck all of them."

"I know. I came close to throat-punching someone in class the other day over a legal debate. But I just go to my quiet place and try to out-think them."

"You've always been a master of that."

"Ironically, it's Will who taught me that. Remember, he used to give us that fucked-up advice when we were in junior high, dealing with bullies? 'Just find their weak spot,' he'd say 'and use it against them.' I did some awful shit to those girls, once I figured out how to do it. I wish I could fix that, too."

"Time to use those powers for good, Jen."

"Yeah, I'll try my best. I wish I could change the past, but there's no going back."

"It is what it is." That old Prairie saying that's always sounded like a weary bit of Zen wisdom to me. Prairie Zen. Is that a thing? I wonder.

The only thing that dampens my anger is the hard times that have landed on my father's doorstep. With so many of the ranch's assets jointly owned by him and Will, and with Will's mounting legal costs, Dad is eventually forced to start selling. Will and Bea's horses were the first to go, back in the fall, and the cow herd follows them. Years of drought means there's not much feed around, and he doesn't get the price he'd have liked. But likely no price would have compensated him for a lifetime's work gone down the road.

Then, in late May, a cow in northern Alberta is confirmed to have BSE, or what most people call Mad Cow Disease, which I'm sure will drive all the farmers and ranchers crazy. The U.S. slams shut its border, as do other countries, and cattle prices plummet. It's a disaster for Canada, which exports most of its beef. I feel awful for my ranching relatives, all the people I know who are still raising cattle.

But I'm resentful that my dad somehow dodged this one, especially since so many better people have been devastated by it. My dad deserves worse.

It's around this time that my dreams change, worsen. I've often dreamt of being lost in the bowels of a jackfish. Sometimes the dream ends when I find a door to the outside. Sometimes an unseen person whispers, "Wake up." But once BSE hits, my dreams take a violent turn, seem more like visions of my own death than dreams.

The most frequent one starts with me lying in bed at night. I sense someone else in the room. There's a weight at the foot of my bed, I realize. But before I can react, the creature pounces. It starts throttling me, and no matter how hard I twist and buck my body, I can't get free or even loosen its grip. I claw and punch at its face and body, but whoever or whatever it is, it doesn't respond. It's as though I'm clawing at stone. Exhaustion creeps in, and my vision darkens, and I slowly give up.

Then I realize I'm alone, and sitting straight up in bed, sweating and panting.

Another night I wake while crouched over my pillow, punching it as hard as I can. I wonder if all those stories about people murdering someone while sleepwalking could be true.

Those nights I plug my headphones into my amp and play my guitar until I've forgotten the feeling of the dream. Sometimes I go back to sleep, but often I don't. I never would have thought I could operate on so little sleep. It leaves me feeling nervy and stretched.

Jason and Char film Ruby and me practising after I've suffered through several sleepless nights. After the practice, they interview me. "I feel like a skinned rabbit right now," I tell them. "Just totally naked and vulnerable, like a few raindrops could hurt me."

But all this practising pays off. That spring Ruby and I get our first paying gig for our duo, Magpie Apocalypse, at a coffee shop near the university. Amber does our makeup that morning, lining my lips and applying the red lipstick precisely with the brush. She lines my eyes in black, smudges on the eyeshadow, blends a red cream blush onto my cheekbones until it fades to a softer colour. I hardly recognize myself when she's done. I look like a model.

"You're so good at this. You should be a makeup artist," I say.

"Nah, I just do it for fun. I'm going to be the most put-together counsellor you've ever seen," she says.

It's my first time singing in public since the throttling, and I'm nervous going in. Jason and Char are setting up their cameras to the side. Char gives me a thumbs up. As we finish setting up our gear, Ruby grabs both my hands, looks me in the eyes, and says, "You are going to rock this set, Darby."

"So are you, Ruby."

I go to the washroom, where I touch up my lipstick and pat powder on my face to keep down the sweat, then take my place with Ruby. I pick up my acoustic guitar while Ruby introduces us to the audience, then opens the set with our cover of Britney Spears's "Lucky." Ruby leads with her pure, smooth voice, makes the song her own with a softer, slower take that picks up the sad thread of the song. I harmonize with her on the chorus. The chatter in the coffee shop dies down. When we finish, it's silent for a moment, and I'm worried, but then the applause begins, builds.

We play two sets of pop song covers, taking turns singing lead and accompanying each other on guitar. I sing solo for the Dixie Chicks's "Wide Open Spaces" and Destiny's Child's "Survivor," switch to keyboards when we get to Tom Waits's "Ol' 55" and "Downtown Train."

There's something about taking a song that everyone's heard a thousand times and stripping it down. The voice is front and centre, every nuance of emotion clear to the audience. There's still some chatter in the audience, but most of them are with us for the whole thing. It's not just the eye contact, the attention—I can feel their energy, the way a flower feels and follows the warmth of the sun.

After, several people crowd around, asking when our next gig is. Ruby takes down their emails for our distribution list.

We have a gig every Saturday afternoon after that, and more and more at other coffee shops and pubs around the university and Whyte Avenue. Jason and Char often show up to gather footage, and their friends start coming, too.

Every time I hear a pop song on the radio, I think about how we can, as Red likes to say, renovate it. It's like putting on a pair of glasses that changes how you see the world. We expand our repertoire into grunge, then old country.

I still put myself to sleep most nights with The Doors, and Jim Morrison starts to haunt my dreams. At first he's just the voice telling me to wake up from horrible nightmares. As the weeks go on, we often walk together on the old railbed running east from Livelong, the poplar leaves shivering overhead. Every walk has the same ritual; at the trailhead, Jim lights a joint, takes a long drag, then offers it to me. After the joint, he offers me everything he knows about music and art and life and the world as we walk. I know these talks are the most important ones I'll ever be part of, but when I wake up, it's all gone.

Nights when I can't sleep, I start writing in a notebook I keep by the bed. I can't even call these scribblings lyrics. They're more like fragments, but I'm grateful that something creative is sparking inside me again. I fill my notebook with things like: *The fish is dark inside.* Or *The room was grey and I couldn't see what it was.* Or *When I'd fought all I could, all that was left was me.*

Ruby loves that last line. One afternoon, in the garage, we take that line, stretch it out, add some meat and sauce and turn it into a real song. It's been so long since I've written a song, it feels like a miracle to me.

You killed my love
Throttled her as she thrashed.
When she'd fought all she could,
You dumped her like trash.
All that was left was us.
You stole my voice
Throttled it right out of me.
And when I'd fought all I could,
All that was left was me.
When I'd fought all I could
All that was left was me.
You tried to take everything,
Leave me with nothing.
But I'm still right here
And now I know everything.
Now I'll tell everything.
When I'd fought all I could

All that was left was me.
All that's left is me.

We joke around about titles ("Fuck You, Will Fletcher" is the top candidate, edging out "Victim Impact Statement"). But finally Ruby suggests "All That's Left," and it resonates in my gut, and I know that's the title.

We start playing with a vocal melody. Ruby insists I sing lead, and she lends her harmonies as I start to find the melody. By the end of the day we've got the whole thing, including the guitar.

"You know what we're going to do?" I ask.

"What?"

"We're going to sing this at the opening reception for Bea's show, at the Chapel Gallery in Battleford. Right when Will's trial begins."

"Yes. Perfect."

FOUR

AS I STAND with Ruby at the edge of the crowd on the night of Bea's opening reception, I cannot stop my hands from shaking. Ruby and I have practised the song a hundred times or more for friends and her family, and they've universally loved it. It even makes some people cry (especially Beth, who had to leave the room right after we first performed it for her). But we haven't played it for anyone else yet, and I'm wondering if that's a mistake. What if it's not as good as we think it is? Or what if I blow it, in front of all these people?

Jason and Char are here, camera equipment set up on two small platforms on either side of the stage, facing at the perfect angles. There are reporters in the crowd, eager for a story to frame the trial, which is starting in two days. They make me nervous as hell. Also in the room are artists and art buyers and local dignitaries, and social workers and administrators who deliver programs for women trying to get out of abusive relationships, and even a couple of women who've survived, and are speaking tonight. Not to mention my own family, some of my old friends, and people from my hometown who knew Bea. Those people, the ones I know, are the ones who make me the most nervous. What if they don't approve of what I'm doing? What if they turn their backs on me? Judge me the way I've judged some of them?

Jen had suggested waiting until after I testified before performing. "It could affect your testimony."

"I'm not going to say anything. I'm just going to sing. It's my version of a victim impact statement."

"Did you ever submit a victim impact statement?"

"No. I didn't want his lawyer getting a chance to scrutinize it beforehand." The thought of them knowing how I felt made my chest tighten. I'd thought about what I'd write a thousand times, but in the end, the song was as close as I'd gotten to expressing what it had been like to survive the attack.

The last dignitary has spoken, and Pauline makes eye contact as she introduces us. Pauline looks good, I think, with her white hair cut into a bob that perfectly suits her heart-shaped face. Still, I wonder if we should have taken Jen's advice. Too late for that, I think. I turn to Ruby.

"Let's do it."

Ruby squeezes my hand, then practically skips toward the makeshift stage. Framing the stage are blown-up prints of several black-and-white photos Bea took as a teenager, provided by her cousin, Helen. Four shots, all featuring a raven. In one, the bird perches on a little boy's shoulder, the bird's weight tilting the boy's whole body. Both stare at the camera solemnly. They're very strange, but the stark photos are the perfect contrast to the vibrant paintings that fill the rest of the room. Below the photos are the negatives, matted and framed. The whole exhibit is called "Negative Space," an idea Pauline and I came up with during a late-night conversation.

"I thought about this a lot right after she died. Every time someone goes, all that's left are the stories and the memories. And in Bea's case, her art. But there's a big hole where she was, and it's surrounded by this other stuff. It's like negative space," I said.

"Yes! That's the title of the show," said Pauline.

I can trace Bea's entire career as an artist by looking around this room. Flanking the raven photos are her early sketches and watercolours, depicting life on a ranch in the seventies. These are followed by the portrait photos of her mid and late teens, a few pieces from art school, where she began experimenting more with acrylics and then oils. The bulk of the room is dedicated to her work after art school, though. Mostly brightly coloured acrylics, landscapes and portraits all conveying strong emotion and a vulnerability that still catches me.

Also displayed are fragments of her life: photos and more negatives she took of family members, old paint brushes, sketch books, receipts for art supplies. Displayed in the centre of the room are her cowboy boots, one upright, one tipped over, as though she'd just slipped them from her feet, and a wooden saddle stand holding her favourite saddle, a saddle blanket, and a bridle. The saddle blanket is flipped upside down, perched on the saddle, and still covered with horsehair, dirt, and dried sweat, filling the space around it with that unmistakable horse smell. Months after Will's arrest, Grandpa Swank had gone to Will and Bea's place and rescued several items from the barn, before the wildlife moved in. When he'd found out from Grandma that we were putting on this exhibition, he'd suggested including the tack and boots. On easels beside the saddle sit a half-finished painting of crocuses and a completely empty canvas.

As I stand on the stage, I gaze at her last finished piece, the same one we displayed at her funeral. Photos of an installation I helped her with at Brightsand Lake. We'd glued tealights to driftwood, dangled shards of mirror from fishing line tied to the wood. Then, by canoe, we'd lit each candle and set the driftwood afloat on the still, dark lake. The photos are beautiful, but they didn't capture the full effect that night. It felt like we were floating in the sky, looking at strange constellations below us. Something about that feeling stays with me now: a feeling of being adrift, disoriented, but filled with wonder.

I take hold of the mic, look out at the crowd. There're Grandma and Grandpa Swank, dressed as though they're going to church. My dad, standing arm in arm with a younger woman—what the eff is that about? Jen and Luke and Sam, my trio of old friends and loves. Jen and Luke's mom, Lena, looking very serious.

I imagine Dad's face on the burly dummy we punch in boxing— for some reason it's called Bob. Then I replace it with Lena's. I don't feel any better, though. Just slightly angrier.

Standing on the opposite side of the room from my dad and grandparents are Grandpa Kolchak, my uncles Henry and George, and a blond woman I don't recognize, but who looks a lot like my mom and aunt. Perhaps the cousin who provided the old photos, I think. Grandpa Kolchak's face is set. He'd probably like to smack a couple of people in this room, too.

Well, this should be an interesting evening.

Then I see Jack. He is standing by himself, at the back of the room. He smiles at me, and I feel that old warmth radiating from my centre. Jack.

"Hi everyone, I'm Darby Swank, Bea's niece, and this is Ruby Hodgkins. We're Magpie Apocalypse. Thanks for having us tonight, it's really important to us that we're all here, to acknowledge what happened to Bea. But also to remember her life, before she became a news headline. I'm not going to talk too much. This first song is called 'Caleb Meyer.' It's by Gillian Welch and David Rawlings, and kind of a twist on the traditional country murder-ballads. It's not real cheerful, but instead of the woman dying, she defends herself against the man who attacks her. Anyway, here it is."

We sing about Caleb's violence and his bloody death, his ghost rattling its chains, our harmonies a counterpoint to the horror of the song. With our two acoustic guitars, we're able to use the same arrangement as the original, although I feel my attempt is a pale imitation of David Rawling's playing.

When the song wraps, there's a smattering of polite applause. Some people look a little shocked. Maybe this wasn't a great choice to open with, but I also wonder what they were expecting, exactly. Grandpa Kolchak, though, is smiling widely.

We play a few more covers of Bea's favourites—Joni Mitchell's "Coyote" and Neil Young's "Helpless" and Leonard Cohen's "Hallelujah." Then we end our brief set with "All That's Left." Singing it leaves me feeling raw and vulnerable, yet also powerful.

I will tell everything, I think.

When we finish, the applause is much stronger. Sam and Luke whoop. Jason and Char both give us a thumbs up from behind the camera. Jack claps loudly, nods at me, then slips out the door. I wish he'd stay, but neither of us want to fire up the drama with Jen and Luke, or to hurt their feelings in any way.

Ruby and I exit the stage. I've already decided I'm going to plead a headache so I can leave early. But before I can take two steps, a strange man grips my elbow. I recoil as though I've been burnt, putting space between us so he can't easily touch me again.

"My, you look just like your aunt," he says, his voice like sandpaper, grating my exposed skin until I feel raw. "I knew her when she was a girl."

"I'm sorry, who are you?" I look him up and down. Black leather jacket, ripped jeans, untucked faded blue T-shirt, long grey hair. I'm not sure how old he is, but he must have least ten years on Bea.

"Kenneth. Kenneth Diamond. I was a mentor, of sorts."

That can't be his real name. "Kenneth. And how did you know my aunt?" I glance over at Char, who has redirected one of the cameras so she could catch me leaving the stage. She is capturing the whole thing, I realize. It's both reassuring and unsettling. I wonder how much of the conversation she's picking up with her mic.

"I'm a well-known photographer. I had a little shop in Maple Creek where I sold prints, that kind of thing. Your aunt used to model for me. So did your mother, in fact. Perhaps you'd like to pose for me sometime?"

What a fucking creep. I realize I'm clenching my fists, and I consciously try not to look upset.

Over his shoulder I can see Jen, Luke, and Sam, waiting to talk to me. But when I try to walk around Kenneth, he blocks my path. Is this guy for real? He's talking, but I can't hear what he's saying—it's like being underwater. He presses a business card into my hand. No address, just a website.

Then the blond woman who'd been standing with the Kolchaks is at his shoulder. She has clear blue eyes and a perfectly calm expression, but there's tension in her body.

"Kenneth? I'm surprised to see you here."

"Helen." He flushes, looks at the floor.

"I certainly hope you're not harassing Darby. That wouldn't be appropriate at any time, but especially under these circumstances."

"I wasn't harassing her. I was offering her ..."

"Offering her what, Kenneth?"

"He asked me to 'pose' for him," I say, passing her the business card.

Helen drops the placid façade, replacing it with a cool anger that tightens the skin around her eyes and mouth. She draws herself up and seems to tower over Kenneth. He suddenly turns on his heel and walks straight out of the gallery.

"What was that about?"

"Long story. I'm your mom's cousin, Helen," she says, briefly touching my shoulder. A soft warmth radiates from my shoulder over my whole body, and I wonder if this is what reiki feels like. "Has anyone told you yet how powerful your set was? That last song ..."

"Thanks." I'm about to tell her that I'm not feeling well, but something stops me. It's partly that she looks so much like my mom and aunt, with her high cheekbones, full lips, and long limbs. But she has a charisma of her own, too, a pull of energy that I haven't felt from anyone else. She is one of the most beautiful women I've ever seen. I follow her to where my Grandpa Kolchak is holding court, telling a small group about the raven in the photos. Ruby trails just behind us.

"Henry decided to make a raven into a pet. They were rare in our area then—this was one of the first ones."

"That's not the whole story. Dad's the one who named him Huginn." Uncle George interrupts.

"I didn't name him. He told me his name," Grandpa Kolchak jokes.

Uncle Henry embraces me in a bone-crushing hug. "Great job, Darby. Your mom and aunt would be proud."

Grandpa and Uncle George embrace me by turns, Uncle George's hug so gentle it's as though he's afraid of breaking me.

"Thanks. Uncle Henry, Uncle George, Grandpa, Helen, this is my friend Ruby."

"Ivan, but you can call me Grandpa if you like," Grandpa says, as he shakes her hand. Ruby laughs.

I can't remember the last time I saw Henry or George. Mom and Bea drove down to Henry's wedding to Aunt Linda, but I hadn't gone with them. I know I've met Linda at some point, can recall her sing-song voice and wide brown eyes easily, but it's been several years. George lives in Saskatoon, not that far away from where I grew up, yet we never visited him or his family either.

Seeing the three of them with Helen, I'm almost overcome with a strange mix of nostalgia and grief. Henry and Helen have the same fair hair. George and Grandpa Kolchak share a darker complexion and black hair, although life has added some grey to Grandpa's thick mane. Together, they look like family, which of course they are. But Helen looks so much like them, it's like discovering a lost aunt.

Jen, Luke, and Sam trail over. Sam is taking quick nips from a silver flask. I'm not sure why he's trying (and failing) to be so sneaky about it when everyone else is drinking openly. Ruby nudges him and holds out her coffee mug conspiratorially, and he pours a little whisky into her mug. There's nothing stopping Ruby from drinking here—she's twenty years old, over the legal drinking age. But she has this way of connecting with people, making them feel comfortable, in a way that they don't even realize is intentional. Next to her voice, it's her greatest gift. She'd be a great therapist, I think.

I watch Sam and Jen carefully, trying to detect any lingering chemistry. When he thinks no one is looking, Sam throws longing glances Jen's way, but there's nothing on her side.

You'd never know Luke and I had ever been together from the way we are tonight, and that feels okay. He asks how I'm doing, tells Ruby he really likes her voice, and doesn't even mention his new girlfriend until Sam brings it up.

"Her name's Meaghan," Sam says. "She cleans everyone out at poker every week."

"You know she cheats at cards, right?" says Jen.

"She does not," says Sam, incredulous.

"Yes, she does. Why do you think I refuse to play?" Luke says. "Anyway, yeah, we met on campus. She grew up near Humboldt. She's a lot of fun, unless you play cards against her."

He pulls his wallet from his back pocket, extracts a small photo. A pretty brunette with a big, toothy smile. "She's studying to be a math teacher. Top of her class."

I wonder if Luke carried my photo around with him. I don't think so. Sadness settles on me as I think about how he bad he must have felt when I cheated on him. What if I'm going to be a serial cheater my whole life? What if something's wrong with me?

Luke asks Ruby about her family. Good old considerate Luke, I think, always thinking about other people.

As long as I'm in the Kolchak camp, no one from the Swank side will come talk to me, I realize. Not a bad thing entirely, but I would like to talk to Grandma and Grandpa Swank. After a while,

I drift to the other side of the room. Again, Ruby comes with me, and Jen, Luke, and Sam slowly trail us.

"So, what does Ivan know?" Dad asks as soon as I approach them.

"Why don't you go ask him yourself?"

Dad sort of scoffs at me, as though I should know better. I do know better, of course. Grandpa Kolchak has a legendary temper, and I've no doubt he'd try to slug Dad for abandoning me in the pasture that day. Not to mention his earlier lack of co-operation with police. Grandpa Kolchak had lost his wife years earlier, then his oldest daughter, my mom, to cancer. Living through his one remaining daughter's murder should have broken him, but he was still here, and he was mad as hell.

"Well, I sure don't want to be your goddamn go-between. Leave me out of your drama," I say, in no mood for it.

At this moment, the woman standing beside Dad steps forward. "Hi, I'm Jacqueline," she says, stretching out a hand. "I've been looking forward to meeting you."

I look her up and down. She looks nothing like my mom. Average height, long face, soft brown eyes, light brown hair with blond highlights, silk blouse, knee-length skirt. I don't think she's more than ten years older than me.

"I'm sorry, who are you exactly?"

"I'm... well..."

Grandma Swank interjects. "Oh, for heaven's sake. She's your dad's girlfriend, Darby. She's from Gimli, Manitoba, but she's been staying with her mother at Turtle Lake. Her mother had a fall, broke her collarbone. I met her at the Mission and knew I had to introduce her to Roy. She's an absolute blessing."

I turn to Grandma Swank, think of all the fights she had with Mom before Mom got cancer. Sure, Mom was hard to get along with—she could be a real bitch to me, if I'm being honest. But did Grandma Swank ever call Mom a blessing, or make her feel the least bit welcome? No, she did not. In one of their more memorable fights, she literally called Mom a heathen and a Cossack.

This is not the time to start fighting with Grandma Swank, though, who's always been good to me. Jacqueline doesn't deserve my bitterness, so I swallow it. "Nice to meet you, Jacqueline."

Jacqueline keeps touching her abdomen. God, is she pregnant? She's drinking white wine, so maybe not.

I can't think of another thing to say, but everyone else quickly fills the gap with introductions and small talk. Grandpa Swank tries to smooth things over, giving me a hug, telling me how much he enjoyed seeing me perform. I thank him, tell him I think his idea of including Bea's tack was brilliant. "It ties everything together," I say.

Grandma Swank hugs me, too. "You're turning into a grand musician, Darby, although I wish you'd picked different songs. They were a bit depressing."

"Of course they're depressing," says Grandpa. "Look at where we find ourselves. We are in the middle of a great tragedy, and it's ripped our family in half. There's no denying that."

"Well, I don't see why we have to make a big fuss about it," says Grandma. "We just have to carry on."

"You know, Grandma, some of us think Bea deserves a big fuss, and we're going to make one."

Suddenly, I wonder if Char and Jason are filming all this. I look back at the stage and see that they're packing up their cameras.

Now I really do have a headache. I glance around the room, see Pauline in a small scrum of reporters in one corner. She'd explained in the press package that I wouldn't answer questions, as I was a witness, but I want to leave now, in case any reporters even ask. I walk toward the door, Jen and Ruby flanking me, the boys bringing up the rear.

FIVE

IT'S A STRANGE thing to be thinking about as I walk into the Battleford courthouse to testify, but it's a beautiful building, inside and out. Outside I'm struck by the brick and limestone, but inside is even lovelier, with oak trim, beamed ceilings, and a gorgeous oak staircase leading to the courtroom on the second floor. The floor on the ground level is a black-and-white chess board. I wonder if the chess board look is intentional, given all the strategic games that unfold in this building.

I am not allowed to sit in on the trial before I testify, in case the proceedings affect my testimony. Too bad, because I'll miss seeing my dad squirm on the stand, along with all the cops and forensics experts. I sit and wait in what Adele, the victim services worker, calls the soft room.

I should be grateful to be testifying in a town big enough to have a soft room, Jen had told me Saturday night over post-reception wine. In small towns that hold court dates at the Legion, there is no soft room or any kind of room. Witnesses must wait outside the building until someone calls them in.

"No way!" Ruby had said.

"It's true," Sam had piped up. "I had to testify for a guy in St. Walburg."

"What if it's cold?" Ruby had asked.

"Tough shit for the witness," says Sam. "It was minus fifteen the day I testified. Lucky another buddy had court too, and he got there early enough to park close by, so I sat in his truck."

"What do you mean, you had to testify for a guy?" I'd asked.

"Long story," Sam had said and left it at that.

Sam's testimony was probably related to someone's DUI or something. They don't deal with those kinds of things at the Court of Queen's Bench in Battleford. This is the place for the big fish, the most heinous offences, the jury trials.

If Will had opted for a judge-only trial, this whole thing might have ended up at the provincial courthouse in North Battleford rather than this beauty of a building across the river in Battleford. This seems like the perfect setting for his defeat.

I wish Ruby, Jen, or even Luke could have stayed, but they'd all had to get back to classes. I was worried about falling behind, but Ruby had promised to help me catch up when this was all over. Jason and Char had gone, too, the morning after the opening at the Chapel. They'd left behind a small camera and tripod and asked me to record video diaries through the trial.

Sam and Ruby had bonded so fast I'd have thought a romance was blooming, except Ruby is a dedicated lesbian. They'd stayed up together all night after the opening reception, and when I'd asked Ruby what they'd talked about, she'd been elusive.

"It's confidential," she had said. I wondered what Sam had told her. Did he have secrets I knew nothing about? I'd known him since we were babies, so it was hard to imagine.

Ruby had taken the Greyhound back to Edmonton two days earlier, leaving me her Chrysler K-car so I could drive in from the acreage I was staying at. The acreage owner, a woman named

Kirsten about my aunt's age who'd loved her art and the horses she'd raised, had offered me a place to stay as soon as she'd heard about Bea's show at the Chapel. Kirsten had a beautiful self-portrait of Bea's hanging in her living room, and two of Bea's nicest horses in her fancy stable. I loved the portrait, but I hadn't been out to see the horses. Every horse reminded me of Bucky, and then I'd start thinking about his final moments, tangled in barbed wire, terrified and in unimaginable pain. And all because I'd been stupid and turned him out into the same pasture with Will's stallion. I hate thinking about it.

Kirsten is a generous hostess. She had even let my four friends crash at her place after the opening, Sam and Luke sprawled out on the living room couches while the three of us girls tucked into one king-sized bed. And she'd invited Sam to stay the week or two for the trial. He'd promised to drive in today, to be there by the time I was on the stand.

I hope he gets here in time. Sam sure drinks a lot these days. I'm worried he'll lose his licence.

I feel very unprepared for this day, when it comes right down to it. I'd assumed the prosecutor would prep me at some point, but all she'd done was send my statement to review. Before she'd left, Jen had given me a few pointers.

"Don't be sarcastic or get mad. It's okay to cry, but they'll hold it against you if you get mad."

"Well, that's horseshit."

"That's exactly what I'm talking about. Don't swear. If the defence attorney asks you something and you're not sure, just say so. Don't guess. They'll try to trip you up on small details to discredit you."

"Okay. Makes sense, I guess."

"If you need a break, or a glass of water, or Kleenex, just ask."

"I'm not going to cry, so I won't need Kleenex. If anyone makes me cry, they'd better start running."

"Don't. Get. Mad. Pretend you're working cows. Even when the cows are total turds, there's no point in getting mad. Same with lawyers."

Jen was so brilliant. I had instantly known what I had to do. I had to go to that calm interior place where I can watch disaster unfold around me without reacting. Staying in that place is easier said than done, though.

At least I had some sort of strategy, no matter how thin. The only other thing I'd done was pull out the old cowboy boots I'd been wearing the day Will had throttled me. Beyond that, I'd opted for new, dark-blue jeans, a brown leather belt, and a crisp white blouse tucked into my jeans. My jeans were starched and pressed with sharp lines. A large turquoise ring that I'd inherited from Bea on my pointer finger, silver rings that came from Mom. No makeup just in case I actually do cry. Kirsten had even braided my hair for me. She was fascinated by the red undertones in my hair, could hardly believe it was natural.

Sitting in the soft room, I fidget with the turquoise ring until there's a soft knock at the door. Adele pokes her head in. She'd wanted to sit with me, but I'd wanted to be alone before I testified.

"They're ready for you," she says.

I stride into the courtroom, trying to project cool confidence and a somber demeanor. The Kolchaks sit on one side of the room, the Swanks the other. There must be at least a dozen reporters, too. I don't see Sam as I take my place on the stand, so I cast about, trying to decide who I should focus on, but give up. When the deputy registrar asks me if I'd rather swear on a Bible or swear an affirmation, I hesitate, then choose the affirmation. I hope no one on the jury holds this against me. As I sit down, I give the jury a good look over. No one I know, of course, but they look like they could be from my hometown.

The Crown asks me about my relationship with Will and Bea. I speak directly to her, tell her about how Bea was like my second mother, especially after my own mother died. I had a good relationship with Will, too, I thought. He seemed smart and generous, giving me money for school trips and that kind of thing. I talk about riding horses with my family, and then later my friend Jen. It suddenly strikes me that my childhood sounds a little like a fairytale. Growing up on the forest's edge riding fast horses, spending time with my beautiful artistic aunt. And my own beautiful mother like a domineering queen. And then the tragedies, which are always part of the old fairy tales—the queen dies, and the aunt dies, and the girl is left alone with the wolf.

That's the hardest part, the part where Bea dies. I don't cry, but my voice trembles as I tell the Crown about the moment I found Bea dead, floating in the lake. How I'd noticed her mutilated hand, the ring finger missing, as though it had been severed. How I hadn't believed she was dead at first, how Luke had held me back so I didn't touch her. I'd wanted to touch her, to fix her hair. Then the betrayal, when I'd realized that she'd suffered from Will's years of abuse and my father and family friends had remained silent around me.

The Crown enters an exhibit. A gold wedding band in a plastic bag. She hands it to me, asks if I recognize it.

"Yes. It's Bea's wedding band."

"Can you read the inscription please?"

"To Bea, my wife. Love, Will."

"Can you tell the court about the circumstances when you found this ring?"

"It was a hot day in early August. We needed to move the cow herd home from the summer pasture. They were out of grass because of the drought."

"I was on my horse ..." I pause again, choking up. "We were gathering the cows, pushing them toward the corrals so we could move them out the gate and down the road. There was a small group of cows bawling, and as I came into the clearing, I saw a bear. It was dragging a calf into the bush."

I talk about how I told Dad about the bear and how he took after it, leaving me alone with Will. I describe how my horse, Bucky, rushed into the bush after a cow. I pulled back on the reins, something I now think threw poor Bucky off balance. Bucky tripped over some deadfall, went down, and I tumbled over his neck, hitting the ground hard. Knocked right out.

It was Will who woke me up, I tell them, by pouring water on my face. He then gave me a drink of water.

"He leaned forward to help me to my feet. I remember the top button on his shirt was missing. And when he leaned forward, the ring fell out of his shirt. It was on a string around his neck. I grabbed it, pulled hard. It broke free. I read the inscription out loud. And I asked him why. And then he attacked me. He punched me in the face. He throttled me." I touch my throat.

"I was about to pass out again. I knew I was going to die. But the horses saved me. Will had an aggressive horse, a stallion. He went after my horse, and as they were fighting, they ran into Will. They knocked him off me.

"I managed to get back into the saddle. Will tried to drag me off my horse, but I lashed him in the face with my reins. And I rode home, as fast as I could."

As the Crown finishes, I glance at the jury. Several are leaning forward, literally sitting on the edge of their seats. My muscles knot with dread as Will's lawyer, Vivian, approaches me.

"Ms. Swank, you had a concussion from the fall from your horse, is that right?"

"Yes."

"And how did that concussion affect your memory that day?"

"I don't think it did."

"Really? You suffered a concussion, which left you unconscious for several minutes, and you didn't suffer any memory issues?"

"I don't know how long I was unconscious."

"Oh, my mistake. You suffered a concussion, and you don't know how long you were even unconscious, yet you say you didn't suffer memory loss."

"Correct." Stay calm, I tell myself. No point in getting mad at cows or lawyers.

"What was Will wearing when you allege that he attacked you?"

"Clothing."

"Can you describe that clothing, Ms. Swank?"

"The top button of his shirt was missing. It was a button-up shirt. Jeans. Oh, and the wedding band he removed after cutting off his wife's ring finger."

"Did you see him sever her finger? Did he tell you he cut off her finger?"

"No."

"Is it possible that she returned the ring to him before she left, and that is why he wore it around his neck?"

"I don't know. Is it?"

She looks at me sharply, then continues.

"Can you give us more details about that day, Ms. Swank? What type of footwear was he wearing during this alleged incident? Did he have a hat? What colour was his shirt?"

"I don't remember. It was over a year ago."

"You don't remember the colour of the shirt of the man you allege throttled you?"

"I was more focussed on trying to survive than analyzing his fashion choices that day." Dammit. Sarcasm. Jen would be displeased.

"You recall minute details, such as one missing button, but you cannot recall the colour of the shirt or whether or not he wore a hat." Vivian turns to the jury with a false incredulity. I want to slap her. Stay calm. Cows and lawyers. Stay calm.

This line of questioning goes on for a full half hour. I have forgotten many details, or perhaps I never noticed them in the first place. I wonder if the jury will hold this against me, think that it's all gotten jumbled in my head. But then again, I had actual physical injuries, which were documented, to prove my story.

"Now, the police report mentions that Jack Cook, your boyfriend, drove you to the hospital."

"Yes, that's right."

"But the same report also mentions a Luke Cherville, who was involved with other incidents that day. It also names him as your boyfriend."

"He was my ex-boyfriend."

"So you were not dating Jack and Luke simultaneously?"

I try not to bristle. "When your client attacked me, I was dating Jack and had broken up with Luke. What does this have to do with anything?" I turn to the judge.

"I'm attempting to clarify the information contained in the police report, Your Honour," Vivian says.

"You may continue," the judge says.

"So, Ms. Swank, you phoned your boyfriend, Jack, who was also your boss, from what I understand. Can you please tell us approximately what time you phoned him, what time he picked you up, and when you arrived at the hospital?"

"Mid to late afternoon."

"Can you please be more specific? I'm trying to establish a timeline. You arrived home at, what, two p.m.?"

"I'm not sure. I wasn't wearing a watch."

"Your uncle's horse had followed you home, correct?"

"Yes, he followed my horse as I rode home."

"And you unsaddled both the horses, and put them in the barn?"

"No. I released them in the pasture." The big mistake that cost Bucky his life. I try to push down the shame and sorrow.

"You walked into the house and phoned Jack. Any idea what time it was at this point?"

"Sometime in the afternoon."

"That is a rather vague recollection, Ms. Swank. Surely you can do better."

I say nothing, wait for an actual question. There is a long pause before she moves on.

"Why Mr. Cook? Why not an ambulance or the RCMP?"

"I don't know. It was just easier to phone Jack, I guess."

"Why was it easier, Ms. Swank?"

"Because all I had to say to Jack was: 'Come get me.' And he did. If I'd phoned 911, I'd have had to explain what happened, what was wrong. And probably give them directions."

"So you didn't want to explain what had happened?"

"I didn't have the energy to explain."

"Or perhaps what happened was not what you ultimately told police what had happened?"

"I don't understand what you're getting at."

"Perhaps you needed time to fabricate a different story. Was that the case, Ms. Swank?"

"No."

"Perhaps these alleged injuries were not inflicted by my client, but by someone else. Perhaps by one of your boyfriends, Mr. Cook or Mr. Cherville, during a quarrel that got out of hand?"

"No. They were inflicted by my uncle, Will Fletcher. That man right there." I point at Will, who drops the smirk from his face.

"He tried to kill me after I grabbed the ring he cut off his wife's hand and kept as a trophy around his neck."

"How do we know you didn't get the ring from Mr. Cook or Mr. Cherville?"

"You seriously think any of us would have a fake inscription engraved just to frame my uncle? It came from your client because he killed his wife!" I've dropped the calm veneer, my rage on full display as I stand, shaking. The judge orders me to sit down, his voice tense and stern. I take a deep breath and my whole body tightens, then relaxes, with the inhale and exhale. And then I sit.

So much for not getting mad. Vivian tries to egg me into more arguments, but I hold my temper for the whole day, even though it leaves me exhausted and trembling. As I walk from the witness stand, I see Sam sitting there, in the front row. Was he there the whole time? I sit beside him, lean into him a little. He wraps an arm around me.

After, as everyone is filing out of the room, the Crown calls me over.

"You're not planning on coming back tomorrow, are you?"

"Yes, I thought I'd watch, now that I'm done testifying."

"You shouldn't do that, in case there's an appeal."

"Why?"

"We don't want your testimony changing."

"It will never change," I say.

"Still, we'd prefer you didn't."

"I'm coming tomorrow, and I will be sitting right here."

After all, tomorrow Lena will be testifying.

I step out of the courtroom, into the hallway, and lean against the wall, trying to collect myself. Both the Kolchaks and the Swanks want to take me out for supper, but I don't want to pick sides. Sam is warming up his truck and the borrowed K-car so we can go straight out to Kirsten's place.

"You did so well in there. Are you okay?" It's Adele, the victim services worker.

"I'm fine," I say, closing my eyes. "I just need a minute." Inside, I repeat my own personal mantra: *I am not a victim. I am a witness. I am a witness. I am a witness.*

I open my eyes, focus on the grandeur of the Battleford Court House. I nod to Adele, and we walk toward the staircase. As we descend, I keep a hand on the oak railing.

Just as we reach the bottom, a familiar voice calls my name from above.

"Darby! Wait, dear girl."

It's my great-aunt Jessie, Will's mother. I turn around, watch her slowly descend. She has aged terribly in the last year and a half, and no wonder, I suppose, with her son's arrest. Her long white hair is so thin there is hardly enough to pull back into a ponytail. She'd once had an imposing presence, but she's shrunk. She looks as though she is folding into herself. As she walks down the stairs, her daughter, Janine, supports her by the arm.

They reach the bottom and turn to face us. We stand there silently on the old black tile floor in the lobby. It feels like we are squaring off, two queens on a chessboard. I wonder if she is still trying to protect her kingdom, and I brace myself for whatever is coming. I'm a queen, I can move in any direction I like, I remind myself, trying to find strength in inner sass. Retreat, attack, evade.

I've played a thousand fictional scenarios like this in my mind already. Aunt Jessie asking me to forgive Will in my victim impact statement, and me responding coolly that I'm not submitting one. My dad begging forgiveness and me refusing. I've obsessed over the meaning of forgiveness, a word I referred to as the F-word when I talked to Jen or Ruby about it. It doesn't mean you're okay with what happened, it just means you're moving on, Ruby always argues. No, I'd replied, that is called me moving on, which I'm doing just fine. It's nothing to do with granting forgiveness.

Jen's definition made more sense yet seemed more miserly. "Forgiveness is not reconciliation," she'd said to me one night. "It's just writing off a debt that you know you'll never collect. After that, you can decide whether you want to try to reconcile, but they're not the same thing at all."

The truth is, just the thought of being asked to forgive stirs a potent mix of power, guilt, and sadness. The idea of withholding ups the power portion of the mix.

Finally, Jessie speaks, so quietly I have to lean in.

"All this time, I didn't believe he'd done what they said, to Bea, to you. Not my boy. My son couldn't have done that," she says. "But now I see the truth of it. And I'm sorry. I should have ..."

She falls into silence. Should have done what? I wonder. Then I wonder whether I want to know what she's done for her son that she regrets. No, I don't want to know at all.

"It's not your fault, Aunt Jessie," I say. It's like the words are pouring out ahead of my brain. "You couldn't have done anything to stop this."

"I should have raised him up better. I should have protected him when ..." Again she trails off, and I realize she hasn't come to me for absolution but for something else. Punishment, maybe. I wonder how often she's sought punishment instead of grace. How funny that I'd been prepared to withhold forgiveness when she would have never taken it anyway.

Jessie's hair is a bit of a mess, as though she's been digging her fingers into it. I have an urge to sit her down on a chair in front of me, brush her long white hair into smoothness, then wind it into a neat bun, the way she'd always worn it. Instead, I touch her shoulder.

"I'll be okay," I say. "All that's over now."

I wonder if this will ever be true for them. Or for me. I want it to be true for me.

I leave Jessie and Janine like that, in the middle of the courtroom lobby. I march out of the building, Adele half a step behind me, into the biting cold. Adele gives me a hug on the court steps. She won't be there tomorrow, but she tells me to call her if I ever need to talk or anything at all, and I say I will. But I know I won't.

—

Sam and I are loading the dishwasher while Kirsten opens a bottle of wine when there's a knock at the front door. Kirsten opens it, and Uncle Henry's booming voice fills the entire house.

"Hi there, I'm Henry. Where's that niece of mine?"

Henry and Helen follow Kirsten into the kitchen. Henry is carrying a brown paper bag. He sets it on Kirsten's counter, pulls a bottle from the bag. Glenlivet.

"Forget that wine, I've got the good stuff," he says to us. Kirsten sets glasses and a tray of ice on the counter. Henry drops one ice cube into each glass, pours the Scotch to the top. He looks at Helen and she shakes her head.

"One of us has to drive," she says.

"Oh, you're welcome to stay the night," says Kirsten.

Henry fills the last glass with Scotch.

"Where are Grandpa and George?" I ask.

"Uncle Ivan's already in bed," says Helen. "He's exhausted. I'm sure he'll be up at five a.m. George stayed back in case Ivan needed anything."

Henry raises his glass. "To Darby. She just won the case for the prosecution."

Helen, Sam, and Kirsten all echo him. I don't know that I agree, but I swallow the Scotch. My first taste of the stuff. It's a little like rye, with a sweet undertone, but more earthy. I can taste the peat and wood. It's definitely smoother than the whiskey I'm used to.

Henry and Helen fill us in on what we'd missed prior to my testimony. Dad had testified right before me, talking about the last-minute trip to buy a bull to replace the one that had crapped out, and how Will had left suddenly, and how Dad had realized later Will had left right before Bea had been killed. But Will's lawyer had ripped him to shreds on the stand, pointing out all the contradictions between his testimony and his earlier statements to police. The lawyer had made him look like a liar, which I guess he is.

Hearing anything about my dad's role in the whole thing makes me so angry, my hand shakes as I drink my Scotch. By keeping Will's secret, he'd left me vulnerable. How was I supposed to have known my uncle was a monster?

But deep down, I feel like I should have known. And deeper down, so far down I don't want to admit it even to myself, I'm disgusted with Bea for not telling me, either. And for not leaving years earlier. Most of all I'm mad at her for marrying him in the first place. It makes me feel small and ugly, this judgement of my aunt, and fills my stomach with acid.

Time to change the subject, I think. I look at Helen. "What was with that guy at the reception? Kenneth Diamond?"

"His real name is Kenneth Bale. Or that's what he used to go by," says Helen.

Henry sets down his glass. "Kenneth was there? That son of a ..."

"He slipped out right from under your nose, luckily for you and him," says Helen.

"Just how redneck do you think I am, Helen?"

She just looks at him.

"Are you talking about the older gentleman at the reception with the leather jacket?" says Kirsten, smiling ruefully. "He was oddly dressed for winter but seemed like a nice-enough man. He gave me his card."

"Trust me, he's not a nice man," says Henry. "Stay away from him. More importantly, keep him away from any teenage girls in your life."

"Oh," says Kirsten. "Oh, I see now. I will." She shivers, and her smile disappears. I wonder what they'd talked about.

"Okay, is anyone going to tell me what the deal is with that guy? He said he knew my mom, and Bea. He said they modelled for him. What does that mean?"

"They did. He also taught Bea a few things about photography. But he was a creep," says Helen. "No, actually, he was more than a creep. He exploited both of them, but especially Bea. He tried to steal her photos and sell them himself, by blackmailing her ..."

I wait for her to finish, but she doesn't. "Blackmailing her with what?"

"It's a long story," says Helen. "We did manage to take care of it ourselves, at least somewhat. Anyway, your grandpa still, to this day, doesn't know anything about it."

"If Dad had found out, he would have called his brother and cousins and strung Kenneth up."

"From what?" Sam laughs. "You don't have any trees down there."

"Oh, Dad would have found a tree. Or a fencepost."

"I don't want to talk about Kenneth anymore right now. Or Will. There was so much more to Bea's life that I feel like we never get to talk about anymore," Helen says. "I used to love coming over to your house. My sisters were both older, and they'd left home by the time I hit high school," she says to me. "I'd go over to May and Bea's, and we'd do each other's makeup and hair. I'd take their measurements for dresses and skirts and tops, and when I went home my mother would help me tailor them."

"Helen's mom was a real seamstress, and Helen is not too bad, either. She made Linda's wedding dress," says Henry.

"Oh, I was so happy to do that for her. It reminded me of learning to sew from my mother. I still love sewing. When work gets out of hand, I just go into my sewing room and focus on colours and patterns."

I close my eyes, imagine my mom and aunt trying on beautiful shift dresses made by Helen. Helen pinning the seams, taking in the waists a touch, then leaving Bea and May to swing the skirts, maybe do a few twirls. I can see the colours, jewel tones that would complement their eyes.

When Henry's not looking, Helen pours her Scotch into my glass, then stands up and refills her own with ginger ale. Henry is too engrossed in a story about Bea and May starting colts with Grandpa Swank to notice. Henry and George had tagged along on their quiet older horses. Bea, not thinking, threw a rope at a calf. Somehow the rope got under her young horse's tail. The horse clamped his tail down on the rope, started bucking, and when that didn't work, took off like a scalded cat across the prairie. Bea hung on through it all. When everyone else finally caught up, the colt had run out of steam, and Bea was laughing.

"'What the hell took you two so long?' she said to us." Uncle Henry laughs.

Kirsten has a lot of questions about Bea's early days as an artist, and Henry and Helen share stories about her sketching, her photography, and later the paintings. "My favourites are her sketches of Mom, baking bread in the kitchen. She was young, probably only about ten, but even then they were good," says Henry.

"Grandma really looked like Mom and Bea," I say, "but blond and fair-skinned."

"Yes, she really looked like her Icelandic grandmother," says Helen. Interesting. I'd had no idea we had an Icelandic ancestor.

After a while, Helen nudges Henry. "You sure you can drive?" he asks her.

"Yes, I gave Darby my drink."

"Sly woman. Okay, we'll get out of your hair."

"Thank you so much for coming," says Kirsten.

"We'll see you kids in court tomorrow," says Henry to Sam and me.

That night, I record a quick entry on the camera Char and Jason left. I talk about my aunt, how wild and brave she was. As I fall asleep, I think of her rip-roaring across the grasslands on a wild-eyed colt, laughing the whole time.

—

I'm a little hungover from the Scotch the next morning, but I'm wide awake by six thirty. Sam and Kirsten are already up, having coffee. They seem awfully chummy. Almost flirty.

On the way into Battleford, I decide to just ask Sam. "Are you sleeping with Kirsten?"

"No. Well, not yet, anyway."

"She must have at least twenty years on you."

"Like you're one to talk. Jack was way older than you."

"Fair enough," I say, my face burning a little. He's right. Who am I to judge?

Uncle Henry also looks a little hungover as I take the empty seat beside him. But when Lena Cherville takes the stand, we're all on high alert.

"And so it begins," Sam whispers under his breath.

The Crown asks Lena the expected questions: how long she'd known Bea and Will, how close she was to Bea, how she found out about the abuse, what happened the week before Bea died. Lena tells us about the first time she met Bea. Dad had brought her into the hospital after Will had beaten the hell out of her. I'd heard this once before, but I listen intently to the details—how Bea was wrapped in a crazy quilt and mostly naked otherwise. The black eyes and serious concussion and ruptured eardrum.

Maybe it's last night's Scotch, but when I think of Bea's injuries, and all the people who knew and said nothing, I feel sick.

During her stay in the hospital, Lena tried several times to convince Bea to call the cops.

"She said they wouldn't protect her, and it would just make things worse. She was embarrassed, too. So I told her to leave him and move back in with her family in Maple Creek. She said he'd kill her and her whole family if she did that. He'd told her that, more than once. But most of all, she said she loved him. She said he wasn't always like this, and she was sure he'd get better if she hung in there."

Lena, already working with my mom, soon grew close to Bea, too. She talked about the coffee gabs with Bea and my mom over the years. How Will tried to cut Bea off from her friends, outright forbidding her to see them at times, but how the three women persisted. Bea would wait until Will was occupied with ranch chores, then sneak over to Mom's for coffee, where Lena would meet them. Or she'd stop in at Lena's for a quick visit on the way home from a grocery run.

"In all the decades I knew them, I can count on one hand the number of times I was at Bea's place, and that was always when the men came, too."

How strange, I think, that I never picked up on those patterns. Now that Lena's said it, it seems plain as day. Except for my mom, and even that was rare, Bea never had her girlfriends over without their husbands.

Lena recalls the times Bea landed in the hospital in the early years of their friendship. Almost always with a story on hand to explain away the injuries, usually involving a wreck with a horse. But anyone who knew Bea knew she was proficient at avoiding injuries, even with rank colts. Doctors advised her to give up the horses, but Lena knew the real story. The next time they'd have coffee, Bea would have an excuse for Will, an explanation of what she'd done to trigger the attack.

"Then one day she stopped making excuses for him. She said she'd realized she turned herself inside out every day to keep him happy, and he didn't even remember their anniversary last year. She decided she was going to leave him. We'd sold a quarter and were able to give her enough cash that she could leave without withdrawing money from their joint account. But as she was leaving, she put her car in the ditch, and someone must have seen her after the accident and let him know. Whoever it was, they probably didn't realize what they'd done until much later ..."

Lena is silent for several seconds, blotting the tears from her face with tissue. Then she goes on. "I never really believed that he would kill her, but she was right. She was right all along."

Lena seems credible as the Crown wraps up. Then Vivian begins her questioning.

"At what point did you tell Sergeant Steele about the abuse Mr. Fletcher allegedly inflicted on the victim?"

"Bea. Her name is Bea."

"Please answer the question, Mrs. Cherville," the judge instructs.

"I decided to tell them when I saw Darby come into the hospital, after Will had attacked her."

"Did you go to the RCMP station that day?"

"No, I wasn't able to with everything going on at the hospital."

"So you went the next day then?"

"No."

"Exactly when did you actually tell the police about the alleged abuse?"

"It was a few days later."

"So *a few days later* you went to the RCMP station, unprompted. Is that correct?"

"Well, Sergeant Steele asked me to come in."

"It took you several days, after your best friend's niece was attacked, to give a statement. And you only did so after being told to come in by Sergeant Steele."

"Well, yes."

"For how many years did you know that Will Fletcher was allegedly abusing his wife?"

"Over twenty years."

"Did you witness this abuse?"

"Not directly. But I treated Bea in the hospital several times in the early years. And she told me about it."

"And you never reported these alleged assaults in twenty years?"

"No."

"As a nurse, did you have a professional and legal obligation to report abuse?"

"Yes, but Bea stopped coming into the hospital once that rule came in. The injuries changed, too. No more broken bones, more sprained wrists or bruising on her body when he'd hit her with a phone book. Not the kind of thing that required an emergency room visit, and that was easy to pass off. Once I became the hospital administrator, I wouldn't have been treating her anymore anyway."

"Still, you knew the abuse was happening. You could have called the police, but you didn't."

"That's true. But I didn't think it was my decision to make. I regret that now."

"Did you urge her to call the police after the initial hospital visit?"

"Yes, several times. But she didn't trust the police."

"Isn't it possible that Will never abused Bea, but you chose to make those false allegations once she was gone to protect someone else? Perhaps your son, after he attacked his ex-girlfriend?"

"That's not what happened. She never wanted to report the abuse, but it happened. Her medical records document those injuries."

"You decided to support your friend's choice while she was alive. What about once she was dead? Why didn't you tell the police what you knew then?"

Lena is silent for so long the judge has to prompt her to answer.

Finally, she says, "I ask myself that question every day. It's hard for me to understand. I was afraid of Will. Bea was dead and there was no bringing her back. I think I was in shock from her death at first, and I was grieving. I regret not going in sooner, before Darby was attacked."

Lena is crying again. She takes a long breath and then wipes her tears with a fresh tissue, which she then tucks up her sleeve.

"Sometimes, when you've held onto a secret like that for a long time, it's hard to let it go."

Someone is sniffling nearby. I glance past Uncle Henry, see Helen dabbing her eyes. I think of Kenneth and wonder what the full story was. What secrets has Helen been holding onto all these years? And will she ever let them go?

—

After Lena finishes, the Crown turns the courtroom over to Vivian, who trots out one expert after another to try to discredit the Crown's forensics experts. It's hard to follow, especially since I didn't see the first part of the trial, but she's trying to throw doubt on the timeline by focussing on the lake's temperature and how fast gas would have formed in Bea's body, causing it to float. It's surreal, hearing people talk about my aunt this way, as though she's a thing, a piece of evidence.

I study the jury during each witness's testimony, trying to gauge their reactions. A couple of them are clearly bored, and one older woman is pale and clearly upset by the gory details. But one guy is leaning forward, listening intently. He's probably in his early fifties, with a slight squint from spending time outside without sunglasses. His face looks a little weather-beaten, too, and I conclude he's a farmer. I create a fictional biography for him: hockey coach, three kids, farm near Hafford, a wife who works as a substitute teacher. He loves curling, secretly dislikes the violence in hockey, and uses phrases like "Hafford dancing boots" and "rarer than hen's teeth." This man, who I call Clayton, is a science nerd, loves the agronomy part of farming. He looks kind. I focus on him whenever the testimony starts to upset me.

I start imagining lives for the other jury members: Sue, the retired school secretary; Terry, a young oilfield worker; Carl, the grocery store manager with a secret life. But then I realize there's something a little strange about this jury. There is not one young woman on the jury. In fact, the youngest woman looks to be sixty or better. I hadn't seen the jury selection, so I don't know what happened exactly, but I bet Will's lawyer struck them because she worried they'd be sympathetic toward Bea. Or maybe toward me.

It's only then that fear grips me. What if he does get off? It seemed almost impossible before I'd noticed the jury composition, but now it's all I can think about. I spend all my time trying to examine the jury's reactions to Vivian's experts, without drawing attention to myself by staring. I don't dare share these thoughts publicly, or on camera, in case it somehow blows back. But before I fall asleep at night, I record my impressions in my songwriting notebook.

> *Clayton clearly skeptical of Vivian's forensics expert today. Terry and Jeanette also seemed skeptical, but Sue shooting Will more sympathetic looks. Edie, who seems to be Sue's friend (she often exchanges looks with Sue), also on Will's side. Rest of jury inscrutable.*

I can't get through a night now without waking after feeling a weight on my bed and hands around my throat. Every night, I wake up already sitting up in bed, gasping for air. One night, I find myself trying to open the back door.

"Darby? Are you okay?" It's Kirsten, Sam right behind her. They definitely have a thing going, I realize. I don't really mind, in a moral sense, but it makes me feel lonely, especially since every time I talk to Ruby, she wants to say hi to Sam, too.

I try once more, half-heartedly, to turn the doorknob, then realize it's locked. If it hadn't been locked, how far would I have walked before I woke?

"I'm fine. Just a bad dream."

"How long have you been sleepwalking?" Kirsten asks.

"I don't know. I don't know what's happening."

"Do you remember talking to me last night? About the girl?" Kirsten is looking at me with concern.

"No. I was talking to you last night? When?"

"I got up in the middle of the night for a glass of water. You were sitting in the living room, looking at your aunt's portrait. When I asked how you were doing, you kept telling me there was a dead girl in here. You were very insistent. I have to say, it spooked me. Then you said: 'It's a bicycle.' And you just got up and walked back to your bedroom."

"I don't remember any of that."

"This trial must be very hard for you," she says.

Sam hands me a mug of something. Tea, I realize. He made me tea just now, and I didn't even notice him doing it.

"This might help you get back to sleep," he says.

"Thanks, Sam," I say, then take a sip. Not tea. A hot toddy.

Sam and Kirsten both seem worried about me, but their concern leaves me feeling embarrassed and weak. I know I shouldn't have anything to feel embarrassed about, but that knowledge makes me feel even worse. I tell Kirsten and Sam that I'm tired, that I'll be fine, and I take my hot toddy to bed. Eventually I slip into sleep again, this time with headphones over my ears and The Doors spinning on my Discman.

I have a dream that is not a dream, but not like the terrifying death visions I've been having, either. It's just as detailed and vivid as those awful experiences, but the horror is replaced by wonder.

In my dream, or vision, I'm outside but not cold at all, even though I'm barefoot and in flannel pjs. The sky is clear; the stars are bright. The moon is nearly full, throwing its silver-toned light across Kirsten's yard.

I have a feeling I should walk toward the river. I don't question what's drawing me there; I follow it. It's like there's a string around my middle, tugging me down the brush trails to the frigid North Saskatchewan. As I walk over the hard-crusted snow, I smell smoke, and soon I can see a crackling fire by the river. There is a man sitting near the fire, but I can make out only his silhouette.

I step out of the brush, onto the riverbank, and stop dead. The man looks exactly like Jim Morrison in the early days of his fame, rail thin and gorgeous. He's even wearing the billowing white shirt, black leather pants, and concho belt I always associate with him. His shoulder-length hair flows in the breeze snaking through the river valley.

"Hi, Darby. It's about time. I've been waiting."

"Who are you?"

"You know who I am."

Stunned, not knowing what else to do, I walk to the fire. Jim lights a joint, passes it to me. I inhale. It's mild sixties pot, not the extreme-THC stuff that people smoke these days. I take another drag, then hand it back to Jim.

"Why have you been waiting for me?"

"I'm here to help you embrace your destiny." He smiles, motions with the hand holding the joint. "Look around you. You have all this light in front of you."

I look up, past the fire, and realize the landscape is, in fact, flooded with light. The moon and stars are impossibly bright, almost as though I'm on a stage. A faint melody floats on the air. It sounds like me singing. Then the light dims and the sound disappears.

"That's your future, man. But before you get there, you need to know something."

"What's that?"

"The war is over. No one is going to hurt you. And I've always got your back. Anytime you need anything, you find me."

It's strange, but as soon as he tells me I'm safe, I feel the tension leaving my body. Muscles I didn't even realize I was clenching relax. I even feel my eyes, my jaw soften. I feel warm by the fire.

Jim hands me an acoustic guitar, picks up a tambourine for himself. He sings the songs I've heard probably a hundred times: "People are Strange," "Love Me Two Times," "Waiting for the Sun." In this place I know not only the lyrics but the chords to these songs. Then he starts singing songs I've never heard, but somehow I know them, too. We play until the fire burns down and the moon fades. Then Jim stands.

"Hey Darby, remember: enjoy the ride," he says. Then he walks east, into the early dawn light, and disappears.

—

The jury is out for nearly two days before they file back into the courtroom to deliver their verdict. I try to guess what they're going to say by their body language. Only one of them, the plump grey-haired woman I've named Sue, looks at Will. She looks him right in the eye as she walks to the jury box.

I glance across the aisle. Grandma and Grandpa Swank sit stoic. Aunt Jessie cries silently into her daughter Janine's shoulder.

Sam pinches my leg and I almost cry out.

"Don't," I whisper.

"Pay attention," he whispers back.

The judge glances at us and we stop. I try to look as innocent as a kitten with newly opened eyes. Then I turn my eyes to Will's back, trying to glare holes into it. Guilty. Guilty. Guilty, I think.

Will, perhaps sensing my evil eye, turns around to look at me. He's still looking at me as the jury forewoman delivers the verdict. Guilty. Guilty. Guilty on all charges.

I smile at Will as his face goes slack. Is he really surprised? Did he really think he was going to get off? Then, as I watch, a snarl twists his lips. He looks at me with an animal hate and he leans toward me, as though he's thinking of leaping at me.

Fuck you, I think. The law's there for your protection as much as mine, you asshole. My body is taut, ready for another fight. I want to scratch his eyes out, smash his nose with my elbow.

"Darby." It's Uncle George. He is holding my left forearm; Sam's got the right. "Take it down a notch."

"Darby, we won. He's going away," says Helen.

I have a flash of the strange dream with Jim Morrison. *The war is over.* It's cost us dearly, but we've won.

"Let her go," says Grandpa Kolchak. "She's not going to do anything."

He's right, I realize. I feel my anger freeze into my bones, numb my skin.

"You take after your grandfather too much," says Henry.

"She's a lot like May," says Helen.

I think of my mom's temper tantrums. "No, I'm not."

I look over at the Swank side of the courtroom. Grandma Swank is standing, her back ramrod-straight, her face tight with resolve. Great-aunt Jessie is sobbing loudly into Janine's shoulder, and Janine is crying, too, as she holds her mother. Dad is holding Jacqueline's hand as he watches Will intently.

Grandpa Swank, who is still sitting even though Grandma stands beside him, has a look on his face that breaks my heart. I can see all his sorrow in his eyes, and I think this is probably how we all feel, deep down. When you get past all the fronting and the distracting drama, what's left is a deep grief that threatens to swallow you whole.

I look back to Will. He is still glowering at me as they lead him away. I wink at him as he goes, just so he knows I'm not scared of him anymore. Rage lights his eyes, and I shiver.

Maybe I'm still a little scared of him.

Grandpa Kolchak insists on taking us out for supper that night to celebrate. We pick a fancy place in Old Battleford, recommended by Kirsten, which was originally a train station. Kirsten joins us, sitting by Sam so they can hold hands under the table. He looks at her with soft, puppy-dog eyes and my stomach knots in worry.

Uncle Henry is jubilant, talking loudly in his warm voice. I wonder if this is what he's like at Canadian Cattlemen Association meetings, where he's been the president since just before BSE broke out. Probably not: he's probably more serious in the board room, I think.

Grandpa Kolchak is happy, too, ordering wine by the bottle for the table and encouraging everyone to pick out appetizers in addition to entrees.

"Don't worry about the cost," he says.

"Dad," says George. "Are you sure that's a good idea?" He looks worried, likely thinking about Grandpa's finances.

"It's not every day that I get to watch my murderous son-in-law go to prison. Let me celebrate," Grandpa says.

I sit next to Helen. After we order, she pulls out a thick envelope of photos, starts rifling through them. "I have some of my photos in here, just a moment. This is your cousin, Brynny. I'm not sure if you've ever met her."

Brynny is a tall blond with turquoise eyes and high cheekbones. Beautiful, like Helen. I feel a pang of envy.

"We named her after your great-great-grandmother, Brynny Jónsdóttir. She came to Canada from Iceland, settled with her family in Ontario, and then on Lake Winnipeg. That's where she met her husband, Charlie Parsons. Bea, May, and I all got to know her when we were young. She was a fascinating woman. A healer. And she would read the runes for us, tell us what fate had set in front of us."

"Really? Was she right?"

"Well, it wasn't very specific most of the time. My older sister swears that Granny Parsons foresaw her engagement and our father's death, all on the same day, but she didn't say it like that, exactly. She'd say something like, 'You have a great love ahead of you, but with that love, you will lose someone very dear.' You never knew what that meant until it happened."

"That's not very helpful."

"No, it didn't help you avoid any tragedy. But when our father died, we all looked at each other and said, 'Oh, that's what it meant,' and it was oddly comforting. Anyway, I thought you should have these. Bea took these when she was a teenager. There are lots of photos of your mom in here, along with the rest of the family."

She slides the envelope to me. I take out the first few photos. They're of Mom, teaching a young boy to make cookies. "Is this Uncle George?"

"Yes, that's him," Helen says.

"Let me see," says George, so I pass the photos to him. "Oh, yeah, I was trying to impress a girl who liked sugar cookies. I'm still a good baker. I think that's how I got my first and second wives," he laughs.

The rest of the night passes in a haze of red wine and steak and stories, mostly triggered by the photos. Neither Helen nor George drink, and so while George ends up driving Grandpa and Henry to the hotel, Helen takes Sam, Kirsten, and me home. We decide to leave Kirsten's car at the restaurant. I'm meeting Grandma and Grandpa Swank the next day for lunch anyway.

As Helen stops in Kirsten's yard, she grabs my hand. "Take care of yourself, Darby. We'll all be rooting for you, whatever you do next."

"Thanks for everything, Helen."

I watch her slowly drive away, the exhaust from her SUV forming clouds in the winter air. Inside, Kirsten and Sam are waiting, but they make me feel like a third wheel. I can't even call Ruby without Sam wanting to talk to her, too, or vice versa, so I walk to the barn instead.

Inside, the barn is warm from the horse's bodies. Their smell hangs in the air, mixing with the scent of hay and manure. A bay mare nickers at me, so I walk into her stall.

"Hey, Liz," I say, sliding into the stall and rubbing her neck. Liz noses around my pockets, looking for treats. "I don't have anything for you."

I remember her as a filly, remember Bea working with her in the round pen, watching her trot and lope circles around Bea, Liz switching directions or walking right up to Bea with nothing more than a shift in Bea's body position. I remember the first time Bea rode Liz out, following me and Bucky along the bush trails and through the open fields. How she'd crow-hopped that day as we broke into a fast canter across the hay field, and Bea had just laughed, pulled the filly's head up, and straightened Liz's body out, keeping her even with Bucky and me. That was the summer before Bea died.

And without warning, all the sorrow I've been holding through the trial pours out of me. I bury my face in the mare's neck and sob. I cry harder than I've cried anytime in my life, more than I thought was possible. My tears drench the mare's mane and neck, until my throat is parched and my eyes are sore and dry. Liz just stands there until I finish. Then she stretches her neck out and yawns out her worry and lies down. I sit down, too, in the warm straw and lean against Liz's back. I stay like that for a long time, until thirst drives me to my feet and back to the house.

PART TWO
2004–2008

The sort of life which I had had previous to this popular success was one that required endurance, a life of clawing and scratching along a sheer surface and holding on tight with raw fingers to every inch of rock higher than the one caught hold of before, but it was a good life because it was the sort of life for which the human organism is created.

—Tennessee Williams,
On a Streetcar Named Success

SIX

IT'S A HOT August afternoon, drought-burned grass crunching under my feet, hordes of grasshoppers like a cloud around me, some as high as my head. I look around at the yard where I grew up. I've already decided it's the last time I'll ever come home.

It's not a hard decision. Soon I'll be in Toronto. And my home is disappearing anyway.

Well, not exactly disappearing. Being auctioned off to the highest bidder tomorrow. Dad and Will had already sold their cows and most of the horses last year, just before BSE slammed ranchers across the country. Uncle Henry, as president of the Canadian Cattlemen's Association, had been in the media more times than I could count since I'd last seen him. It was strange to see him in the paper and on the news. He'd seemed to age rapidly since Will's trial eight months ago, worry blanching his sandy hair to grey.

For over a year, Dad rented out the pastures to another rancher while he tried to decide what to do with the land that had been in his family for three generations. I never thought he'd sell. While

I felt critical about his inertia, it also guaranteed home would be there if I chose to visit it.

Meanwhile, Magpie Apocalypse had picked up steam through the year. Jason and Char had titled their short doc *All That's Left*, after our song, and would be screening it at several film festivals this fall. The song itself had opened doors for us and spurred us to write more of our own songs. We'd recorded an album in the garage, and CKUA had been giving it plenty of airplay, even having us on live. From there, some of the summer festivals in Alberta had booked us.

Ruby and I were about to go on stage last month when I got the call from Dad. He and Jacqueline were moving back to Gimli. He needed to move on, he'd said.

I think he wanted to explain more, a rarity for Dad, but the audience was waiting. "Okay. I've got to go, Dad. I've got a show."

"Where are you playing?"

"A music festival. Pembina."

"I didn't know you were doing that kind of thing."

"Yeah, well, I really have to go, Dad. I'll come home for the auction. I promise."

Ruby watched me closely. "Are you okay? Are you ready?"

I adjusted my guitar strap, more out of nervousness than anything, and took a deep breath. "Yeah, I'm ready."

We were what the festival organizer had called "'tweeners." short for in-betweeners. Performers doing a short set between the bigger acts. Behind us the roadies were setting up the amps for the next act, a rock band out of London, Ontario.

I was just happy to perform. I was glad I'd been able to build my skills on the guitar. I was grateful that my songwriting muse had returned and that I was playing guitar and singing harmony with my good friend on a beautiful summer day. We'd worked so hard for this over the months, playing for Ruby's parents' friends at summer barbeques, covers at corporate gigs that Red booked for us last Christmas, and in every bar along Whyte Avenue or anywhere in the city that would let us. Hours and hours spent writing songs and rehearsing in the garage. No time for any other relationships—Ruby's girlfriends dropped her, one after another, and I never got started with the guys who flirted with me between classes or after the shows. None of them sparked that warmth that Jack had, years ago.

But soon Ruby would move to Vancouver to study music therapy, a profession perfectly suited to her, I thought, as long as she could make a living at it. I had been trying to decide whether to follow her. If nothing else, we'd have this festival performance to look back on, I'd thought.

A small crowd gathered close to the stage as we went through our set, a mix of covers and our own material. By the time we closed with "The Weight," the people gathered at the front of the stage were singing along.

I didn't know it at the time, but Robby Slade, a Canadian alt-country veteran, had watched the last ten minutes of our performance. Slade's solo band was headlining that night. I didn't know it until after our performance, but his main band, Urban Coyotes, was looking for a new guitar player, preferably one who could sing harmony.

Slade had been in the music business for at least twenty years. Music journalists used terms like *blue collar* when describing his career, which kind of cracked me up. It made me think of Robby Slade working away in a coal mine, or on a factory line in Ontario. But I suppose it was accurate in a way. Slade worked like a dog. His tour schedule looked exhausting, especially when you realized he was edging toward fifty. And it was even more impressive when you considered how much good new music he was producing even while touring.

Ruby and I watched his whole set. After, I went backstage, hoping for a chance to meet him. When he spotted me, he made a beeline right for me.

"I caught your set earlier," he said. "You're a decent player. Matt, my guitar player, is leaving in a few weeks. How would you like to fly out to Toronto for an audition?"

"Yes," I said, with no hesitation. "When do you want me there?"

The next week, I'd taken a red eye to Toronto, auditioned for Robby and Owen Wild, who had co-founded Urban Coyotes years ago. Robby and Owen co-wrote songs and took turns singing lead. Also there was Nancy Adams, their long-time manager. I thought it went well, and before I got back on the plane the next morning, I found out I had the gig.

Now, as I lug my duffle bag to the house, the idea of moving to Toronto seems surreal. As though it's someone else moving there, not me.

Dad's not even here, I realize as I walk up the steps. No sign of his truck or him. Oh well. No big loss there. I carry my bag upstairs to my old bedroom.

Standing in the middle of my bedroom, I start mentally cataloguing what I must deal with. Anything I don't want now I'm going to either give away or chuck. Even if it's worth a few bucks. I really don't want people picking through my stuff, trying to decide how much it's worth.

As I work, I fall into an easy rhythm. Keep, gift, chuck. Keep, gift, chuck. The afternoon wears on as I go through books, old clothes, knick-knacks. I keep all my photos and all my music. All the clothes left in my room are scrunched up into garbage bags for the thrift store, unless they're ripped or worn. Those are chucked, even though Grandma Swank would admonish me for throwing out perfectly good rags.

Most of the knick-knacks I chuck. I keep a few favourite books, pile the rest into the give box, for the library in Livelong. As evening approaches, more and more stuff goes into the chuck pile.

I feel very matter of fact about everything until Jen pulls into the yard, driving the same old beat-up Honda she's had for years. It's time to clear my stuff out of the barn.

I hadn't talked to Jen much since Will's trial earlier this year. We had drifted back into our own lives again, exchanging short emails every now and then and a couple of long phone calls. But as time went on, even with that infrequent contact, our friendship felt more comfortable. Before Bea's murder, our relationship was riddled with tension and passive-aggressive slights. I guess Bea's death, and the trial, gave us both some perspective, as we'd dropped the games. Slowly we started to fill the space that pettiness had occupied with a deep loyalty.

So today, even though it's been months since I've seen her, it doesn't feel like much time has passed. We hug, link arms, and walk to the barn.

"Are you sure you want to do this? You might want to ride again," she says.

I just shake my head.

"Okay, well, if you ever change your mind, you'll know where to find your gear."

We load my saddle, bridle, and various other bits of tack and grooming supplies into the back of her Honda. The saddle blanket still smells like horse sweat, I realize. The last moment I saw Bucky flashes through my mind, the soft feel of his ears as I slip the bridle from his head and he opens his mouth and lets go of the bit. For a few seconds, I am back in the pasture, watching Will's stallion take after him.

I can't help imagining how Luke and Sam found Bucky later. Caught in a snarl of barbed wire, bleeding and exhausted, unable even to stand anymore. Sam shot him, put him out of his misery. The stallion was still pacing nearby. Still wearing his saddle and bridle, reins snapped short from when he'd stepped on them earlier in the day. Before Luke could stop him, Sam shot the stallion, too, out of anger,

Two years later, and it still takes me back to that moment where I made the wrong decision. My throat burns, and I feel nauseated and light-headed. I lean into the car for a moment.

I will not ride again. I slam the trunk of Jen's car.

"Well, that's that," I say.

"End of an era. Time for a drink," says Jen. She pulls two bottles of Great Western Light from a cooler in the back seat. We sit on the porch, Bea's old dog, Wilson, at our feet. He rolls onto his back and begs for tummy rubs.

If only this were the hardest part.

—

I don't see Dad until Saturday morning. When I stumble down the stairs, he's at the kitchen table, reading back issues of *Grainews* and *Canadian Cattlemen*, drinking coffee.

"Morning, Darby."

"Morning, Dad."

For a moment, it feels like the last two years have fallen away, like he was the father I always knew. The one who bought me my first guitar. The one who came to see me sing at the Christmas cantata even though he was pretty much an atheist. For a moment, I can see him sitting—clearly uncomfortable—in the pews, almost clapping before remembering where he was.

I start to pour myself a coffee. The silence in the kitchen, which used to feel familiar and even comfortable, now feels oppressive. But I can't stomach the prospect of normal conversation, either. Hard questions stick at the back of my throat. Why didn't you tell me that Will was abusing Aunt Bea? Why didn't you tell the police right away? Why didn't you protect me?

I try making small talk. "Is Jacqueline going to be here?"

"No. She had to take care of some things in Gimli."

I wonder what my mom would think of this Gimli plan. I wonder if she would be happy that Dad is finally moving on from her.

The coffee is acidic in my stomach. I dump it in the sink and go outside, leaving Dad to his farm papers.

—

Light clouds and a breeze keep the temperature bearable for the auction.

Hundreds turn up. They shuffle past the eight-by-ten tables holding boxes of junk, thinking about what they might bid on. How much might that pile of screws be worth? *Those end tables might be nice for the cabin*, I overhear a lady say. I can't place her face. Strangers picking over the farm's carcass.

Dad has washed the old tractor and haybine in the hopes of tempting farmers into higher bids. Even the window trim on the house has a fresh coat of white paint. Grandma Swank has planted, watered, and deadheaded the white-and-purple petunias in the flower beds. The house looks ready to welcome a young farming family, people able to pull their living from the earth. Or perhaps more likely a retired couple ready to escape their hectic urban lives and looking for enough land to tear around on their ATVs.

Dad is standing at the back of the crowd, as far away from the auctioneer as he can get. Drinking black coffee, shaking hands, talking with people. He probably wants a beer, but he's quit drinking entirely. Grandpa Swank comes up behind him, grips his shoulder, and offers him a fresh Styrofoam cup.

Some people are confused by Dad's newfound teetotalism. "He was never a heavy drinker," I hear dad's cousin, Sheila, say. I doubt anyone in rural Saskatchewan quits drinking unless there's a problem brewing, or already ripping apart their lives. Sheila doesn't understand what it's like to stand at the abyss's edge and try to stop yourself from stepping over the brink.

Grandma Swank is handing out the coffee and cold pop, along with the auctioneer's wife.

"Mom, you don't have to do that," Dad had said to her earlier.

"What else am I supposed to do? Enjoy the party?"

So now she's filling the cups, making change. Smiling, but not in a way that reaches her eyes.

Part of me is starting to feel sorry for Dad. Starting to think maybe it's time to forgive him. He started cooperating with the cops right after Will attacked me, even gave them the names of friends and family who might shelter him when he was on the run. They'd picked him up near Moose Jaw, staying with old horse industry friends who said they had no idea what was really going on. Dad was the one who had said Will might be there. If he hadn't done that, who knows how far Will might have got? Maybe all the way to Mexico, or South America. To this day, I don't really know where he was heading.

I decide I'll go stand by Dad, at least. I start walking to where he's standing at the back of the crowd when a young man in flip flops and board shorts, chatting with a pretty brunette in a tank top, collides with me, spilling pop all over both of us.

The guy hands me his used napkin, but I don't take it. It wouldn't help anyway. I feel hot, as though I have a fever.

Then I feel a hand on my elbow pulling me back. I turn around. It's Luke. Jen and Sam are standing behind him.

"C'mon, Darby. Let's get out of here," Luke says.

—

I want to see Bea and Will's house, so the four of us hop into Sam's truck. I call shotgun, gleefully swing into the front passenger seat.

Luke opens the back door, gestures for Jen to get in. "C'mon, little sister. You get to sit at the back with the cool kids today."

Jen snorts.

It should be a two-minute drive, seeing that their place is just across the road from Dad's. But their long driveway hasn't been graded in a long time. The road is pockmarked with potholes and a few fallen poplars, killed by years of drought, block our way. Sam carefully manoeuvres the truck around most of them, but one large white spruce blocks the entire driveway. Sam pulls a chainsaw from the bed of the truck and slices the trunk and branches into manageable chunks that we toss into the bush.

Finally the trees open into a clearing, and we're in the yard. The house, originally the Anglican Church in a nearby town, sits at the top of the hill, the shadow of the cross still visible over the patio doors. One of the stained-glass windows is broken. The wood seems dried out from the sun. The whole thing looks like it could use some paint, or siding, or something.

A raven flies into the clearing, perches on the roof peak above the cross's shadow. It screeches, scolding us as though we've been circling its nest. It even beats the air with its wings while perched, trying perhaps to stir up a dust devil or plow wind to blast us from the yard.

"We're not going anywhere," Sam calls, leaning out the window. The raven screeches again before taking wing above the trees.

Weeds and long grass have overtaken the yard. The spot where Bea had her garden is nearly invisible, except for a few feral dill plants poking their heads over the weeds. At the edge of the yard, the barn doors are wide open. The barn is probably infested by squirrels, mice, and skunks by now. It has been abandoned for years now, I realize. Time has gone by so quickly.

I close my eyes and think of my aunt, her long black hair in a braid, pulling carrots and beets, plucking tomatoes. I remember how she used to laugh at her dog Wilson, who would beg for pea pods. The dog would gobble them up as though she'd tossed him bacon.

Bea would arrange the vegetables in a bowl, set them on a table in her studio on the second floor, and paint a still life. She created a series of these still lives, and the paintings toured as part of an exhibit of her work, just a year before she died. Some machinery company executive bought the veggie series for what seemed to us a fantastic sum. When Bea talked about the sale, she described in great detail the places she imagined her veggie paintings hanging. One in the kitchen, above the marble sink. Another in the chief financial officer's office, overlooking the factory floor. The third in the observation area of the family's personal indoor horse arena.

Sam shuts off his truck, but none of us reach for a door handle. We sit there sweating as the truck turns into an oven, taking in the spooky sight. I wonder how long it will take before it looks like no one ever lived here at all.

Strange how much has changed over the last two years. I haven't seen Luke or Sam since Will's trial. Luke's face and arms are bronzed from a summer of working out of a vet clinic, time spent on farms and ranches in the area. He seems set to work in the local vet clinic, maybe take over the practice one day. He and Meaghan are engaged, Jen told me yesterday, and he looks as happy as I've ever seen him. I feel a twinge of something. Not regret, exactly, for ending our love affair, but maybe nostalgia. I am happy he is happy. Meaghan better be good to him, I think. Treat him better than I did.

Sam, by contrast, looks gaunt and has dark circles under his eyes. He's still with Kirsten—has sort of moved in with her, living with her when he's not guiding hunters or running his trapline up here. From what he's been telling us, it sounds like they both drink a lot. I wonder if he's into anything else besides the booze and cigarettes. Ruby still talks to him often—in fact, she seems to be the only person who reaches out to him regularly.

Seeing him now, I realize he might be in trouble. It's hard to imagine he might need help. He's always been my wildest friend, able to scramble out of any scrape he might get himself into. Without saying anything, I reach across the console and take his hand.

It's so good to be able to sit with my old friends and not worry about past arguments and rivalries. As I catalogue the wreckage of Bea and Will's yard, I wish I could leave behind every other old hurt as easily as the four of us have done it for each other.

"Do you want to go in?" Sam asks.

I shake my head.

I'd intended to take something from the house and leave Bea's wedding band. The Crown had returned it to our family after the trial was done and it became clear Will wouldn't appeal his conviction. Grandpa Swank had mailed it to me a few weeks ago, and I'd slipped it deep into my jean pocket this morning. I dig it out, slide it onto a pinky finger, turn it around and around.

Now the idea of leaving the ring, of going in the house, doesn't feel right. The raven's warnings have spooked me somehow. I don't want to touch my feet to this soil.

"Do you think places hold memories? Does the land remember us somehow?" I look to Sam, the hunter and trapper among us, for answers.

He's quiet for a while, thinking.

"I don't know," he says. "There's a spot near my trapline where I always get a bad feeling. There's this rock, under an old twisted-up jack pine. The rock seems out of place, as though someone put it there. It feels spooky, just like this yard does now. I've asked some of the old-timers, but no one knows if anything happened there. Some of them know the spot, though, and know the feeling."

"Let's get out of here," says Luke. "We're going to roast to death in this truck."

Sam turns the ignition on and starts back down the driveway. I turn around for one last look, and as we drop over a small hill, the yard, the church, and finally the trees disappear from sight.

SEVEN

ROBBY SLADE'S MANAGER, Nancy Adams, picks me up from Pearson. I'd wanted to take the train in, but she'd insisted.

"It will take you forever, even if you don't get lost. You'd have to switch to the subway, then the streetcar."

Nancy drives her Range Rover aggressively on the freeway, cutting in and out of traffic. She seems completely at ease, but I can't help gripping the door. As we make our way, she tells me about the sections of the city we're passing, and about the Leslieville neighbourhood where she lives.

"Umm, where exactly is Leslieville again?"

"East of downtown. A little west of the Beaches. You've heard of the Beaches, haven't you?"

"No."

"Don't worry, you'll be oriented soon enough. And besides, you really won't have time to be overwhelmed by the city. Not with Robby's schedule."

Nancy goes through the house rules as we turn onto Queen Street. It's all common sense. Lock the door when I leave. Don't expect her to clean up after me, she doesn't even do that for her teenage son. Help out a bit. Pay her my paltry rent on time or let her know beforehand if I'm going to be short for some reason. I can't imagine trying to tell her I'm short, since she knows exactly what I'm getting paid.

We turn south off Queen, roll down a side street, and park in front of a small grey detached two-story with a railed porch and an overflowing flower bed in the front.

"My ex and I bought this a few years ago, and split right after. It seemed like the end of the world, but it was good timing. I'd have trouble paying him out on the equity now."

Cole, her son, opens the front door before she's even turned off her vehicle. He is a hulking sixteen-year-old, at least six foot three. He has Nancy's green eyes and sandy hair.

"Hey," he says, as he matter of factly lifts my suitcase and guitar from the back of the Range Rover. "This all you brought?"

"Yup."

"Okay." He carries them up the steps and disappears into the house.

Nancy hands me my key for the front door. "Welcome to Toronto."

—

Later, over a glass of Merlot, Nancy lays out the band rules:

1. Nancy does not work with artists who break contracts. Nor does Robby Slade or Owen Wild. That means I need to show up to every gig unless I am on my deathbed.

2. I need to play well, consistently, no matter what is going on.

3. No creating drama with other band members, roadies, management, or club owners.

4. And finally, Management 101: Nancy is not going to care about my career more than I do.

I wonder if Bea's agent, Pauline, had equivalent rules for the artists she worked with. I wonder what Bea would think of all of this. She'd be proud, probably. And she'd prod my mom to tell me how proud she was, too.

Nancy refills my glass and looks at me. "Is all of this agreeable to you?"

"Oh, yes. Yes, it is."

—

Sometime in the middle of the night I slowly wake. It takes me a moment to remember where I am. Toronto.

There is a weight at the foot of my bed. At first I assume it must be a cat, or even a smallish dog, but then I remember that Nancy doesn't have any pets. And it's something much larger, I realize. I try to focus my eyes, clear my vision. But the shape at the end of the bed remains blurred. Even the streetlight spilling into my room doesn't illuminate its darkness.

Suddenly it leaps on me, crushes me against the mattress. I smell sweat. It's Will. He clenches my neck, right below my voice box. I claw at his hands, but I can't break his grip. I push my feet into the mattress, trying to raise my torso and tip him off me, but he's too heavy. I claw at his face, but he just growls.

I feel my throat collapsing. My lungs feel full, as though I've inhaled water. I am dying.

There is no sudden waking from a dream. Just a gradual realization that Will is not in my room. Slowly my vision sharpens. I take inventory of the things in my new room. The dresser beside my double bed. The small closet with the door that doesn't close properly. The yellow light from the street lying like water on the hardwood floor.

"I am safe. The war is over." I whisper it to myself over and over. But I can't get his smell out of my nose.

—

The next afternoon is my first rehearsal with the Urban Coyotes. I try to shake off the violent dream, but Will's smell lingers through the morning.

"I'd give you a ride, but I have meetings all day," Nancy says over breakfast.

"That's okay, it's not far. I like to walk."

"The easiest way is to cut down Memory Lane," she says.

"Just watch out for the dog behind the pink house," says Cole.

After they leave, I go back to my room and work out. It's a simple workout—skipping, shadowboxing, push-ups, crunchies, burpees, squats. I go through it, over and over, for half an hour, then I shower.

But instead of feeling wide awake, I'm even more tired. I change back into my pajamas, burrow under my covers, and will every muscle fibre to soften into sleep.

I dream of the Urban Coyotes' music. When I wake up, I still have hours to kill, so I pop their last CD into Nancy's stereo system to practise my guitar parts.

An hour later, I'm just sliding my feet into my sneakers when my cell phone rings.

"Hey, it's Robby. You doing anything? I thought I'd pick you up early and get you set up with a custom pedal board."

"Oh, that's okay, I brought a couple of guitar pedals. And I was going to walk to practise."

"Better not walk. There's a mean dog on Memory Lane. And you'll need a custom rig."

"Well, okay then."

I deadhead the petunias in Nancy's front yard while I wait, thinking about the petunias at the farm. Sure enough, four minutes later a vintage Eagle station wagon parks in front of the house. I admire the still-flawless wood-panelling paint job as I walk to the back of the car, open the hatch, and place my guitar inside.

"Where did you get this thing? It must be thirty years old but it looks great."

"Friend of a friend. Now, just so you know, here's what we're going to do at the rehearsal." Robby gives me a quick rundown of the afternoon—he'll introduce me to the band, and we'll review the older material (purely for my benefit, I'm sure). Then a break, and we'll go through their new songs, the ones they'll be recording soon. But first, we'll head over to the pedal board guy to get a rig that I can take on the road, Robby says.

Robby steers the Eagle down Lake Shore Boulevard, drives west. My stomach is in knots, but I don't know why. I try not to show it. I try to memorize every street name as though they're the crumbs that will show me the way out of the forest and back home. After five minutes, Robby parks in front of a red-brick warehouse.

"It's in here," he says.

I look at him doubtfully.

"No, really, it is."

"You go first," I say.

I follow Robby into the warehouse and down the dull hallway lined with doors, mostly closed. Robby walks so fast I struggle to keep up. He swerves into an open door on the right, and I follow him into the brightly lit room. Led Zeppelin fills the air. Two middle-aged people, a towering man and a short, plump woman, are assembling pedal boards. The woman looks the young grandmotherly type to me, with white hair in a pixie cut and warm eyes. A soldering iron, a screwdriver, cables and wire litter the worktable in front of them. On the wall facing the door is a bright red sign that says *Cherry Street Rigs*.

"Hey, Robby," says the man, enclosing Robby in a bear hug. The woman follows suit with a gentler hug. I catch a whiff of perfume that I don't recognize, and for some reason the idea of her wearing perfume surprises me. She seems completely at ease with the soldering iron. What a strange assumption about women who like to work with their hands I have been carrying around all these years.

"Jill, Tommy, this is our new guitarist, Darby."

"Hi," I say.

"Congratulations, Darby," says Tom. "Tell us about your sound."

"Well, I play a Yamaha SA800 right now. Sometimes I play it like a Fender, like real twangy. Sometimes I put it on the back pickup and it has a thicker sound, like a Gibson. I can make it sound like a Strat, too, but I haven't been doing that much yet. I don't know, maybe that will change, but right now I switch between that twangy and that bluesy sound, you know?"

"Yeah, yeah, that makes sense," says Tom.

"You'll definitely want something you can check on flights," says Jill.

"Yeah, I guess," I say. Robby nods.

What follows is an hour-long conversation about fractal audio rigs, analog delays, switches, preamps, phasers, and distortion. It's a whole new level of music nerdiness that I've never really experienced myself. By the end, we've settled on a large touring and recording rig with all kinds of effects for the album and touring. I also order a small mobile rig that I can use for solo gigs or stripped-down performances. Jill writes down the specifications on a yellow pad of paper, along with a price.

"How does someone get into that business?" I ask Robby as we walk to the Eagle.

"Tom used to be a guitar tech. Jill was a tour manager. They worked for some big acts in the nineties, and then decided to run away together and start this little family business in Toronto. You name any North American bands that are still touring and they've probably made a rig for them."

Robby glances at his watch. "Good, we're not going to be late for practice."

Robby turns back onto Queen Street and heads east. Again, I work on memorizing street names. We drive past Memory Lane and I note it. Two lefts and we turn down a dead-end street, lined with skinny two- and three-storey houses, many in need of paint. He drives to the end of the street, where a set of brick townhouses sits across from a grey, squat building with a small foyer entrance, like an apartment building. I grab my guitar and follow Robby to the front door.

"This used to be a bakery," he tells me as he waves his key fob at the door. It beeps and we go through to the first floor. "My brother-in-law develops real estate. When he saw that it was for sale, he figured it would be a perfect studio for me. So he turned it into Bakery Studios, but everyone calls it the Bakery. We liked the building so much that my wife and I bought the upstairs suite and turned it into our condo."

"Wow, was it expensive?"

"I never could have afforded a space like this if it wasn't my brother-in-law selling it to me," he says as we walk into the studio. There's a small kitchen area with a big wooden island right by the door. "That was the front counter for the bakery," he says, pointing at the island. "People like to have the kitchen when they're recording an album. Everyone gets sick of eating out."

I hardly ever ate out, not even in Edmonton. It's still a treat. I wonder if I'll feel different about it after our first tour.

We walk past the island, through the next door, and into the studio itself. "This whole thing worked out pretty good for my brother-in-law, Greg. He's actually a partner in the studio, so he makes a little dough when we rent it out, and he gets to be a patron of the arts."

The studio itself looks a little like a living room. Carpeted, with a big sofa and a couple of armchairs, perhaps to help absorb the sound as much as anything. Black foam bass traps and acoustic panels sit and hang in strategic spots to absorb the echoes and other errant frequencies rattling around the room. A drum kit, bass guitar, acoustic guitar, and microphones stand ready in the centre. At the back is a large window into the recording engineer's room. I walk to the centre of the room, plug my guitar into the Traynor amp, tune it up.

"This room sounds great," I say as I play a few chords.

"Thanks. We'll be doing a small show here on Wednesday—that will be your first show. Just for friends and family, mostly, and a few industry people, so less pressure. It's a nice room to play in, so I thought that would be a good way for you to get rolling."

"Yeah, thanks. I'm pretty nervous."

"If you're not nervous, you're either bored or cocky. I'll take nervous any day," he says.

"We'll see if you're still saying that after I've puked on your floor."

"Nervousness is an energy. Just run it through your guitar."

The rest of the band drifts in over the next fifteen minutes. I have their bios memorized, the way a kid memorizes stats from baseball cards.

Carl, the drummer, is the first to arrive. He's short and wiry with long, dark blond hair pulled into a ponytail. Late thirties, originally from Chicago, played in various alt-country bands before hooking up with the Urban Coyotes ten years ago.

He walks right up to me, shakes my hand, smiles widely.

"Welcome to the band, Ms. Swank."

"Thank you, Mr. Edwards," I reply. "It's good to meet you. I'm a fan."

"Now you're a colleague," he says.

Owen Wild, pedal steel and guitar player, strolls through the door just then. He's about six feet, medium build, wearing a black cowboy hat. Underneath the hat is a weathered face that adds ten years to his real age. He and Robby are the only original band members and have seen it all. But Robby quit partying hard about a decade before Owen, Nancy told me. Owen hit rock bottom about five years ago, and the band took a break. She thought it was going to be permanent, but Owen emerged clean and sober.

"The thing about Owen was that for the longest time he could play even when he was drunk," she'd said. "And then he couldn't."

"Is that why he quit?"

Nancy had paused, refilled her wine. "No, but that's not something I can share with you. The point is, Robby and Owen have sailed through their share of gales and somehow kept the ship upright."

And with that, she'd sipped her wine, and looked at me intently. "Surround yourself with good people and you have a better chance of weathering the storms."

Owen removes his hat as he shakes my hand. "Nice boots," he says, nodding toward my worn-out tan cowboy boots. "Glad to see you wear them the right way, not with your pants tucked in."

"You are never going to let me live that down, are you, Owen?" Robby's voice is gruff, but his eyes are laughing.

"It was a terrible thing, Robby."

"It was the eighties! Everyone was wearing them that way!"

"Not everyone, Robby. It's those kinds of choices that reveal a man's true character."

Robby waves his hand dismissively.

The four of us chat as we check our instruments and plug in. Robby has just glanced at his wristwatch when the door opens and Austin Hicks hurries into the room, gig bag slung over his left shoulder like a hunting rifle. His baby face is bright red from exertion. He's seven years older than me, but he could probably pass for my younger brother if his shoulders weren't so broad.

"Robby, don't you dare look at your watch! I'm not late yet!"

Robby grins, taps his wrist. Austin clutches his heart.

"Extroverts," scoffs Carl. "Stop drawing so much attention to yourselves."

This is the group of guys I'm going to be on the road with thirty-two weeks a year. This is my band.

"Okay, everyone ready?" Robby looks at me. I nod. Channel that energy.

Carl counts us in with the drums. One, two, three, four. And we're all playing. I'm playing with the Urban Coyotes. We are playing "Rodeo," one of my long-time favourite alt-country tunes, a song I've sung on many long car rides and played in Red's garage.

We reach the chorus. I lean into the vocal mic slightly, harmonize with Robby:

> *This ain't her first rodeo and she ain't no clown.*
> *If he had any sense, he'd get outta town.*
> *But he's spoilin' for a fight and he'd go any length.*
> *Common sense never was his strength.*

The song ends with an upbeat riff. It feels good to be playing with these guys. It feels like I fit. As the reverb fades, I glance around at the rest of the band.

"You've got a hell of a voice," says Owen. "Robby, don't you think it would be better if you two sang it as a duet, to get more of the female perspective?"

"Yeah, you're probably right. What do you think Darby?"

"Uh, yeah, sure."

"Let's do it again. I'll take the first verse, you the second, we'll keep alternating and sing the chorus together."

We play it again, and I feel the band's energy flowing through me like a river of sound, every vibration a ripple in the water.

"Wow," says Owen. "No offence, but I haven't felt that good playing with you guys in a long time."

"Maybe Darby's channelling something," says Carl. "Maybe she's a medium."

I wonder if it will always feel like that, and instantly worry that it won't. Maybe the energy is a one-off, or maybe playing the same songs with the same people will become a drag.

But the energy is there again for our first gig on Wednesday. In fact, it's even more intense. It runs through us and to the audience and back to us, like a circuit. The hairs on my arms and the back of my neck are on end through the whole show. The feeling grows through the show until we play the encore, "Rodeo." As Robby and I sing the chorus, I have a sudden irrational fear that we're all about to be struck by lightning. I close my eyes and focus on the song.

After the last chord, the circuit breaks, the electricity vanishes, and I'm drained and suddenly shy. It's clear there are more industry people here than Robby originally indicated, although I suppose many of them are likely friends, too. A bald forty-something man ferries drinks to the band as we set down our instruments. He offers me a drink, a Russian mule, and I take it.

Robby and Nancy introduce me to one industry person after another. I repeat each name in my head, over and over, before being introduced to the next and the next. Karen, a slim woman in her fifties, runs a folk series in Toronto at an old church somewhere on the north side. David, who looks like he's around my age, introduces himself as a producer on a satellite radio show.

"I see you left your charming host at home," Robby says.

I give Nancy a confused look.

"Marilyn Poe," she whispers in my ear.

"Oh!" I try to hide my surprise. Marilyn Poe is the creator and host of the premier arts and culture show in Canada, with reach into the U.S.

David grimaces and takes a long swig from his Russian mule. "I shouldn't say this, but I don't like being seen in public with that woman. One of my co-workers, she throws up at work several times a week, just from the tension. I don't know how much more I can take."

"I know of something opening up that might be a good fit for you," Nancy says. "We should get together for lunch next week."

"Yes, we should. Anyway, when you meet her, watch your back," David says to me. "She's a terrible human being."

"Okay, thanks," I'm not sure what else to say. Marilyn Poe a terrible human?

A young Asian woman with fine black hair takes David's arm. She hands David another Russian mule, and he takes another long swill.

"I loved your set," she says in a voice so smooth and pleasant I want to listen to her all night. "It felt like being in church, in a good way. I felt connected to everyone here, you know?"

"Wow, thanks," I say. "Do you sing?"

"No. People ask me that all the time, but I can't really carry a tune. I'm a poet."

"This is Flora Kim," David says. "She's going to have a book show on the radio."

"David! You can't tell anyone that, nothing's finalized yet! And besides, it's not just a 'book show,'" she says, adding air quotes. "It's more about literature as performance, you know? Oral traditions, storyteller traditions, what that looks like today. And poetry slams, and that kind of thing ..." She launches into a detailed description of the show.

"It sounds great," I say. "I hope they pick it up. I'd love to listen to it."

"Thank you," she says. She looks like she's about to say something else, but David is tugging at her elbow, and then they are gone, their space filled by someone else for me to meet.

The evening continues on like this. People keep offering me more drinks, and I down two more mules before we leave. I feel loose and relaxed, but I can't help slurring my words a little. Finally, it's all over. Nancy drives us home. I brush my teeth, remove the dark eye shadow and red lipstick from my face, put on my flannel pajamas, and tuck myself into bed.

On my nightstand is a well-worn black paperback with gold writing. *Women Who Run with the Wolves*. I open the front cover and a note falls out.

> *Just finished this last night. Kind of a different*
> *one but thought you'd like it. Maybe material for*
> *songwriting? Consider it my first book swap suggestion.*
> *Congratulations on your first show.* — *Nancy*

I'd completely forgotten about the book swap. My second night here Nancy had told me about how she and her friends swapped books. "I love going to used bookstores, flea markets, garage sales. I'm a reader," she'd told me over a glass of good Malbec.

"I'm in," I'd said.

I study the cover, then the back, to get a handle on what kind of book I'm looking at. Jungian psychology combined with myths. I wonder what Ruby would think, and Amber and Beth. It sounds like something Amber would devour. I'd never thought it was possible to talk about archetypes until I lived with them. I don't know if I buy into the idea completely, but it's interesting to think about. Maybe I'll phone Amber once I've read the book.

I decide not to read it in order. Instead, I start with the chapter on being a feral woman, on avoiding leg traps. Part way through, I start to think I'd better avoid Russian mules and other life-sucking temptations at industry events.

No horrible visions disturb my sleep. I dream of playing guitar around a bonfire on the lakeshore. I am safe.

I sleep well but wake earlier than I'd planned the next morning and start thinking about exercise. As much as possible, I want to stay in shape and work out my extra energy. Best to form the habit before my schedule is completely crammed. Over breakfast, I go through the phone book, looking for a boxing club. I find one that seems close, on this side of the Don Valley. I pack a gym bag and walk.

A brisk twenty minutes takes me to the gym, housed in a two-storey red-brick building. I go inside, ask about a membership, pay in advance for two months.

The woman hands me the forms to sign, goes over the basics. I thank her and go change in the locker room. I savour the smell of sweat as I warm up by skipping, then doing push-ups and crunches, and finally the speed bag. When I start hitting the heavy bags, I first think of my uncle, then of nothing but the motion and rhythm of punching. I hit as hard as I can, my hands aching. Then I loosen the throttle and focus on the combinations, my footwork, whether I'm too close or too far from the bag.

Jab. Straight. Hook.

Jab. Jab. Straight. Hook. Hook.

Time breaks down into three-minute increments. Sweat runs into my eyes.

Finally, when my arms can't take it anymore, I step away from the bag. I skip again for a few minutes to cool down, spend about fifteen minutes stretching. I grab my gym bag from the locker room and walk home in my sweaty gym clothes.

No one is there when I walk in. It feels a bit lonely, and I think about calling Jen or Ruby, or even Beth or Amber, but they'll all be busy with their regular lives. So I decide to take a shower and carry on.

After showering, I sit on the porch for an hour, just noodling around with my acoustic, trying to weave some chords around a weird melody that's stuck in my head. But it's not quite working with the guitar, and the afternoon is losing its heat, so I head inside to try Nancy's old bench piano instead.

Bench pianos are a dime a dozen, and I suppose you can't give most of them away these days, but this one is a beauty. The mahogany glows red, and the curved legs give it an almost sensuous look. I stroke the keys and feel a little like some pervy guy in a movie. I start out by playing scales to loosen up my hands. Then I start playing some Urban Coyotes songs. Finally, well warmed, I move into some stride tunes, numbers like "Harlem Strut," played as fast as I can. My hands fly up and down the keys. I make mistakes, but I keep going, just enjoying the sound. This isn't a recital, after all.

Then I slow just a bit, to the speed of a freight train roaring across the Prairies, and start humming this melody that ranges from a sparrow's highs to an earthly growl, and try to match the piano. No words at first, until after about a half hour I switch to the minor key and slow the pace at the bridge. I let my voice soar, and the words spill from my guts.

> *Just a feral*
> *looking for a safe space*
> *in a world of leg traps*
> *and poisoned bait*
> *looking for a den to call her own.*

The words keep coming, then, and soon I have something that sounds like a song. I run through the whole thing, top to bottom.

> *Prairie coyote in the big city*
> *stalking stray cats and little dogs.*
> *Sometimes it's not pretty*
> *when nature meets domesticity.*
> *Take the coyote out of the wild*
> *and she's still a disciple of wind.*
> *Even broken and skinned*
> *she remains undefiled.*
> *She haunts the ravines and back alleys*
> *but she's waiting for the right time*
> *to get back to the open skies and green valleys*
> *that she still thinks of as home.*
> *Just a feral*
> *looking for a safe space*
> *in a world of leg traps*

and poisoned bait
looking for a den to call her own.
Take the coyote out of the wild
and she's still a disciple of wind.
Even broken and skinned
she remains undefiled.
She doesn't want to be your muse.
She won't fall for your ruse.
She wants to fill her belly with meat
and feel soil and grass beneath her feet.
You can take the coyote out of the wild
but she's still a disciple of wind.
Even broken and skinned
she remains undefiled.

As the last notes hang in the air, I feel a surge of homesickness. I close my eyes for a moment.

Then I think: I better record that feeling in my stupid journal—a suggestion from Ruby. I don't feel like buying something, so I dig out my songwriting book. I write the lyrics to my new song, then write how I felt and what I did today.

That night I dream I'm in high school again, but the building is full of strangers. I wander the halls, searching for Luke, Jen, Sam. Finally I glimpse a blond girl walking ahead of me, ponytail bobbing just like Jen's did when she was sixteen.

"Jen!" But she doesn't turn. I walk fast, then run, trying to catch her. She turns a corner, and when I turn the same corner, the entire hallway is empty. The entire school is empty.

When I wake up, I turn on my lamp, and I record the dream in my songwriting book, underlining words that might work for song lyrics. If nothing else, I'm going to mine this hollow feeling for music. Then give Jen a call.

EIGHT

ABOUT A WEEK before we start recording the new album, I get a call from Jill at Cherry Street Rigs. My pedal boards are ready.

When I walk into their shop, Jill and Tommy are looking intently at a half-assembled pedal board and talking in low voices, like doctors examining a patient with a rare condition. I strain to hear what they're saying, but Tommy catches sight of me, calls a greeting, and walks toward me with arms outstretched. Both hug me, and then Jill waves me over to my pedal boards.

They're both beautiful, with candy-coloured pedals set in neat rows on the black base, edged in silver aluminum. Someone has painted a small silver horseshoe at the top of each board.

"Did you do this?" I ask Jill, pointing at the horseshoe.

"Yeah, I did. We heard you were a cowgirl and thought you'd like that little touch."

"It's perfect. Thank you."

The next few days are a blur. Two more band rehearsals, purely for my benefit, I think. I arrive an hour before the band to practise and figure out all the features of the studio rig I've just shelled out for. And then we're cutting tracks at the Bakery.

The first three days go great. The days are long—thirteen, fourteen hours—but I'm just so happy to be recording music, I don't care at all. How is it that I ended up here, straight out of school? I wonder. People with more talent, who have put in more time, would kill for this opportunity.

More than that, the guys in the band are nice to me. It's fun playing with them, even when it's the same song repeatedly. Recording is different from playing in front of a crowd, without that steady hum of energy, but sometimes it comes in bursts, like electrical shocks. Carl plays drums in a separate room to control the sound. The rest of us play in the studio, with Robby and Owen taking turns playing producer in the control room and filling in more guitar or pedal steel later on. Finally Robby and I take our turns in the vocal booth. When Robby's singing, or Robby and Owen are discussing some producer thing or another, I hang out in the kitchen with everyone else, sipping tea and snacking on whatever's lying around.

On day four, Robby is in the control room while the rest of us lay down the instrumentals for a new song. We do three takes, and then Owen sets down his guitar.

"Go take a break, guys," he says, and walks back to the control room.

Carl and Austin exchange a look. I wait until we're in the kitchen before I open my mouth.

"What's up?"

"Not much. Just the usual snag," says Carl.

"What's that mean?"

Austin inhales slowly, puffs up his cheeks, then lets out a long sigh. "This is the part where our band leaders start trying to wrest creative control from each other."

"Oh. So, like, what do we do?"

"We wait," says Carl.

An hour passes. I wonder if they're yelling. No way to tell, given that the control room is soundproof. I find some scrap paper, start writing lyrics. Carl and Austin are both reading, Carl a book on the founder of Scientology and Austin *The Red Pony* by John Steinbeck.

After an hour and a half, Robby sticks his head in the door. "Sorry, it's taking a while to figure some stuff out. We'll get you back in there soon," he says.

Carl and Austin nod and mutter vague agreement, barely looking up from their books. Austin finishes his novel, digs into his gig bag, and pulls out another one. *Light in August*. I eye the thick book with alarm.

"How long are you expecting to sit here?"

Austin hands me *The Red Pony*.

I read for an hour, then take a break and make Denver sandwiches for Austin and Carl.

"Should I make a couple for Owen and Robby?"

"Absolutely not," says Carl. "You don't want to make this more comfortable for them or they'll take even longer."

"But they must be hungry. Maybe we should take them water at least?"

"Didn't you hear the man?" Austin says around a mouthful of toast and omelette. "This is a siege, and our only hope of ending this is to starve them out. There's no room for empathy in war." He pauses to finish chewing. "This is really good, by the way. If you weren't a musician, I'd say you should open a restaurant."

"You have no idea," I respond, laughing, as I plate my own Denver. Then I start telling them stories of my days working at the Horseshoe, the little restaurant on Turtle Lake where I'd grown up, where I'd met Jack. Stories of my customers. Old Larry, who ordered toast with his fries so he could make a fry sandwich. Georgina, who always tipped me extra if I sang a Dolly Parton song so she could join in.

"What song did you sing?" asks Carl.

"Usually '9 to 5.' She'd join in on the chorus. So would other people. It was a lot of fun."

I don't tell them about the crappy parts: aching feet, grumpy customers, grumpy co-workers, the smell of grease in my hair, working with no air conditioning.

Austin stands up, goes into the studio, and returns with Robby's acoustic Martin. Carl pulls out a pair of spoons and strikes them against his leg, rattling out a beat. Austin lifts the guitar strap over his head, checks that the guitar is in tune, and starts playing "9 to 5." I tap my fingernails on the counter in time and sing. Both Carl and Austin join in on the chorus.

We pass another hour this way, taking turns playing favourites from The Band, Gillian Welch, Neko Case, Wilco, Lucinda Williams, Blue Rodeo. Austin takes us into the East Coast, from the Rankin family to Joel Plaskett. At about one thirty, Carl checks his watch. He's about to comment when Robby opens the door.

"Sorry for the delay, guys. We're ready to go again."

"You're right on schedule," Carl says.

Robby laughs as we file back into the studio.

Over the next two months, the Bakery sets the rhythm of my days. We'll work long hours for several days, then take a day, or two, or three off. I start waking up at five a.m. to get in a morning boxing workout a few days a week, except for after the late, late nights.

There are more creative conflicts between Robby and Owen. I never know what they're arguing about, but the conflict is always resolved within half a day, and then it's business as usual. I pack my notebook, just in case. As I read *The Red Pony*, I write down lines I like, to build lyrics around later.

In the middle of all of this, Jason and Char's short screens at film festivals in Calgary and Edmonton. Jason sends Ruby and me an enthusiastic email about how much fun they're having, how much people love it, with links to glowing reviews. When I saw the final version before I moved to Toronto, I was impressed by how they wove a story out of our interviews and footage, but I felt oddly self-conscious about people investing so much time and effort in telling a story about me. But it's not just about me, I remind myself. It's about Bea, too. I send Jason an email telling him how happy I am that it's doing well, and turn off my laptop.

As we near the end of recording, Austin asks me if I want to join his other band, Cyril Sneer's Revenge. The singer just moved to Vancouver, leaving Austin and the drummer in Toronto.

The thought of playing more gigs, in an entirely different band, sends a wave of excitement and nervousness from my stomach up to my throat. Then I think, what the heck, anything to log another thousand hours of playing, so I say yes.

"Great, we're playing Thursday night at the Cameron House," he says.

"That's only three days away," I say.

"Don't worry, I'm in the neighbourhood, I'll bring you a CD. You'll do fine."

He drops off the CD the next evening, and I pop it into my beat-up old Discman and go for a long run. It's high-energy rock, with a slight East Coast feel. I listen to the whole thing twice on the run. I listen to it a third time after showering, and now I'm singing the lyrics. Then I start faking my way through the guitar parts.

Two nights later Austin picks me up for the gig in his PT Cruiser.

"Nice car," I say.

"Is that sarcasm I detect?"

"Nooooo," I say, while nodding my head yes.

As we walk toward the Cameron House, I point at the giant ants mounted on its exterior.

"What's with the bugs?"

"In the eighties, the Cameron House got into a spat with the city about whether they had illegal tenants in the upstairs rooms."

"Oh, yeah, didn't Handsome Ned live here?"

"Yup, lots of musicians did. Molly Johnson used to watch Ned's set from a hole in the bathroom floor while having a bubble bath. Anyway, an artist installed ten ants to represent the tenants. Ten-ants, get it?"

"No, why don't you explain it to me again, but more slowly this time?"

The Cameron House is a holy place, no doubt about it. The painted panels on the ceiling remind me of the Sistine Chapel, but a little more rock and roll, with clouds and imps and rearing horses. Soft red velvet curtains on the stage make me think of a David Lynch film. A sign hangs in front of the curtains, proclaims it the Grand Ole Cameron.

"Would it be lame if I sing 'Crying?'"

"Only if you sing it like a lame-o," Austin replies.

"I'll knock the windows to the street with my voice."

"Let's do it," he says.

Just then a bear of a man looms in the door. He must be close to seven feet tall, with long black hair and squinty brown eyes.

"Darby, Reggie," says Austin. Reggie puts down the drum cases he's carrying and takes my hand, shaking it gently. My hand looks like it belongs to a doll next to his.

The three of us haul in the amps, guitars, cables, and drum kit, and set up on the stage. Over the next half hour, people begin drifting in. By the time we've finished, there are about thirty people, mostly friends of Austin and Reggie. At least four of the guys have Buddy Holly glasses with thick black frames. A new trend, I guess. Another woman is wearing the exact same red-and-grey plaid shirt as me. I nod at her, but she pretends not to notice. I should have worn the turquoise one, but then there are a couple of those, too. I need to develop my own style or I'm going to look like every other girl in the crowd.

The three of us sidle up to the bar. One of the Buddy Holly guys offers to buy me a drink, but I turn him down. Austin and Reggie each order a rusty nail, neat.

"You should have one," says Reggie. "It's tradition."

"No, thanks. How about you have one for me?"

Reggie swallows his drink in two quick gulps, sets down his glass, and nods at the bartender, who mixes him another. He downs that one, too.

"Let's play," he says.

We hit the stage. Austin somehow manages to play lead guitar and bass with his foot pedals simultaneously, most of the time while sitting on a stool. I mostly play rhythm and sing but manage to play lead on a couple of songs. Reggie pounds the drums nearly into oblivion. There's a small group right in front of the stage singing along to the choruses, dancing a little, drinks in hand. We end the first set with a loud version of "Crying," and the audience whoops and hollers.

During the break, I give in to Buddy Holly and let him buy me a rusty nail, neat. It seems like an unlikely drink combination, and frankly, it is terrible. Definitely not something I'm going to overindulge in, like the Russian mules.

"I'm Trevor, by the way," he says, running a hand through his slicked auburn hair. Trevor has the softest brown eyes, flecked with gold. If he were a horse, Bea would say he has a nice eye or a kind eye, and consider it a sign of an even, forgiving temperament.

"Darby."

"I know. I'm friends with Austin."

"Are you a musician, too, Trevor?"

"No, a journalist. With the *Daily Herald.*"

"Oh, yeah? Do you cover arts stuff?"

"Nah, current affairs, mostly. I love music, but I don't think I'd want to write about it. It would take the fun out of going to shows if I had to critique my friends, you know."

"Yeah, I totally get it."

I can see Reggie moving toward the stage, his head and shoulders above the crowd. He looks like a moose wading through water.

"I gotta go, Trevor."

He hands me a business card. "My cell's on here. Call me sometime, if you want."

I feel myself blush a little, hope the lighting is dim enough that he doesn't notice.

The crowd is a little looser for the second set, some of them half-cut. We play fast and loud, sweating under the lights. Austin and Reggie have a no encore policy for some reason, but we close with a cover of "Maybe Tomorrow," the theme song from *The Littlest Hobo*. We play it slow and soulful, and the crowd joins in. Tom and Wynne, two of Austin and Reggie's friends, jump on stage for the singalong. The three of us lean into the mic.

Trevor stands near the front with a beautiful girl in plaid and another guy with Buddy Holly glasses, all three swaying in time to the music. He wraps an arm around Pretty Plaid Girl, and I feel a pang of jealousy, but then close my eyes and lean into the song, feel the vibrations from the guitar and drums resonate in my stomach, chest, throat, and re-emerge from my mouth.

It's a silly song from a goofy show. I can't think of anything more Canadian kitsch than singing it with a crowd of plaid-clad hipsters in a Toronto bar. But there's something powerful about the barroom choir, some weird alchemy that transforms the irony and nostalgia into a higher experience, a moment of communion. It's moving. When we finish, Tom folds Wynne and me into a group hug, and then Reggie and Austin join in, Reggie wrapping his wingspan around the entire group. The audience is hugging, too.

"Thank you everyone. Peace and love to you all, and have a good night," I say, flashing the peace sign.

"Best show yet, you guys," says Trevor. "I think you should keep the singer."

"Stop flirting and wrap some cords, man," says Reggie.

We pack up and, because Austin is tipsy, I drive him back to his Chinatown apartment. Reggie follows, and the three of us carry gear upstairs into the one-bedroom apartment, which squats above a convenience store. Inside, the black-and-white lino floor is so worn the sub-floor shows through, and the walls, painted red, have a pink tinge in certain light, brush strokes visible.

"Why do you still live in this hole, man?" asks Reggie. "You're not a struggling musician anymore."

"You know why. The rooftop patio," says Austin. The three of us troop upstairs. I'm expecting a spectacular view of the downtown, but the building isn't high enough for that. Instead we peer down at the bright awnings and brash lit-up signs decorating the red brick of Chinatown. Pedestrians amble along the sidewalks, ducking into the late-night restaurants for an after-bar snack. All those people, hanging out with their friends, fill me with a sudden loneliness, even though I'm not alone, not really, at the moment. But no one in this city has known me for more than a few weeks, and they don't really *know* me. I'm lucky that Nancy and Cole have taken me in, although we're all often eating supper on the go, too.

I miss my old friends, Jen and Sam and Luke, the people who've known me since childhood. I miss Jack, the man who helped me when I needed someone the most. I miss my fractured family, my dead family. I miss my songwriting partner Ruby, who took me into her own family. They are all so far away, so far west from here. My limbs weaken with the feeling.

"It's beautiful," I say.

Reggie offers me a joint, but I decline. After twenty minutes on the rooftop, the neighbourhood's charm is losing the battle to the night's chill. I leave Austin and Reggie there smoking and drive Austin's car back to Leslieville. The lonely feeling persists.

When I get home, I want to wash the bar smoke from my hair, but I don't want to wake Nancy and Cole. It's a school night, after all. I tiptoe without so much as a creak from the old stairs, brush my teeth like a ninja, and use moist towelettes to wipe the makeup from my face.

I feel exhilarated by the show, but also hollowed out by loneliness and the lingering worry that something terrible is going to happen to me. Sure, things are going great now, but things could shift any time, through my own weakness or through fate. Perhaps there is a leg trap in my future, waiting for me to take a wrong step.

But then I realize that I am going to make myself sick thinking about how everything could fall apart. If everything falls apart, I'll just pick up what I need and keep going.

"I am safe," I whisper. "And I am here."

NINE

WINTER HITS ME like a sledgehammer when it comes.

I had been looking down my nose at Toronto winters when I should have been bracing myself, I realize as I trudge through cold slush that seems to be a permanent feature of Leslieville these days. Winter in Edmonton, or back home, is colder. But there really is something to that whole dry cold versus wet cold thing.

Still, it's not the sogginess of this winter weather that I hate the most. It's the fucking salt. It chews through leather boots and stains the legs of my pants.

"Just get a car," Cole advises. "Then you won't wear out your boots walking everywhere."

"You mean I should pay for a car, and gas and insurance, and then watch the salt eat my car, so I can save on boots?"

Cole peels potatoes while I chop carrots and onions in preparation for a stew. I'd started cooking at least twice a week, and it had piqued his interest. He has a natural talent for cooking—a dexterity when it comes to cutting and peeling, and an enviable ability to balance flavours.

I braise the stew meat while Cole cuts the potatoes into smaller pieces and minces garlic, still full of unhelpful advice on handling salt. We throw everything into the slow cooker and turn it on. When Nancy walks in the door two hours later, the smell is driving us mad with hunger.

Nancy has impeccable table manners. She keeps her fork pointed tines down, and when she's talking, she places her cutlery on her plate. Sam handles his cutlery the same way, a knife in his right hand and fork in the left. Nancy has never said anything critical about my table manners, but she's raised her eyebrows a couple of times. It makes me feel a little awkward and uncouth, and no matter how hard I try, I can't quite give up using my fork as a shovel.

After we've eaten and cleaned up, Nancy hands me a padded envelope. "This came for you today," she says.

I don't have to see the Vancouver address to know it's a tape from Ruby. I thank Nancy and take it to my room upstairs. I grab my little boom box, sit on the bed, and rip open the envelope. Slide the tape out and play it.

Ruby's high, pure voice fills the room. She talks about her music therapy program at Capilano, about Vancouver. She talks about nearly getting hit by a bus twice within a week. Queen of Near Misses, she says.

"I loved your song about the coyote, Darby. I have one for you now, too. And I even tuned my guitar before I began recording." She strums her acoustic for emphasis. Then she starts playing, and her smooth voice fills my room.

> *Every time it rains in Vancouver*
> *I think of you.*
> *Your bright face*
> *on a cold winter day.*
> *Northern su-un.*
> *I miss you on those long June days*

the way you'd
push away the dark
keep the night at bay.
Northern su-un.
I mourned you on winter nights
I mourn you now
Every time the rain
washes out your light.
Northern su-un.

I find myself singing Ruby's lyrics over the next few days. But my melody evolves. One night I sit down with my guitar and sing them into the tape recorder, but with a rockabilly rhythm. Then I pull out my notebook.

"Okay, Ruby, I have a favour to ask. Or maybe a challenge. How would you finish this song?"

I sing a few words, then hum in the blank spots, fragments of lyrics and melody more than a song.

"Things we can't say ... mmmm mmmm ... Bite back my words, swallow my rage, save it all for another day ..."

I finish the song fragment, chat into the tape recorder about everything I've been up to—finishing recording, doing radio spots to promote the new album and the upcoming tour.

"Next Friday we're on Marilyn Poe's morning show. I'm singing a duet with Robby. I am so nervous, especially about the interview."

What I'm really nervous about is the tension between the band and Marilyn. After we'd wrapped the album, we'd sat down with Nancy and Courtney, Nancy's assistant, to talk about the promotion schedule and the tour. Nancy and Courtney had saved Marilyn for last.

"You're booked into Poe's morning show in two weeks," Courtney said.

"Jesus," said Carl. "Must we? I can't stand that woman."

"Yes, you must," said Nancy.

"No offence, Nancy, but you'll have made it worse, helping David get out of there. Marilyn is pissed," said Austin.

"How would she know Nancy helped David get the job at Strut Music?" I was skeptical of their anxiety.

"That woman is like the KGB," said Owen. The edge in Owen's voice sets me back on my chair. "She has all these little rats all over town, giving her information in exchange for a few crumbs of cheese."

"Listen, we all know Marilyn's game. She will yank your chain, off and on air, looking for a reaction," said Nancy. "So how do we respond?"

"Don't bite back. Be nice," the rest of the band said in unison, like schoolboys. Even Courtney mouthed the words.

"That's right, don't bite," said Nancy. "And yes, she will be cranky about David going to a better place, but if it wasn't about David, it would be something else."

The meeting moves on, but I can't stop thinking about the Marilyn Poe thing. No doubt, there was something else going on between the band and Marilyn, besides Nancy's rehoming of her former producer. Wild guesses raced around my mind like a herd of feral horses, but I couldn't think of a realistic inciting incident. Maybe, rather than a single dramatic event, it was a series of slights, eroding any good will.

I hesitate now, on tape. Best not share all that with Ruby. A person can't be too careful, especially if Marilyn really is like the KGB. Far away as she might seem right now, the music community was a tightly woven web, coast to coast. Ruby knew touring musicians from Toronto. And Ruby, for all her good points, is an incurable gossip.

"Anyway, I sure miss you, Ruby. Think of me next time you dig into a Smarties blizzard ..."

I eject the tape, slip it into a padded envelope, seal it, and write Ruby's address on the front. Then I open my journal. I've started writing letters to people I can't talk to, or won't talk to. The first one was to Will, and it was filled to the brim with venom and fuck-yous. I've written to Dad, and to Mom as well. But most have been to Bea.

Today I ask her what she was like when she was young, starting out as an artist. Lately I've realized that I know very little about her life, what she was like, before I knew her. Was she a wild teenager or was she a nerd? Mom was the queen of the school, but Bea would have been different. Did she ever feel like an outsider?

I still feel like an outsider, even in the middle of all this action. I could be famous, and successful and rich, and I would still feel this way, I think. But maybe that's part of what makes me a musician, that small piece of loneliness that makes me feel different from everyone else. That thing that makes me turn inward but want to connect with others at the same time.

One thing that's strange to me is that Bea never talked much about her mentors. I know she had an art school instructor who supported her, and Pauline Brooks, her agent, believed in her work early on. There's that creep that showed up at her show last winter, Kenneth, but I don't know if he counts. What I want to know was whether there was anyone else to nudge her into art when she was younger, the way Bea, Grandma Swank, and Dad pushed me into music. I had emailed Helen, and she didn't recall anyone other than Kenneth taking the time to mentor her (or whatever it was he did—Helen still won't talk about him), but then she had been very shy at that time. It wasn't until she went to art school in Calgary that she started learning directly from other artists, Helen had told me.

Bea's work has been touring steadily again across Canada since the first exhibit at the Chapel Gallery in North Battleford. Just last week it had been in Toronto, where I'd performed at the opening. It was mostly strangers at the opening, although Austin and Reggie had come. After I'd finished singing and done a couple of interviews, I'd meandered through the crowd with my two bandmates, watching their reactions to Bea's work.

"Your aunt was really something," said Austin. "Looking at her paintings, I feel like I know her."

We pause in front of a landscape piece. A thunderstorm rolling in, clouds the purple of bruises. "It's really heavy, man," says Reggie, then wraps me in a hug. I stiffen at first, then relax into his giant body.

The exhibition is coming back to Saskatchewan right after Christmas, to the Mendel in Saskatoon. Pauline really wants me to fly in to speak at the opening. I'm still on the fence about it. I told her I'd let her know by the day after tomorrow at the latest, as she really needs to get the information to the press.

"Do you think I should go?" I write. I stop writing, waiting for a little voice with an answer. Nothing. I guess I'll have to make up my own mind. Then I think: If Bea was alive, she would be my biggest fan. She'd come to every show she could. So maybe I should do this for her.

I put down my pen and call Pauline.

—

Three days before Christmas, Cole knocks softly on my bedroom door.

"Hey Darby, there's some Trevor guy here to see you."

As I pad downstairs, I hear the soft sound of a cork being pulled from a wine bottle, followed by the glug-glug-glug of a glass filling. For a horrified second, I think Trevor has helped himself.

Then I hear Nancy's voice.

"I'm such a big admirer of your work, ever since you started covering the Mad Cow crisis. That rancher you interviewed—where was he from again?"

"Maple Creek, Saskatchewan. Ivan Kolchak and his son Henry. Henry is the president of the Canadian Cattlemen's Association, the group that represents Canadian ranchers."

I start. Henry had been in the media steadily since BSE hit, but it's hard to believe that Grandpa Kolchak actually talked to a reporter. Trevor must wield more charm than I'd imagined.

"Yes, that's the one." Nancy pauses to sip wine. "Imagine, that ranch has been in his wife's family a hundred years and he's worried about losing it. The weight of such a thing. Have you kept in touch with him?"

"I talked to Henry a few weeks ago after the Bank of Montreal released a report stating BSE has cost ranchers about five billion dollars since the crisis began. Did you see the article?"

"No, I missed that one!"

"I'll have circulation send a copy to your office. They keep the old issues for a while."

"So the Kolchaks are holding on?"

"They're tough people, that's for sure."

Nancy doesn't even know that I'm related to them. How weird, considering I've been living in her house for months, but I guess it's understandable since I don't have the same surname and haven't talked about them. The other day, Cole had made a remark about me keeping my cards close to my chest, but I hadn't given it much thought. Maybe I should.

"That's my family." I blurt it out, right there, before I even consider what I should say. Before I can pretend that I just walked into the conversation, instead of lingering on the stairs, clearly eavesdropping. Nancy and Trevor stare up at my feet. I stand for another moment, then pad down the stairs, the occasional creak punctuating my silly behaviour.

I walk downstairs, brace myself for questions from Nancy about my family. But the questions don't come. Instead, Nancy wraps me into a hug.

"Oh, sweetie. I'm so sorry your family has had to go through this, too."

My knees wobble a bit, but I maintain my poker face after she lets go.

Trevor takes me to a pub a few blocks away. It feels like the world's longest drive because the shocks on his old sedan are shot.

"Not really what I pictured you driving," I say, stroking the dash.

"Not that it's your business right now, but I'd rather have no debt than a nice car," he says sharply. I've found a sore point. Maybe something an ex said?

"Well, I'm not judging. I don't even own a car right now. And the only vehicle I have ever owned was a very old AMC Jeep."

The Jeep piques Trevor's interest, so I describe the sunshine-yellow paint and green vinyl seats of my old pickup truck. "I sold it to a guy from Lamont for five thousand dollars," I say. "He was nostalgic."

Trevor's brow furrows briefly.

"Lamont is east of Edmonton," I add.

"Oh, okay."

We pull up in front of a pub on Queen Street and hustle out of the cold weather into the dimly lit interior. It reminds me of an Irish pub on Whyte Ave, and I'm hit with a wave of nostalgia for Edmonton. I used to think of Edmonton as a big city, but it feels so much smaller now that I'm in Toronto.

I haven't been on a first date in so long, I'm not sure how to act. In fact, I haven't really ever been on a first date. I just sort of fell into relationships with Luke and Jack, fell into a few other flings.

Then I stupidly blurt this out.

"I don't think I've ever been on a first date."

Stupid, stupid, stupid.

"I mean, I don't know to make the right impression," I add, trying and failing to sound like less of a moron.

The server, a huge man wearing a plaid shirt and trucker hat, asks for our orders. I order a dark ale and Trevor asks for an IPA.

The server lumbers off, and Trevor turns to me, a serious look on his face.

"Well, you can just be yourself. Or you can play the ingénue. Or the vamp. Just let me know which game we're playing."

"Hmmm." I purse my lips and suck in my cheeks. "I choose vamp." Then I take a sip of beer, but accidentally inhale it, triggering a coughing fit.

"I think that's a fail. Are you okay?" Trevor is trying to look sympathetic, but he keeps laughing, which is not helping.

We talk about music and politics, and it's all sort of pleasant and banal. Trevor likes weather metaphors. He likes weather in general and can rattle off the different cloud formations and what they foretell. He says he's been fascinated by weather since he was a kid and a tornado destroyed a cottage a few streets over from where his family huddled in their cottage's bathroom. He tells me about the danger of anvil clouds, how they can throw lightning bolts thirty miles away. He tells me that a system shaped like an archer's bow can create plow winds or even derechos, which are widespread, severe plow winds with the force of a tornado or even a hurricane. It's the kind of conversation that doesn't reveal too much about him, except perhaps how he managed to get my weather-obsessive grandfather to agree to an interview.

We each order another pint and a plate of nachos. As Trevor clasps the glass, I glance at his hand and notice how much thicker his fingers are than my own. His hands look strong. A short burst of electricity sparks at my sacrum, travelling up my spine and out along my nerves.

A second date would be nice, I think.

When Trevor drops me off, he leans over and kisses me lightly. He starts to pull away, but I pull him back, just for one more moment.

There will definitely be a second date.

Three days later, Trevor sends me copies of clippings of his articles on BSE. "Ranchers ready to ride out Summer of Mad Cow" is the first one, published in June 2003. I read about Uncle Henry and Aunt Linda's ranch, and my little cousins Reata and Jake. Reata sounds like a little hellraiser on her Shetland pony. Sure enough, Grandpa Kolchak is there too, talking about his wife's parents losing their ranch during the Depression, expressing his worry about how this crisis will affect his son's family and younger ranchers across the country.

"This damn BSE thing, it's our generation's Great Depression. Any of us might go under."

They'd even brought Trevor to a branding, and local ranchers had talked about their worries, about trying to bring in other sources of income through off-farm jobs or selling beef directly to consumers. Aunt Linda had two part-time jobs, and Uncle Henry had started training young horses for other people. I hadn't realized how much they'd been working outside the cattle business.

Other articles talked about the economics, the lost international markets. The series had ended by circling back to ranchers in Alberta and Saskatchewan, talking about the stress of it all. There was a quote from Aunt Linda: "It's hard. Neither of us sleep anymore, from the worry. I'm afraid Henry's going to have an accident haying or riding colts, he's so sleep-deprived. I would never leave, but if I could go back, I don't think I'd choose to do this again. Maybe I'll feel differently once we're on the other side of it."

I think about her quote for a long time. I think about what I'd choose, where I'd go back and change things if I could. If my parents had never met years ago at a barn dance south of Maple Creek, I wouldn't be here, but then again, Aunt Bea never would have met Will, and so she would be alive and making art. And maybe my mom would have never developed cancer, without having to worry about her little sister.

I wonder if this thing with Trevor will go anywhere, whether I'll regret it in five or ten years or be glad for it. How will I feel when I'm on the other side of whatever is coming next?

I write a fragment of a song in my notebook, then call it a night.

Worry keeps her awake through the night
Tugs at her sleeve all through the day
Sometimes she wishes she could take flight
But she'll wait until she gets to the other side.

TEN

*Good morning, Canada. You're tuned into Poe's
Morning Show, in case you didn't know. This morning
we're joined by Canada's original alt-country band,
The Urban Coyotes. And if you're thinking you've
heard it all, wait until you hear Darby Swank, their
newest guitar-slinging, jazz-infusing, harmonizing
Saskatchewaaan cowgirl. Saskatchewan may be the
hinterland, but Ms. Swank is anything but provincial,
let me tell you ...*

I KEEP SMILING as Marilyn Poe continues her venom-laced introductory
monologue. David did warn me.

She's not a beautiful woman—her face is too long and thin,
her hazel eyes too large and wide-set, her rosebud mouth too
small in proportion to her face—but those same things make her
interesting to look at.

Her patter usually sounds smart and edgy to me. But it feels
different sitting in the studio.

It's not just the snark on steroids. Something about her leaves me unsettled—a feeling more than anything concrete. Maybe it's the monologue or maybe it's Owen's reluctance to be on the show. I glance around at the rest of the band. Robby smiles widely and Carl looks serious. Austin appears relaxed and unconcerned, but a few minutes before we went on air, I noticed him quietly doing his breathing exercises.

Owen smiles, too, a wolf's smile, designed more to show sharp canines than put anyone at ease.

I suddenly notice that every muscle in my body is tense, as though I'm bracing myself. I try to relax, but my body refuses my brain's directive.

Marilyn is asking me a question, and I snap my attention back to her quick-paced conversation. She asks me about my musical influences, and I list Neko Case, Bob Wills, Joni Mitchell, talk a little about their music. It's a lie by omission, because it's simply impossible in thirty seconds to list all the artists who've shaped my mind.

"What about your aunt, Bea Fletcher? What influence did she have on your life as an artist?"

For a moment, I'm surprised that Marilyn even knows about my aunt, but then I think that she must have read the article from the exhibit in Toronto. I was quoted quite a bit, although I didn't think I'd said anything particularly insightful. I'm still not sure why she wants to ask about Bea, but my only choice is to answer the question.

"Well, she's a great artist in her own right. She wasn't a musician, but the way she painted, the way she looked at the world, shaped my perspective. She taught me to look beneath the surface of things, to watch how deep currents create movement that's sometimes hard to track. The whole idea of negative space is something I think about a lot, especially when I'm writing a song. If you leave some space, listeners can layer their own experiences over the song."

"Your aunt's last exhibition is touring in Toronto right now, a collection titled 'Negative Space.' Tell us more about how that concept relates to this exhibit."

I think back to the opening at the Chapel Gallery in North Battleford and my brief encounter with Kenneth Diamond or Bale or whatever his real name was. What had Helen meant when she'd said Kenneth had tried to blackmail Bea? And how did my aunt, one of the bravest people I've ever known, get tangled up with a creep like Kenneth, and a monster like Will?

"Every death leaves a hole. But I still have so many questions after my aunt's death, I feel like I have very little that's tangible sometimes. Instead of filling in the gaps, the gaps are framing my memory, you know?"

"As though the things people aren't talking about are more important than the things they do discuss?"

"Yes, exactly. The things left unsaid."

"And the exhibition includes your memories of those paintings, of her process?"

"Yes, in a sense. She would work manically sometimes. She was extremely creative in those periods, and she got a lot done. But it came at a cost, because eventually she'd get slammed by a migraine. Now I think it reflected the building tension in my aunt and uncle's relationship, followed by a violent fight, but I'll never really know for sure. More gaps, you know? More places for me to make my own interpretation."

"It's a good guess, though, because your uncle is in prison for her murder."

"Yes, he is." I should have known where Marilyn was steering this line of questioning. The last thing I want to do is talk about Will, and I don't want to dominate the interview, either. I glance at Robby, wondering how to steer the conversation to the new album.

"Darby's a brave young woman. Her testimony helped put her uncle in prison. And that emotion, that courage comes through in her playing," says Robby. "The first time I saw her perform, I was blown away by her connection with the audience."

"Still, that must have caused some tension, with Robby recruiting this young hotshot and then giving her such a prominent place in an established band. Owen?"

"No tension at all. Fuck, I wish he could've recruited her twenty years ago, but then I guess it's probably not ethical to take a little kid on tour, with the child labour laws."

Owen's unexpected F-bomb hits me like cold water. Even though she's on satellite, Marilyn likes to run a clean show, at least during the interviews. I glance around, and Carl and Austin both look surprised, too. Robby seems mildly amused. Owen smiles, showing all his teeth.

Marilyn scowls at her producer, a baby-faced young woman, who acts quickly to remove the swear in the brief delay before it bounces from the studio to the sky to people's radios.

We go to a break. Marilyn is still scowling. "You catch that one, Paige, or did it slide right on by you as usual?"

"Got it, Marilyn," she says over the mic.

"Good. And you." She looks pointedly at Owen. "Watch it."

"Sorry, just slipped out. Bad habit."

"You've been doing this for twenty years, Owen. Don't give me that garbage." Marilyn pauses, as though considering, and I wonder what she's thinking about doing. I feel a chill. Someone needs to roll over and show their belly to placate this woman, I think.

"Did I sound okay? That was my first big interview," I say, widening my eyes slightly. Austin looks at me as though he doesn't recognize me.

"You sounded great," Marilyn says, still sounding pouty but perhaps less malicious.

The break will end soon, so we take our places at our instruments. We're playing the title song, "Light," a duet with me and Owen. It's one of Owen's songs, really, but I got a songwriting credit because

I came up with a lick on the guitar and the lyrics for the bridge: "In the darkest night, you always bring the light."

I am proud of that simple line in the bridge. It's powerful. "Light" is, I think, the best song on the new album. My alto blends smoothly with Owen's baritone, and when Robby adds his tenor to the chorus, it gives me goosebumps. The simple lyrics and the instrumentation weave together perfectly. As soon as we released it as a single, Nancy started getting calls from music writers wanting to interview the new girl with the rich voice.

Sometimes a little voice inside tells me I should be humble about my talent, but then I think fuck it. I don't know how long this is going to last, but it's fun right now, and I'm going to enjoy it while I can. It's not something I'd ever thought of myself doing, but I start creating a swashbuckling cowgirl persona in these interviews. It doesn't feel false—more like a magnification of something that is already inside me.

I've repressed that persona this morning, instinctively, to avoid threatening Marilyn, I realize. It feels oddly insincere.

When we come back from the break, Carl counts us into the song. I think of nothing but the music. I listen carefully to Owen, making sure I'm matching him for volume, hitting all my notes, and getting the phrasing right. When we finish, I look up at Paige, the new young producer, who is now smiling widely, and I can tell she's really impressed. Marilyn seems a little cool, but I care about Paige's opinion more than hers.

The rest of the show goes well. Robby does a lot of the talking about the new album, the upcoming tour, the way the band's sound has evolved over the years, where he thinks we're going. Austin and Carl chip in with a couple of amusing anecdotes about touring and recording (taking care not to mention the traditional standoff on every album between Robby and Owen). We play another song, this time one of Robby's.

Marilyn plays nice with us until the very end. Then she turns to me again, and before she says a word, I know by her clenched jaw that she's about to get mean. Maybe I made the wrong move earlier. But before I can think about it anymore, she's talking about Bea again. About my hometown.

"... hard for me to imagine the betrayal you must have felt, learning that so many people had covered up the abuse."

"Yeah, it was. I still haven't forgiven a lot of those people." I don't know what else to say, and the silence hangs a beat too long for radio.

Then, in a sneering tone: "Of course, that level of abuse and isolation, of cover-up, must be a particular problem in insular rural communities. It's something hard to comprehend coming from an urban environment, where people are more sophisticated about these issues."

Where the hell does she get off, making an ignorant statement like that? It's one thing for me to criticize my people, but she's an outsider. From Toronto. Just because she saw it on the news doesn't mean she has a right to judge. Anger quickens my pulse. I glance at the digital clock to my right. We're nearing the end. I consciously drop my temper to the temperature of steel in a Canadian winter.

"Domestic violence is a problem everywhere. In small towns, people are more isolated, and there aren't as many services. And yeah, sometimes people want to sweep it under the rug, just to get along, I guess, or because they're afraid. But urban people can easily turn a blind eye or miss the signs. And insular communities exist in cities, too. Silence is the enemy everywhere. Anyone who tries to argue otherwise is just damned ignorant. Maybe even willfully ignorant."

Owen gives me a wink. Marilyn's composure doesn't even flicker. She brings the interview to a smooth close, we play one last song, and she wraps up the show. But as we leave the studio, she glares at me, and I know I've got a target on my back.

The rest of the band is jubilant.

"There's the Darby I know," Austin crows. "You know, last week Darby and Reggie helped break up a fight after our show ended."

"Where were you?" Carl asks him.

"In the can."

"Whatever that woman tries to do to us, it was worth it," Carl says.

"Not my first rodeo," I say, then point to my old cowboy boots. "I even wore my lucky shitkickers."

It's true. They're the same boots I wore that day we moved cows, when I came off my horse, got a concussion, was attacked by my dirtbag uncle, but somehow survived it all, even if my horse didn't. The same ones I wore to court when I testified against Uncle Will.

Owen loops a long arm over my shoulders as the four of us walk out the door.

"Welcome to the team, kid."

—

After our first show in Barrie, Ontario, I pull the little blue tour booklet from my backpack. It's a handmade, hand-stapled tour itinerary that also has the names of the crew, booking agents, contacts for every venue and every other piece of information we'd need. The cover has the band name, tour name ("Light"), and tour dates.

"Don't lose this, it's your bible," Courtney had told me as she handed me my booklet. "I made only a few extras."

"It's beautiful," I'd said.

"Awww, you're cute. Baby musicians."

I open the booklet to the front page and examine the schedule. Tomorrow we're at the Sanderson Centre in Brantford. Twelve days straight of shows, a different city every night except for two nights in Kingston, and then a final show in Toronto at the Horseshoe.

I love it. I'm exhausted right now from the show, but I love it. I tuck my tour bible back into the side pocket of my backpack and pull out my book.

Even the most comfortable touring bus is a little claustrophobic after a while. I counter the tight space by reading *East of Eden,* which Trevor is also reading, back in Toronto—our own little book club. We'd been on only a few dates before the tour started, but I really liked him. I'd thought love had to be illicit to be interesting, but then my experience at that time was limited to Luke, the guys I cheated with while still with Luke, and Jack. Trevor is a different animal altogether. There's so much about him I don't know yet.

The book club was his idea, a way for us to feel connected when we're apart. So far, every time I checked into a hotel on this tour, there was a postcard from Trevor waiting for me at the front desk. Quick notes about how he missed me, sometimes a comment about the weather in Toronto that day during his run, maybe a funny observation about something from work, or from the book (the last one about Kate's nasty biting). I always mailed one back.

Tonight, after I finish reading, I select a new postcard, this one showing a ski trail at Barrie.

> *How can one book contain so much space?*
> *Geographical space, the reach of time. When I read*
> *Steinbeck, I have the feeling that each of my breaths is*
> *like a great wind roaring off a mountain, while at the*
> *same time feeling that I'm as insignificant as a blade of*
> *a grass on a sparse mesa.*
>
> *Also: I love being on stage. I don't want to come*
> *home. Can you get a job as a rock journalist and join*
> *our circus?*

Most nights, I read in my berth until I fall asleep. Sometimes I go to the lounge at the back of the bus, where Austin and Carl are smoking pot and watching movies. Every now and then, Robby and

Owen join in, too, and we all crowd into the little lounge. Owen always argues for a Clint Eastwood movie, but he's usually overruled by Austin, Carl, and me, who prefer something from the nineties. But one night he talks us into *The Good, the Bad and the Ugly.*

"Shit, that was a good movie," Austin says at the end.

"You've never seen it?" Robby is dumbfounded. Owen snorts, as though he didn't expect any less.

"No."

"I'd never seen it either," I chime in. "But now I guess I know what all the fuss is about."

"Just call me Angel Eyes," Austin adds, batting his long, dark lashes.

"Angel Eyes," says Carl. "Sounds like a keeper to me."

—

As we sleep, the bus driver sips coffee all night, keeps us between the lines. The crew's bus tails us. These buses carry us to theatres all over Ontario. The thick velvet curtains and graceful rounded stages give me the feeling of being in vaudeville. We are the spectacle. We are giving the people what they want, which is a hell of a show.

I am not used to these shows with seating. I'm used to playing country hall dances and bars and little summer festivals. Intoxicated crowds, crowds puffing marijuana smoke, crowds of bodies moving, dancing, occasionally fighting, bellying up to the bar for more drinks. These theatre audiences are more stationary, more staid.

Their stillness seems to concentrate their emotion at times, to the point I can hardly stand it. I want to break the connection, to distance myself from the intensity. Instead, I lean into it.

People who jump horses, God bless their crazy souls, have a saying: *Throw your heart over the fence and the horse will follow.* Every night, I fling my heart to the audience, and the music follows.

January ninth finds us in Hamilton, Robby and Owen's old stomping grounds.

Hamilton is a departure from the rest of the tour. No theatre gig in this town—we are playing Copps Coliseum. When the band discussed it months earlier, it had been a short discussion. Copps was tradition, the venue they'd played since they'd had enough fans to fill it. And they had more fans in Hamilton than anywhere else—play a smaller venue and everyone would revolt.

It's close enough to the previous night's gig in London that we stay in a Hamilton hotel. I order room service and watch Jon Stewart, then take a long bath.

I have the best sleep in months, maybe years. My dreams are vague and fuzzy and not at all memorable. I sleep until the phone rings beside my bed. For a moment, I'm not sure where I am.

"Hello?"

"You up yet, Darbs?"

"Austin? No. I'm not."

"Well, hurry up. It's time for breakfast."

"What time is it?"

"It's after ten. We're all waiting for you in the lobby, so get your ass outta bed."

"Okay, be right down, Angel Eyes."

When I get down to the lobby, the band is gone. I look to the clerk at the front desk, and she points to the door. "They're in the white minivan out front."

It's one of those slushy, windy winter days that somehow feels worse that a dry minus twenty Celsius. I pull my silk scarf closer around my neck. As I approach the minivan, the side door slides open.

"Come over here, little girl, I have some candy for you," Carl says menacingly. I think about screaming but decide that might be taking this horrible joke too far.

Owen is in the driver's seat. "Is this your mom's van?" I ask.

"Yeah," says Owen despondently, and we all laugh.

Owen is such an aggressive driver that most of us usually refuse to ride with him. But he drives his mother's van sedately. In fact, he's driving so slowly I'm tempted to urge him to step on it. We drift along Hamilton's slushy streets like a boat caught in a lazy current until Owen swings the van into the driveway of a two-storey brick house, big garage in the front, burlap-wrapped roses under the bay window.

As Owen cuts the engine, the front door swings open, revealing a big woman dressed in black slacks and a loose-fitting tunic covered with bright rectangles and squares. Big gold earrings glisten underneath long, thick grey hair. She smiles, revealing the same sharp canines as Owen.

"Well, hello there," she calls to Owen, who walks right up there and wraps her in a hug. Then, she hugs Robby, and then Carl, and Austin. After they've all had their hugs, they part, and I stand in front of her. She looks me up and down. I feel very uncomfortable under her sharp eye, but I stand tall, chin up.

"Mom, this is Darby. Darby, this is my mom."

"I have a name! It's Louise, dear. You don't have to call me Mom unless you want to."

"Nice to meet you, Louise," I say, extending my hand. She shakes it. Her hands are so big. I wonder if she's really strong.

Louise ushers us inside. I slide my boots off, pad in my sock feet across the tile floor of the foyer and into the formal dining room. Place settings for seven are laid out. China, painted with blue and pink flowers and edged in gold. In the centre, plates with stacks of waffles, fruit, bacon, and eggs.

A grey-haired man comes in from the kitchen then, pot of coffee in hand, and starts filling the teacups. "Darby, this is Frank, my boyfriend," she says. "Well, that's not quite true. He's actually my fiancé."

Owen looks momentarily stunned. Robby grins, thumps Frank on his back. It's a move with enough force to have caused a smaller man to spill the coffee, but Frank is built like a retired linebacker, still formidable. He and Louise are well-matched, I think.

"Well, Owen, aren't you going to congratulate us?" asks Louise.

"Of course, congratulations," says Owen, shaking Frank's free hand. "When's the big day?"

"Your mother is running a little ahead of schedule, which is nothing new," says Frank. "Let me finish with the coffee, then we'll all sit down and eat, and talk about our plans."

I place one waffle on my plate and reach for the fruit. Louise tuts, shakes her head at me. "You are too thin! Take another waffle."

"Oh, no, I'm fine," I reply, suddenly uncomfortable. I hate people pushing food on me. It reminds me of my own mother. I glance around the table, but the rest of the band is digging in. They all have at least two waffles, or in Austin's case, three, plus scrambled eggs and bacon.

Louise reaches across Frank's plate, lifts my plate, and sets another waffle on top of the first. Then she shifts the waffles to the side, adds eggs and bacon.

"You can't go all day on one waffle," she says, reaching over Frank again to set the plate in front of me.

"Mom, take it down a notch."

"Now, you listen ..."

"Louise, Frank, tell us about your wedding plans," Robby interrupts.

"Yeah. Do you want us to play at the reception?" asks Carl.

"We were thinking about asking you, but we didn't want to impose," says Frank.

"No imposition," says Austin. "It would be an honour."

"Absolutely," says Robby.

"It will save me having to mingle," Owen adds.

"Well, good then." Louise puts her cutlery down. "I want you to know that we really appreciate it."

"So, when's the big day?" Owen asks.

"Well, it's going to be in three weeks."

Everyone stops chewing for a moment. "Really?" Owen asks. "Couldn't you give everyone a little more notice?"

"We just got engaged the day before yesterday," Louise says.

"So what's the rush?" says Robby. "Give yourselves some time to plan. Give everyone else time to make arrangements."

"We've got everything booked. The reception is going to be in the Legion. And we don't want to wait!" Louise says.

"We don't know much time we have, at our age," Frank adds, placing his hand over Louise's. They look into each other's eyes.

"None of us knows how much time we have," I say.

"Ain't that the truth," says Frank, raising his coffee cup as though to toast me.

—

At four o'clock, I walk onto stage for the soundcheck. I stare out at that empty hockey arena, rows of seats on multiple levels plus the floor. It's a sold-out show, something like twenty thousand fans. I start to feel a little sick.

We play a couple of the songs on our set, then launch into some favourites by other artists. Handsome Ned's "Put the Blame on Me," which makes Owen and Robby a little sad for their old friend. It's not a song they'll ever play for an audience, but we play it every soundcheck, for ourselves. Then we play some Stray Cats, a few old Wilco songs, and on for an hour, finally ending with "Mule Skinner Blues," where I always try to yodel. I've progressed from terrible to not bad to pretty good. By the last yodel, I realize that I've played out some of my nervousness.

After, instead of hanging out with the rest of the band around the catered food, I head to my own dressing room, so I can sweat out the last of my nerves. I change into my sweats and a grubby old T-shirt, put Garbage on my little boombox, and start working out.

I warm up with skipping, burpees, sit-ups, and push-ups. Then I start shadow boxing, losing all other thoughts in the rhythm of Shirley Manson's anger and my combinations, each strike punctuated by a sharp exhale.

Jab. Straight. Straight. Hook
Jab. Jab. Hook. Jab.
Jab. Straight. Hook. Uppercut.

Keep your hands up. Stay light on your feet. Move around. The dressing room, used by countless hockey teams, smells like sweaty socks and cleaner. It's easy to imagine I'm preparing for a title match rather than a show.

After I finish, I try to call Trevor, but it goes straight to voicemail. I leave him a quick message, tell him I miss him, and ask him to call me later tonight if he's still up.

Thinking of Trevor makes me think of the first supper I'd had at his place, over a month ago now. Trevor lives one block from Austin, in Chinatown, above a pharmacy. As I'd walked up the stairs to his second-floor apartment, I'd expected a replica of Austin's dingy place. I'd held my breath as I'd opened the door, then exhaled in relief.

Trevor's place was clean and well-cared for. The white lino floor was relatively new, and so clean it sparkled. Prints hung on the white walls. One, right above the kitchen table, looked like a Tom Thomson piece, a ragged pine on the shore of a Canadian Shield lake. On the adjacent wall was a portrait of a cowboy with a raven perched on his shoulder. Something about it was familiar, but before I could look more closely, Trevor had hurried forward to take my coat, which he hung on a black hook made from a bent horseshoe.

"You want wine? I have a nice Malbec," he said.

I nodded, and he poured the wine into a light blue glass. The air smelled of ginger and garlic. "Whatcha cooking?" I asked, surveying the chopped vegetables and sliced chicken.

"Just a stir-fry. Nothing fancy," Trevor said.

I made my way back to the paintings by the kitchen table. The first was definitely a Tom Thomson. The second looked like one of my aunt's.

It was different from her work that I was familiar with. So realistic and sharp it almost looked like a photo. The man in the cowboy hat was my grandfather when he was younger. His hat was tilted at such an angle that one eye was in shadow, but his other sky-blue eye was piercing. His face was just starting to turn to old leather from time out in the wind and sun. A raven perched on his right shoulder, its face turned toward him, as though it were speaking in his ear. It must be Henry's pet bird Huginn, I realize. A second raven flew overhead.

In the bottom right corner was my aunt's signature with her maiden name and the title of the work: *Huginn and Ivan.*

"Did you get this from my Grandpa Kolchak?" I asked.

"Yeah. He has a whole stack of your aunt's paintings and drawings in his attic, from when she was in art school. I bought this one off him for five hundred dollars. I'd offered to lend it to the exhibit, but Pauline turned me down."

"I wonder why she'd do that. You should ask her again. It's really good."

I suddenly felt a little light-headed and sank into a kitchen chair. "This is so weird. I can't believe you have one of my aunt's paintings. Have you been stalking my family for years?"

"Pretty hard to stalk them from Toronto," he quipped.

Learning something new about a loved one who is gone is a gift. I stared at the painting for what felt like a long time, imagining what my aunt must have been like when she was young. I imagine her in a bright dress made by Helen, ready for a night out on the town. Or in art school, wearing a man's button-up shirt, sleeves rolled up, over top of old blue jeans, all stained with paint. I imagine her looking happy and carefree in her studio, the way she looked most of the time riding horses.

"This painting is so different from her later work, stylistically. Her lines were usually softer, like watercolours, and her work got a bit more abstract as she got older," I said. "This looks like a reproduction of her photos. Pauline really should have included it."

"Your grandpa said it's the only one like this. She wasn't happy with it, so she never did another painting in this style."

"I get the feeling you know my family better than I do."

"Nah. I just collect people's stories like a crow collecting shiny objects."

I looked at the painting one last time. It was beautiful, but my grandpa looked so sad. Sadder than he did in real life. I wonder if he really was that sad or if that emotion came from Bea. Or both.

Later, after we'd eaten supper and washed the dishes, Trevor asked me about boxing. "Do you picture yourself punching someone?"

"I used to, but after a while I just started focussing on the combinations, on moving my feet. I like it because you can forget about everything else and be in the moment. Music is like that, too. Otherwise I'd always be thinking about everything that's happened, or worried about what's going to happen next."

"Maybe good things are going to happen next."

Trevor is right, I think now. The good things are happening, right now.

I look at my cell phone, tempted to try to calling Trevor again. But that might be a bit much. Instead I tap out a text on my little flip phone: *getting rdy now ttyl*

I think about phoning Ruby or Jen, but I don't feel like making small talk, and I don't know how to voice the loneliness I feel. It's always been there, but right now it drags at my heart more than usual.

Nothing for it but to get ready for the show, I tell myself, flipping my phone closed, stripping, and stepping into the shower. I sing Hank Williams's "I'm So Lonesome, I Could Cry" as loud as I can, with as much twang as I can.

—

When I first step onto the stage, the curtains are down and I can hear the audience talking and laughing, a few people singing. There are thousands of them, and they are the most dedicated of Urban Coyotes fans. What if they came to boo me into oblivion?

I have a strong urge to turn around and walk off again. Owen, seeing my nerves, walks over and squeezes my shoulder.

"You're going to be great, Kid. Don't worry."

And once the curtains lift and we start playing, all my nerves are transformed into the same energy that flows between us and the audience and back again at every gig, except amplified. It feels like we could power every home in the city. Every person in that audience knows the words to every chorus, at a minimum. Many know every word to every song. Their voices resonate within my gut and through my limbs.

When Robby sings the opening lines of "Cold North Wind," the audience's emotion threatens to overwhelm me. I close my eyes as he sings.

> She said, Baby, I'm cold, I'm heading for the sun.
> You can take it or leave it, but I am done.
> And I let her walk out that door,
> 'cause I just couldn't fight anymore.

As he hits that last line, I open my eyes. People in the audience are holding up lighters and cell phones, swaying slightly. I walk over to Robby, take a deep breath, and lean into his mic as we sing the chorus together.

> And now that cold north wind's blowing.
> I can feel its chill right through the door.
> Yeah, that cold north wind's howling
> And I wish I'd begged her to stay once more.

After we finish our last set, we head backstage, waiting for the cheering to build up a bit before heading out for the encore. Carl collapses into an armchair and chugs water. Owen and Robby sip warm water with lemon and ginger.

"Is that any good?" I ask.

"Try it," says Robby, pouring me a steaming mug from the teapot. "It's good for your voice."

"Good for your soul," says Owen, chuckling.

I take the mug, sip it. It's fairly good. "Not too offensive," I say.

"Another rave review from the Kid," says Owen.

"Good enough for me," says Austin, pouring himself a cupful. "Mmmm-hmmmm. My soul feels better already."

After a minute, Carl springs up from his armchair. "Let's hit it," he says, striding for the door. We follow him through the corridor and toward the stage. We're about ten feet from the stage when we hear the rhythm of Carl's drums. The crowd begins to roar.

"What the hell?" says Carl, sprinting the last few feet, the rest of us right behind him.

There, on stage, playing our instruments, is the crew, playing The Band's "The Weight." What is it about that old song that always makes me feel like the whole world is inside my heart?

As the song moves toward the chorus, we step onto the stage. The crowd cheers louder. Austin switches on a mic and the five of us crowd around it, singing the chorus along with the crew and the crowd. It feels like being back in church, singing with the choir.

The crew hands over our instruments, to riotous cheering. We play two more songs, nice and mellow to bring everything down, and exit the stage. I power walk back to my locker room for a quick shower and change of clothes, then head to the green room. I'm so hungry that my stomach is eating itself, and there's a real spread laid out in the green room: BLTs (Owen and Robby's must-have for the rider), cheese pizza (Carl's request), tons of fruit (band consensus), ginger snaps (Austin's sole request), Reese's Peanut Butter Cups (my request).

Other people start to filter into the green room. A DJ for a local radio station, friends and family of Owen and Robby, musicians from the area. I smile, shake hands, make small talk between bites of pineapple and strawberry.

The local radio guy introduces two teenage girls who've won passes through some sort of contest. Kayla and Brittany. They shake hands with Carl, Austin, and me. Then they hand me a small gift bag.

"We made this for you," says Brittany.

"We do screen prints," says Kayla.

"Oh, wow," I say, reaching into the bag and pulling out the soft T-shirt. It's black with a red line drawing of a running horse, his mane and tail dancing in the wind. White lettering forms the ground he runs over: *Life is a journey. Enjoy the ride.*

"Do you like it?" asks Kayla.

"I love it," I say. "It's just what I need." I'm not one for hugging strangers, but I hug them, and then the radio guy takes our photo. Kayla and Brittany pepper me with questions about music, about my guitar, how I got this gig. I try to answer them as best I can, then start asking them questions. Are they musicians?

Brittany and Kayla *are* musicians, in fact. They have just started a country trio with another friend, Candy, who couldn't come tonight because she's sick. Candy plays drums, Brittany bass, Kayla guitar and pedal steel. All three girls sing. They mostly play for their friends right now, but the local radio station has played one of their songs as part of the contest.

"Do you have a CD?" I ask.

"Not yet. We're on MySpace, though," says Brittany. She pulls a postcard from her backpack. It's another line drawing of a horse running, but this time the lettering that forms the ground spells *The Greatest Show on Earth.*

"Thanks," I say. I tell them I'll find them on MySpace, which I have been thinking I should join myself. We hug once more, the girls move on, and I chat with a few other fans and industry people.

After a while, the crowd starts to thin out. I stack my plate with fruit, peanut butter cups, and a BLT, collapse into a chair, and eat quickly.

At the end of the night, I grab my duffel bag and boom box and climb back onto the bus.

"Hello, Ms. Swank," says the bus driver, as I make my way up the steps.

"Hey, Craig," I say.

"Happy to be heading home for a day?"

"I don't know. I think I could do this forever."

"Oh, that will change. The miles wear on you," he says with a gentle smile.

"Maybe it will, but right now, I love it."

I climb into my bunk and read the last pages of *East of Eden*. I read Adam's last word, *timshel*. Thou *may* triumph over sin, not thou must or thou will, as it is usually interpreted. In other words, it's up to you to decide how you'll live your life, whether you'll murder your brother as Cain did, or not. That is free will, a keystone of Christianity because it allows for redemption.

If Steinbeck had written a novel about my own family, what would happen next? I wonder. Would he find redemption for Will as he sits in the Prince Albert prison, or would Will continue to rot away from the inside out? What about my father? Can a man who has concealed such evil ever be redeemed?

If I were still a Christian, I might talk to a pastor, and he would probably tell me that redemption is always possible. Every breath, every moment offers another chance at redemption. And that true redemption is not for us to judge but is between God and man (or woman, if the pastor had any feminist qualities).

And I understand that, but where does it leave someone like me, who still carries this sadness and anger, whose bile rises every time she sees her father's phone number on her cell phone?

The pastor would probably tell me that I must turn the other cheek and forgive my father, at least, if not my uncle, for the sake of my immortal soul and own mental health. But what if forgiveness, at least as it's presented in the Bible, doesn't mean what we all think it means? What if we've been misinterpreting that one word for centuries, just like *timshel?* What if it's separate from reconciliation? What if Jen's interpretation of forgiveness, writing off a bad debt, is truer to the original meaning?

I think of the shirt the girls gave to me tonight. *Life is a journey.*

Maybe forgiveness is about leaving behind heavy baggage.

After all, if you're always journeying, maybe it's best to pack light.

ELEVEN

THE WEDDING. LOUISE and Frank's friends have strung white lights all over the Legion. They run along the walls, hang artfully in the bare branches of the fake trees, and snake along the edge of the stage where we stand.

We play a lot of country standards—Hank Williams, Carter Family, Patsy Cline, that type of thing. Owen and Robby want to socialize, so I do a lot of the singing. Louise and some of her girlfriends sing in the church choir, so they often get on stage and sing along. They have beautiful voices, and when I sing with them, it feels like a powerful wave coming up behind me.

As I clutch the microphone and look out on the crowd, it reminds me of the country dances of my childhood. Little kids balancing on the feet of adults as the grownups two-step them around the dance floor. Some guy by the bar laughing with such force his body bends backwards, like a tree in the wind. Two women sitting at a table right by the dance floor, trying to have a conversation, which means yelling in each other's ears to be heard over the music.

Dozens of little tealights flickering on the deep blue tablecloths, reminding me of starlight. It's all lovely, really.

Louise and Frank have a full house, with Owen and his younger sister and her kids. Robby stays at his brother's place. The rest of us stay at a hotel. I didn't think anything of it when Nancy was making arrangements, but when I'm alone at the end of the night, I feel very lonely. I should have pressed Trevor to come. He would have, if I'd insisted, but he already had plans and I hadn't wanted to seem clingy. Now, alone and a little drunk, I find myself unable to sleep, so I watch TV until sometime after four, when I finally drift off.

—

The next night I'm at Trevor's. We've just finished supper and are about to start a movie.

"I have an important question for you," he says, handing me a jewelry box.

I say nothing as I flip open the lid. Inside is a copper-coloured horseshoe on a copper chain. I carefully lift it from the box, hang it in front of me. Each end of the chain is connected to the end of the horseshoe so it hangs correctly, to catch the luck.

"Yes. I will accept this gift," I say.

"I thought you could wear it on the road, so you'd have a horseshoe with you. But that wasn't really my question," he says, suddenly serious. "Darby, will you move in with me?"

"This is moving really fast," I say. I start thinking of all the reasons we shouldn't move in together. We've only known each other a few months, I'm on the road all the time, I'm afraid he'll break my heart. Or that I'll break his.

"I know, but we're both old enough to know what we want, don't you think? I know I want to be with you. I'm in love with you."

It's the first time he's said it. "I love you, too." It's out before I have time to think about it, to even decide if it's true.

Trevor pulls me to him, nuzzles my neck, and I'm flooded with desire. "I'll shack up with you," I say. He says nothing, kissing my mouth and pulling at my shirt. Just like that, the issue is decided.

—

When I tell Nancy and Cole I'm moving in with Trevor, Cole looks so sad I almost change my mind.

"Will you still come over for supper sometimes?" he asks.

"Yeah, of course. You can come over to our place, too." *Our place.* It sounds strange rolling out of my mouth like that, but I like it.

Nancy gives me a hug. "I'm happy for you, but we're sure going to miss you. Let's have Trevor over for supper one night before you go. And I'd like to sit down with you to talk about your career in the next week."

"Okay."

It doesn't take me long to pack up. I still have only one large suitcase full of clothes, a box of books and pictures, another box of CDs, one guitar, and an amp. After I've finished everything else, I take down my horseshoe from above the door and pull out the little gold hook and nail that held it up. I put the hook and nail in a small pocket in my purse and the horseshoe in my CD box.

Downstairs, Cole and Nancy are cooking supper for Trevor and me. I'd wanted to help, but they insisted on doing it alone. I put a Sadies CD on my little ghetto blaster, run a bath, throw in a couple of cups of Epsom salts, pour myself a glass of red wine, and settle in for a long soak.

I let the twangy surf music wash over me and think.

Am I making the right choice? What if it doesn't go well? What if we don't get along?

But what's the worst that can happen? If we break up, I either move into my own place or move back in with Nancy and Cole. I could probably afford my own place by now anyway.

What if things go really wrong? Like, Uncle Will and Aunt Bea kinda wrong? Then what?

Well, either I leave or I'm dead. But Trevor's not like that. Or I don't think he's like that, anyway.

Who would help me if I needed help here? Would Jen come, or Ruby and her family? Beth and Red would come, I think, and arrange for Amber and Ruby to get on a plane, too. But they're all so far away, and I don't have many friends here. I'm closest to Nancy and Cole, followed by Austin. I haven't made a single girlfriend, I realize suddenly. I don't even know the names of the other women at the boxing club, or not most of them. Everyone I really know is in the music industry. It's like living in a small town in the middle of Toronto, but hardly anyone invites you over for supper.

I'm starting to feel really lonesome with all this thinking, when I should be happy that I'm about to go all common-law with a guy who appears to be healthy and normal. A guy I happen to be in love with, and who's in love with me. Why else would he want me to move in, unless he's going to go all *Silence of the Lambs* and use my skin for his woman suit?

Stop it, I tell myself. That is not what's going on.

I have already drunk one glass of wine. Better have another, as my thinking needs improving. I love the *glug, glug, glug* of the wine into my glass. I swirl it around a bit, the way people do at all the music industry parties I've been to, to aerate it or whatever. I can't say it makes a difference to my coarse tastebuds, but it's fun to do. Then I take a sip.

Okay, everything is going to be fine, Darby, I tell myself. If things don't go well, you either work it out with Trevor or you leave. That simple. You're not Bea. You're yourself, and you know what to watch for, and you know you can leave. You have your own money. You can just hop on a streetcar and hightail it back to Nancy and Cole, or the airport, or wherever you want. You survived your uncle. You survived his lawyer during the trial. You can survive anything.

Once the CD ends, I lift my body from the cooling water and drain the tub. I towel-dry my hair, then weave it into a French braid. I think about applying makeup, but then I hear the door open downstairs and Nancy greeting Trevor.

Trevor limits himself to one small glass of wine, but I have two more over the course of supper. It's a new recipe that Cole got from his girlfriend's mother. Curried chicken and homemade naan.

"Oh my god, this so good. Cole, when did you get a girlfriend?"

"Like, a month ago. Where have you been?"

"On tour, I guess. What's her name?"

"Sherri."

"Have you met her, Nancy?"

"Actually, yes. Her family lives three blocks down. Cole has been friends with her and her older brother for years."

"Awww, that's nice."

Cole scrunches up his face at me. Trevor gives me a look. "What?"

"He's not a little kid," says Trevor.

"I know. I just ... I'm sorry."

After supper, Trevor and Cole haul my things into Trevor's car while I help Nancy clear the table.

"I'm going to miss living with you," I say.

"You're a sweetheart, but I have a feeling you'll be over us soon. Besides, I'll see you tomorrow for lunch, remember? To discuss your career options?"

"Yes, okay."

I've just finished wiping down the table when Trevor calls. "Babe, we should get going. I don't want to leave your guitar in my car."

"Okay." Nancy wraps me in a hug, and I walk to the door. Cole is waiting there. He bear-hugs me, and then I'm pulling on my boots, and then I'm gone.

The first thing I do when we get to Trevor's apartment (my apartment) is hang my horseshoe, right side up, over the front door.

Between this horseshoe Jack gave me, the horseshoes Trevor uses for a coat rack, and the one hanging around my neck, we should have nothing but good luck here.

—

Nancy texts me the next day at twelve thirty, and I meet her at a Vietnamese restaurant around the corner. It's still pretty busy, but we find an empty table at the back. I order spicy beef satay soup and a Vietnamese iced coffee.

"And a big glass of water," I add, trying not to look too hungover. The server nods.

Nancy orders a soup as well, and green tea.

"So, let's talk," she says. "Did you know that Clint Andriachuk is playing in a band called Cyril Sneer's Revenge on the West Coast?"

It takes me a moment to process this. Clint Andriachuk ... the former lead singer of Austin and Reggie's band, Cyril Sneer's Revenge.

"Oh. No, I didn't. Is he playing their songs, too?"

"Yes."

"Is there anything we can do about that?"

"Change your band name," says Nancy. "Clint was the primary songwriter and his new band sounds more like Cyril Sneer's Revenge than you do, anyway. I know you have your own material. If you start performing that, develop your own sound, you'll be better than Clint's band ever could have been."

"Okay, well, I'll talk to Reggie and Austin about it."

"Great. On this next leg of the tour, work on your songwriting on the bus, if you can. Experiment a little, see if you can get a sense of what your sound will be. Think about band names, who you want to add. You won't be able to do much more than that for the next couple of months. But once the Urban Coyotes tour is over, I want you three to rehearse, start to nail down your sound. Then I want to send you west for a couple of months, after the Urban

Coyotes are done their festival schedule. I want you to get in your thousand hours as a band, just like the Beatles in Hamburg. And if it all goes well, I want to get you into some international showcases next year."

I look at her, stunned. "Really? You think we can do that? I mean, are you sure I'm the right front man for a band like that?"

"Listen to me, Darby Swank. You need to take yourself seriously or no one else will."

Just then the server arrives with our soups. After she's set them down and walked away, I pick up my spoon, then lay it back down.

"Can I tell you something, Nancy?"

"Of course."

"I don't really feel I deserve all this. There are so many musicians out there more talented than I am, and they never get these kinds of breaks."

"Well, the truth is you *are* lucky. But it's also true that you're talented, and you've worked hard. Everyone feels the way you do sometimes, and that's okay. Just don't let that feeling keep you from walking through a door that's opened for you. And then, when you're established, you can pay it forward to other artists who deserve a break. Not that long ago, women had to break down the door for these opportunities. I was one of those women, and let me tell you, it was tough. I'm grateful to be able to open the door for women like you today."

"Thanks, Nancy. I'm glad you were able to break down those doors."

—

Trevor's still at work when I get home, so I decide to nap away the last remnants of my hangover and the road fatigue. Just as I'm lying down, my cell phone starts ringing. It's a Saskatchewan number I don't recognize, but I answer it anyway.

"Hello, Darby? It's your Uncle Henry. I got your number from Trevor."

"Oh, hi Uncle Henry. How did you know to call Trevor for my number?"

"Your Aunt Linda reads these music websites. She's been following your whole tour. Anyway, one of these blogs or whatever is more gossip than anything, and yesterday she read that you were shacking up with this reporter fella, Trevor Murphy."

"People are writing about me in gossip columns?"

"Don't you have the Internet there in Toronto? We don't have it at the ranch yet, but Linda reads it in town, during her lunch breaks at the bank."

"Oh. Well, yeah, I am shacked up with Trevor Murphy. I guess you know him already."

"Your Aunt Linda jokes that he's stalking our family. She has poor timing, your aunt. She made the joke in front of your grandpa, and he didn't find it all that funny, what with Bea and all." Uncle Henry delivers this in a flat, dry tone, as though trying to scrub away the high emotion that must have followed Linda's joke.

"I've been saying the same to Trevor for weeks, so you can tell your wife not to feel too bad," I reply, mimicking his tone and his way of referring to our relations. "How is everyone?"

"Oh, we're getting by. Reata is obsessed with Temple Grandin. Both the *Grainews* and the *Cattlemen* ran articles on her this fall, and one of them mentioned the hug machine she built for herself in college."

"What's a hug machine?"

"It's sort of a squeeze-chute type contraption that helps people with autism de-stress or feel connected, from what I can figure out. Anyway, Reata was set on her own hug machine. It's all she talked about for a week. Finally, her mother said, 'Reata, me and your dad are your own personal hug machines. Anytime you want a hug, you just ask one of us.' So that solved it. I told Linda I married her for her smarts, and she agreed."

We chat about family (Grandpa Kolchak is still as energetic as ever, and still mad as hell at my dad and Will), talk about BSE (it all sucks, and Uncle Henry is particularly steamed about people calling it Mad Cow disease, but he's looking forward to being past president instead of president). Henry and Linda would like to come to a concert, and I offer to put them on the list when we play in Calgary in a few weeks. I haven't talked to Uncle Henry much, but he's an easy conversationalist and an hour passes quickly.

When I close my flip phone, I realize I'm running late for my band meeting with Reggie and Austin. I pull on my boots and winter coat, grab my purse, and speed-walk to Kensington. I mumble Reggie's directions out loud, wondering if I'm on the right track. Then I see the grocery store with the green awning. And across the street the pawn shop that buys gold and has been hustlin' since 1965, according to its signage. And right beside that the little bar.

I walk inside, take in the orange walls, bright yellow and orange chairs, and Jackson Pollock-inspired splatter tabletops. Then I spot Reggie and Austin near the back. They dwarf the table they're sitting at so much that it makes me think of adults playing teatime at a toddler's table.

I wave, walk up to the bar, and order a Has-Been dark ale. Then I saunter over to Reggie and Austin.

"Hello, fellas," I say in my worst possible Chicago accent.

"Hiya, doll," says Austin. Reggie clinks my glass with his.

"I was just telling Austin that Clint has started a West Coast Cyril Sneer's Revenge."

"Nancy told me the same thing at lunch today," I say.

"I guess I misunderstood him when he said he wouldn't be using the band name," says Austin dryly.

"I knew this would happen, but let's move on," Reggie replies. "We need a new band name. We can still play some of our old stuff, but we should keep writing. We're better songwriters than we were even a few months ago, and now we've got Darby. We're a different band."

"I have a band name," I say. "The Hug Machine." I explain my cousin's obsession with Temple Grandin, my aunt's solution.

"I kind of like it," says Austin. "Maybe."

"Darby Swank and the Hug Machine," says Reggie.

"There it is," says Austin, raising his glass. We clink and we drink. We talk about where we're going to jam. Reggie's older sister and her husband have just bought a house with a heated garage a little west of here, just off Bloor, that we can use anytime from late morning to mid-afternoon. We'll all bring our material and start working on some songs before Austin and I go back on the road.

"Hey, and did I tell you about this Amelia I met? She works here, actually." Reggie says.

"The singer?" Austin asks.

"No, Amelia can't sing worth a damn. You're thinking of Becky. Becky doesn't work here, she works at the Cadillac."

"Okay, no, I have no idea."

"Amelia's decent on guitar. But she's a killer lap steel player."

"Are you two dating?"

"Not yet, but hopefully soon. But she's really good. You should hear her, man. She's just like Jimmy Roy with the Ray Condo band."

"I say bring her to rehearsal and see what happens," I say.

"I'm good with it, too," says Austin.

"Okay, I'll bring her tomorrow."

"It'll be good to have another gal around," I say, again with a poorly done accent.

"Yeah, you know, I never see you hanging out with other girls," says Austin.

"That's because I don't know any here. Because I have no life."

"Oh, by the way, she's from Chicago, so start working on your accent," says Reggie.

I walk home alone. A few blocks from Trevor's apartment, a little blue car slowly passes me, a Corb Lund song blasting, with two guys in cowboy hats singing along. It reminds me of Sam, and a wave of homesickness crashes over me. I stop walking, close my eyes, and think of racing down a forest trail, Jen's horse just a little ahead of me and Bucky, light dappling the trail. I think of summer evenings at the chuckwagon races, Sam, Luke, and me cheering on whoever Jen was outriding for. I think of frying breaded jackfish Sam had just plucked from the lake, the smell of the fire, the warm feel of Luke's hand on my knee. I think of when the four of us were in our early teens, playing kick the can in the bush at night.

It's not that I felt innocent or even safe then, not with my mom's volatile behaviour. But none of us knew what was ahead of us then. Not that we know now, either, I suppose.

Someone bumps into my shoulder, so I open my eyes and carry on in the present. Back to Trevor's, where I make myself a pot of tea and get started on the lasagna. In a short time, the smell of garlic and pasta permeates the apartment.

—

Trevor is one of those crazy people who likes to run before work at least three days a week, even in the cold slush of early spring.

My second morning at Trevor's, his alarm wakes us both up at six a.m. Trevor yawns, stretches, then rolls out of bed, stands, and briskly starts pulling on his running gear: long johns made from some sort of fancy thin material, wind-proof jogging pants with reflective striping, a black base layer to wick moisture, a shirt over that, and a wind-proof shell with reflective striping.

"You were serious about the run."

"You bet your bippy I was. Want to join me?"

Fuck no, I think. I say, "No thanks. I'll do some yoga or something."

I follow Trevor to the door, watch him lace up his shoes. "Don't fall," I say.

"I'll be fine. It's not even slick right now," he says, kissing me on the cheek.

"Okay, well have fun, crazy person."

Once he leaves, I look up a morning hatha yoga routine on YouTube. Sun salutations. I never thought I'd get into yoga, but it's become a necessity. When I'm not slinging a heavy guitar, I'm boxing or sitting on a bus, and all that adds up to tension and stiff muscles. I follow along for twenty-five minutes, stretching those muscles for all they're worth. Trevor is still running when I've finished, so I cook some oatmeal and thaw a bowlful of frozen blueberries in the microwave. Then I grind the fair-trade coffee beans (Trevor is a coffee snob), boil some water, add a shot of cold water to bring down the temperature a touch, and pour the grinds and hot water into the French press. When Trevor walks in the door, the whole spread is laid out on the small kitchen table.

"What's on your sched today?" he asks between bites of oatmeal.

"We've got a band rehearsal at one thirty."

"Seems pretty early for a bunch of musicians. Will Austin even be out of bed?"

"Amelia, the one who's thinking of joining, starts work around suppertime. I can't remember what time. What about you?"

"Oh, you know, the news. Trisha is still in BC covering that slide in North Van. I'm meeting one of my sources on the Judy Sgro debacle."

"What was that about again?"

"She's the one who handed out immigration permits to the woman who worked on her campaign."

"Oh, yeah, the stripper."

"Not very politically correct, Darby. But yes. She quit last week, after it came out that she tried to get free pizza in exchange for intervening in an immigration hearing. And the *Star* broke that story about her credit card fraud."

"Do you really think she was handing out favours for free pizza? I mean, that seems pathetic."

Trevor shrugs. "There's probably more to it, but on the other hand, people surprise me all the time. Anyway, I gotta run. I'll probably be late again tonight. The newsroom has been a zoo lately. Thanks for breakfast, my love. Have a good day."

I wash the breakfast dishes, then curl up on Trevor's old denim-coloured couch and pull out my laptop, along with the band postcard Kayla and Brittany gave me backstage a couple of weeks ago. I log onto MySpace and look up Kayla and Brittany's band, The Greatest Show on Earth.

There they are, with their friend Candy. I'm immediately struck by the images on their page. It looks like they've been taken by a professional photographer.

Not only that, but they're obviously carefully crafting an image. All three girls have their hair pinned up in loose Gibson Girl styles. Pinned into their hair are fascinators full of feathers and small gears. Their clothing is a strange combination of Old West with an edge: ruffled blouses, long skirts, leather corsets, leather arm guards studded with metal. It reminds me of the Will Smith and Salma Hayek movie *Wild, Wild West*.

I click on one of their songs, expecting something bluegrass tinged with beautiful harmonies. Instead, I get high-energy cowpunk, with the girls singing in unison. Soon I'm singing along to the chorus.

> *I don't wannna be your baby.*
> *I don't want you for my man.*
> *I'll do whatever I want, thank you,*
> *just because I can.*

I listen to three other songs. The third has Kayla singing lead with the other two harmonizing. It's a little slower, a sweet ballad about a city girl in love with a farm boy.

They are so talented, and so obviously tech-savvy, I feel a little insecure.

Just then my brand-new hot-pink flip phone chimes. A text. Who is texting me?

> *Heeeeyyyy cuz! its brynny grant. mom gave me your cell i luv your music!*

Brynny ... Helen's daughter. That would make Brynny my second cousin. Or first cousin once removed? I'm not sure.

> *hi.*

> *hows toronto?*

> *good just on a break from touring*

I pause, trying to remember where she lives.

> *you still in Calgary?*

> *yup, finishing my degree this yr*

> *what are you studying*

> *religion with psych minor*

> *huh. you going to be a cult leader or something?*

> *im going to start my own church*

> *sorry bad joke*

> *no worries. theres a fine line btw religion and cult*

> *where is your church going to be?*

> *next time you r in calgary, come out to millarville and*

see me preach. as a horse person you'll like it.

why, is it some sort of horse cult?

something like that. check it out

A url pops up. www.shortgrasschurch.com.

i gotta run darby talk to ya later

thx.

I type the url into my laptop and click on the video.

My cousin, who looks a lot like a younger version of Helen (or a fairer version of my own mother), pops onto the screen. She is wearing tan English riding breeches, tall black riding boots, and a crisp white blouse. Her reddish-blond hair is arranged in a neat bun. She stands confidently in the middle of an indoor riding arena. The camera must be on a tripod, as it's too steady to be handheld.

Brynny starts walking to the left. The camera follows her smoothly. A bay quarter horse, loose with no halter, comes into the frame. The horse's ears are forward as it looks at Brynny, then approaches her. Brynny strokes the horse's neck.

"Do you want to get right with your horse? With your family, your friends? With your Lord? Do you?"

The crowd murmurs yes.

"I can't hear you."

A louder yes, just below a shout. The horse's head shoots up and it looks at the crowd.

"Did you see how this mare just walked right up to me? She doesn't do that to everyone. She is what you would call a 'challenge' to catch," Brynny preaches, adding air quotes as she says *challenge*. "You walk up to this mare in the wrong frame of mind, she will run circles around you, tail in the air like the most high-strung Arabian you ever saw. Ask Bryce, he'll tell you."

"Yes, she will," a man, off-camera calls out. "Anyone lookin' to buy a horse?"

The crowd laughs. The horse looks at them again, but quickly refocusses on Brynny.

"What is this mare's name, Bryce?" Brynny asks.

"Her barn name is Badger," says Bryce. "Sire was a Tivio-bred reiner, mare is off of Shining Spark."

Nice bloodlines, I think.

"Good bloodlines," says Brynny, as though she's echoing my thought. "This little mare is full of potential. But all the potential in the world is worthless if you can't catch her. If she won't even approach you in the round pen, never mind a ten-acre pasture."

"She is tricky," Bryce confirms.

The camera backs up a little, and I can now see that Brynny is actually in a round pen. The small, round corral has been set up with corral panels. Vertical planks form a solid wall on three sides.

"Bryce, I don't wanna pick on you, but do you want to come down here with a halter and show us how to catch this mare?"

"I can try," he says. "I had to lure her in here with a bucket of oats this morning, so I'm not sure she's gonna let me catch her now."

Bryce comes into view. He's a lanky man dressed in Wranglers and a black cowboy hat, looks to be about thirty. He picks up a halter before opening a small man-gate into the round pen. Brynny exits and he enters. As soon as he steps into the pen, Badger's head shoots up and her nostrils flare.

"Bryce, I know you, and you are not a mean man, but that mare looks nervous around you. How are you feeling right now?"

"To be honest, Brynny, I am a little frustrated with this filly. I haven't been able to work with her much, and I'd like to get her started, but she just gives me the finger."

"Just try to catch her like you usually would."

Bryce lifts a pail of oats over the panel and shakes it at the mare. Badger works her mouth, as though she can taste those oats, but when Bryce walks toward her head, she swishes her tail and whirls away. He flips the rope at her rear, and she breaks into a faster canter, circling him, with her tail so high she really does look like an Arabian. Bryce steps toward her head again, probably trying to turn her, but she just blows past him. He tries again, coming in closer this time, but she leaps past him again. It seems like she would run right over him, and my stomach tightens.

"Okay, Bryce, I'm going to stop you right there. Give me those oats, then back up into the middle again, let her run for a moment. Before you do anything else, I want you to go back to how you're feeling."

"Well, to be honest, I'm a little angry and kind of embarrassed."

"Thank you. I appreciate your honesty. But you have nothing to be embarrassed about. There is nothing so humbling as a horse. Sometimes we feel great pride in our horses, but they were put on this earth to humble us, to remind us how to be present in every moment. Every minute is a fresh start with a horse.

"Now, we all grew up on stories like *Black Beauty* and *The Black Stallion*. But I'm here to tell you there's no magic to working with horses. It all starts with what's in your heart. Bryce, I'm going to talk you through it, and I guarantee that by the end, you'll be a little better at catching this mare. And you'll be a little better in other ways, too. It's the start of being better spiritually."

Brynny tells Bryce to breathe from his diaphragm. "That anger, frustration, embarrassment, it is blocking your heart. I want you to focus on exhaling all that emotion. Visualize a warm white light moving with your breath, through your body."

Meanwhile, Badger is still cantering at a good clip around Bryce, but I notice she isn't wringing her tail as much—it flows behind her now, a flag in the wind.

Brynny continues talking to Bryce in a way that reminds me of a yoga teacher, with a slight Christian flavour. Breathe. Relax your chest, your shoulders, your neck, the muscles on your face. Horses read body language and energy, so you need to project a calm energy. You need to be the leader, but that doesn't mean being aggressive.

"Jesus said all who take the sword will perish by the sword. You can understand that literally—it makes sense, right? But you can understand it metaphorically, because if we embrace violence, it corrupts us emotionally, morally, spiritually. That's not to say we can't feel anger. We are only human. Feel it, recognize it, then exhale."

By now Badger is trotting slowly, working her mouth, one ear trained on Bryce. Brynny tells him to think *slow*, to visualize the word, to breathe *slow*, to relax. Badger slows to a walk.

"Now, Bryce, the thing you don't want to do is walk right up to her head."

"I know that, but I still do it. I always think, 'Well, I can walk right up to my other horses' heads, and they practically stick their faces in the halter for me. This mare should do it, too.'"

"Right. Stop thinking in 'shoulds.' That won't get you anywhere. The world should be fair, spring should be here, yadda yadda yadda. Think 'is.' This mare is a little threatened when you march up to her head. She doesn't even like strong eye contact—it makes her move. Drop your gaze to somewhere around her hocks, turn a quarter turn away from her."

Bryce complies, and Badger stops, turns to look at him.

"Now walk slowly toward her hip, but keep your gaze down."

Bryce walks toward her hip. The mare swings her butt away from him.

"Do it again."

This time, for some reason I can't discern, instead of stepping her hind end away, Badger starts running in a circle again.

"That's okay. Any idea why she did that?"

"Well, I was feeling in a bit of a hurry because my coffee's getting cold."

The crowd chuckles.

"You will reap the harvest if you do not give up. That's Galatians. Be patient, and you can rewarm your coffee later."

Brynny continues directing Bryce and preaching. Over the next ten minutes, he's consistently able to move Badger's hind end away, from either direction. Brynny explains that a horse's mind is connected to its feet, so if you can direct the feet, you can direct the mind. If you can get a horse to cross over its hind legs as it moves its hindquarters away from you, you also start to loosen up those muscles in the hindquarters, which relaxes the horse a little. At one point, Badger yawns, and Brynny has Bryce stop because yawning is a horse's way of releasing tension from her belly, she says.

Eventually, Bryce is walking steadily toward Badger's hind quarters, and she is pivoting on her front legs, her head toward him, as she steps her hind end away.

"Now step back, three steps," says Brynny. Bryce backs up. Badger follows.

"Again."

Bryce backs up three steps, and Badger follows.

"Now turn your back on her and walk away."

Bryce walks away and Badger follows him, her nose at his shoulder.

"Pet her shoulder, talk to her quietly." Bryce strokes Badger's shoulder, murmuring. "Now slip the halter on, secure the latch, pet her, then take it off and walk away.

Bryce holds up the halter and Badger sticks her face in as he does up the latch. He strokes her mane, then walks away. Badger follows closely behind.

"Now give her some oats." Brynny lifts the bucket over the fence.

"Why not give her the oats while she's got the halter on?"

"You can. There's nothing wrong with that. But today, I want you and Badger to both realize your relationship is not transactional. Oats alone are not going to catch that mare, you know that."

Badger, meanwhile, buries her face in the bucket, then lets out a big sigh.

"Now that is a content horse. But don't take this to mean you'll be able to walk out into the pasture tomorrow and catch her in thirty seconds. This is just the beginning. You need to practise this every day. And I don't mean the exact technique, because you will have to adjust your methods to the horse and the day. I mean the stuff in here," she says, tapping her heart.

"If you want your horse to be light, to be soft, you need to be flexible and warm-hearted. If you're hard, your horse will be 'bracey.' And so will the people around you."

I close the laptop and lean back into the denim couch, thinking of skittish mares and frustrated cowboys and my second cousin, leader of a Jesus horse cult. What a strange world.

—

Amelia's blue-black hair reaches her waist, even in her loose braid. She is tall, with long legs and arms and a longish face that reminds me of Cate Blanchett. Her red lipstick is perfectly done, not bleeding from her lips in the slightest. She wears dark-blue jeans, with a sharp crease in the front, and a loose cotton shirt.

I shake her hand. Her grip is strong.

"I'm Darby," I say, as though she didn't know that. She smiles.

Austin introduces himself as well, waving with his right hand as his left grips the stand-up bass.

"Thanks for inviting me," says Amelia. "I've been looking for a band for a month. I moved here with my boyfriend—we had a duo—but then he became my ex." She glances around the garage. "This place seems like it will work really well. Who put up the sound treatment?" she asks, pointing at the old blankets over the garage door.

"I did, before you came," says Reggie. "We just have to take down the blankets and roll up the carpet when we're done. My brother-in-law needs enough room to park."

"What about the drum kit?" I ask.

"I can leave it in here as long as it's out of the way," says Reggie.

"Okay, down to business," says Austin. "Who's got a song?"

"I've got a drum track," says Reggie. He picks up his brushes and starts playing a four-beat rhythm with a touch of jazz. Amelia, sitting in a hard-backed chair with her lap steel, starts improvising and Austin follows her lead. I close my eyes, listening carefully. Reggie approaches the end, stops. I open my eyes.

"What do you think?" he asks.

"I like the beat," says Amelia. "I like the energy."

"Play it again," says Austin.

Reggie starts again. I close my eyes again, start playing. Amelia and Austin join in. We all follow Reggie's lead, sometimes adding a little flair, but mostly just following the beat, until we reach the end.

I open my eyes again. Reggie is grinning. "That's starting to sound like something. Let's do it again."

I close my eyes, as we begin again.

We play for three hours. By the end, we have a solid foundation for Reggie's song, and I've started working out a melody. Reggie gives me a ragged piece of yellow foolscap with lyric ideas, and I agree to work on it later. We've also worked on one of my songs, and one of Austin's.

"Do you have any songs, Amelia?" I ask.

"None that I want to do right now," she says. "Most of what I have I wrote with my ex. I want to start something new here."

Reggie nods approvingly. "Makes sense," says Austin.

As we're packing up, I ask Amelia if she wants to grab a coffee or something.

"Oh, sorry. I have to get ready for work. But I'm off tomorrow, if you want to do something."

"Sure, that works."

"Great. You know, I don't really have many friends here yet," she says.

"Me neither."

"Listen, I'm a little broke right now. Can we go somewhere cheap for coffee? I don't want to pay ten dollars for a latte."

"Why don't you just come over to my apartment? We have good coffee."

"Sure."

—

Amelia arrives promptly at ten the next morning.

"Hey," she says as I open the door. "I'm not late, am I?"

"No, you're right on time."

"Good. I'm not a morning person. More of a night owl."

"I'm a morning person, but I wish I was a night owl. It would be easier as a musician. I'm just always tired now."

"Maybe you'll switch. It smells good in here."

"I was doing some baking this morning." A couple of days ago I'd shopped, picking up muffin tins, mixing bowls, measuring cups. Trevor had been skeptical I'd have time to bake. I'd decided to prove him wrong.

"Are those chocolate chip cookies?"

"Yeah. Just the way Mom used to make them," I say.

"Your mom doesn't bake anymore?"

"She died when I was in high school. Cancer."

"Oh, I'm sorry. I can't imagine. I still talk to my mom every day."

"It is what it is," I say, shrugging. I don't feel like getting into a heavy conversation about my family with Amelia, at least not yet.

Amelia plucks three chocolate chip cookies from the pan, explaining by way of apology that she hasn't had breakfast, while

I pour her a big mug of coffee, add cream and sugar. Then I make my own coffee, and we sit at the table.

"Hey, I want to show you something," I say, pulling my open laptop toward me. The MySpace page for The Greatest Show on Earth is open. "What do you think of their clothes?"

"Oh, they're steampunk," she says.

"What is that?"

"It's sort of a cross between science fiction and Old West or Victorian fashion, if that makes sense. Like a sci-fi version of our past."

"Oh, I get it now." I pause, take a sip, consider. "I like it, but it's not my style. It does make me think maybe I should have more of a look, though, you know? For when I'm onstage. Nothing that out there, but just maybe something more than a T-shirt and jeans."

"It sounds like you want to go shopping," she says.

"Oh, I do."

—

"Here, try these." Amelia flings several shirts over the top of the dressing room door. Sparkly, sequined tops, all bright colours. I pull a red tank top over my head.

"I don't know," I say as I pull the door open. "It's maybe too much."

"It's not for everyday use ... it's just for onstage, to catch the light," she says. "It looks great on you."

"I don't know ... I feel like I'm going to the club. And it's too different from what the rest of the band wears."

"Hmmmm ... yeah ... maybe we should take it down a notch. Give me a sec." And she's walking back to the store. I go back into the change room, pull the tank top over my head.

"Here, try these instead." The first three shirts disappear as Amelia pulls them from the top of the door, and a new batch appears in their place. Solid white, blue, and turquoise tops, made of flowy material. I pull down a white sleeveless top. It has a smattering of sequins around the neck, but that's it. I slide it over my head, emerge from the dressing room.

"This is way better," I say, admiring myself in the long mirror.

"Yeah, I like it. But you know, you shouldn't be afraid to draw some attention, take up some space on the stage," she says.

We spend the afternoon travelling from place to place. By the end of the day, I have bags of solid white and jewel-toned shirts, silver bangles, big silver hoop earrings, dark blue jeans, a couple of blingy belt buckles. Plus one tank top covered in red sequins.

TWELVE

ONE SATURDAY MORNING late in the winter, Trevor takes me for a drive. He drives east, to the Beaches, and keeps going along Queen before turning toward the lake. We park beside a great brick structure that sits atop a hill like a queen on her throne.

"This is the water treatment plant," he says.

"How romantic," I reply.

"Clean water is terribly romantic," he says. Then he tells me all about the history, how the plant was built in the 1930s, how it remains the largest water treatment plant in Toronto.

"And the most stylish," I quip.

"Let's go for a quick walk around it."

We walk around the plant, and I have to admit, it is beautiful, with its grand arched entrance and banks of windows, all on the shore of Lake Ontario. We stare out at the lake, so big it seems like an ocean to me, although I've never seen the ocean, so what do I really know. I let my imagination fly past my gaze, skimming the air just above the waves. Then I dive below the surface, retreating from the light, exploring the lake's rocky depths.

But then the wind comes up, and I'm shivering from the chill, despite my layers of clothes.

"We'll come back in the summer," says Trevor. "It's nice to walk around then."

"I'm glad you brought me here," I say.

Once we're back in the car, Trevor pauses before he puts the car into gear. "I need to tell you something," he says.

I brace myself, wondering what bad news he has in store. "What is it?"

"I thought you should know, I'm planning to write a book."

I exhale. I didn't even realize I was holding my breath. "Oh. Well, that's great."

"I just want you to know, because it's going to take a lot of my time. But I'm going to try to do a lot of it when you're on tour."

"What are you going to write about? That stripper scandal or whatever?"

"No, it's going to be about Fred Adams and his family." And with that Trevor launches into a story about a Canadian businessman, now dead, who had built a fortune only to watch his business empire fall apart when his children became involved. He had ten children in all, with three different wives, and they formed different factions.

"No one could have written a book about it while Fred was still alive—he was too litigious. But his youngest daughter, Lexi, has been a good source for some of my business stories. She has all her dad's files, including his daybooks—she worked as one of his assistants when she was in university—along with old newspaper clippings, photo albums, even old emails her mom printed out."

"Why would she hand all that over to you? I mean, won't that book be embarrassing to her family?'

"Lexi's interesting. She's about the only person I've met who truly doesn't care what other people think of her. And she thinks that other families in business together can learn from their mistakes, or at least realize they're not alone."

"What about her siblings?"

"Lexi thinks she can get them on side. She's the only one they all talk to. I've talked to my agent about it, and she thinks it's worth the risk."

I didn't know Trevor had an agent. When did that happen? But I don't say anything.

"I think it sounds great, Trevor."

"Thank God. I was so worried you'd be against it. It's going to be a slog."

"I don't know how I could be against it when I spend so much time on my own music. I want you to be happy."

"I'm worried we won't be able to spend enough time together."

"Then let's try to spend our time together well. Can we go for brunch now? I'm hungry."

He leans over and kisses me. "Yeah, let's do that."

The next several days are a blur of songwriting sessions with the Hug Machine, songwriting sessions on my own, running errands, and going out at night to see music. Trevor has exchanged his morning runs for morning writing sessions, and I make him coffee and breakfast while he's writing. It's a cozy routine.

Trevor, Austin, Reggie, Amelia, and I are often together at night, like a pack. Trevor is not getting much sleep, but he seems to have even more energy than before.

Reggie and Amelia haven't said anything, but they're always touching, hands brushing arms, leaning into each other. Every time I see it, I lean into Trevor, just to feel the circuit close and the electricity flow between us for a moment.

One night, Trevor and I are taking a cab home, when he turns to me and says: "Are you going to be close friends with Amelia?"

"Probably. I mean, we're in a band together. Why?"

"She's just a bit into the drama."

"What do you mean?" I start replaying the night in my mind. Our arrival at the crowded bar, ordering our drinks, the swirl of people, David and Flora meeting us there, Flora complimenting me on my new turquoise shirt (which Amelia had helped me pick out), Amelia rolling her eyes ...

"Are you talking about the thing with Flora? She hardly did anything."

"Didn't you hear what she said? Flora did."

I think back, but I can't remember hearing everything. "No. I saw her roll her eyes, I mean, not the most mature, but ..."

"She asked Flora when her radio show was going to be picked up. And pretended not to know what had happened when Flora looked upset."

It was rumoured Marilyn Poe had inflicted her revenge for David leaving her satellite radio program through Flora. Even though Marilyn didn't work at the station that had agreed to pick up Flora's artsy book show, one of her college friends was brass at the station. Most convincing, at least to me, was that Marilyn had sent Flora a condolence email before Flora found out from the station they were killing the show.

"Well, so? How could she have known that Poe had Flora's show killed?"

"Oh, she knew. David had just told her and Reggie while Flora was in the bathroom. He asked them not to mention it because she's still really upset."

I think back. I must have been grabbing a Scotch with Austin when this all went down.

"Well, there must have been some misunderstanding."

Trevor gives me a look, like *Are you really that naive?*

"No, seriously, I don't think she would do that on purpose."

"You've known her for what, five days?"

"Yeah, I've spent about twenty hours with her in that time. I think I'm a pretty decent judge of character."

"Okay, well, just don't say I didn't tell you."

"Nothing's happened yet and you're already saying 'I told you so.'"

"I just don't want any part of the drama."

"Why is it 'drama' when women don't get along, but it's a 'disagreement' when it's a couple of guys?"

"Guys don't snipe at each other the way girls do."

"Fuck, whatever." I feel my temperature climbing quickly, probably a result of the Scotch. "Maybe I'll just get my womb cut out now so I can remove my hysteria."

"Did I say hysteria? And did I say anything about you? This is about Amelia. I'm just telling you to be careful."

I stare out the window, sulking.

Trevor's criticism of Amelia draws a pall over the evening that lasts into the next day. I don't get up early to make him breakfast, preferring to mull everything over in a state of half-sleep. After he's showered and dressed for work, he kisses my forehead, but I snuggle farther into the blankets.

"Okay, well, have a good day," he says.

I *will* have a good day, I think, my inner voice sarcastic and sulky.

I get out of bed, sort through the pile of mail on the kitchen table as I sip my coffee and eat an apple. Bills for Trevor, mostly. But for me, a package from Ruby. I rip it open. Inside is a short letter and a cassette tape.

Dear Darby,

Things are going well in Vancouver, sort of. The program is great, but I broke up with Lara. Another one gone. I think I am cursed in love. She didn't like all the time I spent at school and volunteering on the Downtown Eastside, at the music group in the addiction centre. I didn't really know what to do with that, so that was it. She has been backstabbing me to our friends, and a few are looking at me sideways. I guess she's telling people I cheated on her with some hipster dude and that's why we broke up. Can you believe that?

Anyway, since we broke up, I've written three songs! And I worked on yours, too. You need to write the last verse, maybe a bridge?

Oh, and I won't be in Vancouver when you're here. But I will be in Calgary so can you put me on the list? I'm going to be there over the weekend to visit Amber. You should see my credit card right now, it's kind of scary, especially since I don't know if I'll have a job in my field when I finish. But I'm having fun.

I did get mugged last week, but I only had five dollars in my wallet, so I just cancelled my cards and carried on. Another near miss.

Hope you enjoy the song.

Lots of love,
Ruby on Tuesday

I pop in the cassette tape, press play. Ruby's sweet voice fills the room, hitting all the high notes. As I listen to the lyrics, a chill runs through me. It was like she was with me, that day I fought my uncle for my life.

You left me there, standing alone
with the monster I thought I'd known
as friend, as blood, as one of my own.
That day my heart sank like a stone.
Things we can't say.
Bite back my words.
Swallow my rage.
Save it for another day.
I had to fight, I had to run,
I bled under that summer sun.

I dug my hands into the mud
and cried until I came undone.

I think for a moment, of my life here in the big city. I think of the old water treatment plant, drawing from the vast lake. Then I write.

Now I stand here on the shore
and I can't go home anymore
'cause you left me fighting a war
that hollowed me from the core.

But I still need a bridge. The song is in C major, so we'll switch to A minor, slow down for the bridge. But what to write?

I keep humming the melody, as I rummage through my box of old photos. At the bottom, in a plain envelope, is Aunt Bea's wedding band.

It's such a strange thing to think about what happens to evidence in a murder trial after everything's done. What does a family do with those artifacts? Are we supposed to carry them with us forever, as long as we can stand it, then pass them to a new family member? Or bury them in a drawer, hoping to forget the sorrow and horror?

I take out the plain gold band, look at the simple inscription inside. "To Bea, my wife. Love, Will."

Love.

It was a lie, I think. A betrayal, right from the day he slipped that ring on her finger. I feel my insides tighten into knots.

I write:

Tell me about love. Tell me about love.

I play it through on my guitar a few times. Then I record it on my cassette player, write Ruby a note offering condolences on Lara, and prepare the package for the mail.

The whole morning leaves me drained, but I fill a travel mug with coffee and set out for a long walk, hoping the city will distract me from the thoughts racing in my head and the sadness clutching at my insides.

—

The day before the Urban Coyotes tour, Trevor takes the morning off and we go out for breakfast, lingering in the restaurant long after we've finished. I feel bad about the argument over Amelia and have tried to make it up to him, even promising to jog with him when the weather turns. He says it's fine, that he was wrong too, but he hasn't said Amelia's name since, and I wonder if it hurt him more than he likes to admit. I want to fix it, but maybe I can't.

Trevor leaves straight from the restaurant to meet someone for an interview. I think the waitress must be annoyed by our loitering, even though she doesn't show it, so I tip her well. I go home and finish packing for the tour. Three days earlier, Amelia and I shopped for new makeup. Amelia's sister is an actor on Broadway, so Amelia knows lots of tricks for applying makeup in a way that brings out a person's features on stage, under that strange lighting. I pack my new blushes, lipsticks, eyeliners, and eye shadows, even fake eye lashes. It's going to be a whole new me.

I head to the boxing club in the early afternoon. It's quiet today, just the regulars. The rhythm of skipping ropes and gloves pounding the heavy bags fills the gym. I warm up by skipping, then work through intervals of push-ups, speed skipping, burpees, sit-ups, and mountain climbers before hitting the bag. All the anger I used to direct toward the bag is long gone, replaced by focus and a steadier energy.

After, I stretch out on the mats in the corner. Susan, a respiratory therapist who is maybe five years older than me, joins me. Black bruises underline her eyes.

"How was your match last week?" I ask.

"Oh, I lost," she chuckles. "I dropped my guard in the second round, and she nailed me."

"That sucks."

"Just part of the game, I guess. I walked away without a concussion, so I think I'm still ahead. You training for a fight?"

"No. I really don't like getting punched in the face."

"Oh, I didn't realize you'd had a match already."

"I don't know if I'd call it a match," I say, trying to decide whether I want to elaborate. I don't really know Susan. I don't know how she'll react.

"Sorry, I'm a bit thick sometimes," she says. "You don't have to explain, I get it. You're not the only one here."

She thinks I got beat up by a boyfriend, I realize. But it doesn't matter, not really.

"Thanks. I'm okay now."

THIRTEEN

WE ARRIVE IN Calgary the day after a chinook. I stuff my winter coat into my suitcase before leaving the airport.

It's our third stop on the west tour, and I occupy the stage with more confidence than I did on the first leg. Between the new clothes, more makeup, and the experience, I feel like I belong up there with the bright lights shining down on me. I love the sound of my new Gretsch, the way it hangs on my guitar strap. And I feel better able to handle the energy and emotion flowing from the crowd.

Doug Wilson, the tour manager, pulls me aside in the hotel lobby before the show. "You're killing it, Kid."

Carl interrupts. "Hey, Doug, what time do we have to be at the venue?"

"Working with you guys is like being a kindergarten teacher. Check your itinerary," says Doug, before turning back to me. "Anyway, keep it up, Kid."

"Thanks, Doug," I say.

The afternoon passes uneventfully. I nap, and sleep deeply. I dream that I'm riding a black horse through a desert at a dead run.

I don't know where I'm going or why we're running—I'm simply a passenger. When I wake, I don't have time to ruminate on the dream. My new makeup routine adds nearly an hour to my prep time, although Amelia assures me it'll take less time as I get used to it. I shower, dry my hair, then lay out my brushes and tins of creams and powders. Various flesh-coloured shades to cover flaws and contour, red blushes and lip creams, lip and eye liners, primer and powder to absorb oil and prevent shine, highlighter to add light in the right spots. Eyeshadows darker than I'm used to, but Amelia says it works on stage.

The show goes smoothly. The theatre is packed, the crowd appreciative. I felt tired before we took the stage, but the music lifts me out of my fatigue. But there's an older man in the front row leering at me. He has dark grey hair and is built like an oak—tall and thick, though not fat. He tries to get my attention, waving at me; I pointedly ignore him. It's not just the leer that makes me uncomfortable. He has a fevered look in his eye, yet seems disconnected at the same time. Even when he's staring at me, it feels like he doesn't really see me.

Afterwards, Uncle Henry and Aunt Linda are the first to arrive backstage. Henry's cowboy boots are polished and his black hat looks new. Linda is wearing a long, airy tunic with a Navajo-type print. She is wearing nearly as much eye makeup as I am, and it looks great, making her big brown eyes seem even larger.

"Thanks for coming," I say. "I know it's a bit of a drive for you."

"We made a trip of it. I can't remember the last time I spent a night away from the ranch. It's been a nice break," says Linda. "Henry had meetings at the Canadian Cattlemen's Association office this week—he's off to Ottawa for their AGM tomorrow. After that, he'll be past president. I'm sure looking forward to that. I visited my sister most of the week. We all had supper with Helen's family last night."

"Oh, how's Helen?" I look around for her, expecting to see her at any moment.

"She's well. She sends her regards. She'd planned to come tonight, but something came up at the hospital. Brynny should be here, though."

Just then, Ruby arrives, toting a small suitcase. We hug. She's wearing a new perfume that reminds me of fresh-cut alfalfa.

"It's so good to see you," I say.

"You, too. You were amazing tonight. Sam says hi, by the way. I'm worried about him. I think he's drinking way too much. You should call him."

"Oh, okay. I don't know what I can do."

"Just call him. He's not getting along with his family these days, you know. They had a big fight a few weeks ago." My head is spinning a little. I had no idea Sam had had a falling out with his parents. "Hey, can I bunk in with you? I need a break from Amber and her roommate ... well, mostly her roommate."

"Yeah, sure. How's Amber doing?"

"She did my makeup tonight, you like it?" Ruby asks, pursing her pink lips. "She likes her classes, but her roommate is driving her insane. The girl is a slob. She left so many dirty dishes in her bedroom they ended up with fruit flies."

"Ugh. That is something else."

I introduce Ruby to Henry and Linda. Robby comes by just then, makes a bit of small talk, signs their CDs. Doug waves him away after a couple of minutes.

"Make sure you introduce them to the rest of the band before everyone splits," says Robby.

"I will," I say. Austin and Carl are likely smoking a joint, and Owen always needs a few minutes by himself to decompress after a show.

Linda asks Ruby what she does, and Ruby tells her about the music therapy program, which leads to an explanation of what music therapy is. "I was handing out resumes this afternoon at the hospitals," she says, "but I'm not having much luck."

"You should talk to Darby's cousin, Brynny," says Linda. "Maybe that's something her new church would be interested in doing, once they're set up. Brynny is really into ... what's the term ... social welfare?"

"Where is Brynny, anyway?" asks Henry.

Just then there's a scuffle near the door, a man yelling indignantly. I crane my neck to see what's going on.

The creepy man from the front row is being dragged out by two burly security guards. "I need to see her! You have no right!" I wonder what he's talking about, then realize he's referring to me. But nothing about it makes sense.

There's a tall young blond woman standing near the ruckus. She walks forward, as though to intervene, but her companion, a handsome man in a cowboy hat, grabs her arm.

"Brynny, you stay out of it," he says with alarm.

"But they're hurting him," she says, then looks at the security guards. "You're hurting him!"

The security guards don't respond at all, but the creepy man hears her. He glances at Brynny, looks toward me, then back at her. He's still staring at Brynny as they pull him from the room. I shiver.

"What was that about?" asks Ruby.

"I don't know, but that guy was leering at me through the whole show. He's a creep." Someone touches my elbow just then, and I turn to see Doug. "Can I talk to you a sec?"

We step away from my family, and Doug fills me in on what he knows. The man's name is Rex Baskin. He somehow bluffed his way backstage at first, saying he knew me. But just before he reached us, he literally bumped into the crew as they were carrying our guitars to the bus. One crew guy, Pat, told him to watch where he was going, and he took a swing at Pat, knocking his glasses to the ground.

"Is Pat okay?"

"Yeah, he just grazed him, fortunately. Do you know this guy?"

"No, I've never seen him before tonight," I say, telling Doug about seeing him in the front row.

"Okay, well, he's gone now. I'm going to call the police in the morning and report him. Even if they don't charge him, there will at least be a record."

I turn back to my group. Brynny and the cowboy have joined them. Brynny is holding out her hand to Linda, displaying a bright blue rock on her ring finger.

"I've never seen a sapphire," Linda says, pulling Brynny's hand for a closer look. "Well, congratulations," she says, releasing Brynny's hand and hugging her. Henry shakes the cowboy's hand.

Ruby is gazing at Brynny as though she's just stepped on a butterfly, which I can't quite understand since they've just met. Just then, Brynny looks her way, and the two of them make eye contact. They hold each other's eyes for several seconds.

What is going on?

Brynny introduces me to her fiancé, Cody. "Cody's a bull rider," she says. "He won at national finals last year."

Cody looks a little embarrassed by her introduction but extends his hand. "Pleased to meet you," he says. "I'm a fan."

"Nice to meet you, too," I say. "How did you two meet?"

"My cousin brought me to one of Brynny's services last year," he says. "By the end of her sermon, I knew she was the girl I'd marry."

"Well, I certainly hope you don't have the same effect on everyone in your congregation or you'll be a polygamist," Linda quips. Uncle Henry gives her a bit of a look, as though he's trying to get her to tone it down, but she just smiles at him serenely.

"Are you a United Church minister?" asks Ruby.

"No. I lead the Church of the Shortgrass. It's not any particular denomination."

"Oh. Is it new?" Ruby continues.

"Yes, but it's also very old in a way, tied back to the true teachings of Jesus," says Brynny. "Did you know Jesus had female disciples? That it was the women who brought news of his resurrection? For centuries, churches have tried to remove women from true leadership positions within the religion, contrary to the original teachings. Jesus was a feminist."

"Well, that is certainly not what I learned in church," I say. "But I might be able to get behind that."

"What church did you go to, Darby?" Brynny asks.

"It was a Foursquare church. Great choir."

"Did they tell you that church was founded by a Canadian woman? Aimee Semple McPherson."

"No, they never mentioned it at all."

"She had a beautiful temple in Hollywood, with pageants and music," says Brynny. "Charlie Chaplin said her service was the best show in town."

"Why don't they mention her in the church I went to?"

"Well, she had a big scandal with a married man. She also flirted with the Klan," says Brynny. "She was flawed, but they should have the grace to acknowledge their founder. It's in our weaknesses that we see God's power."

Grace. Another word to ponder.

"You should come to my service tomorrow," says Brynny.

Tomorrow is Sunday. I pull my itinerary from my messenger bag and check. We have the day off, so I have no excuse. "Okay."

"We'll pick you up for brunch," says Linda. "And you're welcome to come, too, Ruby."

"I'd love to," Ruby says.

The next morning, Ruby and I climb into the backseat of Linda and Henry's pickup. The truck looks a little worse for wear—I wonder if they are nervous driving it all the way to Calgary—but I don't want to insult them. Henry drives south through the city, with Linda occasionally offering directions.

We have brunch at the Chuckwagon Cafe in Turner Valley. The outside of the restaurant is painted like a red barn. Inside, the wood-finished walls gleam softly. The smells of pancakes and eggs and bacon make my stomach growl. By the time we sit down and order, my hunger is a raging beast. I order huevos rancheros. Uncle Henry orders a huge stack of buttermilk pancakes. Linda asks if they have oatmeal.

The waitress just looks at her.

"I'm on a diet," Linda says.

"I'll see what we can do," the waitress says.

"I'll have the eggs Benedict," Ruby says.

Linda gets her oatmeal, and the rest of us eat until we're stuffed. Then we pile back into the truck, and Henry turns north, back toward the city, before turning again, this time toward the mountains.

"Oh, that's it, there," says Linda, pointing to the left. A burnt-wood sign proclaims *Bluerock Ranch*. White wooden fence lines the long driveway, leading to a large, indoor arena, with a red barn beside it. Behind the arena, on top of a hill, a log house overlooks the yard. Henry signals left, but there's a lineup of cars coming from the direction of Calgary turning right. He waits patiently, and someone in an SUV waves him in. Linda waves at the SUV.

Inside, the arena is spotless, with only the smell of hay to indicate that horses might be present. Sunlight streams in through windows high up on the walls. A single row of box stalls, presently empty, lines two of the walls. Grandstands and washrooms take up the rest of the space outside the arena.

"What is that?" Ruby asks, pointing at an enclosed floor with windows overlooking the arena. "Box seating?"

"They've probably got a kitchen in there, so they can sell food during events," says Henry. "Oh, there's Helen waving at us." He walks toward the bleachers and we follow.

Helen is sitting at the very top of the bleachers, her hair in a loose bun, looking put together in a pressed blue Western shirt, jeans, and a silver belt. Today, I notice that although Helen looks like she could be a sister to my mom and my aunt, she has a soft, contented look they never did; my mom always looked pinched with anger, Aunt Bea with anxiety. A groundswell of sorrow for my aunt and my mother threatens to overwhelm me for a moment, but I stay afloat, keeping my eyes on the horizon, until it passes.

The man sitting beside Helen stands and reaches across her, shaking my hand. "Rob," he says. "Nice to see you, Darby."

Cody is sitting on the other side of Rob. He tips his hat at us. Linda introduces Ruby to Helen and Rob. Everything about Rob is round—his eyes, his face, his torso—but the overall effect is pleasant. He reminds me of a teddy bear.

Helen and Ruby sit next to each other, and soon they're chatting away about health care. Helen gives Ruby a few new ideas for places she might want to apply.

"There aren't many music therapy positions, unfortunately," she says. "I think you're probably looking at contract work. You know, Brynny might be able to send some work your way in the future."

"Is she going to keep holding services here?" asks Ruby.

Helen and Rob glance at each other.

"She has an announcement planned today, but we can't say anything more," says Rob. "She'd be upset if we ruined the surprise."

"Shush," says Helen.

Below us is a small stage with a microphone and a screen behind it. To the left is an old grain truck, with shiny red paint, probably from the sixties or seventies. The box on the back has been replaced with a flatdeck, with two rows of chairs, handrails, and wooden stairs leading to the deck.

"Here comes the choir," says Cody. Several women walk, single file, into the arena and onto the deck of the grain truck, standing in the front row. Then the men take their place in the second row.

A middle-aged Black woman with a powerful alto starts singing a gospel song that I've never heard, about love in the name of Jesus. The choir repeats the line. They continue this call and response, and then the tempo picks up and they all sing together. It's just their voices, not even amplified, filling the arena, and it sounds beautiful.

Brynny walks to the stage at this point, dressed in her tan riding breeches and a spotless white shirt. She motions for the congregation to get on its feet. Everyone stands, and many in the congregation sing; the sound is powerful. As they sing the last notes, Brynny pulls the mic from the stand and starts preaching.

"Thank you, Carol, and everyone in the choir. Praise the Lord for blessing us with your talent today.

"Last night, I met my cousin Darby for the first time. I see she's here today. Hi Darby, give everyone a wave."

I wave, and several people turn to look at me, smiling and waving back.

"Darby used to go to a Foursquare Church, but she'd never heard of that church's founder, Aimee Semple McPherson."

Brynny tells us about Sister Aimee's good works and wonderful accomplishments in Los Angeles. She cared for unwed mothers and helped the poor. She had a vision for an earthquake-proof temple, and then had it built according to that vision. She was one of the first to preach on the radio. She put on wonderful, dramatic pageants, complete with costumes and music, to illustrate her sermons.

"Given all of this, why wasn't she a household name in Darby's home church? Is it because she's a woman who excelled at a traditionally male role? Perhaps that's part of it.

"But it's more, or perhaps less, than that. You see, Sister Aimee had flaws, the kind of flaws that would make you want to turn your back on her." Brynny goes on to tell us all about Aimee inviting the Klan into the church (which was confusing because she also preached racial justice at times). Then she tells us about Aimee's suspected affair with a married radio engineer, how she disappeared for months, claiming later that she had been kidnapped, when many suspected she was on a long sojourn with her lover.

"Sister Aimee was far from perfect. We don't know all the circumstances. Perhaps she suffered from depression or bipolar disorder, perhaps mental illness was a factor in some of her poor decisions. We'll never know for sure. But whatever the circumstances, and whatever you might think of some of her actions, ask yourself this: does God demand perfection from us?"

Brynny pauses, looks at the packed bleachers. "Well, does He?"

"No!" Several people shout, and it startles me.

"No, He does not. He shows us grace. Please turn to Corinthians 12:6." Brynny pauses while everyone in the congregation pulls Bibles from their purses and bags and flips pages. Then she recites the passage from memory.

"'In order to keep me from becoming conceited, I was given a thorn in my flesh, a messenger of Satan, to torment me. Three times I pleaded with the Lord to take it away from me. But He said unto me: My grace is sufficient for you, for my power is made perfect in weakness. Therefore I will boast all the more gladly about my weaknesses, so that Christ's power may rest on me.'"

Brynny pauses again. "Power made perfect in weakness. God's greatest power is love, of course. That is the essence of grace. It is not that Aimee deserves the Lord's gifts any more than you and me; our Lord chooses to bestow them on her, and on all of us, despite our weakness. Because it is through our mistakes, our frail humanity, that we come to a deeper understanding of His love. And if there is one thing the world needs more of, it is grace."

The service continues with a few hymns, the lyrics projected onto the screen, and readings by a couple of the kids. I slip into a daydream about riding into the foothills surrounding the arena. I'm riding through a mountain creek, trout slicing the water around my bay horse's legs, when Brynny tells us she has an announcement.

"Can I get the church board up here, please? Dave, Beth, Andrea, Blaire, Clint, Becca, Leslie, Kurt, Levi?"

Several people stand and walk toward the stage. Some look to be in their twenties or thirties, others in their fifties or up. A few of the men have the look of ranchers, with their worn but clean cowboy boots. The others might be teachers or bankers or city councillors, for all I can tell.

"As you know, we applied for charitable status many, many, many months ago," says Brynny, turning to an older man on the board. "Dave, I know you warned me it would take a long time, but I have to say, that wait, it was something else."

Dave chuckles. "Patience is a virtue," he says.

"Yes, yes, it is. And our patience has been awarded. We just found out last week that Church of the Shortgrass has been awarded charitable status!"

A logo appears on the screen behind Brynny. It shows a simple church with a cross, mountains behind it, prairies in the foreground. Everyone claps, and there are even a few whoops. This is not Grandma Swank's church, I think. I will have to call her and tell her all about this.

"And that's not all. Many of you were waiting for this moment, waiting to show your generosity. Thanks to this congregation, we have already raised $170,000 toward our new church! All of our wonderful donors, stand up please and join us on the stage."

Helen and Rob stand up before us. So do another thirty or so people. The congregation goes wild, whooping and cheering. I feel like I'm at a hockey game.

The screen changes, listing the donors and their donations. Helen and Rob alone have donated fifty thousand dollars. I let out a low whistle.

Brynny waits for the raucous crowd to quiet down before continuing. "There's one more thing. And this is a big one. Bryce and Michelle, can you join us up here, please?"

A couple from the front row stands and walks to the stage, two little boys in tow. Bryce is the man from the video, I realize, the one with the cagey mare named Badger. The woman, Michelle, is wearing so much turquoise jewelry it looks heavy enough to hold her down in a strong wind. The boys wear white cowboy hats, jeans, and Western shirts. Even from the top stand, I can tell that all their jeans are neatly pressed, the creases sharp.

"Most of you know Bryce and Michelle Carpenter and their sons Dakota and Chase. They were among the first to join this congregation, and for the last year, they've generously offered us the use of this beautiful facility at Bluerock, free of charge. They share our vision of a church that hews closely to the true teachings of Jesus, a church free of pretension or prejudice. A church with a love for the land, and all the people in it. We are blessed to have them in our congregation."

Bryce looks a little embarrassed with all the praise. Michelle seems to glow, as though she's absorbed the praise and is now turning it back to the audience.

"But their generosity doesn't end there. No, it does not. Their generosity runs deep, my friends. You see, Bluerock Ranch is donating forty acres to us to build our new church, to build a youth centre and a retreat centre, to do the Lord's good work in this beautiful corner of the world!"

The congregation erupts. They're on their feet, cheering and hollering and praising Jesus. The wildness of it makes me uneasy, as though I might be swept off my feet by the current of their excitement and washed right out to sea.

Charisma, magnetism, whatever you want to call it, Brynny has it, in abundance. People talk about Robby Slade's charisma, but that is an everyday, showman-type charisma. Robby is like an old potato next to my shining cousin. She pulls the crowd after her with a force that feels as natural as gravity. Part of me wants to follow her, but something inside me also resists, even though I can't pinpoint why I feel uneasy. Something about her power feels dangerous to me.

But I stand and clap enthusiastically, because to do less would likely garner strange looks, and it is a generous donation, after all.

After the service, everyone goes upstairs to the concession for a meal of chili and a bun. Brynny is surrounded by a crowd, but Ruby wants to talk to her a bit about music therapy, so I leave Ruby to weave through the people to reach my cousin.

Cody and I sit close to a window overlooking the arena, eating our chili and talking about horses. Cody knows the Carpenter family, and he tells me about their cutting and reining horses. It's been years since I talked quarter horse bloodlines with anyone. I tell him a little about Bea and Will's program.

"Hey, isn't that the guy from last night?" Cody nods his head toward the arena. Below us, a lone figure sits on one of the bleachers, staring at the stage. I narrow my eyes.

"I think so. Rex Baskin is his name," I say.

"What's he doing here?"

"I don't know. He's apparently obsessed with me, but I didn't notice him during the sermon."

"You want me to talk to him?"

"No, it's okay. Maybe he'll just leave."

Rex stands up and walks into the arena, onto the little stage. He stands in front of the mic, then touches it.

"He better not steal that mic," says Cody.

But Rex just stands there for several seconds, his big hand wrapped around the mic. Cody raps on the window and Rex looks right at us. My instinct is to flip him off, but I remember I'm at church.

"What's going on?" Brynny is standing beside Cody, looking into the arena below.

"It's that guy from last night. The one who got kicked out of the theatre," says Cody. "He's obsessed with Darby."

Rex stares up at us for what feels like several minutes. I glare at him with all the contempt I can project. Brynny sits down across from me and studies Rex, not with disgust but with curiosity.

"I wonder why people become obsessed like that," she says. "Have you had other obsessed fans?"

"No. Well, not that I know of. I hope not."

"Is it flattering at all?"

"No. It makes me feel like a zoo animal when he leers at me."

"Who's staring at who now, psycho?" Cody says to the glass.

I look down at Rex once more and suddenly get the feeling he's not looking at me after all. In fact, I think he's staring at Brynny. Something tight inside me loosens, and I feel relief, then guilt at the relief. Then confusion, because perhaps I'm imagining that he's staring at Brynny. Or perhaps I'm mistaken about Rex all together. Maybe this is all innocent.

But I can't ignore last night's kerfuffle or Doug's assessment of the situation. Doug has been around the block, and Rex is far from the first weird fan he's dealt with. Last night in the hotel bar, the rest of the band and crew had regaled me and Ruby with stories of stalkers who had haunted them or people they knew over the years. One woman had harassed Owen for twenty years.

"She used to send me pressed flowers from her garden," said Owen. "The first time, I made the mistake of sending her an autographed photo. The next week, she showed up outside my apartment building. Then at my mom's house."

"Wow. How did you get her to stop?" Ruby had asked.

"I didn't. She died in a car accident last year," he'd said. "That woman drove me to drink for a while. For a long time, I blamed her for ruining my marriage."

"But she destroyed her own life, too. Her sister contacted me to tell me what had happened. Even most of her family wouldn't talk to her anymore, they were so upset by what she was doing. It was sad all around."

I'd instantly wondered how many years Rex might have left in him. He looked to be at least sixty, but what if he lived to be a hundred?

Will's enraged face flashes in front of me, and the smell of his sweat fills my nose. I can almost feel his hands around my neck. I close my eyes, feel the hard floor under my feet, my fingers on the window ledge. I am safe here, I tell myself. I am safe.

"That's it, I'm going to talk to him. This is too weird," Cody says, pushing his chair back with a scrape as he stands. But just then Rex starts moving. As Cody starts to walk downstairs, Rex heads for the door. By the time Cody reaches the arena, Rex is long gone.

—

Ruby is morose after the service. After an hour and a half of sitting in my hotel room with her working on our songs, I'm about ready to throw myself out the window.

"Okay, what is up with you?" I say finally. "I've never seen you so mopey. Some of these songs are sad enough as it is."

"I don't know. I just feel silly even thinking about it."

"Oh, just tell me. I think I know anyway."

"Is it that obvious?"

"Brynny," I say. "It's all about the Prophetess."

"Don't call her that. She's not claiming to be a prophet," says Ruby.

"Okay, I'm sorry. I won't call her the Prophetess, at least not out loud. Now, why don't you tell me what's eating you up so much?"

"Well, I just feel silly even saying it out loud," says Ruby. "For one thing, she's engaged. To a man. So logically, I have to think my chances are about zero."

"Plus, you're still in Vancouver," I say. "With over a year to go before you graduate."

"Yeah, exactly. But really, the bottom line is, there's nothing to indicate she'd be the least bit interested in me. Yet, I can't help it.

I want nothing more than to bust up that engagement and sweep her off her feet."

"Well, I don't know what to tell you. You're probably right, but at the same time, stranger things have happened. Maybe Brynny doesn't know she's a lesbian, or bisexual. Maybe she knows but she doesn't want to admit it, because of her chosen profession."

"A lesbian woman preacher," says Ruby dreamily. "That would be something else, wouldn't it?"

"Honestly, that would be way less of a surprise to me than what is already happening there. I am not comfortable with so much passion in a service."

"You're just too conservative, Darby. You should loosen up a little."

I pause. No one's called me conservative before. Growing up in a fairly conservative province, I've been more likely to be called a leftie or hippie. I decide to ignore the comment.

"I wouldn't fold just yet, but I wouldn't bet the farm, either. Just sit tight, maybe something will shake loose. Though I'd sure feel bad for Cody if things went your way. He seems like a nice enough guy."

"Love and war ... all is fair," says Ruby. "Maybe we can turn that into a song."

"Maybe. So are you going to come out to Toronto some time so we can cut an album or what?"

"You paying for my ticket?"

"I might be able to swing that."

"Well, okay, then. That sounds great."

"You know, you could probably get work in Toronto. You'd be welcome to crash at our place for a while. We've got a fold-out couch in the living room. And I'd introduce you to people."

"Awww, thanks Darby. I'll think about it for sure."

"Seriously, think about it. I miss you, Ruby."

"I miss you, too. I will think about it."

Ruby's mood has improved, and when we go back to our music, it feels magical. No one's voice blends with mine so beautifully as Ruby's. She has the pure, high song of a white-throated sparrow, a voice that can sail above my alto effortlessly.

That night, we go out for supper with Austin and Carl, consider drifting by the YMCA where Owen and Robby are playing basketball, something they do whenever they can on tour. But instead, the four of us smoke a joint with the waitress out the backdoor of the restaurant, then walk back to the hotel. I fall asleep watching some horrific film Ruby's picked on the pay-per-view—some gruesome *Child's Play* sequel or rip-off, I'm not sure—but my dreams are of Ruby moving to Toronto.

But when I wake up in the morning, the first thing Ruby asks is for Brynny's cell number—she's already lost the slip of paper Brynny gave her yesterday. And I know it will never happen. My charismatic cousin already has a stronger hold on my good friend than I ever will.

FOURTEEN

OVER THE NEXT several months, when I'm not on tour or playing with the Urban Coyotes, I'm playing with the Hug Machine. We write songs and rehearse our brains out, then start playing gigs in the clubs around Toronto. We even play a few shows with The Greatest Show on Earth. Kayla, Brittany, and Candy dress in their steampunk gear and are nearly as polished with their live show as in their videos. At the end of our set, the trio joins us and the four of us sing Loretta Lynn's "Coal Miner's Daughter." The crowds love it.

We're starting to get some good buzz and Nancy is booking dates for us out west in the late summer.

"Have you heard of Danceland?" she asks me one day.

"Yeah, at Manitou Lake in Saskatchewan. They have a horsehair dance floor, right?"

"Yes, that's the place. You're playing at a western swing festival there."

Before we go west, we play Flora and David's engagement party, followed by the launch party for a new literary journal. The first issue includes a whole suite of Flora's poems that seem to be about Marilyn's abuse of David, and her murder of Flora's fledgling show. The language is sharp and visceral, yet it would be almost impossible to say any one poem is about Marilyn unless you knew the situation.

Flora invited Marilyn to the launch party, using our new band as bait, and it worked. It's clear Marilyn knows what the poems are about—I can't decide if it's awkward or delightful, watching her flush as Flora reads the poems about her. The Marilyn poems splash into the literary scene, garnering plenty of media attention, and soon Flora has a publishing deal. She tells me all about it one night over a glass of red wine on my rooftop patio.

"Are you worried about her suing you?" I ask.

She shakes her head. "She threatened me, but she has no case, really. I mean, if she could prove they were about her, then she'd have to admit she did all that stuff, or at least explain why she thinks the poems are about her. Besides, she doesn't want any more attention than she's already got."

"Really?" I ask. "Are you sure?"

"Yeah, I'm sure I'm safe. We did have to cut one of the best ones because it was libellous and I had no way to prove it, without dragging other people into it. I was upset at the time, but I still read it to David sometimes."

"Can you read it to me?"

"I can." Flora stands up, still holding her wine glass. We're on my patio rooftop, and the neon signs of Chinatown cast their garish spotlight on Flora as she begins to recite the poem from memory.

Monster

When I was a child
a monster
lived under the basement stairs.
Scabby, green skin,

leaving an oil slick behind him
he was easy to see.
You wore your wide eyes
and shiny smile
as camouflage.
But I've met the ones you maimed,
whipped, cracked, bruised, broken into
small pieces.
A wolf splintering bones.
They didn't find out
what you were
until they were in your jaws.

Did she say whipped? Does she want me to ask? Do I want to know?

I decide I don't want to know, so I clap and tell her it's great, and disturbing. Flora looks like she's about to say more, but I cut her off.

"I think I need another glass of wine," I say, getting up to open a second bottle. "You want another one?"

Even with the poem and the wine, Flora and I never grow really close. I like her, and we get along, but I don't have the time needed to nurture the friendship. We mostly see each other at industry events with David, the occasional party.

The other thing is that Amelia hates Flora. I don't know why, can't see any reason for it. Flora has never said a mean word to Amelia, nor does she share her animosity, as far as I can tell. In fact, I'm not even sure if Flora is aware of Amelia's disdain. Her hatred simmers for months at a level the rest of us can ignore, right through the engagement party gig. Once Amelia finds out that Flora has been to my place for a glass (or three) of wine, Amelia's anger boils.

"Well, you could have invited me," Amelia says.

"Why? You don't even like Flora," I say. "You're always cutting her down."

"I can't help it. It hurts me to even be in the same room as her. Physically hurts."

What a fucking drama queen, I think but don't say.

"Okay, well, you don't have to like her ..."

"I don't like her. And I don't see why you have to hang out with her."

I look at her in amazement. What fucking next?

"You don't have to like her, but I don't want to hear about it anymore. I'm a big girl. I don't need you telling me who I can and can't hang out with."

Amelia doesn't say anything, but she misses the next gig. I don't hear a word from her, and neither does anyone else, for days. Even Reggie, who has been dating her for weeks, is frozen out. He is completely bewildered.

"What are we going to do about this?" I ask as we sit on Austin's rooftop patio after the gig, smoking a joint.

"I think she's out," says Austin. "I don't want to deal with this shit."

"Maybe we should give her one more chance," says Reggie.

Trevor, having hung back to fill a cooler with ice and beers, emerges from the stairs with the cooler. He's listened to me complain about the whole situation, without once saying 'I told you so,' although he's surely been thinking it.

"You'd better talk to Nancy," he says.

"We don't even know what happened," says Reggie. "Maybe she's in the hospital or something."

Trevor looks at me, and Austin catches the look. "What's going on?" he asks.

I tell them about the drama over Flora.

"Fuck," says Austin.

"She's so good. Why would she torpedo her career over you having a glass of wine with Flora?" says Reggie.

"She is a jealous bitch," says Austin. "Haven't you heard about what happened with her last boyfriend? They broke up after five years because she didn't like him talking to his brother on the phone. He'd already moved to Toronto and given up all his friends for her because she decided she hated everyone in Chicago."

"I don't know if I believe that," says Reggie, but I can see the gears turning.

Nancy is very matter of fact about the whole thing when I tell her the next day. She'll call a meeting at her office to go over the tour, she says, and we can talk to Amelia then. Nancy will personally call Amelia and let her know.

I don't think Amelia is even going to show up for the meeting, but she does. Nancy goes over the tour details with us before bringing up the missed gig.

"I owe you an apology, Amelia, because I did not make this clear when you joined the band. I expect you to care about your career with this band at least as much as I do. If you don't care, I'm not interested in managing you. That means showing up when you're supposed to show up, treating the crew and the rest of the band with respect—"

"But Darby—" Amelia starts.

"Don't interrupt me. I heard what happened and I'm not interested in hearing any more about it. Darby can drink wine with whomever she wishes. You are expected to follow the same rules as everyone else. Because you can be replaced.

"This is not junior high. I am about to send this band on its first tour, and I expect it to go well. I expect you all to consistently play your best. I expect you to honour your contracts. I expect you to treat everyone you meet with respect. I expect professionalism. Can you do that?"

Amelia pauses as though she's thinking about arguing, but she changes her mind. "Yes," she says. "Sorry."

"Thank you." Nancy passes thick envelopes to each of us. "Inside are the agreements for this tour. Please read them carefully before you sign and date them. You'll also find your itineraries and plane tickets. Please do not lose your itinerary."

I look through the little blue booklet, titled "West Tour." Tour dates in Edmonton, Camrose, Calgary, Fort Macleod, Lethbridge, Medicine Hat, Moose Jaw, Regina, Manitou, Saskatoon, Lloydminster, North Battleford, then Gimli, Winnipeg, and home.

We all sign our contracts. With that, the band stays together. But Amelia doesn't talk to me much outside of our gigs. I am, again, without a close female friend in Toronto. I call Jen, but she doesn't pick up, so I leave a rambling voice message, tell her how much I miss her.

FIFTEEN

A NARRATIVE ABOUT Brynny and Ruby threads its way through the first part of the west tour. It starts the night of our first gig at the Sidetrack in Edmonton. Beth and Red Hodgins come to the gig and take me out for breakfast the next morning as the rest of the band sleeps in before we head to Camrose.

"We've been hearing a lot about your cousin Brynny," says Beth. "She's an interesting young woman."

"She is," I say. "Have you been to her church?"

"No, not yet. Ruby wants us to go together as a family next time she's home," says Beth.

"The choir sounds pretty rocking," says Red.

"It is."

"I'm a little worried about Ruby," says Beth. "It seems like she's mixing her personal and career aspirations together too much for my taste."

"I know. I offered to help her out if she came out to Toronto," I say. "And she's supposed to come out one weekend to cut a few songs with me."

"Well, that's good, Darby," says Beth. "Maybe she will take you up on that offer once she's done school."

"Maybe, but I doubt it," says Red. "Hard as it is, we have to let her make her own decision, Beth."

Beth frowns slightly. "I know. I want what's best for her, but I know."

When they drop me back at the hotel, I don't want to say goodbye. I hug them hard, then stand, sniffling, in the parking lot as they drive away, waving all the way to the end of the block.

At Camrose we play on the stage of the Bailey Theatre for an hour as openers for a couple out of Nova Scotia who play as a duo. He plays drums and sings, and she sings and plays bass pedals with her feet, along with banjo, guitar or accordion. I have never seen anyone so coordinated.

After the show, Amelia and the drummer disappear. The woman is pissed but hardly seems shocked, and I wonder if this is a regular thing, and if so, how they can tour together. Reggie is heartbroken. I'm relieved when Ruby calls my cell. I amble away to take the call.

"Hey, what's new?" I ask. "Still celebrating?"

Ruby and her friends were thrilled with the Canada-wide legalization of same-sex marriage earlier in the summer. I wished I'd been able to be with Ruby when that change came through.

"Oh, yes, we'll be celebrating the rest of our lives. Listen, I have another song for you, but I was wondering if I should wait until you're back from touring before I mail it?"

"Nah, you can mail it. Trevor will get it."

"Oh, good. Mom said she took you out to breakfast today."

"Yeah, it was nice of your parents to do that. It was good seeing them again."

"Did you hear that they broke ground on Brynny's new church?"

"No, I didn't." Ruby proceeds to explain in detail everything they have planned for the land. The church, which is somewhat circular in shape, almost like a horseshoe, with the entrance at the flat part of the shoe, and the sanctuary in the round bottom. The round part will be all windows and will face west, so the congregation will look at the mountains throughout the service.

"Why facing west?" I ask. "I mean, besides the appeal of the view?"

"Brynny had a dream, I mean a vision. Something to do with all our water, our weather, coming from the west," she says. "I don't totally get it."

The church will be two storeys, with services held on the first floor and other programming on the second floor. The board is seriously considering creating a music therapy program to serve people in the area, says Ruby. One of the board members has a grandchild with Asperger's who has really benefitted from music therapy. Another has an aunt with a brain injury who regained her ability to speak through music therapy.

"So, how would it work?" I ask. "Would the clients pay you directly or ...?"

"No, the idea would be to raise money through donations and grants so they could offer it freely to whoever needs it, and they would just pay me by the hour, I think."

"Wow, that's incredible," I say. I've edged far enough away from the rest of the band that I'm now on the stage. I watch my bandmates wrap up the last of the cords. I look out at the empty seats from the grand old stage, close my eyes, and for a moment imagine I'm an actor, or a musician in a vaudeville show. Or just myself, enjoying the thick curtains and the space of the stage, while Ruby chatters away. I want to be happy for her, but Ruby is so selfless and Brynny is so ... well ... not selfish, but not exactly selfless either. Brynny is all-encompassing, and I'm afraid that she'll either string Ruby along for years or consume her entirely.

We all hang out in my hotel room for a couple of hours, swapping stories and drinking until someone from the front desk phones to tell us to quiet down, there've been complaints. Amelia never reappears, and I assume she spends the night with the straying man. Would Nancy consider this drama? I wonder. Amelia doesn't say a word about it on the bus the next morning. Instead, she pulls out a deck of cards and starts dealing.

"What are we playing?" Austin asks.

"Poker. Chicago style," says Amelia, then explains the rules. Rather than betting, we track points, with different poker hands adding up to different points. The pot is literal pot, with each player contributing a couple of joints each hand.

"I'd rather bet," says Reggie.

"We must behave professionally," says Amelia pointedly.

"Do you think it's professional to fuck half of the opening act?" asks Austin.

Amelia gathers the cards and her joints, stands up, and walks to the back of the bus. She doesn't say a word for the rest of the drive to Calgary.

Cody, Brynny, and Amber all show up at our gig in Calgary. They're right at the front of the stage through the whole show, and once we finish, I step down to talk to them. Brynny looks a little like Grace Kelly, with her smooth blond hair and white button-up shirt tucked into a dark pair of Levi's, sapphire on her hand. Cody, though a handsome man, looks a little outclassed beside her tonight in his dishwater-grey T-shirt and ripped, bleach-spotted jeans.

Amber looks more mature than the last time I saw her. Her hair is platinum blond, cut into a pixie style. Like Cody, she's wearing distressed jeans, but with her fitted, sleeveless red top the look is stylish instead of rundown.

"You look great," I tell her. "I love your hair."

Reggie and Austin step off the stage, and I introduce them. Amelia waves limply but doesn't come over. Instead, she starts rolling up mic cord.

"Listen, I better help pack up," I say, glancing nervously at my Gretsch, which seems very exposed on its guitar stand. "I'll just be a few minutes and then we'll grab a drink."

By the time we finish up the crowd has thinned out. The bar will be closing soon, but the bartender hasn't called last call. Everyone is sitting at the bar, and I take an empty stool and order a vodka soda with lime, plus a big glass of water. The bar is sweltering in the late summer heat, and the stage lights have bumped my body temperature even higher.

As soon as I sit down, Brynny starts telling me about the music therapy program they are going to start. Apparently, the board has approved a subsidized version, with a sliding scale requiring some clients to pay, some to be subsidized, and those in need to have free access. Brynny is confident they can raise the money for the program by next summer.

"Can we please talk about something else?" says Cody. "Music therapy is all you talk about lately."

Amber and I exchange a look. "Ruby and her parents already filled me in," I say.

"So, Cody, what do you do?" asks Amber.

"He's a bull rider," says Brynny. "In fact, he won at—"

"Actually, I'm starting university this fall," Cody says, cutting her off.

"Oh, don't say that," says Brynny. "Cody had a rough summer. One of his friends—"

"I really don't want to talk about this right now," Cody interjects.

"—got stepped on by a bull. Broke his pelvis. He'll walk again, though. I keep telling Cody not to let that kind of thing set him back. You have to stick—"

"Jesus Christ, Brynny," I say. She stops, surprised. "Why the hell would you encourage someone you love to climb onto a keg of dynamite, especially when he doesn't want to anymore? I mean, how many injuries have you had already, Cody?"

"Lots," he says. "Three concussions, broke my ribs twice, broke my left hand once, screwed up my right knee ..."

"But he has a God-given talent," says Brynny. "It's brought him great blessings."

"You really think God wants him to keep strapping himself to Brahma bulls? I mean, that's about the stupidest thing I have ever heard. Bull riding is reckless to start with, but I guess if it's really someone's passion, they're going to do it. But for you to push him to do it? I mean, what the hell, Brynny? Stop keeping up appearances."

There's an awkward silence. Brynny looks stunned, as though she's not used to someone contradicting her opinion. In fact, she even looks a little hurt. I instantly regret the "keeping up appearances" bit, even if it's true.

I don't know why I'm so vexed, because it's really none of my business, and I haven't thought much about bull riding before now. But Cody seems like such a sweet guy. He reminds me of Luke, in fact. And I can see something of myself in Brynny—the look of a woman who is not really in love with her man, even if she wants to be.

"What will you be studying, Cody?" Amber asks, trying to fill the awkward silence.

"Animal science. I think I want to work as a bovine nutritionist."

Well, I'll be damned. He could be Luke's brother.

"Hey, Darby, you remember Rex?" Brynny asks.

"Yes, but I haven't heard a thing from him since last time I was here. The cops didn't think there was enough to press charges, but they have a file on him. Why?"

"Well, he's joined our congregation. He made a hundred-thousand-dollar donation to the new church. It turns out he's very wealthy, and quite passionate about his faith," she says.

A cold finger runs down my spine. "What? He's part of your church?"

"Yes. He's kind of weird, but I think he just lacks social skills," Brynny says.

"I don't know about that," I say.

"The man is a creeper," says Cody. "He doesn't look at you when you're talking to him, he looks through you. And he stares at you constantly, Brynny."

"Ugh. He made me feel like prey, the way he looked at me at our show," I say, shivering again at the memory.

"I wish you hadn't let him join the congregation," says Cody.

"It's not up to me to turn him away," Brynny says. "Besides, we are a church built on inclusivity. We won't turn anyone away from the word of God."

"He can find the word of God in his own Bible," says Cody.

"Please, just be careful," I say. "I just have a bad feeling about that guy."

"You two are as bad as my mother," Brynny says.

"Maybe you should listen to your mother more often," says Cody.

Amber changes the subject again. Soon she and Brynny are sharing notes on psychology courses, as Brynny has just finished her degree and Amber is working toward a graduate degree in social work so she can be a counsellor afterwards. By the end of the night, they've all exchanged phone numbers.

Amber gives me a lift to my hotel on her way home.

"That Cody, he's pretty hot," she says.

"Yeah, nice guy too."

"If my sister breaks up their engagement, maybe I'll scoop him up," she chuckles.

"I don't even know what to say to that. Do you think she'll do that, your sister?"

"I don't know. It's not something she's ever done before. But you know, I don't think they're really in love anyway. Or she's not in love with him, at least."

"Yeah, I had the same thought."

—

This tour is exciting, and there's a good crowd at every venue that seems to really love our music. But we have fewer luxuries than an Urban Coyotes tour, and it makes everything a little harder. Some of the venues have food waiting for us, but sometimes we have to forage. There's no tour manager and no crew travelling with us. The bus is just an old school bus, with no sleeping berths. And we have to share hotel rooms to save money, which means I have to share with Amelia the whole tour. She's relatively civil, but pointedly chilly toward me.

"You know, I wish we could still be friends," I say to her after the Calgary gig.

"I can't see it happening after that meeting with Nancy," she replies.

"That had nothing to do with you and me. That was about you missing a gig."

"I don't agree," she says. "If you had an issue with me, you should have talked to me directly instead of calling a band meeting behind my back."

I want to point out that it's impossible to do that if she doesn't show up to gigs or answer her phone, but I decide I don't want to throw fuel on the fire, so I apologize.

Amelia doesn't say anything. She switches off her lamp and rolls over. I sigh, switch off my own lamp, and scooch over to the far side of my bed.

At most stops I get to catch up with some family or old friends; Uncle Henry and Aunt Linda bring the kids and Grandpa Kolchak to Medicine Hat to hang out before the show. Reata, now ten, thinks she's old enough to be left alone with her little brother, but Linda stays with them at her cousin's house in the Hat while Grandpa and Henry come to the show. By the time the show is over, Grandpa looks exhausted, but he thanks me for the free tickets and says he thoroughly enjoyed the music.

"I just wish I could still dance," he says, a little sadly. "Your grandma, she loved to dance."

In Regina, Jen takes a night off from studying law and brings a few of her friends. She's dating this guy, Phil, also a law student, aiming for corporate law. He's too smarmy for my taste, and I'm not sure what Jen sees in him, other than his future earning potential. But I don't say anything.

Luke brings my Grandma and Grandpa Swank and his wife, Meaghan, to the Saskatoon show. Meaghan is polite to me, but not friendly, and I realize my wedding invitation didn't just get lost in the mail. Not that I blame her, really. I have no desire to be chummy with any of Trevor's ex-girlfriends.

In North Battleford, we play at an old bar that has recently changed ownership. It's a place I only visited once before moving, but what I remember most was the missing doors on the stalls in the women's washroom. The new owners have rectified that, and done some renovations, but it still has the rough edges you'll find in a lot of old bars on the Prairies. They've left the old wood finishing behind the bar, a decision I don't understand, until I take a close look and see the bullet holes.

Jack and I had planned to meet here, and I soon spot him sitting alone at a table in the back corner. I don't even realize that Sam is here until a fight breaks out, and I realize he's at the centre of it, taking a swing at a big Cree guy. The Cree guy whoops his ass, and they both get kicked out by the muscle-bound bouncers.

Jack helps us pack up after the show and gives me a ride back to the hotel. We make small talk on the short drive in his old truck, mostly about the restaurant and its customers.

We find Sam waiting for me at the hotel bar. He's nursing a fat lip and a broken nose. His eyes are bloodshot and his knuckles raw. He already has the bloated look of an alcoholic, and as we talk, he drinks his rye-and-coke highballs like ginger ale.

Sam tells us he's broken up with Kirsten, moved in with a drinking buddy at Turtle Lake. He's still guiding, but I wonder if he'll manage to hold onto that for long.

"You should see the burnt areas around Turtle Lake," he says. "The poplars and shrubs are all popping up. The fireweed's painted it all purple. And the ospreys are nesting in the scorched tree trunks."

"It sounds beautiful," I say.

"You should come home sometime. No one comes home anymore. Not even Luke that much, even though he's just in Saskatoon."

"He'll be home when he finishes school."

"Yeah, but then he'll be too busy being a vet to hang out with me much and soon him and Meaghan'll have kids, and that'll be it." He swallows most of a highball in two gulps, motions to the bartender for another. "I kinda got left behind."

"You're only twenty-four, Sam. You can still do whatever you want with your life."

Sam shakes his head sadly. Then changes the subject.

"Hey, you know your cousin Brynny? Ruby's in love with her."

"Yeah, I know Sam." I suspect Sam talks to Ruby nearly as much as I do. How does Ruby manage to pull all these hurting people into her orbit so easily?

"I think she's a closet lesbian. You know those religious types, all scared of hell and shit."

"Yeah, you could be right."

"I have a sense for these things," he says, tapping the centre of his forehead.

After two more drinks, Jack and I manage to talk Sam into leaving his car in the hotel parking lot for the night, bundle him into a cab, and give the driver his cousin's address.

"Sam needs help," Jack says as we watch the cab pull away.

"I know. Do you think we should do an intervention?" I picture Sam's old friends gathering, then pouncing on him. "I don't think that would go well."

"No, just ... someone just needs to talk to him. Get him into a treatment program, if he'll go."

"I don't know if he will." I don't want to do it, to be honest.

We talk for another hour. Jack asks if I'm happy and satisfied. I tell him I feel like I'm swimming upstream. I tell him I have no female friends in Toronto, not since Amelia dumped me. I tell him I am wildly happy at times, especially when I'm on stage.

"Before you go, I have something for you," I say, reaching into my messenger bag and pulling out a book-sized flat box. I hand it to Jack, watch him open it and pull out the horseshoe he gave me years ago.

"It's brought me a lot of luck, but I have another one now." I tug the chain around my neck, show him the horseshoe charm Trevor gave me.

"I'll hang it up at the restaurant again, with a little plaque about its famous owner," he says.

For a moment, I want to fall into him again, to blow up my whole life.

But I don't want to blow up my life. Not this time. Not right now.

"Thanks for everything, Jack," I say.

"Take care, Darbs." He squeezes my hand, then walks away.

—

The next morning, I call Ruby to see if she knows of any treatment centres for Sam.

"You know, I've talked to Brynny about it already. Brynny's going to be funding spaces for one south of Calgary, but he needs to come out here. More importantly, he needs to want to quit. I don't think he's there yet."

"Yeah, I agree, but I just want to know what the options are. I can probably help pay for it, too." I do some quick math in my head, adding up what's in my savings account, what I'm likely to bring in in the next few months. "Not for the whole thing, but a few thousand."

"Sam's welcome to come to a few services and some of the weekday programming we'll be starting. Someone will take him in. I'd take him in, actually. It would be less pressure, and maybe a change of scene would be good. I'll talk to him about it, but I don't think he's ready."

"I know. I just want us to be ready when he is."

The miles pass, and soon we find ourselves in Manitoba. Dad and Jacqueline show up at our Gimli show, which is a rare afternoon show in a little bar just a couple of blocks from Lake Winnipeg. Grandma Swank had told them about the show and Dad had called me the day before, so I knew they were coming, but it seems strange to see him after two years.

He hasn't lost the extra years that settled on him after Bea's death, but he looks happier than I've seen him in a long time. His eyes are somehow more relaxed.

After the gig, they invite the entire band over to their house for a barbeque. Even Amelia agrees to come and is in an ebullient mood the whole time. She seems to like Jacqueline, maybe because she knows I'm still feeling torn about my dad. I'm trying not to show it, but I'm suppressing waves of anger and grief all evening. My mouth feels dry, no matter how much water I drink. I'm sure Amelia notices my discomfort. I told her everything that happened with my family after Bea's murder within a few days of meeting her, just as she'd spilled her experiences growing up with her mom and sister in Chicago. But I don't even care that she may be enjoying my pain, as long as she behaves.

Dad is in his glory, talking to Reggie and Austin about music. Austin shares stories about touring with the Urban Coyotes. They were way past the hard partying days by the time Austin joined up, but he has stories of meeting Neko Case, Wilco, Carlos Santana, Willie Nelson, and many others. My dad eats it up.

Jacqueline comes out with potato salad and corn on the cob. I follow her back into the kitchen to help her ferry out the rest of the food, plates, and utensils.

"We were hoping you'd come over for brunch tomorrow, if you have time," she says.

"I guess I could," I say, feeling trapped. What I really want to say is *Fuck no. Why am I even here after the shit he's pulled?* But I don't.

"If you have time, I could take you to the museum as well. I'm not sure if you knew this, but your mother's ancestors settled in Gimli for a while."

"No, I didn't know that. Where did they come from?" Also, how the hell does she know this? I wonder.

"Iceland," she says. "And England. Brynny and Charlie Parsons. Brynny was Icelandic, Charlie grew up in Ontario, but his family was English."

"I think my cousin in Calgary is named after her," I say.

"Helen's girl? Yes, that's right. I've talked to Helen about their family history."

So that's how she knows about my mother's family. She's in contact with Helen. I can't be mad at Helen for talking to her, no matter how much I'd like to be. Helen is like Teflon—everyone else's bad feelings slide right off her.

"I don't think I will have time tomorrow. We have to get to Winnipeg for our next gig." This is a lie. I have time. But Jacqueline doesn't need to know that.

"That's too bad. Next time, then. I volunteer at the museum, so I can give you a tour."

"Okay," I say. Even from halfway across the country, it's going to take effort to maintain the estrangement, I can see. There are too many forces trying to pull me back, including Jacqueline.

Amelia's cheerful mood lasts right through our final gig in Winnipeg the next night. It's not until we're seated on the plane that she turns to me and says, "I could quit any time, you know. I've had other offers."

"You'd quit now?"

"I could. I could line something else up like that," she says, snapping her fingers.

"So are you going to quit?" I'm not sure where she's going with this.

"Not for now. I just want you to know that I could."

"Okay. Got it."

"If you ever have Nancy scold me in a band meeting again like that, I will quit on the spot. Next time you have a problem with me, tell me instead of going behind my back."

"Listen, I've apologized for that already, and I'm not apologizing again." I am starting to wonder why I apologized the first time.

"Okay. Fine," she says.

"Okay then."

Conversation concluded, Amelia starts her flight ritual. She rubs lotion on her hands and arms, spritzes something on her face, and slips on an eye mask. Then she puts on her headphones and starts playing her MP3 player.

I wait until the seat belt sign flicks off, then stand up to use the washroom. Inside, I splash cold water on my face and touch up my lipstick. Back at my seat, I pull a copy of Alice Munro's *Lives of Girls and Women* from my bag and tuck into it the way I'd tuck into a good meal.

SIXTEEN

WHEN WE ARRIVE at Pearson airport, I feel ready to drop from exhaustion. I'm grateful Trevor is here to drive me home. Austin's new girlfriend, Tara, is with him. I've only met Tara a couple of times, but I like her. She's unpretentious and straightforward, if a little intimidating. She's nearly as tall as Austin and, as my Grandma Swank would say, too thin for her own good. But then she's a model, trying to become an actor, so perhaps she's not too thin for her own good.

Tara grew up in Montreal. She's mixed race, her mom coming from Iroquois people, Austin had told us on the tour, but she doesn't like stupid questions from white people.

"What's an example of a stupid question?" Reggie asked.

"Does she pay taxes, is one," said Austin.

"Well, what's the answer?" Reggie asked.

"Yes, she pays taxes. She doesn't live on the rez. And her mom lost her status when she married a white man."

After this conversation, both Reggie and I are fascinated by Tara but wary of asking her about these things.

Today I'm too tired to do much more than say hi as Tara and I stand together while the guys collect the luggage.

"How was the tour?" she asks.

"It was a lot of fun. But exhausting," I say.

"How was that one?" she asks, nodding toward Amelia, who is collecting her luggage.

"She was okay." A lie, but I don't want to start something.

"Good. If I miss photo shoots for no reason, my agent drops me. That's the real world."

I shoot an anxious glance at Amelia, but I don't think she's heard Tara. Although I agree with Tara completely, I don't want to get into it with Amelia again.

The day after we get home, I get up at nine a.m., have coffee and a muffin, and go for a long walk.

Trevor's apartment is starting to feel too small for us. He's finished the first draft of his book, but he's starting to get caught up in perfectionism. I try to tell him it will never be perfect, that perfect doesn't exist, but that doesn't seem to help. Plus he's getting annoyed with my things taking up space. Never mind the space his things take up. For some reason, that doesn't seem to count with him.

I walk in a big circle, back to Kensington Market, then start walking through the streets surrounding the market. There are a few places for sale, some for rent. I imagine being able to buy one of the houses with the little porches on the front. A house where Trevor could have his own office to spread out the documents he needs for his book, and a bit of space for my instruments and things. Maybe it's too soon to buy something, but surely we could rent a bigger place.

When Trevor gets home early that evening, I tell him we need to move to a bigger place.

"I don't know. Can we afford it?"

"Yes, we can afford it," I say. "I'm making as much as you. So we should be able to afford something at least double the cost of this place."

"Austin might be upset. We've lived beside each other for years."

"Austin can move in with us for all I care. Then we can get something triple the size."

Trevor's eyes brighten, and I quickly backtrack. "I mean, maybe not right in with us. But he can afford to move, too. He's got more money than we do."

"Let's talk about it later," he says.

After we talk with Austin, it's decided that we've all outgrown our little Chinatown apartments. The three of us, with input from Tara, settle on a neighbourhood a short walk from Reggie's sister's place, which we're still using as practice space. We find a house broken into suites for rent. Trevor and I take the three-bedroom suite on the main floor, and Austin takes the smaller top-floor suite, with two bedrooms. We have a fenced-in backyard with a firepit and a covered porch on the front. The rent is more than Trevor wants to pay, but he's outvoted by the rest of us. By the end of the week, we've all signed the leases, with plans to move at the end of the month.

—

After we sign the lease, Trevor and I decide to take a week off together. Trevor needs some time away from work, and the book, which is really just work he hasn't been paid for yet. Robby has invited us to his cottage in Prince Edward County. I keep calling it a cabin, and Trevor keeps correcting me.

"Why do people in Ontario say cottage and westerners say cabin?" I ask.

"No idea," he says. "To me, a cabin needs to be made of logs."

"Purist," I say.

Trevor grew up in Belleville. His parents, upon retiring, moved out of town and bought a vineyard. I ask whether we should stay with them, but Trevor says they wouldn't let us share a room, since we're not married.

"For real?"

"Oh yeah. Mom's a very strong Catholic. Dad goes along with it, for the most part."

I knew they were Catholic, in a vague way, but not that she was a "strong Catholic."

"What did they say about your series on the priest in Toronto abusing kids?"

"They were more upset with the Church than anything. It almost broke Mom's faith, she told me, but she decided her faith was not in the Church, it was in God. They still go to Mass, but she doesn't tithe anymore. She gives that money to other charities instead."

I fall asleep on the drive, and when I wake up, the landscape of green meadows ringed with aspen, pine, and spruce momentarily makes me think I'm home.

"What do you think?" Trevor asks.

"Oh—hey—those jack pines look just like the ones Tom Thomson painted!"

The week passes pleasantly. Trevor's parents, Trina and Colin, are nothing but kind to us, hosting a few elaborate dinners with us and Robby and his wife and kids. We sample copious amounts of their wine and agree that it is all excellent.

I feel slightly removed from Trevor's parents, as though there is a pane of glass between us, but no ill will permeates the glass. They may have misgivings or hesitation about their only son shacking up with a heathen musician, but they don't say anything.

Back at Robby and Camille's cabin/cottage one night, just as we're going to bed, I ask Trevor whether his parents like me. He hesitates before replying.

"Of course they like you. Why wouldn't they?"

"You're a terrible liar," I say.

"Okay, well, to be honest, they've never liked any of my girlfriends. But they'll get over it."

"I don't want to be a wedge between you and your parents."

"You won't be. They're not like that," he says.

I don't think Trevor is being honest with me, but I don't know what to do about it. I can't make his parents like me, and if no one wants to talk about it, I don't know how to resolve the situation. Maybe I'll just have to follow Trevor's lead and ignore the problem. Hopefully it doesn't fester.

We make love, very slowly, very quietly. The slow pace, the knowledge that his parents don't approve, and the feeling that we're getting away with something make me crazy. It's the best sex I've had in years, I think. Maybe ever. After that, we have sex every night, sometimes faster, but always hushed and furtive.

Robby's wife, Camille, is a writer, primarily fiction. She and Trevor have been talking shop, but it's not until the second day, when the two of us are sunbathing on the beach, that something clicks in my brain and I realize who she is.

"Hey, did you write *Black Crows*?" I ask.

"Yes, that was me," she says. "You know, I used to go to the writing retreats at St. Peter's Abbey in Muenster, Saskatchewan. We would visit with the brothers over meals. One day, one of the brothers told us about the journals of one of the founders of the Abbey. He wrote about eating badger, about the hard winters. I moved the setting to Manitoba, but that was the inspiration for the book."

"I love that book."

"Thank you," she says.

"Are you working on anything right now?"

"I just submitted a new novel to my publisher, so I'm taking a break. Maybe a long break. The well is dry."

I don't know what to say to that at first. I think of what it was like for me a few years ago, when the songs wouldn't come, and my chest tightens. But Camille doesn't look worried. She looks unconcerned, even peaceful with her book and her sun hat.

"You don't look worried about it."

"It happens every now and then after a big project. I think creativity is seasonal. I'm in the quiet season. It's time to rest, recharge, read at the beach."

"That sounds nice, actually."

"It is."

Robby and Camille's kids, Rosie and Jerry, are in their midteens. They sleep late into the morning, stay up late talking to their friends at the next cottage, and spend afternoons lying on the sand, languid, like reptiles trying to warm their blood in the autumn sun. Both are agreeable, not only polite but interested in adults, when they're not texting their friends.

Meals are not elaborate at the Slade cabin. Everyone grabs their own breakfasts and lunches. Sometimes we barbeque burgers or steaks or chicken, make a salad, but often we're foraging through leftovers for supper, too.

Robby and I talk shop only when Camille and Trevor are talking shop. We talk about the Urban Coyotes' American tour, scheduled for later in the fall.

"Nancy said you and Austin are going to be recording an album with the new band," he says. "Where are you recording it?"

"We were thinking about using Reggie's sister's garage," I say. "We haven't asked her yet, though. We'd have to do more sound treatment to improve the acoustics."

"You're welcome to use our recording studio, free of charge," Robby says.

"I was hoping you'd say that. Thank you so much."

By the end of the week, the sun has painted red undertones into my hair, and despite plenty of sunblock, I'm sunburnt. As Trevor drives us back to Toronto, I feel relaxed in the warm car. Sleep keeps tugging me down, and I finally give in, bundling my coat under my head and closing my eyes as it pulls me down. I don't wake until we're well into Toronto, surrounded by city traffic and city buildings.

SEVENTEEN

I HAVE THIS feeling of falling in love while recording The Hug Machine's first album. Working with the Urban Coyotes in studio had been thrilling and tedious by turns. To cut the tedium, Amelia, Reggie, and I decide to record our debut album live off the floor instead of overdubbing each track separately.

"Don't polish it up too much or you'll fuck it up," Reggie tells Cara Rooney, our recording engineer and producer.

"Do I look like someone who is going to polish too much?" she asks.

Cara is the most rock-and-roll person I've ever seen. I think every inch of her skin below her chin is covered in tattoos. From what I can see, all those tattoos are music related: lyrics from Nirvana and Elton John, Janis Joplin howling into the mic, a Flying V guitar. Every day, with different outfits revealing or concealing different patches of skin, I notice something new.

Ruby flies out so we can record the songs we wrote together. She makes it clear right off the hop that she's not joining the band and isn't interested in touring with us, but might make some guest appearances, depending on how our mutual schedules look. I understand, but I'm a little disappointed. I had hoped I might be able to persuade her to run away with the circus.

When Ruby and I sing "Love" together, shivers run from my toes to the top of my head.

> *You left me there, standing alone*
> *with the monster I thought I'd known*
> *as friend, as blood, as one of my own.*
> *That day my heart sank like a stone.*
> *Things we can't say.*
> *Bite back my words.*
> *Swallow my rage.*
> *Save it for another day.*
> *I had to fight, I had to run,*
> *I bled under that summer sun.*
> *I dug my hands into the mud*
> *and cried until I came undone.*
> *Tell me about love. Tell me about love.*
> *Now I stand here on the shore*
> *and I can't go home anymore*
> *'cause you left me fighting a war*
> *that hollowed me from the core.*

Ruby and I haven't been able to sing it together since meeting up in Calgary, and she hasn't sung it with the band, but we nail it on the second try. The power of the song is incredible, the way I imagine surfing must feel—as though we're being lifted and thrust forward at great speed. Cara has us play it together twice more, just to be safe. After, I feel drained from the emotion of the song and need a break.

Cara comes out of the control room crying.

"Are you okay?" Reggie asks.

"I just love that song," she says. "It's so sad, and the music is so beautiful, and your voices ..." She breaks down.

I look at Ruby. I knew it was good, really good, but I wasn't sure if other people would see that.

Even Amelia's ill will seems to soften as the album starts to take shape.

"I like your friend, Ruby," she tells me one day as she makes herself tea in the kitchen. "But I don't know about her thing for your cousin."

"Me neither," I say. "Brynny's still engaged."

"Is she even a lesbian? I don't get it." Amelia stirs milk and sugar into her tea, then sets the spoon at the edge of the sink.

I take a sip of my own tea and think. Ruby is in the studio right now, on the phone with Brynny. She's perched on the arm of the sofa, everything in her body radiating joy. Ruby's not dumb. If there was nothing there, she wouldn't look so happy, I don't think. But I'm worried that Brynny will smash her heart.

"Well, there's definitely chemistry between them. You can feel it. And there's not much chemistry between Brynny and her fiancé, Cody, which is weird because he's a real catch."

"Hmm. It sounds dangerous," says Amelia.

"That's exactly it," I say. "It feels like it could blow up."

"I'm sorry for being a bitch about Flora," she says. I drop my spoon on the counter, and the clang makes me jump, causing me to spill tea.

"You don't have to look so surprised," Amelia says.

"I just wasn't expecting it," I say.

"It's just that a friend of mine, Rae, has some history with Flora. She did something really horrible to Rae in university. It ruined her life."

Do I really want to know what that history is? Can I trust Amelia to give it to me straight, or is it going to be slanted? No, of course I can't trust her. And I'm tired of her drama triangles.

"I'm sorry to hear that. I'm sorry for Rae. And I just remembered something I need to talk to Cara about."

I set my tea on the counter and leave.

The next day Owen drops by to see how we're doing. When we take a break, he comes into the studio, admiring the chord progression I'm playing. He asks me to play it again, so I do, while everyone else filters into the kitchen.

"You look like you've got a hide full of ticks," he says.

"I do feel a little itchy," I say, thinking about a tick-infested moose I saw once, bald patches marring her body. "Between you and me, I'm getting tired of dealing with Amelia."

"She's still playing games? Why do you keep working with her?"

"Because she's talented. I mean, she's brought so much to our band."

"So? There are plenty of other people who are just as talented, waiting for a break. Look at those girls you used to play with ... what was the band's name?"

"The Greatest Show on Earth."

"Right. All talented, all professional and agreeable. And doesn't one of them play pedal steel?"

"Yeah, Kayla does." I think about what he's suggesting. "I just get the sense Amelia hasn't had it easy, you know. I mean, she hasn't said much, but ..." Where has this idea come from, exactly? Has Amelia been dropping hints or have I made it up? I'm not even sure anymore.

Owen snorts derisively. "Join the club, Kid. No one's had it easy, including you. Would you treat other people the way Amelia treats you and everyone else in the band?"

"Well, no." I think of how I used to cheat on Luke and feel a wave of guilt. "Not anymore, anyway."

"Listen to me. It will not be all smooth sailing ahead. Your band is a ship, and you are the captain. You need a crew that will help you avoid the reefs, not steer the ship toward them."

"You're not going to tell Nancy about this conversation, are you?"

"No, Kid. We're all adults here. Including Amelia, even if she doesn't act like one. Don't forget that."

—

The Hug Machine's first album, *Love*, hits bigger than any of us ever expected that spring. Before the CD officially launches, the Americana and college stations in the U.S. start playing it. When Nancy calls to tell me it's getting a lot of play in the U.S., even more than the Urban Coyotes, I'm suddenly afraid.

When I tell Trevor that night, he says "Anvil cloud. Get ready for a bolt out of the blue."

"That sounds like a song," I say.

Leading up to the CD launch, we film a music video for "Love" at Canada's Wonderland. Tara stars as the betrayed woman, wandering through the fair alone or, in flashbacks, with her ex, who is by turns chivalrous, winning her prizes, and abusive, as he grips her wrist or glowers at her. I have to remind myself it's not real, but I can't help feeling tense during these scenes, every nerve activated, every muscle primed for action.

The park is closed during the week this time of year, but they let us film and bring in extras for the happy flashback scenes. Other days it's just us, and the park is eerily quiet and cold. One day Tara and her ex-beau are on the roller coaster, then the Ferris wheel, with the rest of the band in the cars behind them. I wonder if it's going to look like Tara is being stalked by an alt-country band.

In the middle of all this, Trevor has just got a publishing deal for his book on Fred Adams, and he's already started the second one, a book about Bea's life and her art. I read what he's drafted during the breaks. The idea came from Pauline Brooks, who has been putting together Bea's archive. Trevor's been talking to my family over the phone, and we've already made one trip together to Maple Creek and Calgary.

My entire family has embraced him as one of their own, holding nothing back in their memories of Bea. So far, even my dad has been completely open about everything that happened, saying he'll hand over journals Mom kept, that I didn't even know existed. Trevor wants to go to Gimli next month to visit my dad. I'm hesitant, but then I think maybe I should just go and bury the hatchet.

Asked what it was like knowing the abuse was going on for years, Dad said, "We tried to do something about it in the early years. Before Darby was born, Bea would spend the night here sometimes while Will cooled off. May wanted Bea to divorce him, but Bea was afraid he'd come after her, and whoever sheltered her. I physically dragged him off her more than once."

"I don't think it got better for her over the years, but Will got smarter and it was less visible. I know this sounds terrible, but it just became part of normal life, something we all had to live with. I didn't know how it would end. If I'd known the cost, maybe I would have done something differently. I wish I'd known Bea was leaving that day. I would have run interference. But she was probably afraid I'd give it away. Will is very smart. Smarter than I am, truth be told. It was hard to get one by him."

Reading those notes one weekend morning while sipping coffee with Trevor, I couldn't help feeling a little bitter about Trevor's access to my own family.

"That's more than he's said to me about it in years."

"Hard for him to say anything to you when you don't take his calls, Darby."

A flash of rage. "Fuck, whatever. I don't need to hear his excuses."

Trevor's face tightened, and he looked like he wanted to bite back, but he was silent for several seconds. Finally, he sighed. "The war is over, Darby."

Then he walked through the patio doors, back into the house.

Trevor still has to figure out how he's going to write about Kenneth Bale, the man who "mentored" Bea while simultaneously grooming and eventually sleeping with her when she was only sixteen. He'd done the same kind of thing with my mom, I've found out through Trevor's interviews with Helen. I don't think Helen would ever have told us what really happened, but as Bea's fame has grown since her death, Kenneth has started to publicly position himself as Bea's mentor and the source of her inspiration. He's told reporters that he "discovered" Bea and even alluded to a Lolita-type romance between them, which pretty much made me puke in my mouth the first time I read about it in the arts and entertainment section of one of the big dailies.

The truth is that Kenneth's "relationship" with Bea was abusive. He had managed to talk Bea into posing nude for him, and later used those photos to blackmail her so he could take credit for her photos and sell them in the store. Helen had somehow made him stop, but she had refused to go into details on how she'd done it.

"I did a little research, found out about another girl he'd done it to before Bea. I prayed on it. Then I just ... well ... I made him an offer he couldn't refuse, as they say."

"Did you threaten him?" Trevor had asked.

"I wouldn't say that. I just pointed a few things out to him about the reality of his situation."

Trevor, Helen, and Pauline all think it's important to write about Kenneth to correct the record. Also, people aren't well informed about what sexual abuse of children or young people looks like in the real world. I hadn't realized how insidious that kind of abuse was either, until Helen told us how Kenneth spent so much time teaching Bea about photography, how he gave both her and May part-time jobs in his shop (along with other girls, too). He never did anything inappropriate in front of other adults, and people thought he was a talented photographer who cared about up-and-coming artists. He even mentored some boys. The thing is, Bea learned from him, Helen said. That made the whole thing worse, because art was such an important part of her identity.

"But it was all a strategy to get access to teenage girls," says Helen.

Trevor is a little worried about getting sued by Kenneth, but he's going to make sure it's bulletproof before he even sends it to a publisher. But more than that, he doesn't want the book to be what he calls "trauma porn."

I'd argued against including Kenneth at first. "I don't want people to draw a straight line between Kenneth and Will. I don't want them to think she was 'damaged.' That she brought it on herself."

"Only an asshole would think that," says Trevor.

"Well, there're lots of assholes out there. Don't give them a weapon."

"Look, Kenneth happened, and like it or not, he's part of her story. But he's not her whole story, and neither is Will." Trevor sets down his cup so hard it sloshes coffee all over the table. "Despite everything, she kept creating. She was an artist through and through, and no one ever took that away from her. And she was brave and kind, and a hell of a horsewoman. And she was loved by you, and so many people, and she loved them too. THAT is her story."

I'm still uneasy about it, though. I don't want people to think my aunt was fated to fall into another abusive relationship, or to somehow excuse Will because of her history. I want people to remember her as more than a victim. I want them to remember her art, and her spirit. I think that those awful men were drawn to her not because they thought she was weak and vulnerable, but because they wanted her light. They had none of their own, and they wanted to possess it, take it from her. And eventually Will did.

God, I miss Aunt Bea. And my mom, even though she could be so mean to me. I don't know how to fill the gaping holes left by them. One night, I stay up late, writing notes on postcards to the other people I miss. Jen. Ruby, even though I've just seen her. Beth and Red, all my grandparents. I stamp them and set them aside to mail.

Then I write a letter to my mom, and another to Aunt Bea, and in the cold, dark early morning, I light them up in the fire pit in the backyard and watch the sparks and ashes float skyward.

At the end of the week, Ruby flies out for the weekend and we play a concert for the video. There are about two hundred people who responded to the ad for free tickets forming the crowd in front of us. It's a warm fall day, and we're actually sweating under the lights. The crowd moves to the music, and soon there are even a few couples dancing, whirling each other around the makeshift dance floor.

I'm not sure what the video is going to look like, but in the end, it's beautiful. All the scenes with Tara are in black and white, the tone sad. But the scenes with us playing to the crowd are in vivid colour. And it doesn't look like we're stalking her at all, in the end. When the video is released just ahead of the CD, it starts climbing up the MuchMusic countdown, quickly cracking the top ten, then the top five. Tara gets a call to audition for a pilot being filmed in Toronto, and she gets a good role, although the pilot never gets picked up. But it's okay, because her agent's phone is ringing off the hook and Austin is sure she's just a week away from her big break.

Soon Nancy is getting so many requests to talk to me, to have the band on various radio and TV shows, she has to add people to the team. Overnight, Courtney has an assistant to answer media calls and handle scheduling, and another person joins the marketing team.

"We're looking at playing a few dates in the U.S. in the summer, and maybe a second tour in the winter," Nancy says during our band meeting.

"Can we go somewhere warm in the winter?" Reggie asks.

"Sure. But for now, I was thinking we might start in Chicago, since Amelia has roots there," says Nancy.

Nancy starts talking about dates in the U.S. It will be a three-week tour. Ruby will have graduated from her music therapy program by then, so she can join us for the whole tour, as a guest, and she's committed to several gigs through the year, in between her work at Brynny's church's music therapy program. We'll actually have a tour manager this time—a younger guy named Theo, a friend of Reggie's. Then Nancy starts going through our media schedule over the next two weeks. I have at least twenty interviews a week. I start to feel ill.

"Darby? Are you okay?" Courtney asks. "You look like you're going to be sick."

"Just give me a sec," I say. "I need a bit of air."

I step outside the conference room, and Courtney follows me. "Here, come sit in my office," she says, leading me into a room down the hallway. I haven't spent much time in Courtney's office, I realize, looking around the room. In the corner is a record and CD player. One wall is records, floor to ceiling. Another is CDs. I start looking at the various albums. She has everything from the Carter Family to k.d. lang to Martina McBride. It's the most complete collection of country music I've ever seen.

I sit in a plush chair, and Courtney offers me a bottle of water. "Feeling overwhelmed?" she asks.

"Uh, yeah, just a little. Not long ago, I was a music student. I wasn't even the best vocalist in my class. Then I was in a cool Canadian band. And now I'm ... well, I don't know what I am. I don't want to say it."

"You might be the next big thing," says Courtney.

"I just don't understand how it's happening so fast. It doesn't make sense."

"Fame isn't a logical creature. It's emotional and impulsive. It doesn't usually embrace bands on their first album, but then this isn't Austin or Reggie or Amelia's first album. It's not even your first. Something about this band, and these songs, is hitting with people. We can break it apart, say it's the songwriting, the melody, the guitar parts on track four. And there's some truth to that, but it's not getting at what makes this album magic." Courtney pauses.

"Well, what is the magic?" I ask.

"I think it's the emotion on the album," she says. "It's so raw. Listening to it, sometimes I feel like crying and laughing and celebrating all within the same song. It reminds me of what I loved about music when I was a kid, you know?"

"Yeah, I know."

"Listen, I know all this is overwhelming, and it's going to be hard in some ways, but we've got your back. If you ever need anything, you just call us."

"Thanks, Courtney."

—

Nothing is the same after *Love* comes out. We're not rich, mind you, but we are all famous. During a break in touring, Amelia and I go shopping one day—the first time we've shopped together since our spat over Flora—and everywhere we go, young women are asking if they can have their pictures taken with us. If any of us go to any bar, we can hardly pay for our own drinks. It's thrilling and disconcerting at the same time.

Trevor finds it as intrusive than I do. Somehow my personal cell phone number leaks to an obsessive fan, and he starts calling me at all hours of the night. Trevor answers, every time, in case it's an emergency, and every time he unloads on the guy. We both lose sleep, especially once my night terrors return. Eventually I change my number and don't give it out to anyone outside our small circle of friends and family.

One day, a reporter Trevor works with, while writing a feature on the band, describes the neighbourhood where we all live, including the name of the coffee shop around the block where Austin and I sometimes meet to talk songwriting. Trevor is furious with the reporter, sure that some stalker is going to firgure out which house we live in. A few fans show up at the coffee shop, but no one comes to our house, thank God. I don't want to move right now.

What this really means is that there are many people listening to our music, and that amazes me. I imagine specific fans: a teenage girl picking up my album from A&B Sound in Edmonton; a middle-aged teacher from small-town Saskatchewan opening it as a birthday gift; in the future, a college kid in Chicago buying it at our show.

It also means that Austin and I, especially, are busy all the time. Between the two bands, we work most days of the week. If we're not touring, we're songwriting, doing press, or playing on someone else's album. Soon, Amelia and Reggie are more and more in demand, too, both appearing in other alt-country bands. Within a few months of *Love*, Amelia starts getting calls to play sessions in Nashville, which leads to steady work. I'm jealous, but I try not to let it show. She's always wanting me to come down with her sometime, so we can go to the Grand Ole Opry together and I can meet some people, but I find it intimidating, and so I hide in my workload.

In the middle of all this, I get a call from Jen late one night. Since she's started practising law, she doesn't call late at night, so I know instantly something must be wrong.

"What is it?"

"It's Sam," Jen says.

Sam has finally found the bottom, she tells me. He showed up at Luke and Meaghan's after a two-week bender in Saskatoon. "Luke took one look at him and drove him to emergency," says Jen. "He had alcohol poisoning."

"God, I thought we all got past that after the Grade 11 incident."

"Sam wants to be back in high school. That's what he told Luke."

"He's said the same to me," I say.

Sam is now a full-on addict, Jen continues. Probably has been for a while. But the problem is that if he quits drinking, withdrawal smashes him over the head—bad enough to kill him.

"Really? God, I had no idea he was that far gone," I say.

"Oh, yeah, it's bad. Real bad. He's in a detox centre right now, but we don't know what to do after that. Luke is willing to help any way he can, but Sam has too many friends around there who are drunks. How are we going to keep him on the wagon?"

"What about his parents?"

"They want him to move back in, but it's the same problem. Too many drinking buddies back home. And to be honest, his mom is a bit of an alcoholic. They can be volatile together."

"Wow, I had no idea about his mom." I wonder if Ruby knew. "Listen, I know this might sound like a crazy idea, but what if Sam could get a completely fresh start? Somewhere he'd have a community to support him, programming to help with his addiction. But no drinking buddies."

"Where?"

I tell her about Ruby's idea to bring him to Calgary.

"But he doesn't know anyone there," says Jen. "Is that really a good idea?"

"He knows my friend Ruby. She's out there now, and she'd be happy to have a roommate."

Jen's not sure it's fair to saddle Ruby with Sam, but I think it's Sam's best shot. Besides, Ruby would probably be mad if we didn't give her a chance to help, I say. "She's not built like you and me, Jen. She's actually kind."

"Ha ha, you're funny as shit. Well, okay, maybe we should look into it."

When I call Ruby, she's already heard from Sam and made the same offer. She's feeling lonely in Millarville, I suspect, still pining over Brynny, whose engagement to Cody seems to be never-ending. Maybe it will be good for both of them.

Sam, for his part, takes a few days to think about it. Then, not seeing any better options, he agrees. Luke decides to drive him to Millarville instead of leaving Sam to the bus. He seems too vulnerable to get there on his own.

I get a flurry of texts from Sam and Ruby over the first two weeks as Ruby tours Sam around. They take long drives through the foothills and into the mountains, have breakfasts at the Chuckwagon Café, and attend Sunday services together. Sam is instantly pulled into Brynny's church, which surprises me, because he was never a church-going guy and neither is anyone in his family. Maybe it's the kindness of the other people who attend. Carol, who owns a bed-and-breakfast in Millarville, brings him a basket of baked goods to welcome him. Within a few days, Sam has signed up for Alcoholics Anonymous and is helping out at the church. Soon he has a part-time job cutting grass and doing maintenance on the grounds. It's going so well, I feel like it's too good to be true.

I blurt this out to Sam one morning on the phone and instantly feel horrible for sticking my foot in my mouth. But he laughs.

"Don't worry, it's hard as hell and I know it. I still want to drink every minute of the day. The therapy is really hard—it's so much fucking work, I feel like I'm back in school. I like the work, though. I like being busy. And I like the people."

I'm glad Ruby's taken Sam in, because the truth is I don't have time to help. I'm on the road more and more. It's a grind, but while the band is travelling, someone is always there to take care of our every need. Good food appears backstage. The tour manager steers the ship, pointing us toward our destination each day and making sure we get there on time, usually. Our crew packs and unpacks our gear, over and over. Everyone around us is there to do something for us. Months pass, mostly on the road, as Nancy coordinates tours for both bands.

Being in a band is no way to travel, but it's also the only way to travel. It means long days on a bus in all kinds of weather, but even the trials inspire nostalgia later. We play a lot of poker and a bit of crib. Theo and Amelia are the best card players. I do suspect that Amelia is counting cards, maybe outright cheating somehow, but I can't be sure.

Sometimes we watch movies. Sometimes we write songs or just play old favourites and sing along. Anything that anyone can play on the guitar is a potential singalong in either band, no matter the genre. Just to keep things interesting, sometimes we pick an era or an artist: Dolly Parton night, Rolling Stones night, nineties night, Cash and Carter night. Amelia does the best version of Johnny Cash's "A Boy Named Sue" any of us have ever heard.

The day the Hug Machine's bus loses wheels, we're on our way to Chicago, our second time there. The night before we had played a gig at a Detroit club. We are all a bit hungover and singing along to the Rolling Stones' "Gimme Shelter." Reggie and Amelia are looking very cozy—I'm pretty sure they hooked up last night.

I am doing my best to harmonize with Merry Clayton's vocals. Merry and I have just belted out the line about rape and murder, our voices breaking with sorrow, when I glance out the window and see a wheel roll past. A moment later, another wheel follows its mate, and the back corner of the bus drops, sparks shooting in the air. Reggie, sitting beside me, starts swearing like I've never heard anyone swear before. Everyone else is totally silent as the driver tries to ease the wounded bus to the highway's shoulder. I watch apprehensively as the wheels cross to the other icy lane, into oncoming traffic. A pickup fishtails as its driver brakes hard, then takes the ditch, narrowly missing the wheel. A black SUV follows it into the ditch.

I close my eyes. There are moments that are like asteroids, knocking you off orbit or obliterating everything. This, I think, is one of those moments. I imagine the people dead in other vehicles, their families destroyed. I can see their bloody, twisted bodies, smell the death.

Then, I don't know why, I think of my mom, my aunt. I see my mom dying in her narrow hospital bed, pale, with dark bruises under her eyes, the cancer having consumed most of her by then. Then I see my aunt floating in that lake, bloated, her mutilated ring finger.

I want to remember Aunt Bea with smudges of paint on her cheek and under her nails, a far-off look in her eyes. And my mom laughing hard at one of Lena's stories, a cup of hot coffee in front of her. But I can't get these images out of my head.

My vision starts to go black, and I'm afraid I'm going to pass out. I lean forward, put my head between my legs, and throw up.

Once the driver, Bill, manages to stop the runaway bus, Austin and Amelia sprint across the highway to tend to the wounded, confident in their first aid training. I am such a wreck that I can hardly stand at first, and Reggie helps me off the bus. The cold, wet wind rips through my body. Bill is right behind me. I take one look at his devastated face, start sobbing, and hurl into the grey slush edging the highway. There's nothing left in my stomach but bile, yet I keep vomiting, throat burning.

It turns out no one is dead or critically wounded, although an ambulance does haul away the driver of the SUV. But I can't stop crying. I kneel at the side of the highway, howling into the wind, soaked by the wet snow. I can hear and understand what people are telling me, but I can't get any words out myself for all the crying.

Eventually a guy named Dale, who stops by in his minivan, offers to give me, Amelia, and Reggie a ride to Chicago while everyone else waits for the next bus. I don't understand why Reggie is coming with us; then I realize he's there in case shit goes down at some point, because I'm obviously a mess and Amelia, for all her bitchiness, is no fighter. I snuggle into Reggie's giant side and cry softly the whole way while everyone else tries to talk around me. Eventually the sheer awkwardness gets the better of them and they stop trying to make small talk.

When Dale drops us off at our hotel, we find out a fire early that morning has caused enough smoke damage that none of us have rooms. The whole lobby reeks of smoke. My sobbing has receded to pathetic hiccups, but I'm at a loss as to what to do. Amelia, however, commandeers a phone in the hotel's business centre, where she starts calling friends and family with a room to spare.

In the end, I end up staying with Amelia's aunt Alejandra, a choreographer with a condo in downtown Chicago. Alejandra, a tiny Venezuelan woman, hugs me on sight and takes my duffel bag from me. Inside, she makes me rose tea with heaps of sugar and teaches me to feel my pulse in my wrist, breathe deeply, and focus on my pulse and breath. I do this for an hour, sprawled on her couch with a pack of frozen peas on my swollen eyes.

Alejandra zips out to buy some groceries—she wasn't expecting company—and Jim Morrison appears. How strange. I don't remember falling asleep.

"Am I insane?" I ask him.

Jim lights a joint, inhales deeply, exhales slowly. Then he offers me his hand. I take it, and he pulls me off the couch, into a dance. The dance is unfamiliar to me, the rhythm wild, the steps erratic. Jim spins me, and I whirl away from him, through the wall, above the street, into the sky. And I'm gone.

I wake some time later to Alejandra shaking my shoulder. "Please, wake up, Darby. You will be late for your show."

I sit up slowly, yawning, trying to hold onto a strange, beautiful melody that is already leaving my head. A few fragments of a strange dream linger: a beautiful tree, so tall I have to crane my neck to see the lower branches. Its bark a gleaming white, the leaves silver and sparkling. Delicate pink blossoms that emit sparks like shooting stars. The mother tree that connects everything, holds everything together.

"I'm sorry, I tried to wake you a half hour ago, but you would not leave your sleep. Did you take a sleeping pill?"

"No … I just had a strange dream. It's like I went somewhere else."

Alejandra nods as though she knows, and passes me a large glass of cold water. I realize that I'm very thirsty and start to chug it.

"Slow down a little," she says, and I pause between gulps of water. When I finish it, she brings me more sweet rose tea. "You'd better get ready," she says as I sip the tea.

"Is there anything in this tea that would make me high?"

Alejandra laughs. "No, it's just tea."

I have a quick shower, dress, and dry my hair. Amelia must have told her aunt about our pre-show routine because she insists on doing my hair. So I sit on the little bench seat in front of Alejandra's oak vanity, carefully applying makeup as she weaves my hair into something medieval. By the time she's finished, my locks are a plaited fairy crown. She sends me out the door with a travel mug of sweet rose tea.

Our show that night, at a little bar with a huge back room, is like nothing I've ever experienced. I am in a trance, my mood swinging from sorrow to ecstasy, and I pull the whole room along with me. People start to dance, hesitantly at first, but with each song, they commit a little more, losing themselves to the music, to the joy of movement. As I sing the last words of "Texas Swing," a song we like to cover, I hop from the stage to the floor and find before me a young man wearing cowboy boots. He dances me around the barroom floor as the band plays an instrumental extension.

We do several encores, playing until I feel like I'm going to collapse from exhaustion. I have nothing left in the tank. We are done. The crowd is done, too. They whoop and holler, but they don't ask for more, and when I look at their faces, they're drained.

I lean on the mic stand, and Reggie swoops me in his arms, carrying me from the stage and depositing me at the bar. I want a drink badly, but something warns me not to start tonight, so I order a club soda with lime, then stagger outside into a cab with Amelia, up to Alejandra's condo, and collapse into bed without even bothering to wash my face or brush my teeth.

I wake up at noon, and even though I haven't had a drop of alcohol, my skin aches, my head pounds, and my mouth is dry, dry, dry.

Amelia is on the pull-out couch in the living room, but she is sitting up, talking to her aunt as Alejandra cooks French toast. They are speaking Spanish, but I think they're talking about last night's show, based on Amelia's gestures. I say hi, then head straight for the bathroom and a shower.

I emerge fresh-faced, my hair still plaited, my body feeling like I've been on a three-day bender. "Why do I feel so awful this morning?" I ask as I sit down at the table. Alejandra offers coffee, but I wave it away. Acid sloshes in my stomach—I think coffee would tip it over the edge.

"I don't know, but that was the most intense show I've ever seen," says Amelia. "It was like some sort of spiritual experience."

"Maybe we should start a cult," I joke.

"Oh, speaking of cult, your cousin Brynny phoned while you were in the shower," Amelia says. Alejandra gives her a sharp look. "What? She's leading some kind of Christian horse cult. Just ask Darby."

"Yeah, she really is."

"Perhaps charisma runs in your family," says Alejandra.

"Oh, no. My cousin is way more charismatic than I am. I've never seen anything like it."

Alejandra raises an eyebrow, then puts on the kettle. More tea, I think.

I flip open my phone, select Brynny's number. She picks it up on the first ring.

"Hi, Darby, I have something important to talk to you about."

"Jesus?"

"Ha ha, very funny, no. It's about Ruby."

"What is it?" My stomach clenches as I imagine every horrible thing that could have happened to Ruby.

"Well, listen, I don't want to shock you, but I think I have feelings for her. Like, romantic feelings. Even sexual feelings."

About time, I think. "Yeah, I kind of figured that was the case."

"Really? How did you know? Is it that obvious?" Brynny is so loud that Amelia and Alejandra can hear every word over the phone. Alejandra leans against the counter, her eyes wide with interest, slowly raising her coffee mug to her lips.

"Yes, it is pretty obvious. Sorry, I guess that's not very sensitive."

"How many other people have noticed, do you think? I mean, do you think the whole congregation knows?"

"Well, listen, in all fairness, I've been paying attention only because I know Ruby's nuts about you."

"She is?"

"Yes—wait, haven't you talked to her yet? I mean, isn't that what you called to tell me?"

Alejandra pours hot water into a tea pot, and the scents of rose tea and coffee mingle in the air.

"No, I haven't talked to her. Cody called off the wedding last week. He said it wasn't going to work, he could see I was in love with someone else. When I told him that was ridiculous, who could I possibly be in love with besides him, he said Ruby. I started to argue with him, tell him that we were just friends, that she was like a sister, and I really believed that. But then I thought about her voice on the phone and how it created this warm feeling in my belly, and I knew he was right."

"Wow. How's Cody doing with all of this?"

"He's broken-hearted, and he's mad at me for being so obtuse, he said. But we had coffee yesterday, and you know, he's so clear-eyed about the whole thing. He seems to know exactly what he needs to do—get away from me! I'm just the opposite. I feel so bad for him, and so guilty, and so confused. I don't know what to do next. All I know is that warm feeling in my stomach, you know? I haven't told my parents why Cody and I broke it off. You're the only one who knows, outside of Cody and his best friend, Ty. They won't tell anyone else until I do."

"Your parents will be okay with it, won't they?"

"Yeah, I'm sure they will. We've always been a church-going family, but Mom and Dad have always been open-minded about this kind of stuff. And Mom's never taken the Sodom and Gomorrah story at face value."

"Are you worried about the congregation?"

"Some of them will be upset for sure, especially if they think I've been hiding something. I'll lose some people ... I think I know who I'll lose for sure, and there are a few that will be on the fence. Cody and I talked about it. He's going to keep coming to the church because he really believes in it, and he wants to show that he supports me. Who does that after such a rotten breakup? I'm such a fool for not wanting to marry someone like him."

"No, trust me, I've been there. Kind of. You'd be a fool to tie yourself to him when you don't really love him. Someone will snatch up that guy in about five seconds, once he's ready. And by the way, Ruby is just as kind, so be good to her, please."

"Are you worried about Ruby getting together with me?"

I pause, think about how to say it. "Well, yes. I'm mostly worried she'll be too much in your shadow. If you get together, please promise me you'll let her shine, too."

"I can do that," she says, but the way she says it, so lightly, I wonder if she really knows what I'm talking about.

"What are you going to do about your congregation? I mean, are you going to step into the pulpit and tell everyone you're a lesbian?"

"No, I'll probably wait. I don't know what I am. I thought I liked men, but then Ruby came along ... although I guess she's not the first woman I've found attractive. I don't think I need to spill the mess inside my head from the pulpit. Just, when I know, when things are kind of official, if they ever become official, I won't try to hide anything. That's all I know. Anyway, everyone knows our engagement is off because I wasn't wearing my ring last Sunday. I've given it back to Cody."

Brynny hesitates. She's quiet for so long I wonder if my phone has dropped the call. "Hello?" I say.

"I'm still here. Something happened after the service on Sunday, and it's so weird, I don't know what to make of it. I don't really know how to talk about it. Do you remember that Rex guy?"

"Yes."

Alejandra hands me a mug of tea, and I take a sip to fortify myself.

"He followed me home after the service let out. Right to the end of my driveway in Millarville."

"You live in Millarville now?"

"Yeah, Mom and Dad co-signed a mortgage for me. Cody was supposed to move in after we were married. Anyway ..."

"What did Rex do when you got there?"

"He just sat there in his pickup, watching me as I walked into the house. I locked the door behind me."

"Did you call the police?"

"No. Should I?"

"Yes. He's a creep. Maybe you should start keeping a log. Ask for a restraining order or whatever the hell they call it."

"Doesn't that seem a little melodramatic? I don't want to draw unnecessary attention to the whole thing."

"Doesn't it seem melodramatic for some old guy to follow you TO YOUR HOME as soon as he figures out you've broken up with your fiancé?"

Amelia's eyes widen. Worry lines appear around Alejandra's eyes and mouth, across her forehead. She whispers something to Amelia in Spanish.

"Well, when you put it like that ..."

"Listen, man, I know this is going to sound weird, but I am very in tune with my own intuition and the universe at the moment.

And I am telling you, this motherfucker is trouble. I have thought that since the moment I laid eyes on him. There is a big hole in the centre of him, and he's always trying to fill it. And if he tries to fill it with you, or his idea of what you should be, it's going to be like a star imploding, taking down everything in its gravitational field. You need to knock him out of your orbit, or yourself out of his orbit, however you can, whatever it takes, no holds barred."

Brynny is silent for a few beats. "I'm just worried about how it will look to the church. And I can't make sense of it. I don't know what to think."

"Who cares how it looks to the church!" I feel a hand on my left wrist and realize Alejandra is standing in front of me and I am yelling into the phone. She turns over my hand, takes my pulse, mimes breathing. I slow down.

"I'm sorry, Brynny." I pause, drink some tea, then breathe. "What is your gut telling you? What do you feel when you think of Rex at the end of your driveway?"

"Confused. But scared. He scares me."

"Then act accordingly. Please."

We chat a little bit more about nothing much, as a chaser to the tough conversation we've both had to swallow. When I hang up, Amelia and Alejandra are staring at me.

"Are you okay?" Amelia asks.

"I just ... I just have a really bad feeling."

PART THREE
2009

Hey, remember wild horses running on

With the morning in their eyes.

Ears pinned back on a free land,

Under free blue skies.

— JT Nero/Birds of Chicago,
Remember Wild Horses

EIGHTEEN

"**YOUR LIFE MUST** be radically different since you released *Love* and it
skyrocketed to the top. *Cease Fire* looks like it's going to surpass
your first album. People have labelled you a shaman, a guru. It's
a level of worship we don't really see these days, especially in the
alt-country sphere. What is that like?"

I stare blankly at the young man sitting across from me. Robin.
We're sitting in the old town of Albuquerque, New Mexico. Earlier
in the day, Austin and I had driven out to the petroglyphs scrawled
into volcanic rock. As we climbed to the top of the hardened lava,
we speculated about what the glyphs could mean.

"Maybe it's just ancient graffiti," Austin said.

"Seriously?"

He pointed to a drawing that resembled a spaceship. "We're
still doing it."

"Okay, fair point."

Sometimes I wonder if people are reading more into our music
than is there, just like the glyphs. Or more into me than is there.
But I can't say this. This guy is with ... shit, which rock mag is he

All That's Left

writing for again? I can't keep track. God, I must come across as so arrogant.

I take a slow, deep breath before I answer his question.

"You know, I'm glad people connect with our music. But I hope they don't put me on a pedestal. Or at least when I fall off it, they give me some grace. I'm not magical. I'm as human and flawed as everyone else."

"Yet you somehow convey this openness, vulnerability, while maintaining a certain mystique."

"Mystique?"

"Your shows are like spiritual revivals, but as soon as the show is done, you slip on your poker face. You convey your biography, even traumatic events like your aunt's death, with a newsreader deadpan. Your music is transcendent, but when I sit down to interview you, you seem removed from it. It's hard to make sense of it."

"Well, I mean, I guess no one has ever put it to me like that." I could try to make sense of myself in a way I can explain to this writer, but opt to sidetrack him first if I can. "Did you like last night's show?"

"In the plaza, here? To be honest, even though I pitched this story, I wasn't really expecting much. I mean, a fundraising gig for domestic violence sounds like an opportunity for lots of lectures more than anything."

I bite my left cheek.

"But it wasn't like that at all. I tried to take notes, but I was just caught up in it. It felt like you split me wide open."

"Well, good."

"I just can't reconcile the Darby who was on stage last night with the Darby sitting here now. You seem almost flat."

"Because I'm tired, man. Do you know how much it takes out of me to create that music and perform it? When you're making it, you have to create this bubble so you can let out your deepest creative urges, your fears, your passions, all of it. And then when you play that music in front of an audience, you have to let them in and split yourself wide open—as you put it—while still performing. It's exhilarating, there's nothing like it, but it's also really, really hard and draining. If I was in that state all the time, I'd be like a raw nerve, in constant pain, you know? Don't get me wrong, I know it's all part of the deal, and I'm eternally grateful that people love our music. I just can't be that vulnerable offstage all the time."

Robin's next several questions are standard fare, the kinds of things I've answered a million times. I am on autopilot, answering by rote, when Robin asks about Ruby and me getting married. I must have misheard.

"Sorry, can you repeat that?"

"Oh, I was just asking whether you have a queer following, given that you and Ruby are getting married next week. I would have loved to see her perform with you."

I laugh and Robin looks confused.

"Well, we do have a queer following, but Ruby and I aren't getting married. Ruby and my cousin, Brynny, are getting married next week. Brynny is a preacher in a church near Calgary, Alberta. Ruby runs a music therapy program through the church. She's been busy getting ready for the big day."

"I'm sorry ... I got that mixed up."

"No problem. I can see how it's confusing."

We talk about the legalization of same-sex marriage in Canada and whether it's coming to the States with Obama in. We talk a little about Brynny's church, how she lost a good chunk of her congregation when she first came out as lesbian. But since then more people have joined the church, and some of the ones who left came back. We talk about the Church of the Shortgrass, about their activism to keep resource development out of the ecologically sensitive foothills, how that issue has brought together their congregation, local ranchers, and First Nations along with other residents in the area. The Hug Machine has played a couple of awareness-raising concerts, plus a fundraiser for Ruby's music therapy program.

It turns out a photo from the fundraising concert is the source of Robin's confusion. Ruby had kissed me smack on the lips onstage at the end of the show.

"That was just a kiss between friends," I shrug with a *What are you going to do?* look.

My mind wanders back to the church. It's strange, I never thought I'd find myself in church again, but Brynny's Jesus/Horse Cult makes me feel connected to something bigger.

"Jesus/Horse Cult?"

"Oh, did I say that out loud? It's kind of an in-joke. In the early days, Brynny preached in an indoor equestrian arena, and sometimes she'd literally bring a horse into her sermon, work with the horse and draw all these spiritual parallels."

"Horses, environmental activism ... it sounds like your cousin is very connected to the land."

"She is, in a way. I think a lot of it comes from the people in her congregation. There's one woman who knows a lot about native plants, uses them for medicine. She delivers sermons sometimes about the spiritual significance of plants. That church is kind of its own beast, you know? I don't think there's anything else quite like it."

Robin and I chat for a while longer, then he takes a photo of me standing in the square. I try to look energized, but I probably look wiped out, with dark circles under my eyes.

That afternoon I'm on a plane, sitting beside Amelia, smelling her lavender skin lotion and looking at her cooling eye mask. She looks very relaxed. Maybe I need an eye mask for flights.

I close my eyes and turn up my iPod just enough that I can't hear the drone of the plane's engines. Gillian Welch's mournful voice fills my world, leaving me in my own imagined version of some hard times. I sleep until the plane bumps the pavement of Salt Lake City.

The journey from Albuquerque to Calgary is a real milk run, with a two-hour layover in Utah followed by several hours in Minneapolis. The Salt Lake City airport is bereft of shopping, so I lean against Reggie's bulk, staring at the mountains.

"Do you think I'm depressed?" I ask him.

"You're just tired, Sweet Pea," he says, patting my head like a dog.

"I'm always tired unless I'm on stage." It's true. Even the idea of going into the studio leaves me exhausted now. And forget real life—I can't so much as boil water these days. Trevor tells me it's like I've forgotten how to do normal stuff, like load the dishwasher or do laundry. I'm just lazy now, I always reply. The road has made me lazy, with tour managers to organize my life, people putting food in front of me. It's like living with a teenager, Trevor says. I want to say something sharp, but can never think of anything, so I end up gathering my dirty laundry from the bedroom floor in a sulk.

On the road, I miss Trevor sometimes so much it hurts, but that longing is tempered by relief at being away from him. We still send each other postcards, still read together in our own little book club. But when I'm home, we drive each other crazy. We fight over chores, the space my stuff takes up. It's become a pattern I can't change.

"You just need a nice long vacation, Sweetie Pie. You've been on the road for years," says Reggie. I wonder if I've been talking again without realizing it.

Between the two bands, it's been one album after another, like babies born too close together, each accompanied by its own, progressively bigger tour. I'd been to Australia with the Coyotes, all over Canada and the U.S. with both. I'd played dive bars, theatres, private gigs, festivals, and stadiums. No more than a few days off, ten days at the most, here and there.

"I'm fucking tired, Reggie. Can you carry me to the plane?"

"No, that would be weird, and they probably wouldn't let us on."

I taste the worst coffee in my life at the Minneapolis airport—watery and a little hinky. Have I become a coffee snob? I chuck it in the garbage after one sip.

The beer selection, however, is very good, so the four of us sit and drink for two hours. When I stand up, I feel unsteady, and wonder why, then try to remember how many drinks I've had.

"I'm going for a chiropractic adjustment," I say. "I'll be back."

I walk with great focus to the airport chiropractor, trying to project an image of sobriety. Will she adjust me if I'm tanked? Is that unethical? If so, how do they treat alcoholics?

The chiropractor is an athletic woman with strong arms and thick, wavy auburn hair. She is very no-nonsense as she asks me where I'm tight, has me fill out a form and sign waivers. I lie on the drop table, hear the metallic clang of the table falling out from under me as she adjusts me. Then she has me sit up and move my head, my arm, as she squeezes various muscles, wringing out the tension. By the end, I feel fantastic.

"Thank you so much." I toddle off to the washroom, then back to the bar, with the rest of the band. We order food to sop up the alcohol, and more alcohol. Austin doesn't look the least bit drunk, but then he has a tolerance like nothing I've ever seen. He could drink my old friends from Saskatchewan, or Edmonton, or anywhere else, right under the table. It's not even his size—Reggie can't match him—it seems like he just inhales it, then exhales it, and keeps going. I can't wrap my head around it.

By the time the plane lands in Calgary, we are very, very drunk. Amelia barfs twice in the airplane bathroom before we land, drawing some looks from other passengers that I feel are a little judgemental. I wish there had been a first-class option so we weren't crammed in so tight.

The bottom line is that Reggie has to half-carry Amelia off the plane. I wonder if they will sleep together tonight. Tara is waiting for us, flashing her canary-yellow engagement ring as she poses for a photo with a fan. When we reach the gate, the attention shifts to Amelia and Reggie, and the cell phones turn to them, their fake digital clicks grating on my nerves.

"Relax," says Austin. "We're all rock and roll, not investment bankers or some shit."

"Fair enough," I say. Tara and I air-kiss, a ritual that started as a joke about being posh.

"Trevor's renting us a car," she says. "I told him to get us something bitchin'."

"Good. Very good," I reply.

Trevor does not rent us a bitchin' car. He rents an ugly van that has a dent in the door. It was the only thing available that could carry us and our luggage, and he had to beg for it, as it was supposed to be pulled from the fleet on account of the dent, he tells us.

"Good job, man," Reggie says, slurring slightly, as he fist-bumps Trevor.

"Are you all smashed?" Trevor asks.

"Nooooo," Reggie, Austin, and I say in unison. Amelia hiccups, then starts laughing.

"Okay, well, I guess I'll drive," Trevor says, sighing.

"Thanks, dear," I say, kissing his cheek.

Trevor navigates Calgary's evening freeway traffic, hurtling us south, toward Millarville. I text Ruby, tell her we're on our way. She texts that she'll see us in the morning. I'm a little disappointed. We haven't had a good talk in ages, but I understand she's tired and probably stressed.

At last, we reach the hilltop bed and breakfast, right on the edge of Millarville. I stare down the hill, trying to see if Brynny and Ruby's light is on. It's dark.

Carol, the bed and breakfast owner, is in bed, as it's after midnight, but she's left the door unlocked. We've rented out the whole place, as we've done in the past for the church fundraisers, so we each head to our usual rooms. I'm a little disappointed that

Carol didn't stay up either, but I don't blame her, as she'll be working by five a.m. Along with running a bed and breakfast, Carol is the choir director for Church of the Shortgrass, so she is busy.

By the time we get to our room and I wash the feeling of airports and airplanes and travel off my skin, I'm just as glad that Carol's in bed and that Ruby didn't want to hang out. I'm so tired I brush my teeth half-heartedly and curl up beside Trevor in bed.

The next day I wake with a start. For several seconds, I'm not sure where I am. Then I remember: Ruby and Brynny's wedding is just a few days away.

I have no sense of what time it is, and Trevor is gone. Damn. I'd promised to start running with him. I reach for my iPhone. Holy hell, it's after lunch. I lurch out of bed, dress quickly, twist my hair into a bun, and search for the others. No one's around.

I could walk down the hill, toward Brynny and Ruby's place. Then I have a sudden urge to call my old friend Jen, who I haven't talked to for months. She's likely working, even though it's Saturday. Family law waits for no one. Screw it, I call her. She picks up on the second ring.

"What's up?"

"Not much. We just haven't talked in a while, and I wanted to hear what you've been up to."

"Morning sickness, that's what I've been up to. I have to say, being pregnant is a pain in the ass."

I hadn't even known Jen was pregnant. I listen to her talk for a long time. She tells me all about her family law practice, which sounds like hell to me, but then Jen always was an adrenalin junkie. She's switched leaping on top of revved-up thoroughbreds and tearing after the chuckwagons for shielding her clients from malicious spouses—although sometimes her client is the one oozing malice.

"What about you? What are you up to?"

"Oh, I'm in Millarville. Ruby and Brynny are getting married in a few days."

"Oh, yeah, Sam mentioned that to Luke. Sam's excited to be in the wedding party. Hey, whatever happened to that guy who was obsessed with Brynny? Sam said something about it to Luke, but I think Luke got it mixed up."

"Rex. He kind of comes and goes. I haven't heard much lately—I think he kind of backed off when they got engaged. Or I hope he did, anyway."

"Did they try getting a peace bond?"

"Yeah, the police told them they didn't have enough evidence for a peace bond."

"That's a load of crap."

"I know, and they know it, but what are you going to do?"

"Well, they can go before a judge and ask for one themselves. Tell Brynny she can call me if she wants. I can connect her with a colleague in Calgary who deals with this kind of stuff."

"Thanks. I better go join the real world."

"Okay. Hey, whatever's going on, I hope you're okay."

"Thank, Jen. I'm just burnt out."

When I get off the phone, I find Amelia outside smoking.

"I thought you'd quit."

"I did, until I heard about Robby."

"Oh, God, what happened to Robby?"

"You haven't heard?" She exhales slowly, as though she's buying time. "He had a heart attack. They don't know if he's going to make it."

—

Owen picks up on the first ring.

"Is Robby going to be okay?"

"I don't know," he says. "They're going to try to do surgery, but they're still trying to stabilize him."

"I can't believe this would happen to him. He's so healthy!"

"I know. It should have been me. The crap I put my body through, I'm surprised I've made it this far. Robby's been careful, but you know, that's because it runs in his family."

"Did his dad die of a heart attack? He never told me the full story."

"Yeah, that's exactly what happened."

"How's Camille doing? Can I do anything?"

"Nothing you can do. Camille's holding up. I'll tell her you called."

—

Over the next few days, we're recruited to do everything from assembling centrepieces and decorating the hall in Millarville to giving the church a spit and polish. It is stunning, with the wall of glass behind the sanctuary framing the mountains. As I dust the pews, I keep stopping to stare at the view.

My iPhone buzzes with a text from Owen. I look over at Amelia.

"Robby's through surgery," I tell her. "It sounds like he's going to be okay."

"Oh, thank God."

My phone buzzes again, a text from Austin saying the same thing. I feel lighter knowing Robby will likely recover.

Ruby, however, looks extremely stressed. With everything going on, I haven't had a chance to talk to her alone, and I don't want to ask in front of everyone else why she looks like hell. Her nails are chewed to the quick. And today, the way the sun is shining through the windows, it looks like her hair is thinning. Can that all be from the stress of wedding planning?

Brynny, on the other hand, seems to thrive amidst the action, delegating and jumping in as needed. They have this way of holding hands, where Brynny just touches the tips of Ruby's fingertips, that seems beautiful. I catch Trevor noticing it, and he smiles at me, brushing a stray piece of hair back from my face.

"Maybe we should get married," he says.

"I don't think I'm that traditional," I say, half-joking, half not.

"I'm serious."

"We'll talk about it later."

I know Trevor's parents have been unhappy about us living together, but I don't want to get married to please them. They don't say anything horrible to me, but we're still not allowed to sleep in the same room if we visit, and I am tired of being treated like a teenager.

For a moment, I imagine trying to plan a wedding with Trevor. No way I'd get married in a Catholic church, and that would surely send Trevor's parents into shock. I have nothing against rank-and-file Catholics, but I can't stomach the atrocities the Church has committed, from the times of the Inquisition and burning witches right on up to today. Residential schools. Priests abusing children, only to be moved to a new community when their superiors find out.

Do I really want to join a family that sees our relationship as illegitimate unless it's confirmed not only in a church, but a church of their choosing?

I have such mixed feelings about religion in general. Even though I'm enmeshed with the Church of the Shortgrass, I feel uneasy calling myself a Christian. I would never have become so involved if Ruby hadn't joined first, drawn by Brynny, and then Sam.

Sam. What a Hail Mary sending him here had been. No one knew if it would work, but here he is, doing well, working construction. Usually sober. He's relapsed a couple of times, but Ruby is always there for him, along with others in the church.

Sam is convinced that God and Ruby have saved his life, and he's probably right. Today he looks fit and tanned as he cleans windows.

The hours pass quickly. Relatives and friends start pouring into Millarville. Uncle Henry tows his "new to them" fifth wheel. Sam directs him as he slowly backs it into Brynny and Ruby's driveway. Linda, Reata, and Jake pile out of the truck, followed by Grandpa Kolchak, who is moving slowly these days but still getting around without even a cane. When people express amazement at how well he's doing at his age, he gets cranky.

"No one talks about how well the dog's getting around," he grumps, nodding toward Brynny's old border collie, Molly.

"Some people don't get that choice at your age, is all," Linda replies.

One of Brynny's uncles from her dad's side starts talking about how they had to take away his mother's licence. He pulls a cooler from the back of his truck as he talks, offering beer and hard lemonade to everyone. I notice Sam says no without hesitation.

Grandpa looks at Linda and Henry. "Don't you even think about pulling that crap with me," he says.

"Dad, no one's talking about taking away your licence. You're no worse a driver than you've ever been." Henry chuckles.

"I'm an excellent driver," Grandpa says.

"Well, you're a little heavy on the gas. And the brakes," Henry replies. This is putting it mildly. Grandpa is like a wartime transport driver trying to evade craters and bombers.

Molly, upon making eye contact with Grandpa, picks up a stick and drops it at his feet. Grandpa picks up the stick and tosses it across the yard, and Molly tears after it. "C'mon dog," he says. "Us old farts gotta stick together. You better watch it, next thing you know they'll be trying to take that stick away from you."

"Actually, I don't really like her playing fetch with sticks. I don't want her to hurt her mouth," Brynny says.

"Sorry, I can't hear you. I'm old and deaf." Grandpa walks off, Molly running circles around him, stick in mouth.

Jake soon finds two other boys around his age, and they detach themselves from the adults, chasing frogs in the creek that edges Brynny and Ruby's yard. There are no teens around, though, so Reata glues herself to me and Amelia, asking us about music.

"Do you sing or play?" Amelia asks.

"I sing a little," Reata says shyly. "Mostly, I just like music."

We enlist her and Amber to help with the centrepieces, which involve a branch of pink flowers submerged in a tall vase with a tea light floating on top. There are hundreds of them to assemble in the new equestrian centre where the dinner is being held. Soon more people join us, a corps of decorators setting up tables with white linen cloths, setting out the centrepieces. and stringing white lights from the arena's railing and the makeshift stage at one end. As we near the finish, Helen directs a few people to grab brooms and sweep the temporary flooring covering the arena's sand.

"How many people are coming?" I ask Ruby.

"I think about a thousand to the ceremony and dinner, more to the dance afterwards."

"Wow."

One morning Trevor and I find ourselves with an unexpected break in the action. I mention this to Carol. "Want to go see John Ware's original homestead?" she asks.

"Yes, yes I do," I reply.

"Just a sec, I want to bring my camera and recorder," says Trevor. He's been looking for another project since finishing his book on Bea.

"You don't mind being in print, do you, Carol?"

"Honey, I've been in print since before you were born," she laughs. I guess Trevor is thinking about another book, or at least a print feature, on the freed slave who came to Alberta in the late nineteenth century on a cattle drive and never left.

Reata texts me as we're heading out the door. *What ya doin?*
Going to see John Ware's homestead.
can I come
Yes, we'll pick you up in one minute.

By the time we reach Brynny's street at the bottom of the hill, Reata is standing at the end of the driveway waiting. I introduce her to Carol as she clambers into the backseat of Carol's baby-blue truck.

"Nice to meet you. Thanks for picking me up," Reata says.

"No problem at all, Reata," says Carol.

Reata's lips are burgundy this morning, the lipstick perfectly applied. She looks gorgeous with her shining auburn hair, porcelain skin, and full lips.

"Where'd you get the lipstick?"

"Ruby—she found a new tube in her coat jacket and gave it to me. She showed me how to put it on with a brush, too."

"Your parents see you with it on?"

"No, Mom slept in, and Dad and Grandpa went for a drive."

"Okay. Well, we won't tell them, obviously, and it will probably wear off by the time you get home."

"It's supposed to last all day. That's what the packaging says."

"Oh, sweetie," Carol laughs from her belly. "It's time you learned about the broken promises of the beauty industry."

Reata laughs through her nose. Her strange nose laugh is so much like my mom's laugh, it's eerie. I stare at her and she stops.

"Is something wrong? Did I do something wrong?" she asks.

"Oh, no, I'm sorry. It's just that you laugh just like my mom."

"I know. Dad told me that, too. He misses his sisters a lot."

"Yeah, we all miss them. I wish you and Jake had gotten a chance to know them."

"Grandpa tells us stories about them sometimes, and about Grandma Kolchak, and all our ancestors. Or the ones he knows about, anyway. He even took us out to the site of the old ranch by Walsh last year."

"Oh, really? I'd like to do that."

"You should take some time off this summer," says Trevor. "You're done touring with the Hug Machine for a while, and I don't think the Coyotes will be touring anytime soon."

"Nancy said the Coyotes are out for at least three months. I'm still worried about Robby. I haven't been able to talk to him yet. Owen has seen him. He said Robby didn't even feel off until he had the heart attack."

Carol clucks, shakes her head. "It's like a lightning strike from the blue," she says. I think of an anvil cloud. "But you know, he may feel much better now that he's had that surgery. Sometimes we don't know what we need until we're in a crisis."

"Amen," says Trevor.

We pull up to a meadow with a boulder commemorating the site of John and Mildred Ware's homestead. The site is framed by pine trees and hills and, in the distance, mountains. I step out of the truck, inhale the cool mountain air, take in the riot of wildflowers. I imagine a little house, corrals in front with hardy ranch horses, a few outbuildings. I can almost see John on a big, soggy bay gelding, Mildred on the porch in a well-made dress.

"What happened to them in the end?" I ask.

"Mildred died quite young of pneumonia—she wasn't even thirty-five. John died not long after when his horse tripped in a badger hole and rolled over him. Mildred's parents took the kids in, raised them in Calgary."

I remember my own wreck with Bucky, the helpless feeling as he tripped in the bush, sending me sailing over his head. Blinding pain, then nothing, then waking to my uncle looming over me. The realization that I was dying as he throttled me. Did John know he was dying, or was it over in an instant?

I touch the boulder, feel the sun warmth stored in the rock. "Do you think they were happy here?"

"Yes, I do," says Carol. "They had good friends here. Good friends around Rosebud, too. People remember them. That love is still there, you know."

"But they would have faced a lot of racism, too. Why is it that some people can be so good, and others so awful?" I ask, still touching the rock. "Or be kind and loving one minute, and just hateful the next?"

"The Lord gave us free will, and we all make our choices, every moment of every day," says Carol. "Some of us choose love, and some go with something else."

"That's our next album title," I say. "*Choose Love.*"

"How can we make more people choose love?" asks Reata, shyly.

"We can't, sweetie. We can only choose it for ourselves," says Carol. "That's why I go to your cousin's church. Brynny is as flawed as the rest of us, but she understands that choice, right down to her core. And she not only preaches it, she lives it, no matter the consequences."

I close my eyes for a moment, feel the earth solid under my feet, the breeze pulling at my hair, brushing through the late-spring grasses and flowers. "Thanks for bringing us here, Carol."

We're just turning into Millarville when Reata drops a bomb. "Can I tell you about something?"

"Yes, of course," Carol says. "Tell away."

"Okay, well, the last couple of nights, really late at night, like three a.m., I've been waking up. And when I wake up, I can hear a diesel idling at the end of Brynny and Ruby's driveway. It's always a black three-quarter ton. This morning I went downstairs and opened the door because I was going to see who it was, but Molly got out and ran down the driveway, barking her head off, and he drove away. I had to go chasing after Molly in my bare feet. She didn't come back until he'd turned onto the highway by the general store."

"Sounds like Rex's truck," says Carol.

"Did you tell Brynny or Ruby?" Trevor asks.

"Yeah, I told Ruby this morning. She thanked me and said she'd tell Brynny. Amber was there, and she was freaked. She started talking about some psychology stuff that I didn't really get. She was asking if Rex thinks Brynny is sending him messages through her sermons or YouTube or Facebook or anything."

"Does he?" asks Trevor.

"Ruby said she didn't know. She said she doesn't want to crawl inside his head because it's likely full of dark corners and giant spider webs. So then Amber went on Facebook and started looking on Brynny's page and the church's page, and Rex is, like, commenting all the time, having a conversation with her. Like, she wrote about knocking down a wasp nest with a hockey stick, and he wrote 'Sometimes we have to do scary things so we can feel young again.' What does that even mean?"

"Why can't someone get a restraining order?" Trevor asks.

"We've talked at the board level about trying to get a peace bond," says Carol. "The local sergeant has told us that there's not enough evidence for a peace bond."

"That's a load of crap," I say. "I have a friend who's a lawyer in Regina. She's willing to connect you with a good lawyer in this province. You can also just go to a judge for one, she says."

"Well, I happen to agree with you," says Carol, stopping at the end of Brynny's driveway and putting the truck into park. "And so does another of our members, who is a retired Mountie. But Brynny and the rest of the board decided they'd pray on it instead."

"Oh, no," says Trevor.

"They feel that the Lord will protect them, or reveal a path to healing for Rex," Carol says.

"I'm sorry, but if you believe in free will, which is a central tenet of Christianity, you cannot count on the Lord to protect you from delusional psychos," says Trevor.

"Amen," I add.

"I agree, more should be done, but Brynny doesn't want to draw attention to the situation, and neither does Ruby. They are hoping that Rex will eventually move on."

"You know, I think this is the only situation where I've heard of Brynny not wanting to draw attention to something," I say. "She's said the same thing to me, so I believe you, but it seems very out of character for her."

"Brynny needs to be loved by everyone, you know," says Carol. "When the church split after she and Ruby came out, it was very difficult for her. And although we think of Rex as a 'delusional psycho,' he is a prominent member of the community. A *wealthy* prominent member of the community, who has donated hundreds of thousands to the church. He used to tithe a couple of hundred bucks every Sunday, on top of everything else."

"He doesn't still go to the services, does he?" Trevor asks.

"Not lately, not since one of the board members had a quiet word with him. But he sits in the parking lot—sometimes I can hear his diesel idling from inside the church."

"Fuck's sake," I say, my anger growing. "Sorry for the language, Carol, but this is sick."

Carol nods.

"Amber said that Brynny likes the attention," says Reata. "She called her borderline narcissistic. That made Ruby cry. So then their mom, Beth, came in, and I had to tell her what happened, and by then Amber and Ruby were almost ready to tear each other's hair out."

"Well, that's not unusual for them. They're a very expressive family," I say.

"But Beth didn't know anything about any of it, and she was so upset, she started crying, and they were all crying, so I sat on the deck, and that's when I texted you."

"Where was Brynny in all of this?"

"She was jogging. She says she writes her sermons in her head while she's jogging, then she comes home and writes them down on paper. So that's what happened this morning," Reata concludes.

It's a lot for a young teenager to process, I think. "What do you think of the whole thing, Reata?"

"I think everyone should stop arguing about what Rex is thinking or feeling. They should tell him to take a hike, or they'll take him for a walk in the back forty. That's what Grandpa would say to do."

"That's a very clear-eyed assessment," says Trevor.

"Very Old Testament," says Carol.

—

We're almost late to the wedding ceremony Saturday morning on account of Amelia's inability to get out of bed on time, combined with her insistence that she must blow out her hair and apply her elaborate eye makeup.

Finally, Trevor has had enough. "We're leaving now. If you're not outside when I pull out of the driveway, you're hitchhiking."

"Just give me a few minutes!"

Tara rolls her eyes. "Stop being a princess and move your ass," she says.

The rest of us load the gear into the rental van and pile in. Amelia comes strolling out of Carol's just as Trevor is putting the van into gear. She seems to walk slowly on purpose, so Trevor takes his foot off the brake and lets the van roll toward the street. Amelia keeps her pace until he finishes backing up and is facing away. Then, perhaps realizing that he's not bluffing, she dashes for the door.

"You don't have to be a dick about it," she says to him.

"You know what, Amelia? I don't have to put up with your shit just because you think you're some sort of celebrity."

"Are you going to let him talk to me that way?" she asks me.

"Jesus Christ, Amelia, I'm not the boss of him. Besides, I'm with him on this one. I don't want to be late."

Amelia glances around the van for support, but Austin and Reggie avoid her gaze and Tara just shakes her head no. It's a quiet ride to the church.

I think of my conversation with Owen, months and months ago, when he suggested firing Amelia and hiring Kayla. I scroll through the contacts on my phone, look at Kayla's name and number. I could do it any time, I think. But today is not the day.

—

We pull up to the church with about five minutes to spare. A valet takes the keys from Trevor and sets out to park our vehicle by the equestrian centre. Pots of pink-and-white petunias line the walkway to the church and the equestrian centre, which is about a hundred yards from the church parking lot, and congregate at the church's entrance and on the grounds near the picnic benches. Their sweet scent fills the air.

Inside the church, we wait for about fifteen minutes before someone signals the pianist, who begins the processional. Rather than "Here Comes the Bride" she plays "Can't Help Falling in Love."

Ruby is the first down the aisle, flanked by Beth and Red. She wears a dusty pink tea-length dress, with a tulle lace neckline and crystal dragonfly hair pins. Beth, also in a sleeveless tea-length dress, but blue, is crying. Red beams at people on both sides of the aisle. Ruby looks beautiful and happy, and I wonder if I've been worrying needlessly about her. I catch her eye as she passes us.

Flanking her at the altar are the wedding party, including Amber and Sam. In the centre stands the minister, a woman from a United Church in the city.

After a moment, Brynny and her parents enter. Brynny is wearing a long, flowing chiffon gown, pure white, with long lace sleeves and a fitted bodice. Her shining blond hair is pulled back into a loose fishtail braid with several smaller, tighter braids woven into the main braid in a way that I can't quite comprehend. Helen's hair is also a tapestry of braids. They both look stunning, like Viking goddesses.

The minister preaches about God's love for all of us. The tone of her sermon reminds me of Brynny, but her energy is softer than Brynny's. As she reads from Corinthians, I close my eyes and breathe slowly, feeling happy to be here holding Trevor's warm, strong hand.

"Love is patient. Love is kind. It does not envy. It does not boast. It is not proud. It is not rude. It is not self-seeking. It is not easily angered. It keeps no record of wrongs. Love does not delight in evil but rejoices with the truth. It always protects, always trusts, always hopes, always perseveres. Love never fails."

Then she turns to Brynny. "Brynny, do you take Ruby to be your lawfully wedded wife? Do you promise to love and respect her, to honour her always, whatever you may face in life?"

"I do," says Brynny, her face solemn.

The minister asks Ruby the same questions, and she says, "I do," with a big grin on her face.

Then they exchange vows. Ruby goes first. "I promise I will always stand beside you, so that we may face life's greatest challenges together. I promise to bring you joy and music and laughter, and to dry the tears nobody else sees. I promise to love you to the ends of the earth, and beyond."

Someone is sniffling behind me.

Brynny goes next. "I never truly understood what it was like to be in love until I met you. I am grateful that God saw fit to bring us together, and I am grateful that He gave you the patience and kindness to wait for me. You are the one great love in my life. I vow to put you first, to be there for you when you need me. I vow to be there to share your joy and sorrow, your exhilaration and despair. I vow to love you always."

I lean into Trevor and wonder what our wedding would be like, if we were to get married and didn't have to worry about pleasing other people. It seems like an impossible dream.

After the ceremony, we walk over to the indoor arena to set up our instruments and check out the stage. Reggie starts setting up his own cymbals, snare, and bass drum pedals with the rented kit. Someone else has already set up the speakers, amps, and mixers, but they haven't taped down the cords from the guitars to the amps, a definite tripping hazard. Austin is digging through his gear bag for gaff tape when Ruby, Brynny, and the photographer appear.

"They want some shots of me singing," Ruby says.

"Okay, just don't trip on the cords. They're not taped down by the amps," I say.

"Oh, like this," Ruby says, walking on stage, then miming a clumsy cartoon character skipping right over the loose cords in her heels.

"Ruby—" Brynny starts to warn her, but sure enough, Ruby trips over a cord and nearly falls flat on her face, saved only by Austin's quick hands on her shoulders.

"Queen of Near Misses," Ruby says with a shrug.

"Stand in one spot until Austin's taped the cords," I say.

Ray, the sound guy, appears so we plug in. Ray adjusts the levels, and then we play for the sound check while the photographer aims her lens at a crooning Ruby. A few people start to trickle in, and soon we have a little audience standing at the stage's edge. Ray gives us the thumbs up, but we keep playing until the photographer stops shooting and glances at the door. A guy in a black cowboy hat is standing there. When we finish our last song, he says, "The horse is ready," and everyone starts to disperse.

Outside Sam is holding a horse the colour of a new penny, with black points on its feet and a black mane and tail. The horse is tacked up with a black bridle and a black leather side saddle. He hands the reins to Brynny, who holds them in one hand and wraps her other arm around Ruby's waist. They kiss in front of the copper bay horse, mountains in the background, while the photographer snaps away from different angles. Then Sam gives Brynny a leg up and she settles herself into the side saddle, looking elegant and wild at the same time with her dress and hair and the beautiful horse. Ruby stands by the horse's shoulder, and Sam shows her how to hold the reins. Ruby and Brynny gaze at each other, then at the camera.

The photos make their lives look like a fantasy. Brynny rides, of course, but not in a clean flowing white dress with silver jewelry. And Ruby sings, but by the end of the night she's a pool of sweat just like the rest of us. Not that I'm any different—my publicity photos gild me with a glamour that's far from real.

My phone rings just then. It's Robby. I step away from the crowd to take the call.

"Hello?"

"Darby, this is Camille. Robby wants to talk to you, but he can't talk long."

"Thank you, Camille. I've been thinking about all of you. I hope you're okay."

"I'm holding in there. I'm going to pass the phone to Robby now."

There's a pause. Then a very quiet hello.

"Robby? How are you feeling?"

"I've been better," he chuckles. His voice is barely a croak.

"We've all been thinking about you, Robby. We're all worried."

"Don't worry about me. Listen, Darby. I'm taking time away from touring when I'm better. I want to spend time with Camille and the kids. I don't know what I've got left."

"Oh. How much time?"

"I don't know yet. But I wanted to tell you. I'll be okay. We'll talk more when you're back."

"Okay, Robby. Hey, Robby, maybe this sounds weird, but I want you to know, I really care about you. I love you like family."

"I know. I love you, too, Kid."

Robby passes the phone back to Camille then. We chat briefly. Camille sounds exhausted, her tone flat, until the end of the conversation. Then, voice shaking, she says, "We're lucky he's still here. I almost lost him ... I'm sorry, I need to go."

"It's okay. Take care, Camille. I'll see you when I get back."

"Enjoy the wedding, Darby."

I take Camille's advice. We enjoy the wedding, Reggie most of all. He loves weddings. He rocks the drums through our set with an energy that surpasses even our best shows. Ruby has arranged for other musicians to take over after we play a set, so we can mingle and enjoy the reception. When the church's choir singers and musicians play their sets, mainly country, Reggie takes to the dance floor, two-stepping with the brides, their mothers, the kids. One pretty young woman, with huge brown eyes and puffy lips, keeps coming back to him. I watch Amelia to see if she looks jealous. She studiously ignores the woman and focusses on Brynny's handsome ex, Cody.

I talk Trevor into learning how to two-step. Despite his reluctance, he picks it up quickly, and soon he's spinning me on the dance floor, almost launching me into Brynny and Ruby.

"Hey, watch it, buddy," Ruby says, laughing, before Brynny whirls her away.

The first church band announces their set is over, and another group takes their place. The new band members all wear black cowboy hats and black shirts with red roses. They start playing a butterfly. Trevor looks mystified.

"C'mon," I say, grabbing his arm. Reata takes his other arm, and the three of us promenade until the music pauses, then switches to a fast pace.

"Spin me," Reata orders Trevor, hooking her arm into his. He obeys, pivoting and spinning her until she lets go, laughing wildly, and I grab his other arm. Out of the corner of my eye, I can see Austin spinning Ruby violently. She spirals like a top, nearly falling into a table edging the dance floor. Tara looks briefly concerned, then latches onto Austin's other arm.

"This is weird," Trevor says when the song slows and we resume the promenade.

"It's the best thing ever," Reata corrects him. The music picks up again and we nearly collide with Amber, sent into orbit by Sam. Sam and Amber have been dancing together all night, I realize.

It's during this second set of spins that there's a commotion by the door. As I whirl away from Trevor, I catch glimpses of Ruby's pink dress moving rapidly and someone talking to Austin. I stop, look, try to make sense of what I'm seeing. Then I see him and I know.

"Rex is over there," I say to Trevor. Trevor wordlessly grabs both me and Reata by our wrists and pulls us away from the scene.

"No, wait, where's Brynny?" I ask. Trevor doesn't respond, just keeps pulling. I twist my wrist quickly, breaking his hold, and walk toward the scene. I glance over my shoulder, and he is looking at me, fear in his eyes.

"Watch Reata," I mouth. He shepherds Reata away from the chaos.

Ahead of me, a horrible drama is playing out. Tara steps between Rex and Ruby. Ruby looks terrified. I can't make out what Tara is saying, but she is jabbing her pointer fingers at Rex, her eyes narrow and hard. Rex is shouting, and I can't understand what he's saying, either—the sound is muffled, as though we're all under water—but spit is flying from his mouth. He is like a bull flinging snot and slobber right before a fight.

Austin steps between Tara and Rex, blocking Tara from harm. Rex is a little taller than Austin, and he looks so angry, I'm suddenly afraid for Austin. Rex tries to push past Austin to get at Ruby, who is cowering beside Tara. But Austin doesn't budge. Austin pushes Rex toward the door. Rex stumbles backward, nearly falling on the artificial dance floor. He regains his balance and looks like he's about to hit Austin, but Reggie and Sam are both there now, too.

Rex lunges toward Austin, fist cocked, but Reggie steps in between them, takes the punch.

Bad move, Rex. Hitting Reggie is like slapping an elephant with a fly swatter.

Reggie grabs Rex by the back of his shirt collar and his belt, carries him toward the door, and chucks him outside as easily as a ranch hand tosses a square bale. Then he follows Rex outside, Austin and Sam right behind him, along with several other men. Brynny's ex, Cody is among the mob. I don't want to see what they're going to do next, so I turn to Ruby and Tara.

"Oh, God," says Ruby. She is pale and shaking.

"That's my man," says Tara. "He doesn't put up with that shit."

"Where's Brynny?" I ask. And then I see her swooping toward us from the far side of the arena. "Are you okay?" she asks Ruby but doesn't even give Ruby time to answer before she's sailing for the door. "I don't want them sending Rex to the hospital," she calls over her shoulder.

"What the actual fuck?" says Tara.

Ruby breaks down in my arms. "She's so fucking concerned about her church's image. I can't take this anymore."

"Let's take her up to the concession before we get swarmed," I say to Tara, nodding at the enclosed kitchen and seating area that overlooks the arena.

We sit up there with the lights off, looking down on the scene below. Slowly, the men start to filter in from the parking lot. Brynny is the last to re-enter the arena, with Cody and Sam. We watch her look around.

"She's so fucking self-centred sometimes, always worried about what people will think," says Ruby.

"What did Rex say to you?" I ask.

Ruby starts sobbing again.

"He said he was going to shoot Ruby, for 'ruining' Brynny," says Tara. "Then he ..." Tara stops.

Ruby spews out the rest, shaking with anger and fear. "He called me the whore of Babylon and started quoting Revelations at us. He was spitting on us as he talked. I want to kill him. I want to skin him alive. He's ruining my life. I can't go anywhere without him breathing down my neck. If I go for a walk, he follows me in his truck. When I come out of church, there he is, in his fucking shitty diesel, waiting. My world is getting smaller and smaller. I can't even be at peace in the home I share with Brynny, with him sitting at the end of the driveway at all hours of the night. He texts Brynny all the time, even though she keeps blocking his number, he finds a way. He follows her, too. She says she'll find a way to make him stop, but the truth is she feeds off his obsession. It's killing me. I feel like I'm going crazy, especially because it doesn't bother her that much. But then, he doesn't hate her. He worships her. And hates me. I think I'm going crazy. Am I crazy?"

"I'm so sorry, Ruby," I say, rubbing her back as she cries on my shoulder.

"That is fucked," says Tara. "Trust me, you're not the crazy one in this scenario."

The three of us sit there a long time before we hear steps on the stairs leading up to the kitchen. The door opens and Brynny is there. She flicks on the lights. "Why are you hiding out here?"

Tara rolls her eyes. None of us say a word.

Brynny looks at all of us. "Can someone please say something?"

"You're supposed to love me," Ruby says, standing. "But you're willing to throw me to the wolves instead of doing anything that might hurt your reputation."

"That's not true. I do love you."

"Then why weren't you up here with me?"

"I didn't want anything bad to happen to Rex. It would have been bad for us."

"Fuck Rex! He wants to kill me! He just told me I was a whore. And then said he was going to shoot me—at my own wedding reception!"

Beth and Amber have joined us now, wrapping their arms around Ruby, sheltering her. Helen stands beside her daughter, looks at her, heaves a big sigh.

"My girl, you need to decide what you stand for," she says. "Do you care about those you love or what people you barely know think? It's time to choose."

Brynny breaks down in her mother's arms. Helen stands there stroking her hair. On the other side of the room, Ruby is crying, too, encircled by Beth and Amber. Tara and I stand in the middle. I'm gripping her arm, I realize. Slowly, I let go. I've left finger marks behind.

Tara rubs the spot. "That's going to leave a bruise."

—

Sure enough, the next morning, Tara has finger-shaped bruises on her left arm. "I didn't think I was that strong," I say. "Sorry."

"It's okay. It makes me look like a bad ass," she says, flexing.

"You are a bad ass," I say.

"Something smells good," says Tara. "Like cinnamon."

"Let's go see what Carol is making us."

As we walk into the kitchen, Carol is pulling a tray of cinnamon buns from the oven. "Those smell amazing," Tara says.

"Good. You can help me make breakfast. Anyone else up yet?"

"No," I say. "Well, Trevor is, but he went for a run. I'm supposed to be running with him, but here I am."

For the next hour, Tara and I help Carol put together an amazing spread for breakfast. Waffles, bacon and eggs, home-made hashbrowns, roasted Roma tomatoes, fresh fruit, yogurt, plus the cinnamon buns. It's nice to work with other women putting together a meal. The three of us gossip and laugh, Carol directing us a little but not a lot. Tara and I know our business.

We're laying out the food, piping hot, as everyone else starts to sit at the table. Trevor has the pink, freshly scrubbed look of someone who's had fresh air and exercise. Amelia and Reggie look hungover, Austin yawning and sleepy.

"You think Rex called the cops?" Amelia asks the table.

"On who?" Reggie sounds genuinely puzzled.

"On you and Austin for tossing him around," says Amelia. "Who else?"

"He's lucky no one put the boots to him," says Austin. "Well, except Sam. He did get one kick in, but I pulled him back. I'd love to teach that guy a lesson."

"God, you men," I say. "You think beating him up will change anything? He's probably just stewing at home now, getting madder and madder."

"He should be afraid," says Tara.

Trevor, I notice, is taking notes through the whole exchange. He notices me looking and slips a napkin over his notepad. Then he asks, "How do women expect good men, like Reggie and Austin, to react when some sick asshole is threatening them?"

Carol gives Trevor a look. "Sorry for the language," he says.

There are about two beats of silence; then everyone erupts simultaneously, talking over each other, even yelling their opinions.

"That's enough," cries Carol, standing up. "I don't want this kind of talk at my table. Now quiet down while I say grace."

We all stop, close our eyes as Carol gives thanks for the bountiful food and good company.

Later, while Trevor helps Carol with the clean-up, the rest of us call Nancy, putting her on speakerphone as we figure out what we're going to do since the Urban Coyotes are out of commission for a while.

"I can get you more dates this summer," Nancy says. "You only have a couple of festivals booked, and you're in demand."

"Who wants to book us?" Amelia asks.

"Many of the venues that had booked the Coyotes, plus a few others," says Nancy. She starts listing venues all over the U.S. and Canada. I close my eyes, suddenly feeling exhausted. The thought of playing the few gigs we still have, never mind booking more, makes my whole body feel heavy.

"I can't do it," I say. "I need a break."

Everyone else is silent for a moment.

"I'm sorry," I say, feeling awkward. "But I can't do any more than we've already booked. I'm not even going to go back to Toronto tomorrow."

"Where are you going? Are you staying here?" Amelia asks.

I think for a minute. "No, I'm going to visit my family. In Maple Creek."

NINETEEN

A HORSE'S RUN is considered by most a four-beat gait, with all four feet hitting the ground separately. But there is a fifth beat, a quiet pause, when no feet touch the ground. The horse is, briefly, airborne.

Some compare riding a galloping horse to flying, but it's more than that. The other beats, when the horse is pushing against the ground, connecting to the earth, are as thrilling as the moment of suspension. It's the wind in your eyes and nose and mouth as you laugh and whoop. It's the feeling of being balanced on top of a large, athletic animal that is hurling itself over the land with little consideration for rocks or badger holes or anything else that might slow its wild flight.

The horse and I race after my cousin Reata and her sorrel mare, Gypsy, over the hills west of the ranch yard. Gypsy is a thoroughbred and very fit, given that Reata rides the hair off her, as her mom says. The distance between us is growing. I squeeze my calves and loosen my reins slightly, and Foxtrot, a small but hot-blooded quarter horse, lengthens her stride, trying mightily to close the distance. I pray that I will stay in the saddle and Foxtrot will stay upright. I try to forget about that ride years ago, the last time I worked cattle. How my own sorrel gelding tripped over deadfall mid-flight and sent me to the forest floor. How I woke up to my uncle hovering above me.

Then I forget everything except the rhythm of the run, the sound of Foxtrot's breath and hooves pounding the earth, the sight of her ears pinned flat to her head.

Finally, as we crest a hill, Reata sits up and slows Gypsy. I try to do the same, but Foxtrot wants to keep running, and I've almost passed them before she slows down. We trot, then walk, letting the horses air up.

"I wish I could do this all day, every day," Reata says. "I don't want to go to school. I don't want to help Dad with fencing, or wash dishes, or anything else. I just want to ride a hundred miles every day, until I'm in Argentina or something, and then turn around and ride back."

"That sounds great. Or terrible. I'm not sure."

Every afternoon the first week was the same. At three thirty Reata would leave school, walk across the street, and knock on the verandah door of Grandpa Swank's red-brick house. Grandpa and I would be reading our respective books. We would look up as she poked her head in the door and greeted Grandpa. I grabbed my coat and purse, hopped into the old pickup Uncle Henry lent me for the summer, and drove to the ranch. We saddled up the horses, usually Gypsy and Foxtrot, and rode.

Now that school is out for the summer, we've switched to mornings. As the weeks wear on, I get braver and occasionally ride a green-broke horse, something younger but strong enough to keep up with Reata and Gypsy. Then we ride the hair off them.

Sometimes Aunt Linda asks if I want to go with her to Medicine Hat or Swift Current, but I don't. I don't want to go anywhere. The only time I leave the area is for the few festival gigs Nancy had booked for The Hug Machine before Robby's heart attack. I play those shows like Reata rides her horses—full out, dancing and sometimes howling like a coyote and throwing myself into every song. The band and the audience race right along with me. We're all exhilarated and tired and soaked in sweat by the end.

"Are you on something?" Amelia asks me after the first show. "You're like the Energizer Bunny or some shit."

"I've been riding a lot," I say. "That's all."

"Well, you need to bottle that up and give me some," she says. "The only time I feel good these days is when we're playing, and we're not playing much."

I want to say *Wherever you go, there you are*, but there's no point in causing drama with Amelia. Even the little time I spend with her offstage is hard. I never realized how carefully I watched my words around her until I retreated to Maple Creek. I even control my facial expressions, body language.

After a Calgary Stampede show in July, for the entire four-hour drive back to Maple Creek I think about all the shit Amelia has pulled. When I get back to Grandpa Kolchak's, I call Nancy.

"I think maybe it's time to replace Amelia. How hard will it be to get rid of her?"

"When would you want to do it?"

"I think after the summer."

"I'll have to check the contract. Let me get back to you. Any ideas on who you'd want to step in?"

"Yeah. Kayla Swann."

"Very good. Keep this under your hat until we figure out how we're going to handle it."

I feel like I've been carrying a backpack full of bricks for a long time. After I talk with Nancy, it's like I've unpacked a few bricks. But they're soon replaced by worry over Ruby. Ruby says things are okay, that Brynny has finally got a peace bond against Rex, but there's an edge of worry in her voice.

"Do you want to come here for a visit? There's a winery up the road from Henry and Linda's."

"No, I can't. Since we got back from our honeymoon, it's felt like we're way behind. But it was worth it." She launches into a description of Iceland: moss and rocks, lamb, fermented shark, big fishing vessels made small by the vast ocean. Beautiful little horses that she knows I'd love.

"I wish we could have stayed," she says, a note of sadness in her voice. Then, with a false cheeriness. "I have some lava jewelry for you. You should come here for a visit."

"Okay. I will, soon."

—

I know that I'll have to leave Maple Creek eventually, so I develop a routine to make the most of my time here. After riding with Reata, if it's empty, I go to the old Jasper School, where my whole family went to elementary school before it closed in the eighties. Now it's a museum and occasional music venue. Aunt Linda, who volunteers there, hooks me up with a key and permission to use it. There's one room with a piano that's in tune and a tin ceiling. Singing there sounds something like singing in a cathedral—or what I imagine it would be like to sing in a cathedral. A prairie cathedral, I think, one night early in the summer, as I sing an a cappella version of "Cease Fire", our title song from the second album.

> *Bury your dead*
> *Let them rest in peace*
> *Put down your guns*
> *Let the fighting cease*
> *The war is over.*

Tonight is the first time I've actually felt, deep in my bones, that those words are true. I feel at peace in this town on the northern edge of the Cypress Hills. Is it something about this place, or is it just that I'm so tired?

I go through the love letters Trevor has sent me over the years, pull out pieces for lyrics, build on them. Words like *I miss your breath on my neck at night. I miss your cold feet tucked against me.* Sometimes I call Trevor and sing his lyrics back to him in the school.

"Maybe you should move out here," I say one night, half-joking. "You could buy the local paper, make a go of it."

"I don't know if any local paper can make a go of it," he says. He tells me he thinks he's going to be laid off. "Things are getting worse here. The new publisher wants to bring in her own people. I'm grinding my teeth at night."

"What are you going to do?"

"I don't know. I'm so tired of the stress. But I don't know what I'd do without the routine of the job."

"Whatever happens, we'll figure it out," I say.

But it's a half-truth. We would be fine financially for a while if he lost his job. But I can't imagine him without his routine either. It holds him together, I think, in a way I can't. Without it, I imagine him fretting around our small house, moving things constantly. Or running, running, running. Or picking at me, asking me to conform to his way of placing the coffee mugs in the cupboard, or hang my jeans differently, his eyes pinched as he explains why his system is superior. We've been through his compulsive spells before, but nothing's really been resolved. It's been more like an armistice than anything. And if it happens again, I realize, I won't pick up arms again. I'll simply walk away.

By mid-July, I have enough material for a solo album, and it's good. Really good. The best I've done so far, I think. I start thinking about whether I can actually record the album in the Jasper School. I start to think about touring again. Maybe we can organize the tour differently this time, so I don't feel so burnt out. And it will be easier without Amelia, I think.

Or I could launch my solo career, without the Hug Machine. Maybe have Reggie and Austin play on some songs, as guests, but work with a whole bunch more musicians. Kayla and her friends, and Owen, too, and people I've met touring.

Another brick falls from my backpack, and I know I'm ready for a solo career.

One weeknight I finish late, well after midnight. There's no traffic, no pedestrians on the street, just the sound of the wind rustling the trees. My life is so different from a few weeks ago. I'm not waking up in a different bed every night, constantly checking my phone to see if I'm where I'm supposed to be. I hum as I walk back to Grandpa Kolchak's, a swooping, trilling melody, my best impression of a sparrow.

Grandpa's house is dark. I remove my shoes in the verandah, tiptoe across the squeaky floorboards and up the noisy stairs, trying not to wake him up. I shouldn't have worried—as I step lightly past his room, I hear him sawing logs.

When I get upstairs, I look at my phone and realize I have a missed call from Ruby. I try to phone her back, but there's no answer. She must be asleep.

Before closing my eyes, I open *East of Eden*. Trevor and I are both re-reading it right now for our personal book club. I've reached the scene where Samuel is helping Kate deliver her twins and she bites his hand.

Falling in love with someone like Kate is like a slow-motion accident. I wonder if everyone around Bea felt like that with Will, if they could see the disaster coming. I wonder if there's another tragedy waiting for me. A semi somewhere down the highway with my name on it.

The Cypress Hills are not the Salinas Valley, but I love the sweep and the beauty of both landscapes, and the extremes. But the book is sadder than I remember, or maybe I'm just feeling sad because I've been so tired and Robby's still recovering. I think about the secrets people hold in this book I'm reading, and in my own life. My Dad hiding Uncle Will's abuse, even the murder. Helen, Bea, and May keeping Kenneth's abuse a secret for years. It will all be coming out when Trevor's book is published this fall. He's titled it after the song I wrote for Bea, years ago. *All That's Left: The Brilliant Life and Tragic Death of Bea Fletcher.* Even though I've seen Bea's story in Jason and Char's film, and even though I've written songs about her, the book seems surreal sometimes. And other times, raw grief threatens to overwhelm me all over again.

If Trevor and I break up any time soon, it will be horrible for him to promote the book. I feel guilty for even thinking about breaking up with him, although the thought of weathering another compulsive period leaves me bone weary and heavy. But maybe promoting his book will keep him occupied.

Still, if not, I know what I'll have to do. I feel lighter knowing it.

Eventually I let sleep take me. My dreams are troubled, filled with sleet and the blare of a semi's horn and then a train whistle, and I am running down the tracks, fast as I can, but it's not fast enough.

The dream morphs into the same one that haunted me after my aunt's death. My mother's black mare, Magic, is racing down the tracks, toward the train, just like in the Alex Colville painting. The sky is bruised purple, and fields of canola and flax glow yellow and blue. I scream and scream, but Magic strides to her doom.

I wake with a tumbling sensation, find myself sitting bolt upright. My cell phone is ringing. I glance at the alarm clock beside my bed. Four o'clock.

"Hello? Ruby? Slow down, I can't understand you."

"It's Rex. He ..." More sobbing.

Shit. I thought they'd finally slapped a peace bond on that motherfucker. "Ruby? Just take a deep breath."

"He shot Molly," Ruby wails.

"What?" I think of the sweet border collie playing fetch with Grandpa Kolchak before the wedding.

"He shot her ..." The story comes out in a gush. Rex hadn't been around, and they thought perhaps the peace bond had worked.

Then, this week, he started parking on the street at the top of their driveway again. Brynny and Ruby had a big fight about it. Brynny didn't want to report it to the cops—against all logic, she thought he might quit if they ignored it. Ruby had had enough, told her if she didn't do something about it, they were done. So Brynny was staying with her parents in Calgary and Ruby was home alone with Molly. Sam and Amber had offered to stay with her, but Ruby had wanted to be alone.

Something woke Ruby at three thirty. At first she thought it was Rex's diesel rumbling at the edge of the driveway, but as the sleep cleared from her head, she realized it was Molly growling and whining, wanting out. Hearing nothing else, she trudged downstairs and opened the door for the little collie. Molly tore up the driveway, barking furiously. Ruby stared after her, trying to make out what she was after, but the streetlight was out, and it was a new moon. Then, there was a shot, a yelp, the sound of a truck door slamming and an engine starting, and then the rumble of a diesel driving away.

Ruby ran up the driveway. Molly was crumpled on the ground, blood flowing from a shot to her gut. Ruby held the whimpering dog, bawling in her fur until Molly died.

"Holy fuck. Have you called the cops?"

"No."

"Call 911!"

"Can you come here, please? I don't want to stay here but I'm afraid to leave."

"Yes, but you need to call the cops. Do you promise me?"

"Yes."

I scribble a brief note for Grandpa, get dressed, and pack a toothbrush and a change of clothes before hopping in the truck for the four-hour drive to Millarville. I want to drive as fast as the truck will go, but the tires are worn, so I try to keep it to 120. I wish the cruise control worked.

I drive through the dawn. I know that I am steering the truck, controlling its speed, but I have the feeling that the highway is pulling us west, past the little town of Walsh, where some of my ancestors once ranched; through Medicine Hat; on through miles of wide-open prairie, dotted by a few little towns, and then the larger centre of Brooks. I wonder if this is what it feels like to be at sea, with the horizon far off, at the mercy of the currents. Slowly, the mountains come into view and the wild prairie gives way to suburbs and commuter communities, and I skirt the southern edge of Calgary until I arrive at Millarville.

As I turn onto Brynny and Ruby's street, I pass a police cruiser with a Mountie in it, turning back onto the highway. There's another parked in the driveway, with two RCMP just leaving when I arrive. One, a tall woman, waves me over, asks me who I am, how I know Brynny and Ruby, writing my name and phone number in her notepad. I tell her everything I know about Rex from the beginning. I tell her about Rex crashing the wedding early this year, about the death threat. She asks a lot of questions about that, and I wonder if Ruby or Brynny reported the threat, then I think they probably didn't because they didn't want to get anyone in trouble for roughing up Rex. I give the cop Tara and Austin's numbers to corroborate my story.

Then I tell her about the disconnected look in his eyes, as though he doesn't really see you, but is looking past you. And the strange excitement on his face and leering smile he directs at all pretty young women and girls. She takes a lot of notes, thanks me when we finish, and I walk into the house.

Ruby is crying and packing when I walk in. Brynny is talking, talking, talking.

"We can't let him get the better of us," she says. "I'm not going to let him stop me from delivering my sermon."

"You've always put the church before me! For years, I waited, because you were afraid of what your parishioners would think of us. Then I got to live with the fact that nearly half of them left because they didn't like what I was. And then I put up with Rex because you didn't dare criticize one of your biggest funders, a 'well-respected member of the community.' Well, I'm scared and I'm exhausted and I am not staying here! Darby's come to take me to Maple Creek."

"Brynny?" They both turn, surprised to see me. "You're not really going to stand up there today, are you? I mean, the deranged fucker just shot your dog."

"Darby." Brynny hugs me, then steps back. "I won't let him win. Besides, what's the worst he could do?"

"Well, he could shoot you. Like the dog. I'm serious."

"He won't shoot me. I don't know why he shot Molly, but he wouldn't do that to a person."

I feel sick. I take a deep breath, trying to stay calm, trying to summon my most persuasive self.

"You ever hear the saying *When people show you who they are, believe them?* You should believe him."

Brynny turns back to Ruby. "Don't go," she pleads. "We can figure this out."

"I love you, Brynny, but I don't want to wait for Rex to kill me." But Ruby's anger is already giving way to acquiescence.

"I'll just be outside," I say. My own anger is growing, and I don't want to say something I'll regret.

Poor Molly is wrapped in an old sheet on the lawn, awaiting burial. With the shroud and the cops, it's too much like that day we found Aunt Bea's body floating in Brightsand Lake. I remember Luke holding me as I retched and sobbed.

I want to call Luke now, but I haven't talked to him in a long time, and after everything I'd put him through in years past, with my cheating ways, I'm reluctant to drag him into this mess. Plus, it's probably not fair to Trevor. And Luke's wife, Meaghan, would be upset if she found out. Meaghan's been nice enough to me the few times we met, but I don't think she really likes me all that much.

Jen is the one other person who might understand what I'm going through. She lived through the silence and denial in our community around my aunt's murder. And her analytical mind will dissect this whole situation quickly.

I look up at the blue sky, inhale that blue, exhale it to every nerve and muscle and tendon in my body, trying to release tension, to no avail. It's like a fire alarm is ringing through me, blaring *Danger! Danger!*

I wait for twenty minutes, leaning against the truck, my anxiety building. What is taking Ruby so long? Has my cousin lost her mind?

I walk up the driveway, past the smear of blood where Rex shot Molly. There's a sprinkle of glass from the broken streetlight, and I wonder whether he shot it, too, to conceal his truck. Surely the neighbours would have heard it, though. I glance around for the cops and see the young constable is already talking to the next-door neighbour, who is waving her hands in distress.

I keep walking along the street, heading uphill toward Carol's bed-and-breakfast, until the signal strengthens. And then I call Jen.

"Hey, what's up?" she asks.

"How much time you got?"

"Phil and I are going for brunch, but not for a couple of hours. He's working this morning. I should be working, too, but I need a break. Family law ... I love it, but it doesn't love me back, you know?"

"No, but I can imagine. I'm sorry to lay this on you, but I want to hear what you think." I tell her about Molly.

"Did Ruby get a good look at him or his truck?"

"No, the streetlight's out and it was dark. But she heard the truck—he drives a diesel."

"One diesel sounds like another," says Jen. "What about the neighbours?"

"I don't know. The cops are talking to them right now. Can't they, like, match his shoe prints or something? Or the bullet from the dog?"

"The real world is nothing like *CSI*. The cops have limited resources, and that stuff takes time, and it's open to interpretation. Unless they can find someone who got a good look at Rex, or at least his truck, I doubt they'll arrest him for this, at least not today. I mean, he'd pretty much have to confess."

"Are you trying to convince me that it was some other asshole who shot their dog?"

"Oh, I believe Ruby. It sounds like he's escalating. I'm just saying they probably don't have grounds to arrest him today without other evidence. They might get there, but it will take time."

"So what do we do?"

"Get out of town," she says. "I don't know what's going to happen next, but with these guys, you just can't be sure. He's not rational, he's obsessive, he's angry, he's got a gun, and he's willing to use it. He seems to think he had some sort of relationship with Brynny, or a right to one, at least, and now he feels rejected. He's like an angry ex, and those guys are dangerous. It just takes one last trigger, and then they explode, spreading pain and hate everywhere. I see it sometimes in my practice ... they ruin so many lives ..." We are both silent for a moment.

"Just like Will," I finally say.

"Yeah, just like Will. Listen, Darby, if they won't leave, see if they'll ask the cops to watch their house at least, and maybe the church. You said he's been hanging out in the church parking lot during services? If Ruby has a peace bond, he's breaking the conditions, so the RCMP should be able to pick him up for that."

"Okay, thanks, Jen." I pause. "How are you feeling these days?"

"Oh, I'm okay. I'm not puking all the time, at least. Now I just feel big and awkward."

"Well, I'm glad you're not sick anymore."

I say goodbye just as I reach Carol's door. I text Ruby to let her know where I am. Then I knock and Carol answers.

"Well, hello, stranger. What are you doing here?"

"Just came by for coffee," I say.

"Well, come on in."

I tell Carol about the frantic phone call from Ruby, the dead dog. Carol and I are on our second cups of coffee when she gets a phone call from her daughter-in-law.

"She did ... What did she post, exactly? ... Yes, I knew about the dog, Darby was just telling me all about it ..." Carol turns to me for a moment. "Can you pull up Ruby's Facebook page on your phone?"

"Yeah ..." I'm about to ask her why, but she's talking to her daughter-in-law again. So I pull my phone out of my coat pocket, navigate to Facebook.

"Oh, shit." I scan the post. It's a long rant about everything Rex has done, ending with "murdering" Molly and questioning why he's so respected, why people are protecting him. He didn't even earn his fortune, Ruby writes. He inherited it all. There's a growing pile of comments below. I pass the phone to Carol.

"Oh, my, yes I see," says Carol. "And you say people are sharing it? His son saw it, you say? I didn't know he had a son ... Oh, they're estranged ..."

I feel a bitter satisfaction at Rex's public shaming, but also a jab of fear, just like the split second before you start falling, when it's too late to do anything about it.

———

Ruby gives in to Brynny's requests. I'm still at Carol's when I get a text saying she's decided to stay after all.

"Well, you may as well come to church with us, since you're here already," Carol says. "It will be nice to have you in the choir."

"Okay," I say. The feeling of falling is still with me, but I try to push it away. I text Sam to see if he's going to be at church. He calls right away.

"What are you doing here?" he asks.

"Long story. Go read Ruby's Facebook page," I reply.

I call Trevor before we leave but get his voicemail. "I love you," I say. "Whatever happens with your job, we'll be okay. We have savings. Your new book is going to do well, I know it. I'm visiting Ruby and Brynny right now, so don't call Grandpa looking for me. Come out here, please, as soon as you can. I miss you."

I don't want him to worry, so I don't tell him about Molly or my fear of Rex.

Carol drives us to the church. There's no sign of Rex when we pull up, but there is an RCMP cruiser parked near the church entrance. The cops were thinking along the same lines as Jen, then. Inside the cruiser sit the policewoman I talked to, and another young constable with warm brown eyes. I exhale slowly, hoping this is a sign that Rex will be dealt with before something worse happens.

Inside, Carol finds me a spare robe for the choir, a blue gown. It will match the sky in the floor-to-ceiling window behind us. I take a place in the middle row, right behind Ruby, and squeeze her shoulder. She turns and smiles at me.

"Thanks for being here, Darbs. I couldn't ask for a better friend."

"You deserve nothing less. You're worthy of all the good things in life. I love you, Ruby."

We both cry a little, quietly.

I look out at the packed church. Hundreds of people dressed in their Sunday best. Carol's son and daughter-in-law are in the third pew with their three kids. The oldest girl with a scarf wound around her afro, the other girl's hair in tight plaits. The youngest, a boy about three years old, smiles and waves at his grandma in the choir, and Carol waves back.

Near the back are Sam and Amber. They are looking friendly. I wonder if they're dating. No one's mentioned it to me. But then I remember seeing them dancing at the wedding and think that perhaps that was the start.

I see Brynny's parents near the middle, Helen sitting right next to the aisle, gazing at her daughter, while Rob talks to the older lady on his left—his aunt, I think.

Brynny has decided that today's sermon will focus on forgiveness, reconciliation, and redemption, how they're connected but separate. We open the service with "Amazing Grace." It's a relatively understated, straightforward rendition, lacking the vocal flourishes some singers add these days, letting the power and beauty of the song shine through. I can feel the voices of the rest of the choir resonating in my torso, my heart space. It's one of the best feelings in the world. It feels good to be in this beautiful church, where one of my best friends was married just a few weeks ago. But even with the cops outside, my stomach still churns nervously.

As we near the end of the song, a vehicle backfires in the parking lot, *bang, bang, bang.* I flinch. Just someone late for church, I tell myself.

Then the doors burst open and Rex storms through, a ball cap pulled low over his eyes. He's carrying a rifle and has a pistol strapped to his side. He starts shooting, and someone screams.

Sam launches himself at Rex but before he can get close, Rex shoots him in the chest. Sam drops with a moan.

"Sam!" I scream. "Sam!"

Rex keeps shooting. It's not a regular rifle, I think, not like the .22s we used to plink cans or gophers, or even the hunting rifles my friends and family had. There are too many shots, one after another, so close together. I crouch down, trying to make myself invisible, praying that Sam will be okay.

"Run!" someone cries, but too many in the choir are frozen, and we'd have to crawl over each other to escape. I freeze, too, watching with horror as Rex continues his rampage.

"No! No!" Brynny is still at the pulpit, screaming into the mic. I've never heard her scream that way, her voice impossibly high, shrieking.

Rex strides toward the front, shooting anyone who gets in his way. Ruby, seeing Brynny stock-still at the pulpit, dashes toward her. Rex takes aim and shoots. Ruby drops with a cry. He's shot my beautiful friend.

Helen and Rob are crouched between the pews—I can just see the top of Helen's gleaming blond head. I wonder, for the first time, if she dyes it or if it just hasn't gone grey. What a strange thing to think about right now, but the light is filtering through the stained glass and catching Helen's golden crown, and it's stunning amidst the gore.

Why haven't they tried to run, or at least moved away from the central aisle?

Rex discards the rifle—whether he's out of ammo or has jammed it, I'm not sure. That's when Helen throws herself in front of Rex, trying to stop his advance. But he draws his handgun and shoots her in the head. She falls without a sound. Rob tries to tackle Rex, but Rex shoots him, too, and he collapses.

Is this really happening? Are we all going to die here today?

The logjam at the choir's edge breaks and people run from the stage. Some dash down the aisle along the wall, but that means running toward Rex, and he starts shooting at the blue-gowned singers as they try to follow the other fleeing parishioners. I flatten myself to the floor, hoping he won't see me or will think I'm dead. Carol is beside me, and she touches my hand with her fingertips. We lie like that, and I focus on the light touch of her skin as though it's tethering me to life.

I remain there for seconds that feel like hours, trying not to move or breathe. Praying silently. Listening to Rex's footsteps slowly approach the sanctuary. His boots are sharp and heavy on the wood floor, and every footfall sends a shock through my body. I open one eye just a crack and see his black cowboy boots, the sharp creases on his starched jeans. He's standing over Ruby, who is moaning on the floor. Brynny crouches next to her, pressing her robe into Ruby's side, trying to stem the blood.

"We could have had a good life together," Rex says to Brynny, raising the gun.

"God did not put me on this earth to be your trophy wife," she replies, cool as anything. Just like Helen, in the end. I am so proud of my cousin, and terrified for her, and filled with white-hot rage, but I stay still.

Rex raises the handgun, and Brynny closes her eyes.

And then I see Carol's son Ben rushing up the aisle, Rex's discarded rifle in his hands, pointing the butt at Rex like a bayonet. He bashes Rex on the head, once, twice, until Rex crumples at his feet. Ben pulls the sidearm from Rex's hand and several other men rush up to stand guard.

Ben points the sidearm at Rex as though he's going to shoot him. Carol stands up then. "Ben," she says.

Ben looks at his mother and starts to shake. She reaches out a hand, and he gives her the gun.

"Mom. I was afraid he'd shot you. I was afraid ..."

"I know, sweetheart. But I'm fine. I'm just fine."

Ben folds Carol into his massive arms, sobbing.

Brynny is crouched over Ruby but looking out at her parents. Her dad is sitting up, cradling Helen's body and crying silently. Ruby sits up slowly, clutching the wound on her side. "I'll be okay," she says. "Go help your dad."

"I'm so sorry," Brynny says, then goes to her parents.

Ruby, I think, is too strong. No one puts her first. I walk over to her, sit beside her, wrap my arm around her, and apply pressure to her wound. She leans into me. We look out at the chaos, the living crouched over the crumpled bodies of their loved ones, the wounded moaning. The air is thick with the scent of blood and other body fluids, the wet smell of death.

"Can you get me out of here?" Ruby says. "I can't stay here."

"Yes," I say.

I help Ruby to her feet. Carol sends Ben to check on his wife and children, who must be outside. She takes Ruby's other arm. I take one last look at Rex, lying on the floor of the sanctuary, several men standing over him, their eyes glued to him. If I ignored the blood on the back of his head, I could believe he was sleeping. He doesn't look like a monster at all. He looks like any other man.

We start toward the door, slowly manoeuvring around the dead. Past Brynny and Rob, sobbing over Helen's lifeless form. Past Michelle Carpenter, still as a stone, her turquoise rings covered in blood. I suddenly remember seeing her years ago, when Brynny held her services in Michelle and Bryce's riding arena. She was one who stuck with the church when others left because of Ruby and Brynny's love. Her husband, Bryce, strokes her hair, moaning. Bryce, I remember, was the man with the hard-to-catch mare in Brynny's video.

Their two sons lean into each other, faces pale with shock. I want to pull those boys out of that church, away from their mother's body, and fill them with ice cream and blue whale candies, tell them fart jokes until they forget everything that's happened, but I can't. All I can do is help Ruby.

But somehow Carol knows what to do. "Bryce. Bryce, look at me." No response. "Bryce," she says again, loudly.

Bryce looks up at her, dazed. "Carol?"

"Bryce, you need to get your boys out of here. Do you hear me?" Bryce just stares. "Michelle would want you to take care of your boys now. You need to get them away from here, right now. You need to get them out of here. Do you understand?"

Bryce nods. "Yes, yes," he mumbles. He leads his sons away from their mother. We follow them down the aisle.

We reach Sam, Amber leaning over him. His eyes are open, and he looks at me. He's still alive. I fall to my knees beside Amber trying to stop the blood oozing from his chest.

"Sam! Sam! Stay with us," I say. "Please, just hold on."

Amber smooths his hair from his sweaty forehead. Sam looks from me to Amber and Ruby, then back. He reaches for our hands. He opens his mouth, but I can't hear what he's saying, so I lean closer.

"Thank you for being my friend," he whispers.

"Sam, I love you! Don't go, Sam," I sob. "Please, don't go, Sam!"

Sam looks at me. Then he exhales with a shudder, and all the light leaves his eyes.

I feel like someone has ripped out my heart, my guts. Amber keens beside me, a high-pitched wail that I can feel in my bones. I pull her against me, and she wails into my neck. She's covered in Sam's blood. It's even in her hair. I must be, too.

Carol leans over. "Ruby needs you now," she says. "Sam would want you to take care of her."

She's right. But it's so hard to leave him here alone. I unlatch my horseshoe necklace, the one Trevor gave me years ago that I've worn every day since to catch all the luck. I place it around Sam's neck, make sure it's secure, and tuck it under his bloody white dress shirt. I kiss his cheek and close his eyes. Then I follow Ruby, Carol, and Amber outside.

It's then that I feel the blood, sticky on my skin. When we reach the door, I puke off the side of the steps. Then I look up, see the RCMP officers. The woman is slumped forward in her seat—he must have shot her first. The man is sprawled awkwardly, one foot still inside the cruiser, the rest of his body on the dusty gravel, his gun drawn, his head ... I lean over the steps again, my throat and mouth burning with acid.

It's only then that I realize what I thought was the sound of a vehicle backfiring was actually gun shots. The young constables were the first to fall.

"You stay with Ruby," Carol says to me and Amber. "I'm going back inside to help."

The three of us make our way down the church steps, Amber and I almost carrying Ruby. We walk away from the death scene around the cruiser to the lawn on the southwest side of the church where the other survivors are gathering. We sit and face the mountains. We listen to the sound of approaching sirens. I wonder how any of us will be able to go on.

—

The next few days pass in a stupor. Millarville is flooded with media. Brynny doesn't venture out onto the deck during the day, as photographers with zoom lenses wait at the end of their driveway, just an inch past the property line.

I, however, do not give a shit about the media at this point. The day after the shooting, I walk up the driveway to tell them what I think. Instantly, several reporters surround me, microphones aimed at me.

"Do you have to do this?" I ask.

"How is Brynny holding up? Any word yet on when Ruby will be discharged from the hospital?" asks one journalist with perfectly blown-out shiny auburn hair. Her well-coiffed hair triggers unexpected rage. How dare she care how she looks right now?

"You know, Rex used to park right where you're standing when he stalked them," I reply, then turn around and walk back to the house. They replay that clip on the news over and over, and later an

RCMP constable asks me not to talk to the media about anything related to the case.

—

Trevor finds out about the shooting while at work, from the Canadian Press wire service. He tries to call me, not realizing yet that I'm in Millarville, but I've dropped my phone somewhere in the church. Then he hears the message I left him and starts to worry that I'm at the church. When he can't reach me on my cell phone, he really worries. He calls Sam but gets no answer. He calls Ruby and Brynny's land line, but gets a busy signal. He tries Grandpa Kolchak, and Henry and Linda, but their lines are busy, too. He tries calling everyone he knows in Millarville, and finally Carol picks up her cell phone and tells him I'm alive.

Then Trevor stands up, tells his editor he has to go, and leaves, not caring about the job or anything else. He takes a taxi home and tells the driver to wait while he packs. Then he takes the cab to the airport and waits on standby. He lands in Calgary late that night, rents a car, and drives straight out to Millarville. He finds me sitting on the back deck of Brynny and Ruby's home, smoking, and hugs me. I'm so relieved to see him I cry and cry, soaking his shirt.

After my sharp rebuke of the media, Trevor takes over as spokesperson. Every morning he walks to the edge of the driveway to talk to them. He knows a couple of the reporters from journalism school. They like him, even though he doesn't usually give them much, often saying things like, "You'll have to ask the police that" or "I can't really comment on that, since there's an investigation."

I watch him from the living room window every time he does his morning scrum. After, we sit together on the deck on the south side of the house, where they can't get a photo without trespassing, and I lean into his shoulder and stare at the mountains.

Ruby is discharged the morning of Helen's funeral. Beth selects a black dress from Ruby's closet, packs a toiletry bag, and drives with Brynny into Calgary to pick Ruby up and take her to Helen and Rob's house to get ready.

I should have gone with them, but I hang back with Trevor.

"I don't want to go to the funeral."

"You don't have to, but it will give you some closure."

"But then there will be Michelle's funeral, and then the one for the Parker family. And then the big memorial. It's exhausting."

Not Sam's funeral, though. His family has decided to hold a small private service back home. I'm not invited. Nor is Amber, Ruby, or anyone else from the church.

Even though I don't want to, we go to all the funerals, a full week of them, one after another. A week of black clothing and crying. Most of the funerals are restrained in their mourning, the grief muffled by the public nature of it. Helen's service is held in a United Church in Calgary. Trevor and I sit in the front row with Brynny, Ruby, Rob, and the Hodgkinses. Our extended families surround us like a buffer. Trevor sits on one side of me, Ruby the other, each holding a hand. I glance down our row, and everyone is holding hands, like a chain.

The same United Church minister who married Ruby and Brynny performs the service, but I hardly hear a word she says. I am on edge, constantly looking behind me for threats. Every heavy footstep makes me shake.

Earlier, Rob had asked me if I was up to singing at Helen's funeral. I contemplated standing at the front of the room, but immediately, I was back in the church, lying flat on the floor, as Rex's bootsteps echoed through the building.

"I can't," I said. "I'm sorry, but I can't be in front of a crowd like that."

"I understand," he said. "I don't think anyone from the church will be able to do it, but I wanted to give you the option."

His eyes look so soft and so sad. The lines have deepened on his face. I wish I could do it for him, but I can't.

Ruby is the one who comes up with the idea of displaying the lyrics on a screen, so we can all sing together, without anyone going to the front. She organizes the music, too—a playlist of songs Helen loved, with the vocals turned way down, so we can sing along. And most people do sing along to Helen's old favourites—songs from Buffy Sainte-Marie and Ian and Sylvia Tyson. Eventually grief and horror overwhelm me, and I sink into my seat, sobbing, and Trevor sits beside me, holding me. I close my eyes, but images of Helen falling rise. White-hot anger suddenly pushes out the grief, and I stand, and run outside, and scream and scream. I want to break things, smash everything around me, rip it all down. The old truck I've been driving all summer is parked nearby, and I settle on it, pounding the hood, the dented door, kicking the bumper, tires.

Trevor pulls me off the truck and I sob into his shoulder until I'm dehydrated and exhausted.

After, the family all comes to Millarville, along with Carol's family and a few others from the congregation. Relatives and friends fill the kitchen and living room of the log house, spill out onto the deck and the lawn. Some people I haven't seen in years, like Uncle George and his family. Dad and Jacqueline. Jacqueline gives me a long, hard hug, and I think, This is why he loves her. And there are people I haven't met. It's almost like a family reunion. I sit on the stairs of the south side, braiding Reata's hair and watching Jake and Uncle George's kids playing bocci ball with Carols' grandkids.

"Do you believe in heaven?" Reata asks me.

"I don't know. Definitely not the version with angels and harps. I think something of us stays behind, at least for a while. Maybe we go somewhere else eventually. Our bodies break down, but I don't know what happens to the rest of us." I think of the massive tree of light I saw in my vision, its leaves like stars.

"Helen died trying to save other people, though. Don't you think she deserves to go to heaven?"

"More than anyone, she does," I say, trying not to cry. I'm so tired of crying, and thinking of Helen and her warrior death is so hard. As for Sam, I can't even bear to think of him right now.

I finish Reata's French braid, go inside for a drink of water. Dad and Uncle Henry are talking quietly by the front door. Brynny and her cousins are at the kitchen table, looking through old family albums. Helen posing with her older sisters, some of her and my mom and Aunt Bea.

"Mom used to make me the most beautiful dresses when I was a little girl," says Brynny, looking at one of my mom posing with Helen in jewel-toned shifts. Helen must have sewn them. Another shows Helen sitting on the porch steps at the Kolchak ranch, braiding Aunt Bea's hair, just as I was braiding Reata's moments ago. I shiver.

What are the odds that one family would lose two women of the same generation to two different violent men?

Leaning against the counter is my acoustic guitar.

"Your Grandpa Kolchak brought it for you," says Brynny.

I pick up the Gibson, tune it. Then I carry the guitar, along with a big glass of water, to the porch and settle into a wooden deck chair. I play the first things that come to mind, and no one suggests anything different. Classics like "Helpless," "Long Black Veil," "Sea of Heartache." Then newer songs, like Gillian Welch's "Revelator," and on and on. A small crowd gathers, some people singing along. Ruby, Reata, and Carol join me on most of them. Their harmonies are so beautiful, I can feel the sound resonate deep in my chest.

Dad comes out with his own acoustic and accompanies me. It's the first time we've played together since before Aunt Bea's murder. I can't hold onto my anger toward him anymore, however justified. I don't have the energy to carry it.

We play for hours, stopping only to sip water or refill the glass. My mood is solemn even when the songs aren't. Finally, we sing "Will the Circle Be Unbroken," several people joining in, a chorus of voices, and when the last note hangs in the air, it feels like we're done.

Grandpa Kolchak, sitting in a lawn chair next to Uncle Henry, covers his face with his hands and starts to sob. I've never seen him cry like that before. Never seen him cry at all, in fact.

Reata goes to him, sits beside him and wraps her arms around him. Grandpa turns off the sobs as easily as flicking a switch, and that worries me even more. He looks at me, then looks at Brynny, leaning into Ruby and Amber on the step below me, and he speaks.

"When my wife died, I told myself things would be better for our kids than they had been for us. And then I lost my daughters, and I told myself life would be better for my grandchildren and their cousins. Especially the girls. Women have more opportunity now, I said to myself. More rights, and they don't have to put up with so much horseshit. But all it takes is one madman to end everything. I'm so afraid for you girls."

I want to comfort Grandpa, to tell him that everything will be okay, but the truth is I'm afraid, too.

That night, I dream that Sam and I are standing on the fireguard road that runs through the Divide Forest back home. Without a word, Sam steps off the road onto a forest trail and starts walking. I hesitate.

"Are you coming or not?" he asks.

Stepping onto this trail is like stepping into another world. It reminds me of the stories where a sheltered child leaves the village for the first time and discovers a wild, magical place. The forest is completely silent. Poplars give way to black spruce as the trail edges around a huge wetland. Mossy, boggy soil is soft under my feet. I follow Sam wordlessly for miles until we reach the banks of Horsehead Creek. A few feet upstream beavers have dammed the creek, creating a pool that is at least a hundred feet wide, leaving a shallower crossing for us downstream of the dam.

Sam stops then and turns to look at me. "You can't follow me anymore. I need to go the rest of the way alone."

"Sam, please don't go."

"I have to follow the trail in front of me."

"I'm so sorry about what happened to you, Sam."

"Don't worry about me, Darby. I'm going to be okay."

"I'll miss you, Sam. You were always a good friend. I love you."

"I know. I love you, too, Darbs." He smiles, hugs me hard. Then he slowly wades into the water. It reaches his chest, then recedes as he continues to the other bank. He stops there, looks back at me once more, then keeps walking north, and disappears into the dark forest.

When I wake, I don't feel at peace exactly, but I feel like something hard at the centre of my chest has loosened.

—

When we're not at funerals, we're being interrogated by the RCMP, hours at a time, in a windowless room at the local detachment. Sometimes it feels accusatory, and I wonder whether I should have a lawyer. I call Jen for advice. She reassures me that I'm just a witness and don't need a lawyer.

"Just cooperate. Tell them what you know. You can make notes about the interview after, if you want," she adds. "You can ask for water, for breaks. You can ask for support from victim services. You're not a suspect."

At the end of one of the interviews, just as I'm about to stand up, I stop.

"Did you know them?" I ask.

"I was the sergeant at Constable King's first posting, in Virden, Manitoba. He was right out of depot," says the Mountie, his voice flat.

"I'm so sorry for what happened."

"We all are."

In the days after the massacre, we learn that Rex had more guns in his truck, all restricted or prohibited. Someone leaks the list of his targets to the media. A photo of it runs on the front page of one of the local papers. It includes people we don't know, such as his son's ex-wife, who he blamed for the estrangement with his family, and some former neighbours.

The list also includes several people from the church. Ruby and Sam are right at the top. Michelle and Carol are on there, too. I ask Carol why Michelle, and Carol tells me Michelle pushed hard to contact the RCMP about Rex at a church meeting. "She was afraid of him," says Carol. She pauses, thinking. "That meeting was supposed to be *in camera*. I wonder how Rex found out what she said. I wonder who told him."

I'm also on the list, along with Reggie and Austin. We're in our own separate section, off to the side, with question marks after our names. It's as though Rex wanted to shoot us, but didn't know how, since none of us were supposed to be there. Would he have tried to find us in Toronto? That seems far-fetched, but then everything seems surreal right now.

But he must have seen me that day. He would have shot me and Carol if he'd had the chance.

Brynny's name is not on the list. He thought he'd win her over after massacring all the people who stood between them, I realize.

Rex didn't have a firearm licence, but he got his younger brother to buy him ammo over the years. His brother also lent Rex the handgun he used in the shooting. He says he didn't know what Rex had planned, thought it was for target shooting, but the police charge him.

Brynny finds an old essay about a mass shooting at a university in the U.S. from the early nineties and forwards Ruby and me the link. I read it at Ruby and Brynny's kitchen table, covered in dirty coffee cups and unopened mail. "The Fourth State of Matter" by Jo Ann Beard.

I pick up a pen and an unopened envelope, flip the envelope over. *Fuck Rex Baskin,* I write. *Fuck mass-murdering asshole garbage humans. Fuck the people who buy their guns and ammo. Fuck. Fuck. Fuck!*

Then I remove the letter and rip the envelope into the tiniest pieces I can.

Most nights, I have night terrors, Rex's heavy footsteps plodding up the steps, on the floor above us, down the basement steps, until he's a dark shadow in our doorway, or a weight on the bed, or hands around my neck. Sometimes he morphs into Will. I can always feel that I'm dying.

Sometimes Trevor manages to shake me awake, sometimes I wake sitting up in bed, or part way up the stairs, or, one night, crouched over my pillow, punching it with everything I have. I worry about hurting Trevor or myself. Is it possible to kill someone while in the grip of a night terror?

When I can't sleep at all, I leave our basement bedroom, walk upstairs and watch TV with Brynny, who has the news on twenty-four/seven and is simultaneously scouring social media for information and rumours.

"I shouldn't have let him join the congregation. I shouldn't have taken his money. I shouldn't have smiled so much when I was delivering sermons, he thought I was flirting. I should have listened to Ruby."

I tell her to stop it, that it's not helping, but she just continues, almost like a robot, searching for answers, dissecting herself.

A reporter named Margo Nielsen keeps calling the house. One day, while Trevor is out, I answer the phone and it's her. She asks who she's speaking to, and I tell her. She pauses, then tells me she's sorry for what happened to us. She has a warm, calm, low voice, the kind of voice Aunt Bea used when she was talking to a worried colt.

"What you're going through is horrible and I can't imagine how hard it must be. You don't have to talk to me. But if you do, you might be able to help someone else. You might know something that stops this from happening in the future."

I write down her number and tell her I'll think about it.

Later, I talk about it with Trevor, Brynny, and Ruby. Uncharacteristically, Brynny says she doesn't want to talk to anyone.

"I'll talk to her," says Ruby.

"Why would you do that?" asks Brynny.

"Because it's important. It's important that people know how it happened."

Brynny looks at her, hurt.

"What about you?" Trevor asks me. "What do you want to do?"

I think about how I used to feel, playing with the band, in front of an audience. I remember that trust, that connection. The feeling that if I threw them my heart, the music would follow. It was a feeling like love.

Rex has taken that from me.

But I can do this: I can open myself up to this reporter and let her see everything inside of me. I can show her what has been stolen, and what is left. And maybe she can weave all of our pieces into a story. Not a story to make sense of this thing that has happened, or to provide all the answers, but to let people know what's at stake.

"I'll do the interview, too. After the memorial," I say.

Trevor texts Margo and lets her know we'll talk to her.

The morning of the public memorial, I wake at four a.m. to the rumble of thunder. I get up and sit on the south-west side of the wrap-around deck and open a new package of cigarettes. I've promised Trevor I'll quit smoking after today, but I realize now I have no intention of keeping that promise. I am done pleasing other people. Lightning flashes to the west, and I light a smoke, inhaling deeply.

It feels peaceful. It is all done, I realize, except for the aftermath.

Later today, there will be a service at the horseshoe-shaped church. Jen, Phil, Meaghan, and Luke all arrived yesterday, along with Grandma and Grandpa Swank. Austin, Reggie, Amelia, and Tara will be there, too, in solidarity. We won't go inside because the crime scene cleaners haven't done their work yet. But the weather will be fine and we'll gather outside. Brynny won't say much, having decided to turn the service over to others who want to speak. Carol will lead the choir, and I'll join them if I can. We will sing and we will cry, all under the watch of TV cameras and smartphones and gossip bloggers and the RCMP.

That is for later, though. Right now there's just me, sitting on this wooden chair, trying to detect the silhouette of the mountains between lightning flashes, smelling the rain and the decaying leaves and the neighbour's fresh-cut grass.

I sit smoking for a long time, humming a mournful melody. The storm fades and the first light leaks into the sky from the east, and I hear someone in the kitchen behind me. Still I stay a moment longer, until I smell fresh-brewed coffee.

Then I stand and look out on the land, now visible in the early morning. Rain coats the tawny grass, and the leaves have turned. The whole world is shimmering shades of gold, with the silhouette of the mountains framing the grasslands. It's so beautiful, I can hardly stand it.

When I am dead and gone, this land will remain, a constant for everyone who comes after me. I have a sudden urge to walk west, into the foothills, and dig my fingers into the topsoil. If I did, maybe I would find God.

I stub my cigarette, fill my lungs with clean air, try to take in every detail in the landscape before me, every rain-wakened smell, the song of every bird I can't name. Then I turn and walk into the house, where my cousin Brynny pours me a cup of coffee, and we wait for the rest of the day to begin.

Author's Afterword

In her essay "The Fourth State of Matter," published in the *New Yorker* in 1996, Jo Ann Beard describes her elderly collie as "the face of love." The dog wakes her up three times a night, calling her out of her dreams.

Jo Ann writes of the grind of everyday life: heartbreak, squirrels invading her house, a colleague she doesn't get along with, the sorrow of watching her collie failing. Her life seems fairly normal: a stable job producing a scientific journal on space physics at the University of Iowa; a good friend at work; another good friend who is both an ex-beauty queen and adept at capturing squirrels; and a husband who has left.

One Friday in November 1991, Jo Ann decides to leave work early. It's a small decision, but one that likely saves her life. A doctoral student named Gang Lu brings a handgun to that afternoon's seminar, where he shoots Jo Ann's friend and colleague, Chris Goertz. He shoots Bob Smith, the colleague Jo Ann can't stand. He shoots Linhua Shan, Ann Cleary, Dwight Nicholson, and Miya Rodolfo-Sioson before shooting himself. Miya, the sole survivor, is left paralyzed. She morphs into an activist for disability rights and becomes the subject of a documentary before losing a struggle against breast cancer in 2008.

Jo Ann is at home with her friend Mary as the news starts to come in over the phone. She smokes and tries to brace herself, then wonders what that even means, to brace oneself. When a physicist phones her to try to tell her the news, she tells him she doesn't want to talk. He tells her to prepare for bad news.

"I have the distinct feeling there is something going on that I can either understand or not understand. There's a choice to be made," she writes.

More people gather in her home, and as they watch the evening news, Jo Ann sees the names and faces of the dead. She sees Chris's photo and retreats to the bathroom. "It's a good thing none of this happened," she says to herself in the mirror.

The collie is the one who retrieves her, just as she pulls Jo Ann from sleep every morning. Jo Ann and the collie sit together, and Jo Ann takes the dog's long muzzle and works it like a gear shift, as though the dog is a car she is driving around town. It's a game they've played for years, but that night they drive "all the way through town, until what happened has happened" and reality has sunk in.

Jo Ann's collie, "the face of love," stands in opposition to Gang Lu's destruction. She reminds us of the power of unconditional love, the ability of animals to ground us. In *All That's Left*, Darby is reconnected to the earth by Foxtrot, a spicy, very sensitive sorrel mare I lifted from my own life. Darby can feel Foxtrot pushing against the ground and propelling them through the air, while also feeling in tune with a powerful, highly intelligent, and intuitive creature. While it's true that tools such as reins and bits and halters allow us to communicate cues to horses, much of the communication is through body language, shifts in body weight, and perhaps even our energy. The real-life Foxtrot is one of my favourite horses. She loved to run when I rode her (because, deep down, that's all I wanted to do, even though I pretended otherwise), but with another rider seemed almost lazy.

For people facing traumatic situations, animals can be a great source of support, especially given that animals such as dogs and horses are more emotionally sensitive than most humans (at least in my opinion). Yet they can also be collateral damage of domestic violence. Crystal Giesbrecht has surveyed domestic violence survivors on behalf of the Provincial Association of Transition Houses and Services of Saskatchewan. In her survey, about 80 percent of domestic violence survivors reported their animals had been harmed. You can read more about Crystal's research at pathssk.org/animals-ipv.

Even if abusers don't directly harm animals, their partners are often afraid to leave the relationship because they fear their pets or livestock will be killed, injured, or neglected. For those who earn a living farming or ranching, financial issues also come into play, as the abuser may legally own or co-own the livestock. In that way, abusers can weaponize relationships with companion animals or livestock to coerce their partners into staying in the relationship. One can imagine Will doing this very thing to Bea.

Of course, Rex doesn't have a romantic relationship with Brynny in this novel, but he thinks he is entitled to one. He shares a pathological sense of entitlement with many abusers and mass shooters. Often it's a domestic violence situation that explodes, but not always. Jo Ann Beard wrote of Gang Lu's belief that others weren't giving him the respect he was entitled to, and online sources mention his jealousy of fellow student Linhua Shan, who outshone him. I realize there are often other issues at play with extreme violence, such as intergenerational trauma, and perhaps severe mental illness and/or addictions. But there's also a blatant disregard for other people's rights to live their lives free from violence, harassment, and abuse. Combine this with abusers' belief that they are actually the victims, and these abusive personalities become fissile, like an atom in a nuclear reactor about to split and release a great burst of white-hot energy. But unlike atoms, fissile humans release pain and sorrow as they break apart, harming anyone in their vicinity.

There are people working to contain this harm and offer refuge to those fleeing abuse (and even trying to find ways to protect their animals). Again, the Provincial Association of Transition Houses and Services of Saskatchewan is a good source for what's happening in Saskatchewan. Margo Goodhand wrote an engrossing, well-researched book about the establishment of women's shelters in Canada, titled *Runaway Wives and Rogue Feminists*. What has stuck with me long after reading this book is the courage of the people who founded and worked at those shelters, and those who continue this hard work.

The other thing about animals is that they don't judge us the way our fellow humans do. Targets of stalking, harassment, and domestic abuse too often find themselves the subject of unwanted advice, unfair criticism, and pity. Even if people want to help, most of us don't want to be branded a victim. No wonder people find refuge in animals, who connect with us on an entirely different level, free of such notions.

If you are, or have been, a target of abuse, harassment, stalking, or violence, I want to tell you this: you are worthy of love and respect. And you are worth fighting for. So please, fight for yourself, and love yourself, and take care.

Acknowledgements

Thank you to Alexis Kienlen, Edna Alford, and Leeann Minogue—good friends, fine writers, and astute readers—who provided crucial feedback to an early, messy version of this work. It takes a community to raise a book.

I was fortunate to find community both in Saskatchewan and farther afield as I worked on this manuscript. The whole thing started with a self-imposed writing retreat at Jim Saville's lovely bed and breakfast near Ravenscrag, SK, several years ago. While en route, I lost a wheel on the highway near Kyle, SK. Deepest gratitude to Dale for lending me a vehicle while mine was in the shop, even though he didn't know me from a hole in the ground.

That retreat was followed by the Sage Hill Writing Experience at Saint Michael's Abbey near Lumsden, SK. Thank you to Nino Ricci, who led us through the fiction colloquium and helped me find the emotional core of this story. Colloquium members Leona Theis, Patti Flather, Catriona Wright, and Maria Meindl shared key observations on everything from winter in Toronto to Darby's physicality. And a shout-out to my thunderstorm sister Kim McCullough.

This experience was followed by more retreats. One was led by author Gail Bowen at Saint Peter's Abbey at Muenster, SK, and organized by the Saskatchewan Writers Guild. My friend JQ and I then organized our own retreat at Ness Creek, SK. Both were crucial to getting this book to the next stage.

As I was completing the substantive edit, I had the good fortune to receive a bursary to cover the workshop fees at the Iceland Writers Retreat in Reykjavik—many thanks to the donors and organizers of the bursary, to retreat co-founders Eliza Reid and Erica Jacobs Green, and to my mother for giving me her airline points so I could make the trip. Even at that late stage, the retreat provided inspiration and crucial details to this work. Carol Leonnig shared insights from her work reporting on mass shootings and Jessica Key introduced me to Jo Ann Beard's essay, "The Fourth State of Matter."

Thanks as well to the folks in Toronto who shared their knowledge of the music industry: Susan de Cartier at Starfish Entertainment, Lillian Wauthier of Acoustic Harvest, and Jill Snell of Jayward Artist Group. Any errors in my depiction of the music industry are mine alone. Thanks as well to Sonja Kresowaty and Alex for hosting me, and to Alex de Cartier as well for the hospitality.

Many thanks to Nathan Smith for gifting me with "Hug Machine" as a band name. And gratitude to my long-time friends Shannon Goralski and Junelle Dion, whose wonderful homes inspired fictional homes.

A huge thank you to the people at NeWest Press for once again believing in my book, and for their ongoing work at the press: Leslie Vermeer, Matt Bowes, Meredith Thompson, Christine Kohler, and Carolina Ortiz. Your work is more important than ever, given the climate of censorship these days.

And finally, I have a posse of great friends who have given me a leg up and offered encouragement after I've been tossed from my horse (sometimes literally, sometimes figuratively). We've ridden many miles together, and hopefully have many more ahead of us. Thank you.

About the Author

LISA GUENTHER is a writer and editor based in rural northwestern Saskatchewan. She has previously written for *Grainews* and *Country Guide* and served as the editor of *Canadian Cattlemen* magazine. Her farm journalism has received awards from the Canadian Farm Writers' Federation and the North American Association of Agricultural Journalists. Her previous novel, *Friendly Fire*, was shortlisted for a Saskatchewan Book Award and placed second in the Saskatchewan Writers Guild's John V. Hicks Long Manuscript Award. When she's not writing, editing, or reading, Lisa enjoys horseback riding and getting out on the land.